As far back as I can remember, I knew I was different from most people. And so were the rest of the kids, my age and younger, in the Enclave. What the differences was, I had no idea, because nobody said. And I couldn't ask; the hints gave me nothing solid to go on.

But I knew. Every time I had a physical exam, the doctors and nurses inspected the ultrasonic pictures of my insides and nodded as if everything was all right, or else looked puzzled and said things like, "I don't know; we'll just have to wait and see."

"Wait and see what?" I said, one time. "Whether I've got cancer or something?" The younger doctor, the intern, shook her head and laughed. Oh, no, I was perfectly all right: Dr. Gill's voice sounded honest enough, so I believed her when she said these special tests were just part of the project the doctors were working on. And when they had some real answers, they'd tell me all about it.

Except that they never did. But I found out, anyway.

# THE
# BREEDS
# OF MAN

F. M. Busby

**BANTAM BOOKS**
TORONTO • NEW YORK • LONDON • SYDNEY • AUCKLAND

*To Amy and Lou and Tappan*

THE BREEDS OF MAN
*A Bantam Spectra Book / March 1988*

ISBN 0-553-27008-7

*Published simultaneously in the United States and Canada*

*Bantam Books are published by Bantam Books, a division of*
*Bantam Doubleday Dell Publishing Group, Inc. Its trademark,*
*consisting of the words "Bantam Books" and the portrayal of a*
*rooster, is Registered in U.S. Patent and Trademark Office and*
*in other countries. Marca Registrada. Bantam Books, 666 Fifth*
*Avenue, New York, New York 10103.*

PRINTED IN THE UNITED STATES OF AMERICA

O     0 9 8 7 6 5 4 3 2 1

# THE
# BREEDS
# OF MAN

# BOOK
# ONE

"Knowing that one is collaterally descended from a virus can be somewhat humbling."

(From Origins, by Rome dos Caras.)

# I

The Presidential Task Force, Cogdill thought, needed someone who knew how to ramrod. Three days ago they'd called him in from Chicago, and for those three days he'd sat around watching them not make up their minds. As Chairman of the Board for the Phoenix Foundation, Thane Cogdill was used to seeing some action. Here in D.C., to date he'd observed very little.

The subject was AIDS: more specifically, how to combat the fatal scourge. At latest report, more than half the country's population tested positive for exposure; how many would contract the disease, and when, was anybody's guess.

Two years earlier, Gilcorp's labs had produced a vaccine that seemed to stem the threat. But as viruses will do, this one had mutated—had found new vectors and begun to spread by new avenues. Had, in fact, scared the hell out of most of North America and much of Europe. Africa, possibly the organism's original source, suffered between disease on the one hand and famine on the other. From Central and South America, word was sparse. And as usual, neither China nor the Soviet bloc was telling anyone much more than the time of day.

Now, sipping coffee, Cogdill watched and listened as the Task Force's own Chairman, Pete Randall, plowed through old ground. "The question is whether we can, in conscience, bypass normal procurement methods. A good case can be made—"

Cogdill had had enough. "Excuse me, Pete. The question is, do you want to give my people the green light for an all-out push toward an AIDS cure? Or poop around for another six months, shuffling procurement papers and permission documents?"

Some of the Force members looked shocked; Randall merely showed distress. Cogdill went on, "When Phoenix clobbered herpes for you, a time back, it stayed clobbered. Remember?"

"Of course. But that contract went through normal bidding."

3

"And you got lucky; you got Phoenix. With AIDS, you didn't; Gilcorp outbid us."

"That's true, and—"

"And for a while, their vaccine seemed to work." Now Cogdill was getting warmed up. "But then the retrovirus mutated. It couldn't do that spontaneously, not on such a wide scale. The change had to be triggered by Gilcorp's vaccine."

"But how—?"

"Pete, I don't *know* how; I'm an administrator, not a white-coat." Forgetting that he wasn't in his own Board room, presiding, Cogdill slapped his hand down onto the table, hard. "Here it is: do you want to vote a no-strings grant, to get us started on this job as soon as I can get to a phone? Or would you rather stay with the lowest bidder?" He stood. "When you decide, call me at my hotel. Either way, tonight I'm catching my ten o'clock flight back to Chicago."

The woman sitting beside Randall—Laura Casey, her name was—glared at Cogdill. He hated to see her do that; the tall brunette was one of the better, more decisive thinkers in the Task Force. "You're demanding a bottomless purse, no conditions, or you pick up your marbles and go home. That's arrogance."

Aroused now, Cogdill said, "You want arrogance? If the Feen takes this job and doesn't produce, you get a full rebate of all costs. You can write it up that way."

Having said all that he felt needed saying, Cogdill left.

His cab was an electric, and its metered charging circuits were a Feen development. The trick had been to make the interface unnecessarily complex, to foil Charlie Cheater and make sure all energy usage could be properly billed.

Located in a rather unassuming hotel, Cogdill's room was done in middle 1980s let's-pretend-it's-not-plastic. It had, somehow, a nostalgic appeal: even the bas-relief seagulls helped his mood. After he showered, and ordered dinner from room service, he made himself a drink: real bourbon, ice water on the side. Then he watched some Tri-V.

He switched away from the news, because "you can't turn the page." Printout sheets cost more, but saved time.

He passed up horseback basketball, the Grandmothers' Water Polo semifinals, and a talk show featuring two women who claimed to be pregnant by interstellar aliens. Cogdill snorted; if alien visitors ever did show up, all he hoped was that the Feen would manage some kind of handle on First Contact negotiations.

Flipping through the channels, he blinked in surprise before turning back to a very explicit depiction of group sex. After a few more seconds of blurred, writhing flesh, the screen cut to a youngish, florid-faced man whose blond hair was plastered down by an immoderate amount of grease. Introducing himself as the Reverend Jody Jay Tolliver, he said, "What you have seen here, my good friends, is *sin*. And now, what you see next is the *wages* of sin." Then on split screen several people were shown, before and after suffering the ravages of AIDS. Cogdill wasn't certain the befores-and-afters were always the same people—but that was advertising for you, and this was definitely a commercial.

Enough of that; he turned the set off. Dinner arrived; he ate nonpolluted fish from the Great Barrier Reef, and vegetables grown well away from toxic-waste dumps. Or so the menu promised; if it read truly, the considerable tab was worth it.

Then he packed, and waited to see if the Task Force would nibble.

It was Casey they sent. The desk called to announce her, and someone escorted her to Cogdill's door. So she had clout.

And also presence. Instead of the business hairdo, Casey sported a rioting mass of blue-black curls; her stylized office garb was superseded by a sleek Nile-green gown.

If the transformation was intended to divert Cogdill from contract considerations, it failed. A two-year widower, he found he couldn't ignore the woman's striking attractiveness—yet it had no bearing on the matter at hand. Inspecting the papers she'd brought, he bluepenciled the tricky clauses someone had slipped into the agreement; Casey shook her head, saying, "I told Pete you'd catch that stuff, but the lawyers insisted on trying."

"They always do." Business was done; belatedly he offered her a glass of wine, and she accepted. Attempts at small talk went nowhere; it was almost time for Cogdill to leave for the airport before it came to him, what to say. "If you're free to handle it, I'd like you to manage liaison for this project."

"Yes, I could arrange that assignment."

"Good. When you're up in Chicago we can get better acquainted. Take some time for it."

Slowly, she nodded. "I think I'd like that."

When the cab didn't arrive in time, she drove him to the airport and walked with him to Check-in. "Goodbye," and she moved inside the handshake to kiss his cheek.

Boarding the plane, Thane Cogdill felt unaccountably good.

After he reread the grant authorization and accepted a snack from the flight attendant, Cogdill slept for the rest of the subsonic ride. At O'Hare, once he had his luggage and a cab, he decided it was too late to go home; the trip there and back would take time he could use for sleeping.

So he went directly to the Foundation, and dossed down in the *pied-à-terre* suite behind his office. He'd done a lot of that since his wife died. Maybe he should sell the house, but he wasn't ready, just yet, to put away so much of his past.

Feeling energetic next morning he showered, called for breakfast from the Exec Cafeteria, and ate while scanning some reports he'd taken from his desk on the way in. Nothing really new, no problems: he initialed each item and turned on the Tri-V.

A news analyst was discussing NASA's new third-generation shuttle, explaining the changes it would bring to Earth-Moon travel. The Feen held shares in the multinational Lunar Enterprise System, so Cogdill paid heed

A normal Moon trip consisted of four stages: shuttle to low orbit facilities at the 400-km belt, Transfer-A vehicles up to synchronous stations, Transfer-B's (A's modified for extended life support but less cargo space) to lunar orbit, and light-duty shuttles to Luna-surface. What the third-gen shuttles would do, the narrator told in terms suitable for a bright six-year-old, was reach sync height directly from Earth. Existing shuttles, Trans-A taxis, and low-orbit installations would still have their own functions, but not as part of the overall Earth-Moon route.

He switched the set off. It was time for his Board meeting. Time to enter the lion cage.

Two floors below the tower suites, the Board room faced west, away from the major high-rise cluster. The room's large windows looked out over lesser buildings; beyond them, suburban sprawl faded into a blur of hazed air, with no true horizon.

Walking the conference table's length, Cogdill saw that all Board members were present. At the far end he took his seat. With his back to the window's light he saw each face quite clearly—but they couldn't see *his*, all that well.

Having no time or patience for parliamentary niceties, he

handed out copies of the Task Force grant proposal. "Skim it; I've checked out the fine print. Ten minutes; then we'll vote."

But things always take longer and cost more. Thin-faced Roark, chewing his pencil-line mustache, had nits to pick. Beau Slade needed everything explained in kindergarten terms. Amailie duShield wanted time to consult with the law firm that handled her husband's estate. And Cogdill knew the ultracautious temperament that belied Harve Castellan's dashing appearance. Castellan, in particular, hedged at the guarantee clause—until Cogdill said, "Come on, Harve; we've done this before. And when's the last time we had to pony up a rebate?"

Luckily the remaining members were old Blaine, nearing retirement and only wanting the meeting over and done with, plus three of Cogdill's own appointees. So with a minimum of outright railroading, the proposal passed.

"Now then." With the small stuff pushed aside, Cogdill was warming up. "Let's set this project up right away, get it moving fast." He leafed through his notes. "To run the lab side of things I propose Dr. Mareth Fallon. If you don't know her record, look it up; twice she's saved her superiors' butts. At the moment she's largely marking time. All in favor? Right."

Frowning, Ned Roark said, "I'm not so certain—"

"I am." Cogdill slapped the table. "If you're not sure what you're saying, why say it?" With a quick headshake, he continued. "To head the project I propose young Kennet Bardeen."

Quicker this time, Roark said, "Now wait a minute. I want some discussion here. Bardeen's a junior administrator, pure and simple. He knows nothing about physical science, and—"

"I know," said Cogdill. "In his entry-level interview he said, and I quote, 'When it comes to organic chemistry, I got only as far as ethanol.'"

Beau Slade leaned forward. "He's not a drunk, is he?"

By laughing, Cogdill surprised himself. "Hell, no! He's a man who can joke at his own expense. He is also, if records don't lie, a damned good administrator. I think this job may need both qualities."

He looked down one side of the table and then the other. "Motion put to vote: all in favor? Carried." He stood. "Move to adjourn, motion carried."

Leaving the room, he felt a twinge of guilt. *Sometimes I push 'em around too much.* But how else could he get things done?

* * *

Coming to his office by its main entrance, Cogdill saw that his chief secretary had made a good start on her In-basket. "Morning, Glynnis. Anybody need me right away?"

She smiled. "Nothing urgent. How was the trip? Is there anything I should know about it?"

"Not until it hits your desk, I'd expect." That was the good thing about working together more than twenty years: you didn't have to dot all the *i*'s. Glynnis Payne was fifty, two years older than himself but not looking it. If ever she decided to retire, he dreaded having to adjust to someone new.

Now he said, "I want to see Dr. Mareth Fallon in my office as soon as possible. Find out when, and let me know, please."

"Right." She nodded. "Anything else?"

"Not at the moment." Moving toward his own office door, he added, "If any calls come in, my line's open."

Fallon was available at five-thirty; before she arrived, Cogdill rechecked her personnel file. In ten years at Phoenix she'd built an impressive project record. Minor tasks, mostly, compared to this one, but they showed her approach to be sound.

When she arrived, right on time, he looked her over. Mareth Fallon was tall, thin upstairs and heavier below, with a long, ruddy face under sandy hair cut to need little or no maintenance. Her expression was pleasant.

As she sat across the desk, facing him, he handed her the grant proposal. "We have a crash job, picking up after Gilcorp on the AIDS problem. A fairly open budget, and I want you to boss the lab end—the real work. Do you want it?"

Looking not at all surprised, she said, "I knew what it was; things leak. Yes, I do—*if* you can meet some conditions."

"A raise comes with it, of course. What else?"

She handed him a sheet of paper. "Here's a list of twelve researchers I'd like to have with me; I'll settle for any six. They won't be easy to get, so I'm asking that you put money no object." Her smile came lopsided. "If you have to pay any of them more than you're paying me, that's all right, too. Because the name of this game is results; I can't play it any other way."

He looked at her list: some names he knew, others not. He nodded. "I like your thinking. Until we've approached these people I can't make any guarantees. But for now, would you phase out your present work and begin setting up the support team?"

She nodded; he said, "For physical plant I had in mind the

ground floor of Building K-5; we're clearing space from two completed projects, and could vacate the rest of that level within two or three months. Satisfactory?"

Her headshake wasn't negation; she said, "When you move, you *really* move, don't you?"

"Then are we agreed?"

"I think so. One thing, though: who will I be working for? Directly, I mean."

"Does it matter? A manager's a manager."

Her breath came out a snort. "Unless he's a shithead. My file will show that for two solid years I was stuck on a project that got nowhere. Finally I gave up and transferred."

"What happened to the project?"

"After you fired Merle Gravens, it succeeded."

Recall came. "Oh—*that* one." His brief laugh served for punctuation. "Yes. I see what you mean. Well, then—do you know Kennet Bardeen? If so, what's your opinion?"

"I've met him; he seems reasonable enough, which should indicate competence. He even has a sense of humor. So—"

"So you'll take the job?"

Her sudden smile gave her attractiveness. "If you can get me any fair share of the people I've asked for." She stood. "Meanwhile I'll go ahead with the tentative arrangements."

A handshake seemed in order. Cogdill stepped around his desk and shared one.

He smiled. "I'll be in touch."

"Yes. Good luck with your recruiting."

As he watched her leave, Cogdill mused: *Her walk is awkward, but her thinking isn't.*

Sitting again, he called Glynnis Payne. "Get word to Kennet Bardeen. I want to see him here tomorrow morning, nine o'clock."

When she'd acknowledged, he closed down his desk terminal and considered the upcoming evening. His silent home didn't attract him; might as well stay here again, this night.

But not the next. For one thing, he was running out of fresh clothes.

# II

Kennet Bardeen had met the Feen's Chairman only a few times, but rumor said he was a tyrant in the Board room. Enroute to Cogdill's office, Bardeen kept trying to digest butterflies.

After a brief wait the Chairman's secretary sent him in—to a dark-paneled room, not large but free of clutter. The oversized desk carried two computer terminals and a multiline phone console; one of the terminal screens would do the video.

Immediately he put his attention to Thane Cogdill. Seated, the man didn't look as tall as Bardeen knew him to be. Above a thin, weathered face, his greying hair was trimmed closer than the current norm. Not by much, but noticeably.

The man gestured toward a chair near the desk. "Sit down."

No handshakes. Right. Bardeen sat, then waited. After perhaps a minute that seemed more like thirty, Cogdill spoke. "I have Board approval to appoint you director of a major project. We have a government grant, practically no limits except deliver-or-no-pay, to develop an AIDS vaccine that really works. Cure, too, if possible."

"Sir, I thought Gilcorp held that contract."

Cogdill's grin carried a hint of secret triumph. "Not any more. It's a fair guess that *their* vaccine changed the virus so as to give it new vectors. No one has any idea how, but what other answer is there? So they're out, and we're in."

The Chairman paused. "Well?"

*Say it right.* "What I'm good at, sir, is keeping teams on track, monitoring what's working and what isn't, cutting out people—or lines of endeavor—that aren't getting anywhere."

"I know. That's why you're here."

The dry tone and lack of facial expression gave no clues. "But I'm not a lab man. Before I could evaluate the medical reports, I'd need them translated into English."

10

Cogdill's brows rose. "You're not a physicist, either, but your ceramic-engine project proved out."

"I know what physics is *about*; I don't need gravity or voltage explained to me. Except for some of the details. But when it comes to biochemistry I'm totally ignorant."

One eyebrow up, the other down; Cogdill was versatile. "And if I see to it that you're provided translations you can follow?"

"If you can guarantee that, sir, please count me in." He felt he should explain further. "I'm not trying to be difficult; I'd love to have the job. I just want to be sure I can do it."

"Because your career would hang on it."

For no reason he could understand, Bardeen found himself grinning. "That too, of course. But also because this particular job is more important than *any* one person's career."

Standing, Cogdill walked around his desk; Bardeen got up to accept the Chairman's handshake. "I'm sold; the project's yours. If the translations let you down, you're free of it without prejudice. If you screw up on your own, that's something else."

"Seems fair enough, sir."

The other man made a snort. "It should; it's the best offer you're going to get." He rummaged inside a dark, polished wooden cabinet. "If you like bourbon, I think we've earned ourselves a drink. Then I'll tell you how the job begins."

The whiskey was strongly flavored, almost like sour mash; Bardeen enjoyed it. After a moment, Cogdill handed across a piece of paper. "Your lab chief is Dr. Mareth Fallon. She knows you're to head the project, and agrees. Here's a list of people she wants, and where they work now; try to steal at least half a dozen for her, and the more the better."

"Yes, sir. She'd better do the bait letters herself, and Personnel can take it from there."

"Good. Now then—your physical plant will occupy most of ground level, Building K-5. Get with Neal Bratton to coordinate moving his stuff out, and with Fallon for where she wants to start installing hers. Put your own office in a corner nearest the main entrance. You have more questions?"

"No, sir." Those aspects of any project were duck soup.

"Good. I do, though. How soon can you be loose from everything you're doing now, to put full time on this one?"

*Think fast, and don't guess wrong.* It's Wednesday, most of the day left and nothing says a man has to stay home on Saturday: "Would Monday morning be all right, sir?"

An abrupt nod. "Fine. All necessary authorizations will be on your present desk by Friday. Any questions, call me directly." The Chairman stood. He offered a handshake; Bardeen took it.

As Bardeen turned to leave, Cogdill said, "You're a project chief now. The only time you have to call me sir is when you screw up and I chew your living ass out."

There was a lot of Wednesday left to work with; Bardeen set up an afternoon meeting with Mareth Fallon, then began putting all his current work assignments on skids to the people who would inherit them. By noon he was almost sure he wouldn't need to come in on Saturday, after all.

He lunched at the main cafeteria, then met with Roger Forrest, who for some years had been his favorite assistant. Older, baldish and dour-looking, Forrest was never talkative. Now he said, "Something on your mind?"

"Plenty. I know you're doing well, these days, on your own projects; if you want to stay that route, I won't blame you. But I've been handed a big one, and I'd very much like to have you for backup on it."

Forrest's expression didn't change; he leaned forward. "You might tell me more."

The explanation took a time. When it was done, Forrest said, "I'll be with you. Is Monday soon enough?"

Mareth Fallon moved oddly, with an impression of clumsiness. But after a few minutes, talking, Bardeen found himself liking her. As she said, "Get me six or more of the people on the list I gave the Chairman, and I can tackle the job." She gave her long-faced head half a shake. "Less than that, I'd have to say the odds are too long. And I detest hopeless assignments."

"I'm not fond of undersupported projects, myself. But the Chairman assured me we won't have that problem." She still looked skeptical; he said, "Either you're satisfied, or I'm out, too. All right?"

She nodded. "I'll need the ground-floor plans for K-5."

Leaving the cubbyhole, half lab and half office, that was Fallon's current working base, he thought, *Lady, I hope you satisfy easier than it looks like you might!*

When Bardeen got home, later than usual, it was nearly the kids' bedtime. So before anything else, he spent time unwinding with seven-year-old Donald and five-year-old Celia. Then he and auburn-haired Jenny had dinner, highlighted by the baked salmon she did so well.

Not until he brought out the chilled champagne and suggested they take it into their bedroom did Jenny get her first sign that the Bardeens had something to celebrate. Even then, he delayed the announcement for a time.

First things first . . .

By Monday the ground level of K-5 was cleared. Over the next three days Bardeen and Forrest got their adjoining offices into operation, while Mareth Fallon rode herd on every item of delivered equipment like a jealous nursemaid.

Rounding up Fallon's key personnel took longer. One top-rated man, Kurt Denholm, kept adding demands until Fallon said, "Oh, let him go; nobody's *that* good."

The funny part was when Denholm called on Bardeen and tried to backtrack. Bardeen shook his head. "You're too hard to deal with. We don't have time for it."

Before the end of the month, actual research was under way; Bardeen began eyeballing Fallon's reports. Her technical secretary, Aileen Kayler, explained the parts he didn't understand. "Yes, we *are* doing a fast recap of Gilcorp's work. HEW made those reports available, so while Dr. Fallon intends to bypass the obvious blind alleys, she does want to skim through the lines of experiment that led directly to their results."

"What for? Their stuff backfired, didn't it?"

"But we don't know why, sir. And we need to find out."

He nodded. "I suppose so. Seems a waste, though."

The answers took longer than anyone liked, but once found, turned out to be relatively simple. Dr. Fallon didn't even need an interpreter.

"The immune system," she said, "is a tricky thing. You might think it couldn't possibly be too efficient; if you do, you've probably never heard of lupus erythematosus. You become immune to *yourself*; the condition is sometimes fatal, and the course of the illness can be horribly unpleasant."

"But Gilcorp's vaccine didn't trigger anything like that. Did it?"

"No." Fallon shook her head. "Because they didn't go in that direction. Their effort was to beef up the AIDS-produced antibodies, to handle the invasion. But for the reasons I've just mentioned, they were afraid of making the antibody too effective." She shrugged. "So as it turns out, they made it not quite effective enough."

Rog Forrest leaned forward; for the first time since the meeting had begun, he spoke. "In what way?"

MEMO TO THE BOARD OF DIRECTORS, ATT'N CHAIRMAN COGDILL:

Dr. Fallon's conclusions are that the Gilcorp serum killed all except perhaps one in a million of the virus population in a human body. But although it seemed the infection could be spread only via blood or semen, a very small proportion of any virus colony might differ. Before the serum, those variants were so few as to pose no problem; they simply couldn't compete against the overwhelming majority of like organisms.

But when nearly all of a virus group was killed, the few survivors, lacking competition, could multiply unchecked. And those, it seems, were the ones that could exist and thrive in tears or saliva or nasal discharge, and even survive dehydration. Dr. Fallon draws a parallel to the emergence, decades ago, of penicillin-resistant gonococci.

She's not yet ready to specify her own major line of attack. I'm not sure she's figured it out herself. But I strongly recommend she be given ample time to do so.

Kennet Bardeen: Director, Project AIDS

He turned to Aileen Kayler. "Except for the last paragraph, the Board won't think *I* wrote any of that."

The next Monday morning brought a new problem. Walking the two long blocks from his tube station, Bardeen saw Phoenix's main entrance besieged by a noisy mob. A few carried placards, but most didn't. Bardeen glimpsed extra security guards; the situation was in control.

But that didn't get him inside. He backtracked, went around the corner and along the compound's east side to the delivery gate.

There a guard checked his ID and admitted him, saying, "A popular place here, this morning. What's going on up front?"

"A crowd at the doors; that's all I know." After a moment to orient himself, Bardeen headed for K-5.

At the project area only about half the personnel were present, and none working. Waiting, Bardeen learned, for the rest of the crew to come in. Because when they did, the Chairman had a few words to say.

With Cogdill came a technician, who turned on the oversized Tri-V in "Lecture Alley." When everyone was seated, the Chairman said, "I don't know who leaked, but we weren't exactly under secrecy, so it doesn't matter. Anyway, my hunch is that the blab came from D.C. But the info went to our local Tri-V reporter who can't even spell his own name right. I mean that unparalleled horse's hemorrhoid, Steive Dilmarr.

"All right; let's view the tape."

Dilmarr was a flash boy: bleached ringlets and artificial tan. He began, "Big news today, about Chicago's own Phoenix Foundation! Working in secret, that research empire conducts unauthorized experiments on human subjects, risking their lives to a dread disease. AIDS. Yes, fellow citizens—AIDS."

*What a crock!* But judging by the crowd outside, some people believed it.

"Our own government has approved this inhumane research, right here in this very city!" He gave the Foundation's address. "American citizens don't have to put up with—"

Cogdill gestured; the tech cut the set off. Mareth Fallon said, "Then the crowd out there wants to shut us down?"

The Chairman shook his head. "Not exactly. Maybe some do. But most are here demanding to serve as volunteers for this nonexistent program. They're AIDS victims."

Cogdill wasn't done yet. "Now that we've been chased out of the pocket, so to speak, we need to make some changes."

Bardeen nodded. "All right; where do we start?"

"Let's a few of us talk about that in my office."

After dinner, with the kids in bed, Bardeen unloaded some of his frustration to Jenny. "We're going to have to fake it that the project's been moved entirely away from this area. And if asked, play dumb. To get past the pickets, research people will wear tech

coveralls and union badges." He grinned. "Me, I have a briefcase
with a drug company's monogram on it. Anyone asks me, I'm a
hotshot salesman in pharmaceuticals."

Jenny frowned. "All this outside distraction is getting to you,
isn't it?"

"Too much." He checked his watch. "The news is on. Let's see
what Dilmarr tries next."

To Bardeen's surprise, the newsie was interviewing Thane
Cogdill. Lacking makeup, alongside Dilmarr's flamboyance the
Chairman looked like a mummy—a mummy who had led a hard
life. Bardeen whistled. "The old boy doesn't mind taking it to
them on their home grounds!"

"—explanation, if there is one," Dilmarr was saying. "So tell
us, Mr. Cogdill, just what devilish work is your Foundation up
to?"

The Chairman's grin had a skeletal look, but his dry-toned
voice was steady. "Looking for a vaccine, possibly a cure, for the
AIDS plague. What's so devilish—?"

Dilmarr cut in. "Why the secrecy? And why the experiments
on human beings?"

Cogdill shrugged. "What secrecy? You had no difficulty in
learning of the project. Publicity, no. Would you prefer that we
arouse hopes concerning a project that's barely begun?"

It was the reporter's turn to shrug. "If you claim that's been your
motive, I suppose I can't prove otherwise. But—"

Dilmarr had no monopoly on interruptions; Cogdill said,
"Your talk of experiments on humans is ridiculous—and libelous.
You're accusing the Phoenix Foundation of violating Federal
law."

Dilmarr glanced up, toward the wall clock, but Cogdill beat
him to the punch. Standing quickly, he said, "I have no more
time to waste here. Our legal department will be in touch with
you and with this station. Good evening."

As he walked away, the camera also showed, clearly, Steive
Dilmarr with his mouth open but nothing coming out. Even
when Cogdill paused to say, "If you're truly worried about this
city's health, you'll be pleased to know that we're moving our
project to a remote location. I'm sure it's obvious, after the
reaction to your irresponsible statements this morning, why that
location will not be announced." This time he did leave.

Switching the set off, after Dilmarr in his final thirty seconds
had tried—and failed—to restore his aura of confident domi-

nance, Bardeen found himself gently pounding his fist against a chair arm. "Did you *see* that, Jenny?"

"Yes, I certainly did. Your Chairman is rather impressive, isn't he?"

"I've never been to a Board meeting, but I see why he's called 'the lion tamer.'" He chuckled. "If Dilmarr had any knowledge of the Feen's scuttlebutt, he'd never have given Cogdill a shot at him. Makeup or no makeup."

# III

For several days the picketing of Phoenix increased, spreading to all entrances. Then, without comment from the station, Steive Dilmarr ceased to appear on Tri-V news; if he found similar employment, it wasn't locally. Lacking his encouragement, the harassing activity tapered off and ended.

Nonetheless, since both personnel access and supply deliveries had been badly hampered, Phoenix went ahead with plans to reduce vulnerability. By expansion, for one thing, including a land purchase that gave the Feen its own tubetrain station, complete with some rather sophisticated security gates and a short siding track to accommodate its newly purchased cargo cars.

What the commuting public may have thought of the infrequent but inevitable delays, Bardeen didn't know and didn't ask; he had too much else on his mind. Fallon's diagnosis of Gilcorp's failure was still the project's only solid result. Bardeen's tension built; there was nothing he could do personally, but when your name tops the letterhead, you're first man under the gun.

He was not especially pleased, one evening, to see Steive Dilmarr on Tri-V again, broadcasting from a nearby state; the man's new role was doing lead-in for the syndicated evangelist Jody Jay Tolliver, a born-again bigot whose blond hair, in hot weather, tended to ooze grease down his rotund cheeks.

Inexorably, the AIDS plague spread. Worldwide statistics, while hardly accurate, became more and more alarming. From D.C., Pete Randall sent confidential reports of research status in the Soviet bloc. Dr. Fallon reported that it seemed to recapitulate Gilcorp's efforts, mistakes and all. Meanwhile they wanted lots of help, but no publicity about it.

She asked, "Can we send them our own results, Mr. Cogdill? I mean, will a Soviet or joint success fulfill our own grant?"

The Chairman nodded. "I forward our data to Pete Randall. From there on it's the President's decision, but I don't expect an old pol like Bert Norris to play dog-in-the-manger. As to our grant—yes, any results, developed either by ourselves or in cooperation, are acceptable and cost-plus." A tight smile. "I have that in writing. A Congressional committee went retroactive on us once; it won't happen again."

Cogdill was a puzzle of inconsistency. Sometimes he was jovial and considerate, but unpredictably he could turn into a downright abusive martinet. Mareth Fallon's guess was that varying pressures from D.C. made the difference, but Bardeen noticed that when Laura Casey, the HEW liaison, was in town, Cogdill was a lot easier to get along with.

The reasons, Bardeen felt, were none of his business, so he kept his speculations to himself. The project didn't need a gossip mill; it had enough troubles already.

Most of those were the kind he was good at handling: supply foulups, personal differences and backbiting, keeping tabs on the flow and completeness of records, taking the brunt of outside pressures so that they didn't affect the work—that sort of thing. He'd done it all before; now wasn't too different.

A major flap came when the junior Senator from California developed AIDS. Several of his colleagues moved to expel him; only by a narrow margin did he hold his seat. No one thought he'd contracted the disease sexually; the hardworking legislator and devoted family man could hardly have found *time* for fooling around. But scarehead thinking strikes at anything that moves.

Frustrated, the ouster group's leader took aim at the Feen. As Cogdill said, the grant left no way to renege on payment for success—but so long as monies already paid were left alone, Congress could terminate the project at any time.

\* \* \*

For that fight, Cogdill went to Washington and took Bardeen along. Sitting alongside the Chairman in testimony before a joint House-Senate committee, again the younger man was impressed by Cogdill's tactics. "Can you specify," a Senator asked, "that your group will produce a cure? And when?"

"If experimental breakthroughs could be predicted and scheduled, we'd all have an easier time of it, wouldn't we?" Cogdill leaned forward. "But will we produce, you ask? If I didn't think so, I wouldn't have agreed to return all government funds if we fail."

"Fat bit of good *that's* doing for a lot of sick people! Sick, and dying. I—"

"You have an alternative in mind?" Cogdill's words cut like a knife. "I'm sure we'd all like to hear it."

After another hour or so of waffling, the hearing adjourned.

Laura Casey drove Cogdill and Bardeen to a hotel. The three had dinner in the Chairman's room; afterward, more or less tactfully, Bardeen was sent off to his adjoining quarters, to go over his notes from the hearing and then get a good night's sleep. "We'll meet for breakfast here at seven," Cogdill said. "You, too, Laura—we can talk some more before we catch our plane."

Later, ready for bed, Bardeen grinned. He was expected to believe Casey had gone home for the night? In a way, it was nice to know that the Chairman's talent for convincing people wasn't *totally* effective.

Aside from that: whatever kept Cogdill happy, had to be good for the project.

Breakfast next morning was pleasant, and the flight home uneventful. Except for a brief recap on the hearing, the two men didn't talk much.

Predictably, a push came for nationwide AIDS quarantine. Other nations were doing it, was the argument—and proponents ignored the fact that it wasn't doing other nations much good: the virus spread so easily from latents that isolation of actives had little impact. And as one commentator put it: "When half of us are quarantining the other half, who'll mind the store?"

No easy answer existed; risk and fear had to be lived with.

Bright spots did occur. Eighteen months into the project, with little apparent progress except a few promising leads, HEW statistics showed a leveling-off of new AIDS cases. "The mutated virus," Fallon reported, "spreads much more easily, as we know. But with this strain of the virus, the average period of latency must be considerably greater."

"So we have more time than we thought?" Bardeen asked.

Fallon made a thin smile. "Let's say we don't have as little as we'd begun to fear."

It was hardly total encouragement, but better than most of what Bardeen had heard lately.

Shared data or no, the Soviets didn't seem to be getting anywhere. Mostly, Fallon said, they tended to repeat, over and over again, experiments the Feen had tried and found wanting. "I think," she said, "their people are afraid to try anything new, for fear of making new mistakes."

"But repeating old ones is all right?" asked Rog Forrest.

Fallon shrugged. "That's what it looks like."

The trouble, Bardeen thought, scratching an itch under his "flu mask," was that what the project did learn tended to make life more difficult without being truly helpful.

None of the new inconveniences carried any real assurance. On the project itself two active AIDS cases had surfaced: one of Fallon's prime specialists, and a young lab tech. Both were scrupulous in wearing gloves as well as masks, but all the scrubbing imaginable couldn't make Bardeen comfortable at work. Even though there was no proof the contagion had occurred there.

The two-year mark. As Bardeen gathered his gear and started to leave his office, at the door stood Mareth Fallon. "Aren't you staying for our project anniversary party?"

"I don't think so. Have a good time, though."

She put a hand to his shoulder. "You haven't read my latest in-house reports?"

"No translator. Kayler's been home with the flu."

Surprisingly, Fallon grabbed and hugged him; he realized she'd already had a few drinks. "Then hear this, buddy boy! Don't leak it outside the labs, just yet, but the war's taken a new turn. And with today's authorization to test our stuff on volunteers, we're gearing up to win it."

*   *   *

He enjoyed the party too thoroughly to feel safe in taking transport to his car and driving home, so slept in the stopover facility he'd set up behind his office. The next day he found, in his In-basket, notice of his appointment to the Board of Directors.

The day before his sixth Board meeting, Bardeen got a briefing from Mareth Fallon. Previously, because Fallon wanted the breakthrough held under wraps until she could prove virtually total success, he'd had to keep his reports to a low profile.

Now, though, she'd given him the green light. He looked through his notes. Fallon had worked on two fronts: the vulnerability of the virus itself, plus increasing an organism's resistance to it. And when the logjam blew, *both* sides went.

Part A was a synthesized organic factor, more than an enzyme but less than a virus—"protovirus," one report called it—that was harmless to cellular life but inhibited viral potency by nearly eighty percent. Part B, to increase immunity, was a shotgun approach, a nonspecific agent. As Fallon put it, the only good virus was a dead virus. "And I'm not above swatting a few bacteria, if they get in the way."

He ran through it aloud; at the end, she nodded. "You have it clearly enough; I think the Board will understand." They both knew, he felt, that she should be the one giving the report and receiving credit directly—but that wasn't the way things worked.

At the Board meeting he didn't tell it all the way through, after all; as soon as he said "effective vaccine" a flood of questions stopped him, until Cogdill slapped the table to bring silence. "They don't want to know its pedigree, Kennet, only what it does. *What*, mind you—not how."

All right, then: the bare bones. "Aside from the vaccine aspect, existing latent AIDS infections have been wiped out within a week to ten days. The antibodies, that indicate presence of the virus, vanish, and no remaining signs can be found in tissue samples."

Breaking the sudden quiet, Cogdill said, "What about active cases? Any luck with those?"

"With higher dosage—and over a longer time, of course—the factor/agent combination eradicates the virus and stops further damage. Naturally it can't restore tissues or functions already destroyed." He shrugged to break tension out of neck and shoulders. "I've oversimplified, but that's about it."

"Not quite. What about side effects?" Roark again.

"Throughout the course of treatment," Bardeen answered, "moderate dehydration, some lethargy, and a mild fever."

"But you can't know, yet, about long-term effects."

"Hell, no," said Cogdill. "Compared to AIDS, though, who wants to wait?" No one contradicted him. "So if I have it right, now we need to produce enough of this product for about four billion people, and then persuade them to line up and take their shots." He shook his head. "This isn't the end of the project; it's just the start."

"Not exactly," and Bardeen had everyone's attention. "The team knows the logistics of mass injection would be impossible. So a subgroup's been working on an orally effective form."

"Pills?" Slade always needed things stated simply.

Bardeen spread his hands. "If you like. Or powder, or liquid; the form wouldn't be important. We—"

Cogdill cut in. "How's the progress on that?"

"They're close, but nothing firm yet."

"When it is, I want to see you in my office." The Chairman stood. "Meeting's adjourned."

Nearly six weeks later, Fallon gave Bardeen her test results and he took them to Cogdill. The Chairman still had questions. "The oral version works, then." Bardeen nodded. "How about quantities? Possible overdoses?"

"With respect to normal tissue, the stuff seems to be practically inert, and is excreted within a relatively short time—no buildup."

Gradually, Cogdill's thoughtful scowl cleared. "All right; you've produced. Proving that I was correct in putting you on the Board." *But I did no research, I only managed!* "Do you know what to do next?"

"Switch project emphasis from research to production?"

"Well, not quite yet." The Chairman glowered. "Oh hell, if you can't figure it out, I'll have to tell you. Call Pete Randall and have him put you through to MacIlwaine at HEW."

"And tell him what? I don't understand."

Cogdill leaned forward. "Dammit, do you think getting medication into the general public, all of it, would be much easier than giving them shots?"

"But, then how—?"

"In the *food*, Bardeen—and maybe the water. No big ad campaign or educational propaganda—just spread the stuff around and cure the silly pukes, like it or not. But that's going to need government backing and government money. So now you know what to tell MacIlwaine. And when you're done with Pete Randall, have him call me."

"Yes, sir." *Well, he is chewing me out. . . .*

"Don't you want to know why?" Bardeen nodded. "Because the grant's winding up; it's time, now, for mass production. We can't handle more than a fraction of that, ourselves—but I want the main contract, with a lock on all the subcontractors!"

Bardeen left—thinking that Cogdill could be a real sonofabitch sometimes. But he was one *able* sonofabitch.

On the phone, Roth MacIlwaine looked and sounded skeptical. "Just put the curative agent in food and drink, but don't bother to tell the public? Even for Thane Cogdill, that's autocratic."

What *had* Cogdill said? Well, fake it! "The program would be announced, of course. The point is to avoid an expensive educational campaign, to provide the cure in a way that requires least effort from the public. That's hardly autocratic, is it?"

MacIlwaine sighed. "I suppose not. I'm tired, is what, and up against a seminar tomorrow. Look—Bardeen, is it?—tell your boss I'll get on it by Monday and call him ASAP."

Bardeen reached to cut the circuit, but the other man said, "Hold it! One more thing. Tell Cogdill we needn't lobby the FDA for approval. Two of their top people are AIDS-latent."

For the first time in over two years, Kennet Bardeen could take a vacation. He and Jenny and the kids spent ten days at a pair of lake cabins; when he returned to work, he felt like tackling just about anything.

Project AIDS shifted into its new phase; during the process, Bardeen ran liaison with MacIlwaine at HEW in D.C. Cogdill went to the capital only once; on returning, he reported that the Food and Drug Administration's red tape had indeed been bypassed.

Sooner than Bardeen expected, the cure/vaccine began to be distributed: mostly in the U.S. at first, but also to countries most closely allied. A nonprofit arm of the Feen set up a program to get the curative agent out to countries that couldn't synthesize *or* pay for it. The government put no official support behind that move, but the government didn't check on all of Cogdill's dealings with subcontractors, either. As usual, the bureaucracy's left hand never let its right hand know what was going on. In this case, that idiosyncracy was a blessing.

Fallon herself headed the team that went to help the Soviets begin vaccine/cure production. China and India first refused similar offers, then hurriedly reversed their fields. Probably, Bardeen thought, AIDS was getting into the circles of power.

When production-and-distribution had been running for a year and some months, Cogdill told the Board, "Except for maintenance chores and routine supply of product, Project AIDS is wound up. I move we close it out."

The vote was perfunctory; Cogdill said, "You can't know how glad I am that these problems are over and done with."

Slap of palm to table. "Meeting adjourned."

# BOOK
# TWO

"It is common knowledge that nobody is always right the first time."

(From Origins, by Rome dos Caras.)

# IV

Noise woke five-year-old Brad Salich—and scared him, because his mom and dad hardly ever yelled at each other. And never this late at night. Pushing the sheet back because he was sweating, he sat up and listened to the voices from the living room.

"I want another child, Stan, and I intend to have one. Whatever it takes. I—"

"You're crazy! Ulla, we've been to three fertility clinics and they all say I'm okay. So what's the point in—"

"Okay? Sure you are. Along with ninety percent of the men being tested, these days. But still they're stuck, same as we are, with the Only Child Syndrome."

"Oh, come on, Ulla. Lots of people have more than one child." Quieter voices now; no more yelling.

"Born in the past five years or so?"

A pause, then: "Sure. How about the Harpers?"

"One by Edna's first husband; remember? And one by Arnold, two years ago. No more since, though."

"Maybe they decided two was plenty."

Brad's mother's laugh sounded ragged. "Fat chance. Arnold wants a son, not just a daughter and stepdaughter."

"Well, that's just one case. What about—?"

"Oh, quit it, Stan. My support group has hashed this over and over. And checked statistics, for what those are worth. Do you know which groups have beaten the Only Child Syndrome, these past few years?"

"Well, I—"

"Women who divorce and remarry, who have affairs, who shop around a lot. Welfare mothers, some of them, though certainly they're not all promiscuous types, nor the only ones, either. You see the pattern?"

From the way Stan Salich spoke, Brad could almost see his father shaking his head. "I don't want to see it. I—"

"You don't want to see me looking for stud service, and I can't blame you. But the trick seems to be, a woman can have more than one child, but not by the same father. Stan—I *am* going to have another if I possibly can, and if that's what it takes, that's what I'm going to do."

Brad's mother gasped then, and she said, "You wouldn't!"

"Hit you? No. But it was close, Ulla. Close." Then, "When do you plan to start?"

"Not just yet—not while you feel this way. We can talk, Stan. I knew you'd hate the idea—but I had to open the subject sometime, and now I have. So that's a start. Sooner or later you'll see why I have to do this."

"You think so?"

"I'm sure of it. I know you, Stan."

"Oh?" The man made a sound, half laugh and half snort. "I wouldn't bet your lunch money on that, if I were you."

Either the talk dropped below Brad's hearing level or his drowsiness took over. The drying sweat had chilled him; the boy pulled the sheet up and curled into sleeping mode.

Ulla Salich wanted an affair the same way she wanted a good case of poison ivy. What she did want was a second baby. Ulla herself had been an only child, and in retrospect she felt she'd missed a lot. With a brother or sister around, would she have turned into such a loner? She was still fighting her way out of that bag, and knew it.

It was Stan's fault. First he insisted on waiting until they had money saved up—and after Brad was born, two more years before they tried again. And by then, the Sterility Plague had started. The Only Child Syndrome, the media called it. If they'd got the show on the road earlier, like she wanted, she'd *have* her second child. He'd set this mess up, Stan had—not that he'd meant to— so now he could damn well cope with how she handled it. Ulla was all done with taking no for an answer.

It wasn't any dissatisfaction with their son. Brad was a sweet kid—intelligent, outgoing, and no more stubborn than you'd expect from half Swede and half Polack. One nice kid, in fact. But Ulla didn't want him growing up lonesome, the way she had.

All right; she'd laid it on the line to Stan. Now things were up to her. The only question was, *who*? She couldn't cheat on her women friends, so their husbands were out. Irene Tilden might not mind, but Fred's whole family ran to fat.

Ace Corbett was divorced, and healthy enough. He had a big mouth, though. Scratch Ace.

The single guys they knew—Gene the alky, Jimbo the sleaze, Karl the latent gay or maybe not so latent? Al nice enough but not what you'd call bright, Eddie on insulin and maybe it ran in the family. Pete the Fleet, the fanatic jogger; hell, the man was so bashful he couldn't be kissed at New Year's!

Wait a minute; how about the redheaded one who showed up at the Tildens' sometimes? Murphy or something; a little Irish couldn't hurt. But last time, he was high on something. Not that she and Stan minded a little flash now and then—but nothing heavy, that might come back on you later. Or hurt your kids, even.

Ulla sighed. Nobody she could think of, seemed to fill the bill; she might as well go hang out in bars for pickups. And sure to hell she would do no such a thing.

Maybe artificial insemination wouldn't bother Stan so much. But getting a baby from a squirt gun? Ulla shuddered; somehow that idea gave her the fidgets.

*If you're going to do it, do it right.*

Stan Salich thought he understood Ulla's resentments; she'd said them enough. But he had no good answers. Hell yes he'd stalled, until he got the promotion and could *afford* a kid, including a place big enough for the little house ape to run around. Stan said "house ape" so as not to let anybody know how just looking at the kid turned him into warm mush. A man should act like a man, Stan's father always said. Maybe more than he needed to, but there you were.

And then holding off before a second kid. All the doctors said to, and they should know. But Ulla seemed to think Stan should've seen the Only Child thing coming up, before it happened. Well, he hadn't, so now they were stuck with it.

Except, she said maybe he was but she wasn't. She said a lot of things, Ulla did. For one, that he ought to go back to his real name, Szalicz, that his dad still carried. But back in college, before the Army got him for two years, he'd decided Salich was better for business. He still thought so, and wasn't about to change his mind.

Well, anything Ulla really wanted to do, she'd do it. He hoped like hell she wouldn't go get herself somebody else's kid.

But if she did, he'd have to put up with it. Because if it came to that or losing Ulla, he had no choice at all.

Failing to find substance in the demographic report, Roth MacIlwaine stubbed out a cigarette. The entire HEW complex had been put off limits for smoking, but here in his own office they could all go piss up a rope!

His coffee was cold; too much work to microwave it again. He paged back and reread a section that hadn't made sense the first time; his second try didn't help, either.

One problem was that nobody had any good idea when this new trend had begun. Over nearly a decade the birthrate had been down near Zero Growth—due to late marriages and increased use of birth control. And notwithstanding strong attack from various quarters, abortion was still legal.

So when had Zero PG shifted to Negative? Shuffling through the pages, trying to spot some definitive statement in all the jargon-filled text, MacIlwaine snorted his frustration. The report was mostly talk and damned few figures.

Once again he tried the part that claimed to be a Brief Recap. *They wouldn't know brief if it bit 'em in the leg!* But on a third read, bypassing the jargon and feeding the meager facts into his desktop computer, he began to see a pattern.

A surprising number of women appeared to be sterile from the word go. But not so fast: Mac fed in more data, and found that a high percentage of this lot had had abortions. Oops—in most cases, make that one per person. Now why? *There's something here; stay with it.*

Other women who'd been aborted had children later—but again, one per mother. Why? And then, to blow holes in any theory he might have had, MacIlwaine found a few cases of aborted women who went on to have more than one child.

Probably there were other criteria he could have put through the machine, but Mac was pooped, and tomorrow was brief-the-Secretary time. He shut down and went home.

Next day, as usual, Secretary Sheila Granger, Jr., was right on time. Granger seldom had a good press; her dislike of newsies was all too obvious. What she did have was presidential support; Homer Varnell gave loyalty in the same measure he asked it.

The meeting's opening reports carried little cheer. The population's median age continued to increase, and at an increasing rate; when the peak Baby Boomer wave hit retirement, the ongoing Social Security crisis could turn into all-out disaster. "Not to mention," added the Assistant Sec'y, "whether such a diminished work force can keep the wheels turning."

Oh, sure; retirement age could be raised again, with added incentives for people to keep working past it. "But sooner or later," the man concluded, "that stopgap won't suffice."

Frowning, Granger nodded. "This is no surprise. We've been tiptoeing around that certainty for some time; maybe it's time we face up to it and begin looking for some new answers."

Roth MacIlwaine cleared his throat. "There's only one answer I can see. Find out what's *causing* the Sterility Plague, and see if we can do something about it."

Nobody topped Mac's suggestion.

At the President's next Cabinet meeting, Granger took MacIlwaine along. He listened to the initial parts, foreign affairs and such, without much interest. Until an aide from State said, "Concerning the population matter: I'd like to point out that the problem threatens all industrialized countries. Underdeveloped areas actually benefit to some extent. To China and India, in particular, the Sterility Plague is a lifesaver."

Then Defense took over; Secretary Bergson stated that the armed forces were deeply concerned about the future dwindling of available manpower "—of both sexes, of course. HEW has noted the problems of a decreasing civilian work force; while it may go without saying, I want to make clear that this decline also affects our side of the fence."

When Granger got her turn, she made the summary brief. Then, "Roth, why don't you just tell them what you've already told me?"

He stood. "It won't take long. The only avenue of attack I can think of is to research the Sterility Plague in earnest—and then try, all-out, to overcome it."

Homer Varnell said, "Thank you, Mr. MacIlwaine. Sheila, this comes under your department. Rough out the possibilities that occur to you, and fill me in next week."

Walking back to HEW alongside Granger, Mac had only one idea in mind. Give Thane Cogdill a call.

"Look; I don't even want to mention the problem on the phone here. Can you come down sometime in the next few days?"

A pause. Then, "Yes, I guess so, Mac. Something big?"

"You could say that. Now I can't promise anything, but my bet is that the grant contract will be free of budgetary limitations. But—"

Cogdill's laugh carried an edge. "But no results, no pay; right?"

"You've done it before, and always collected."

"Yes, but not in the blind, without knowing what the job is or having a fair idea whether we can do it."

"Once you're here, you'll be told everything we have on hand to date. And of course the travel tab's on Uncle."

"That's good. Because I'm bringing along some help."

Bardeen and Fallon accompanied Cogdill to D.C. Over the three days, each evening he managed to disengage from his traveling companions and spend time with Laura Casey. The last night, she said, "You're pushing yourself too hard, Thane."

Reaching, he stroked her hair and cheek. "A little too tensed-up tonight, I'm afraid; yes. I wish we had more time together—but there's always next trip."

"I only wish there were. I've put off telling you, but I have this offer: an overseas appointment. The promotion is simply too good to pass up."

He couldn't answer; finally she said, "If I can, I'll come visit before I leave."

"Yes." Because he needed time, before he could say goodbye.

All during the trip Thane Cogdill had kept a close mouth. Even so, at their final meeting with HEW, the Chairman surprised hell out of Kennet Bardeen.

Pushing away the folder Secretary Granger had brought, Cogdill said, "The Feen's not going for this package. We simply don't know enough, to take it on a contingency basis."

He gestured interruption away. "The problem comes in two parts. First, identify the mechanism. We could tackle that, but only on this basis: you pay us for our work, results or not, and we rebate you for any help you can feed us from other sources."

He looked around the table. "That's clear enough, I trust." No one disagreed. "Now then—if we learn the cause, Part Two is finding a way to circumvent it. And at this point that's something I won't even consider."

MacIlwaine leaned forward. "Why not?"

"Come on, Mac; you're not stupid! If you have no idea what's wrong, how can you contract to do a repair job?"

Granger hadn't said much; now she did. "You're saying, then, that in this time of crisis you refuse to help?"

"I'm saying we'll attempt Part One, but not on contingency. And nobody with the brains God gave a clam would bite on that kind of proposal for Part Two."

"If you'd like to tell the President your opinion in person," she said, "I can arrange an appointment."

Cogdill shrugged. "No need for that. You're the one who works for him; I don't."

The meeting ended. An hour later, the three boarded a fast plane for home.

The grant for Part One, sans any contingency strings, came through. Pleased to be working with Mareth Fallon again, Bardeen as Project Chief assembled a working team and began equipment procurement. In less than two months, research began.

In a correlated effort, the Feen initiated a program—supervised locally and sponsored nationally—of low-cost prenatal and infant care. Bardeen suspected a PR ploy, but kept those suspicions to himself.

As more people grew aware of the upcoming population crunch:

Demonstrating near the emplaced armored weapons that guarded the White House, the League to Protect Social Security demanded a guarantee of continued full benefits without regard to revenues. Aged anywhere from forties to eighties, crowd members cheered as their speaker ended his bullhorned tirade. "No compromise!"

A Tri-V reporter, of an age to be equally concerned someday, remarked on the hemoglobin content of turnips.

Governments made their own comments, or else kept silence. China's, it seemed, might have accepted the Only Child Syndrome as a gift from heaven, if Marxists believed in such a place.

Religious differences aside, Hindu-Sikh India and Muslim Indonesia showed much that same attitude.

The Muslim world took no monolithic stance. In Iran the Ayatollah Khalaf, third of a sequence of fundamentalist rulers, stated that he found no reason to depart from custom. "As Allah in His mercy has ordained, a man may keep four wives. Should any prove barren in this new way of bearing one child but never another, the man may divorce her and keep the child."

"Typical camel shit," said Jenny Bardeen. Her sister, married to an Israeli, lived in Tel Aviv; she had little love for the Arab nations. "Walk *behind*, woman. That's all they know."

Kennet didn't want to talk politics, let alone religion; he wanted to get himself and Jenny into bed, and the sooner the better. "Pretty stupid, I grant you. If the woman walks behind, the man can't enjoy watching her."

He gestured toward their bedroom. "After you?"

When the time came that Stan's opposition had eroded to grudging acceptance, Ulla Salich went to an insemination clinic. "Bright and healthy is what I want," and the doctor said she'd do her best to meet those criteria.

The process was expensive, and didn't pay off. Ulla couldn't be sure whether Stan was more aggrieved or relieved.

Feed enough data into a re-entrant program, and correlations emerge. As usual, the apparent anomalies gave most of the useful information. For instance: since the Only Child Syndrome began, women who had two or more children never seemed to bear more than one by fathers of the same blood type. "There may be other factors," Bardeen told the Board, "but that's the prime item we have to date. So we feel—"

Cogdill stood. "That's enough, Kennet. Basically, what we feel is that we don't know our ass from third base. Any reason to keep this meeting open?"

With a final handslap the Chairman adjourned it, then came around the table to put a hand on Bardeen's shoulder. "You did fine, Kennet. But at this point, let's not say too much."

On Tri-V the Reverend Jody Jay Tolliver announced that he had fasted and prayed for a considerable period, and that his devout efforts had been rewarded. He knew, he said, the cause of the Sterility Plague—and shortly after the next Important Messages he would divulge it. His puffy cheeks belied any idea that he'd ever fasted for more than two hours, but among his flock of true believers, who was counting?

Following the commercials—one was for dashboard-ready plastic Jesuses—he did indeed tell what he had learned. The Plague's cause was *sin*, and any regular viewer knew he didn't mean theft, vandalism, or armed robbery. Tolliver had his own favorite Commandments—and in his book, sin was spelled S-E-X.

He didn't seem quite ready, yet, to pick specific targets.

"Ova," reported Mareth Fallon, "have become rather picky about the gametes they'll accept as fertilizing agents."

Bardeen frowned. "Any clues to the mechanism?"

"Not really. We're fairly certain it's the attachment of a fertilized ovum to a woman's uterine wall, that signals later ova to reject any sperm cell of the same blood type."

"I don't see how what happens to one ovum could affect unreleased ones."

"Neither do I. There must be some kind of feedback from the placenta to the ovaries. At any rate—the 'immune' ova aren't blocking penetration. The sperm does enter, but conjugation of the nuclei breaks down, midway of the process. The incomplete zygote isn't viable; the partially united gametes die."

Bardeen had an idea. "What if you extract two or more ova and try to fertilize them *in vitro* from the same batch of sperm? That way there couldn't be any feedback."

"No. But it's hardly a practical large-scale solution."

"I suppose not. What approaches *are* you trying?"

"About twenty percent of those we'd like to."

He scowled. "*What?* If the funding's short—"

"It's not that. More a matter of supply and demand."

"Tell me about it. I'll see what I can do."

He told the Board, "Fallon's experimental range is limited because ova are hard to come by." Sure, there was the PR pitch for ovaries to be listed on organ donor cards, but response was sparse. "It's like trying to get organs for transplants—all the money in the U.S. Mint won't increase the supply."

Cogdill nodded. "Wish you'd told me sooner. I—"

Angered, Bardeen said, "I didn't *know,* sooner!"

Hand wave. "All right, all right; sorry. As I was going to say, I'll call Granger, and ask if she can do anything about overseas procurement. If she can, the rebate for government assistance would be well worth it."

Bardeen felt his face redden. "You're right, of course. Let me know what word you get?"

"Naturally."

Government aid speeded Fallon's research. But when she did come up with a partial answer, Bardeen didn't like it much.

# V

**A**rriving home after a rough day at the Foundation, Bardeen didn't appreciate seeing Steive Dilmarr's face on the Tri-V. Jenny cut the sound. "It's that rabble-rousing preacher, on next. Tolliver. Something about Phoenix, Dilmarr said. So I thought I'd better record it."

"Right." Setting his things down, he gave her a quick hug and kiss, then fixed himself a Bushmill's with splash. "My Tolliver tolerance serum needs a booster shot."

"Yes. Here he comes now." She turned the volume up.

Florid face grimacing below greased blond hair, the Reverend Jody Jay was off to a running start. "—these sinners, my friends. These agents of the devil himself. The Lord set his mark on the swine who wallowed in that so-called sexual revolution. AIDS, my good friends. Ten years ago, the Lord He had that revolution stopped square in its tracks. But then those great sinners, that Phoenix Foundation, in utter blasphemy they made *vaccines* against the Lord's scourges, so all those other vile sinners could get away scot-free.

"So what did the Lord do *then,* I ask you?"

Dilmarr reassured everyone that we would all learn what the

Lord did then, right after these messages from our local stations. Bardeen took the opportunity to break out some crackers and dip.

Onscreen, again Tolliver was shouting. "What the Lord did— *I'll* tell you what. He struck Pharaoh's curse onto this sinful world. He said, like unto Moses only not exactly the same—the Lord said, 'Now all you sinners, if ye seek to use these vaccines to escape My righteous scourge, then I shalt smite thee on the other cheek as your Savior might have said. For I am a jealous God, though not as jealous as I used to be a time back, so instead of taking all your firstborn the way I did in Egypt, you can keep those. But that's *all* you get!' Now then," said the Reverend Jody Jay, "do you see, do you understand, the infinite mercy of the Lord?"

During the next commercials, as Bardeen replenished his glass—last one before dinner, this would be—he admitted he didn't understand, really. Jenny voted the same way.

Back for his finale, the Reverend said, "My good friends, I wouldn't ask you to go uproot that sinful Phoenix Foundation, that brought all this woe upon the Godly, nor then to spread its substance to the four winds and leave not one stone standing on another. Although if you just happened to do it of your own accord, I'm sure He would find it in His heart to forgive you. No, all I ask is that you *pray* for those poor sinners. Pray for them in the streets. Pray for them on their very own toll-free phone lines, right to their sinful ears at the far end. Pray for them in their own postage-paid envelopes, so that the good Lord will reap the benefits thereof and the sinners shalt *pay* for it all. And now, my good friends: our blessed sister in salvation, Bountiful Harvest Hatfield, will sing us the Benediction."

Having heard the woman's voice before, Bardeen made haste to kill the sound. Not the holo, though; instead he leaned forward. "Bountiful is a meager word, there."

Jenny laughed. "Maybe she takes hormones the way other people take vitamins." Then she sobered. "That man frightens me; he's actually inciting his followers to violence. How does he *dare* blame the Sterility Plague on the Foundation's work?"

Kennet wasn't smiling, either. "The threats he's making, I'm going to run past our legal department.

"But the worst part is: from the lab results Mareth Fallon showed me today, that insane bastard's guesses may be totally correct."

\* \* \*

Next morning, Fallon addressed the Board. "—no clue, none at all, to the mechanism. But almost certainly, our vaccine caused the Only Child Syndrome."

"How can you be sure?" Harve Castellan.

"Correlations. For a long time, other trends disguised the problem. But it seems clear that the Syndrome began roughly a year after our distribution program started."

"Coincidence!" Bardeen wasn't sure who said that.

Fallon shook her head. "We were working to augment the immune system, and the Sterility Plague is definitely an immune phenomenon." She shrugged off the next interruption. "Women's development of immunity to their husbands' sperm isn't new; it appears in the literature—though recorded cases were too few for any wide-scale study."

Well on stride now, she didn't pause. "And there's more. From data on the lower animals, both inside and outside of laboratory facilities."

"Animals don't get AIDS!"

"But they do have immune systems. And given our oral vaccine, they develop the Sterility Plague."

Clearing his throat, Thane Cogdill said, "Outside of lab facilities, you said. Do you have data on animals in the wild?"

"That depends on what you mean by wild. We shipped a lot of grain, eight years ago, laced with the immunizing agent. Any time food travels in quantity, the rats get some of it."

Cogdill's hand slapped table. "Do you mean to tell me—?"

"That's right. At every seaport where vaccine-enhanced foods were handled, the rat populations diminished drastically."

Bardeen couldn't resist: "At worst, then, we still have a future in rodent control."

If the Chairman felt any amusement, he hid it well.

Later, just the two of them in his office and Bardeen feeling definitely on the carpet, Cogdill said, "We have some decisions to make. And we'd better be right the first time."

"Yes. Uh—what's our first question?" Because Bardeen hadn't the faintest idea.

"To put together a firm position—a stand the Foundation can hold, come hell or high water—and sell it to the Board."

Bardeen didn't know what to ask, so he waited. Until the other man said, "Granger gets the raw facts, because she's paid for them. But what about Fallon's conclusions? Do we turn them over, too, and risk public reaction that might destroy us, or keep them in-house?"

"Cover our ass, you mean? Stonewall?"

At the hinges of Cogdill's jaw, muscles knotted. "That horse-collar, spitlicking evangelist, Tolliver—!"

"I saw him, too. Recorded his spiel. Legal's looking it over, to see if his threats are actionable."

"Good; it may help. But what do we *do*?"

Carefully, Bardeen said, "You know the answer to that; you didn't have to ask. Did you?"

The older man sighed. "I guess not. The Feen has always played it straight; this is no time to switch." He made a tight grin. "And we'll tackle the cure part, too. But not on any government grant; this one's with our own money."

"Well, that's good PR, and we can afford it. But—"

"PR, hell! Sure, it wouldn't hurt us—but there'll be *no* publicity. So we won't owe answers to anyone, until we're damned well ready to give them."

"All right; I'll work up a draft for the Board."

Cogdill said, "Do you realize how many years we've ridden this tiger, off and on, since I got the original AIDS grant?"

Bardeen thought back. "Eleven. It doesn't seem that long."

"No. But how much longer?"

Predictably, the Board had little enthusiasm for a policy of full disclosure, and even less for the Feen's financing its own research. Cogdill left it to Bardeen to make the presentations and take the heat, holding his own clout in reserve until time to force the issues. The strategy worked well, but reminded Bardeen of his role as blocking back, in his high school football days. *You take the lumps while the other guy scores the points.*

But the agenda did move, until it jammed on Lana Pendleton's need to know *why* Phoenix should research the Sterility Plague without backup by a Federal grant.

Bardeen shrugged; this one was up to Cogdill. The Chairman said, "I could give any number of reasons. That we're obligated to remedy a disaster we may have caused. That I'd simply like to keep the government's nose out of our business. That if and when we solve the problem, I want us, not Uncle, to have full control of the solution—including its financial aspects. Or even that since we'll be taking a lot of flak in the media, then by dissociating ourselves from Homer Varnell's administration we're doing his reelection campaign a favor, and we owe him."

The woman looked puzzled. "But which of those is true?"

Cogdill gave a shark's grin. "Who says any of them are? Take your pick. Everyone else will."

MEMO FOR RECORD

SUBJECT: Phoenix Foundation report on biophysical mechanism and possible causative factors in the Only Child Syndrome.

PURPOSE: Evaluation and interpretation of the report and its projected consequences, summarized in layman's language.

I. The Syndrome probably began almost nine years ago, its advent masked by the existent low birthrate and other factors.

II. The timing, and the immunity aspect, indicate that this Syndrome may be a by-product of the AIDS vaccine. The Foundation admits the possibility, but emphasizes that no proof has been found. On balance, our Department accepts that statement.

III. Hypothesis: implantation of a zygote at the uterine wall immunizes a woman against future conceptions, not only by the same father, but against any sperm of the same blood type. This holds true, regardless of whether the embryo comes to term.

IV. Giving no reasons, the Foundation categorically refuses to apply for a grant to attack the problem. Tentative feelers are out to other research centers; although Gilcorp Labs' earlier vaccine is blamed for the second-stage AIDS epidemic, the group's overall success record is second only to that of Phoenix.

V. If it is true that no woman can conceive more than once by a male of any given blood type, the social consequences require careful study.

VI. Conclusion: we must decide which of these data are to be made public, and how to state them. Social upheaval, already under way, can-

not be avoided. What can, perhaps, is social
chaos.

Sheila Granger, Jr.
Secretary, HEW

When the government press releases began, Bardeen kept his
fingers crossed. But the tone of the items surprised him. To
Cogdill he said, "I don't understand. In essence this squib points a
finger at our vaccine, all right. But on a quick read, it puts the
blame on AIDS itself. Why—?"

Cogdill gave a partial smile. "Roth MacIlwaine writes those
releases. And when we put the vaccine into production, his
youngest daughter had just come down with AIDS. Actively."

While HEW sparred with padded gloves, others weren't so
gentle. Jody Jay Tolliver, and his rapidly growing Church of the
Reborn Righteous, used bare knuckles. Reading between the lines
of HEW's releases, Tolliver came ever closer to advocating
outright violence. Phoenix procured a "peace bond" injunction—
one with real teeth in it—against the man's Tri-V fulminations.
But nothing could stop the word-of-mouth campaign he'd
triggered.

The matter came to a head when Thane Cogdill's house was
torched. The fire department minimized damage, but the
Chairman had had enough. Finally he did sell the place, and
moved to augmented quarters in the Feen's compound.

Once again the Foundation increased its holdings, adding a
high-tech security enclosure all around. Some buildings in the
new area underwent remodeling; others were replaced.

Puzzled, Bardeen asked, "What are you after, here?"

"Our own self-contained city," Cogdill answered. "Any more
questions?"

"Sure. Why such a drastic move? Second, do you really expect
the Board to agree? And third, who the hell pays for it?"

The "why" was simple enough: safety. After the arson at
Cogdill's home, Amailie duShield was attacked and beaten in the
supposedly secure garage area of her condo building. Two other
Board members received threats by mail and phone. A package
exploded in Mareth Fallon's mailbox, only minutes before she

would have opened the receptacle. In the debris, police found charred fragments of two threatening letters.

Under siege by predators, the Board agreed to "Fortress Phoenix." Bardeen wasn't worried; he'd always kept his phone and residence anonymous, and his mail went to a P.O. Box. But one day, driving home, a car followed him; a few quick random turns told him the follower meant business.

Feeling a taut grin stretch his mouth, he switched to double ignition and to his racing-type four-wheel drive. Then for the first time in years, he floorboarded the go-pedal. At the first turnoff he broadsided into a narrow, winding road. Speeding between overhanging trees, sun and shade flashing strobelike across his vision, he fell into the never-forgotten rhythm: *slow a bit, broadside, gun out* hard! When he reached a three-way fork with no signs on it, he didn't bother to listen for pursuit. Because so far as he knew, there weren't five cars in the state that could have stayed with him.

"So today," he told Jenny when he got home, "that ceramic white elephant truly paid off. And much as I hate to give in, it's time we take sanctuary. At the Feen."

Not only Board members could move into the compound; all permanent employees had that option.

Cogdill called the financial setup a membership trust; Bardeen thought co-op or commune could fit equally well.

You didn't have to move in, Cogdill informed the Board, but you could. You didn't have to invest your personal assets into the overall Feen pot, either, but you could do that, too.

There were options. Your Feen investments brought returns, sure. A Feen residence, all expenses paid, was part of your salary, so less of that salary would be cash. Bardeen nodded; considering the monthly costs of his own house, it made sense.

The kicker was: given massive employee investment, plus salary savings via company housing, the Foundation could finance the whole project and break even within five years.

Cogdill shrugged. "Depending on fluctuations in the economic indicators, maybe three."

Not even Roark voted against the motion.

Danger or not, Bardeen held misgivings about moving to a new, limited environment. But the architects and landscapers began to rough out an attractive, livable setup.

Such as: *hills* in *Chicago*? Not huge, but big enough to break the flatness. The trees, he thought, looking at the model in the Board room, helped a lot, too.

Fuel and water tanks would be underground; so would the massive backup-power system. Seeing those things on the plans, Bardeen began to understand the magnitude of the siege mentality that possessed Thane Cogdill.

For once, he merely hoped the Chairman was spending a lot more money than necessary.

The time of changing never seemed real to him. Part of the disorientation came from having the entire project moved to new, underground facilities. Over a three-month period, every physical aspect of his life was transformed. About halfway through, he gave a mental shrug and said the hell with it; his job was basically on hold, so why bother? He concentrated on Jenny and the kids, getting them settled in and trying to see that the whole family came up feeling comfortable.

Near as he could tell, things worked more than not. The condo didn't feel like part of a massive, larger building, because every unit opened onto a separate hillside area, isolated by altitude or direction or barriers so that the sense of privacy was absolute. (Now he knew what the hills were for. If you design a hill *around* a building, you achieve luxury.)

Jenny liked the labyrinthine aspects of the new place, and setting the carefully selected plantings from their former home was something she obviously enjoyed. In their personal lives together, these contentments came clear.

The youngsters: at eighteen, Donald had his junior degree; where he went from there was anybody's guess. Celia, fifteen, missed the open landscapes she loved to paint. She'd adjust, though—or so Bardeen hoped.

For the most part, the move seemed to be working.

Closemouthed these days, all Mareth Fallon would say was whether or not she felt she was making progress. That grade of reticence gave Bardeen no ease. Especially at Board meetings.

Alvin Henshaw, the President's press secretary, was a crap artist. Discussing the Sterility Plague on Tri-V, he lamented the growing strains on traditional monogamy, versus "the severe social problems posed by a drastic population decline." Pinned down by a questioner, Henshaw stated that despite condemnation from certain quarters, Homer Varnell's administration found no objection to artificial insemination.

Fine, thought Bardeen, viewing. Except that the process, which cost a bundle, was at best a small-scale answer. And a miscarriage meant the chance was lost permanently.

Henshaw continued. "In the interests of our accepted standards of morality and family well-being, your government can in no case condone promiscuity. We—"

"How about the Baynes-Dennis bill?"

First waffling, Henshaw finally said, "The law to allow group marriages?" Well, *obviously*, so after a pause he said, "Our administration opposes that bill, but should Congress pass it, the President will accept it as the law of the land."

No veto? No. Why not? Waffle-waffle. The real point, Bardeen knew, was that Varnell would accept anything at all, that might help get him off the hook.

For a stuffed shirt, though, Henshaw ran a fair talk show.

# VI

Once the Feen pulled in its horns like a snail retreating into its shell, Jody Jay Tolliver's diatribes began to run out of steam. For a few weeks he made do with condemning sin in general; then, abruptly, he switched gears and attacked Gilcorp.

For after all, hadn't that group accepted an HEW grant "—to try to fight—and a vain fight it shall be, I tell you all—against the Lord's very own scourge? Those vile sinners—what we have to do now, my dear friends—"

Bardeen cut both sound and holo. "You know what, Jenny?"

She looked over to him. "Not in detail. So tell me."

"It's too bad the Sterility Plague wasn't around before Tolliver was conceived."

Her brows rose. "What if he's an only child, or eldest?"

Sigh. "Back to the ol' keyboard." But it didn't really hurt his feelings to see Gilcorp take the crap, for a change.

The idea of "living besieged" had bothered him, but it didn't work that way. Newly built, secure routes left the compound, emerging in neutral areas. If you turn up nowhere near the Feen, who's going to make the tie-in? Sometimes alone and sometimes with Jenny, Bardeen explored all the options.

Mareth Fallon had a handle on something, but she wasn't sure what. The new man from Canada—Ramda Singh, a refugee Sikh—contended that immunized ova rejected specific chromosomes as invaders, stopping fertilization at a midway point.

Well, maybe. Fallon had spent a lot of time, trying to find a pattern that would fit Singh's thesis. Finally one night she decided. *The way to test it is to* disguise *some chromosomes and see if they look like the good guys in the white hats.*

The problem was, how to do it. Shuffling through recent journals, she looked for Blixor's paper on "pseudogenes."

The Board meeting, Bardeen thought, had been a farce; no news *wasn't* good news. Financial aspects were all right; in fact, Bardeen's earlier flippant suggestion about rodent control had turned into a profitable sideline. But the Feen's attack on the Sterility Plague remained stalled at dead center.

Even Cogdill seemed lethargic. Until after the meeting: "Kennet? Let's go talk in my office. In twenty minutes?"

On the way, having found nothing important on his own desk, Bardeen pondered. After Laura Casey went to Stockholm he'd watched Cogdill and expected the worst. But it didn't happen, and after a time Bardeen figured out why his superior took an occasional long weekend and couldn't be reached.

Now he entered the Chairman's office. Bourbon and ice were at hand; this would be one of the friendly talks. "Cheers," and each man took a first sip.

Cogdill spoke first. "I want your evaluation. Are we in a blind alley? Beating our heads against a stone wall?"

No point in asking "What about?" They both knew. Bardeen said, "I'm not qualified. Ask Fallon what *she* thinks."

"I'm asking what you think of her competence. Has she burned out? Is it time for a shakeup?"

Bardeen shook his head. "I don't speak Medical, but I can tell you she's not spinning her wheels; each month she begins new experiments and terminates old ones. And the descriptive language, incomprehensible as it may be, isn't repetitive."

The Chairman sighed. "I suppose that has to do." He drained his glass. "Stay for another? I'm not superstitious about drinking alone, but it's damned boring."

So before Bardeen left, they each had a short one.

After dinner, while he and Jenny sat with coffee, the phone chimed. "I'll get it." The screen stayed dark; either his caller had a voice-only phone or didn't care to pay for picture.

"Is this Bardeen? Kennet Bardeen, at Phoenix?"

*Watch it!* "Who's asking?"

As if aimed away from the phone, the voice went fainter. "Punch for pic, Andrea. Might as well pay the rate." The screen lit; against an office background appeared a man, fortyish, showing signs of strain but well groomed and dressed. "I'm Alex Schofield at Gilcorp. You want to put your own pic on?"

"Sure." Bardeen did so. "I don't think we know each other, but there's always a first time. What's the occasion?"

Schofield ran fingers through his carefully arranged blond hair; it fell back into place perfectly. "Look—we're in competition, sure. But basically on the same side. Right?"

"The same side? Against what?"

"Against that asshole bastard Jody Jay Tolliver!" A deep breath turned to hiccup. "He was on you; now it's our turn. Today a bomb went off in one of our labs and killed two people."

"I—I'm very sorry, Schofield. But what—?"

"What can you do? Tell us how you protect yourselves."

"Sure. But it's going to cost you."

"You'd hold us up for *that* information?"

Bardeen snorted. "Hell, no! It's the protective measures that cost a bundle." He thought further. "The Dlumane people did our systems." *And they learned as much from us as we did from them, but we paid for it.* "Tell you what. We still have Dlumane under contract for maintenance and upgrades; if you want to save some time you could subcontract from us. All right?"

"It sounds good. Thanks, Bardeen."

"My pleasure." A thought came. "Oh, just a minute."

"Yes?"

"While we're doing favors, I could use one."

"I—I suppose so. What is it?"

"I have this bad habit of being curious. Just in general terms, how are you coming along with the Sterility Plague?"

"But—but you *know* that comes under industrial security!"

"And the Feen's security-systems contracts don't?"

Looking as though he'd swallowed a bug, Schofield said, "Don't quote me; I'd deny it. But off the record, all we know at this point is a lot of things that don't work."

"Those could be interesting; I'd like to see them."

"But I can't—"

"I think you'd better. While I'm getting the Dlumane arrangements set up."

Bardeen cut the circuit. His play would work, or not. Either way, he could hardly have left Gilcorp hanging out to dry.

When Ramda Singh spoke, his English was precise. Looking up from the paper he'd just read, he said, "Most interesting, Dr. Fallon, this 'pseudogene' concept. Might we communicate with Dr. Blixor, even induce him to visit and meet with us here?"

Fallon shook her head. "Not possible, I'm afraid. Unfortunately, the man's dead."

"But this paper—"

"Written last year, I expect. He'd been ill, unable to work, for several months before he died."

Singh's frown showed mild regret. "A sad loss." He didn't ask about the cause of death. Instead, "Is there other of his work that I might study?"

Fallon nodded. "A few things, we already have. I know there's more, in journals that aren't on my own reading list. The staff's making a computer search of listings in the field; whatever's available, you should have in a day or two."

"That is well." He looked up at her, then turned aside. "I will now compose a new series of experiments."

"That's fine. See you later." As she walked away, Mareth Fallon thought that she wasn't used to people who could halt a conversation simply and flatly, dismissing the other party, with no need to put any kind of polite frame around the act.

Singh's way saved time—but she wasn't sure she liked it.

Without regard to President Varnell's wishes, Congress passed the Baynes-Dennis bill, legalizing group marriages. The new option didn't raise the birthrate greatly; obviously a fair number of women were already being impregnated extramaritally.

Ulla Salich placed a blind ad, with a P.O. Box number, in the *Sun-Times*: "Wish to meet male Caucasian, blood type O, sound health and heredity, age 25 to 40, fair hair and complexion preferred." When she first had the idea and checked the Personals, she was quite surprised at the number of ads indicating the same purpose.

The first man she met, after the awkward business of getting his phone number without giving hers, seemed to match her specifications. The only trouble was, she didn't like him. Or the next, or the next. Her fourth attempt brought a shy young man, considerably younger than she'd had in mind, to meet her at a small restaurant. After making sure he understood the situation, she told him to bring his medical records next time. They satisfied her. "All right, Leland. Are you free on Wednesday afternoon?" That was when her clock would be at its best point.

He nodded; she said, "I'll take a room at the Emerson. At two o'clock, call and ask for—uh, June Rogers. I'll give you the room number and you can come right up."

His smile looked uncertain. "That's not your name, is it?"

"Of course not. What difference does it make?"

"None, I guess."

"Next Wednesday, then."

She left first, thinking that although she'd been prepared to pay for stud service, with this kid it wouldn't be necessary.

Carrying a suitcase with not much inside it, Ulla reached the hotel a few minutes early and checked in for one night. When she paid cash in advance rather than using a credit card, the clerk grinned wisely—or rather, Ulla thought, like a real smartass! Well, it was none of the woman's business, and Ulla refused to let herself be embarrassed. Well, not much . . .

Leland's call came promptly. Waiting for him, Ulla made herself a weak drink and looked around the room. Decor was Standard Glitz of the previous decade, but the place was clean and the plumbing worked.

Undressing, she felt, was an awkward process, so she did it now, in private, and wore only a light robe. Before donning it, she inspected herself in a mirror. How was this youngster going to see her? Not exactly a spring chicken, breasts showing the effects of Brad's infancy, but still rangy-built and not carrying too much extra weight. She shrugged. Hell with it: if he wanted Sweet Sixteen he could go ask her!

The knock came, and there was Leland with a paper bag. "Champagne." It wasn't chilled, so she sent him to bring some ice; an hour or so should take care of it, she told him.

Then, saying nothing more, she took off the robe.

"He wasn't very good at it," she said, "but at that age they never are. You remember *us*, at first?" She giggled.

She'd had to tell Stan what she was going to do; now she had to tell him she'd done it. Because there was no way to lie about something like this, and she needed at least his grudging acceptance. Each of her first three meetings, ending in her rejections of the men, seemed to take some of the edge off Stan's resentment. Now, near as she could tell, he was listening with very little tension. "But he's a *nice* young fella, Stan; he did his best with what little he knows."

Stan made a snort. "Don't put down my husband-in-law. If we're gonna raise his kid I need to think good of him."

She reached to touch his hand. "If it takes, you mean."

"Yeah. Ulla, if you need it this much, I hope you get it."

"So do I. And *this* time. I'm not sure I could handle too many reruns."

# VII

Kennet Bardeen had been on the moon once before—a long time ago, when the Lunar Enterprise System was first put together. Basically he'd done a top-hush courier run; he hadn't known the content of what he carried, either way, but assumed it had to do with the dickering as Phoenix bought into the System.

Except for the space views at stopovers, he hadn't enjoyed that trip. At his third stop, in lunar orbit, he'd learned how to sleep—but not relax—in a zero-gee "drawer."

Nor had he liked the moon itself, particularly. So that even with the new three-stage system, and improved conditions at the various stopovers, he wasn't looking forward to the encore.

A few weeks earlier the Chairman had booted him upstairs from his Project Director slot, to a position overseeing nearly a dozen projects. He still had overall charge of the Sterility problem, but now at one remove.

And even before he had his work reorganized, Cogdill came up with this moon jaunt. The assignment seemed simple enough; Phoenix was expanding its moonside operation, but Pidge Sutton, in charge at that end, had no grasp of logistics. Put him in place and he'd run things just fine—but don't ask him to design or evaluate a working configuration.

That ability was one of Bardeen's strong points. Which was why he was stuck with this expedition. And considering the plan drawings he'd seen, Cogdill was right. Only on-site inspection could give the necessary answers.

One good thing: this time he knew what the job was about.

Bardeen's first space ride had been in a shuttle updated considerably from the original model but looking much the same. By comparison, the one he now approached was a sleek greyhound, carrying mostly passengers and very little freight. Boarding, he entered a cabin resembling that of a miniature airliner, with forty seating spaces. The seats themselves, hardly airline style, functioned as recliners, acceleration couches, and in zero-gee, restrainers. Checking his ticket, Bardeen located couch twelve, secured his oversized briefcase, and strapped down.

This machine did not lift on huge rocket engines; it would begin flight much like a normal jet plane, rise through the intermediate altitude range in "scramjet" mode, and reserve its rockets' thrust until the low-orbit belt was near. Savings in fuel and weight made profitable reading.

He lay back, but couldn't relax. Waiting for takeoffs always jittered him, and this one was already late. In planes, at least you could look out the window.

He tried to put his mind to the job ahead, but a hand, heavy on his shoulder, broke his concentration. "Excuse me, friend; eleven's my seat and I'd better strap in fast. Lucky they held for me; I got hung up on the way here."

Moving his knees to one side and twisting his feet sidewise, in the automatic airline or theater response, he waited as the latecomer, stepping on Bardeen's foot, clambered across.

The man strapped in, secured his carry-on, and turned to say, "Takeoff's coming up. Later we can talk."

*The later the better*, was Bardeen's thought.

The shuttle climbed like a bandit. Accustomed to flying mostly at medium levels, plus the occasional suborbital run, Bardeen found himself expecting the vehicle to level off, then felt sheepish when he realized it wouldn't. No, it tilted up and then more so; when scramjet cut in, he felt almost as much acceleration pressure as the older shuttles pushed during first-stage burn. It was nice to have these things happening up higher, where there was room for error!

"Your first time in space?"

He'd forgotten the man; now he looked at him. Nothing special: almost well dressed but not quite, and in his expression a kind of humorless intensity. Bardeen said, "On this kind of shuttle, yes. I've ridden one of the older ones."

"How far out? All the way?"

"To the moon, if that's what you mean. Not on any of the special probe missions." *I'm talking too much*.

"The moon, though. Getting there, it's a lot simpler, now.'

"I noticed."

"Why are you going back, anyway?"

"Business, more or less."

"Yeah? What kind?"

"Who's asking?" What the hell *was* this?

The man's voice took on a whining note. "That's the trouble with people these days. Nobody trusts anybody."

"You may be right." The all-purpose answer. And why, Bardeen wondered, did this fellow *irritate* him so much?

Not until the shuttle reached the low-orbit belt, fired its rocket engines for a time, and then began coasting toward synchronous rendezvous, could Bardeen relax.

Crew members handed out food and drink. Bardeen wished they'd done that before the trip went zero-gee. He wished he'd hit the john then, too. Sure, he'd done these things before; not lately, though. He coped better than not, but felt awkward. Eventually he settled down and found sleep.

\* \* \*

He woke earlier than he would have chosen; rendezvous was still more than an hour away. The time passed slowly; he knew docking required a delicate touch, but the approach seemed to take forever: periods of coasting, punctuated by unnerving jerks and nudges. If he could have *seen* what was happening, he'd have felt better. Finally a soft, shuddering impact, then quiet.

The PA speakers told how to debark. "—and take your carry-ons. Your next vehicle leaves in a little over two hours; you have time for a meal, and to freshen up."

"Could have said exact time," his seat-neighbor grumbled. Dealing with his own gear, Bardeen didn't bother to answer. Pulling himself along the aisle-lines toward the exit, he thought, *It wouldn't have hurt me to be civil.* But somehow the man simply rubbed him the wrong way.

Entering the sync station he followed others through an interface to the rotating section, and felt centripetal "gravity" increase as they descended toward the station's rim. At the dining facility he guessed the pull at roughly lunar strength.

The place was at one end of the spinning cylinder. Here were a few actual viewports; outside "the stars wheeled in their stately courses." Not all that stately, though—not at roughly one revolution per minute. Finding a seat at a small table, Bardeen was annoyed to find his shuttle seatmate taking the remaining vacant place. Well, the man had the right to sit where he chose. . . .

The meal was better than Bardeen expected; afterward he found shower and toilet facilities. He couldn't change clothes, but still he felt better. Well before departure time he went to the loading area and boarded. Next came the longest stage of his journey: sync orbit to lunar orbit.

In appearance this shuttle resembled the ones he'd ridden before. Thirty-six seats: on this low-accel run, they were lightly built and lightly padded.

One of the first to board, he took a place at the rear and watched to see who else came in. He hoped his seatmate from the first leg wouldn't show. But he did, and went several rows past Bardeen's seat before pausing to look around. Then hesitated, staring at Bardeen, but finally took the nearest vacant seat.

What *that* was all about, Bardeen neither knew nor cared.

* * *

With Earth's gravity exerting only about two percent of its surface force, shuttle acceleration was only a gentle nudge.

Zero-gee was Lazy Country; on this leg of the trip Bardeen slept more than not, waking to be fed or to eliminate, but dozing away as much time as he could. Eventually the shuttle docked at a "hotel" satellite, riding a four-hour orbit roughly fourteen hundred kilos above the lunar surface.

This station proved to be considerably smaller than the one in sync orbit; its spin was so much faster that Coriolis forces made walking a tricky process.

With no luggage at hand except his carry-on, Bardeen was tired of wearing the same sweaty clothes. A quick wash in a very stingy shower helped some, but not enough.

The dining area was cafeteria-style and the food looked to be standard college-dorm grade; he loaded a tray with small portions of the least-unappealing items. Seeing his former seatmate approach, he scuttled for the last vacant seat at a four-person table, and got there without spilling anything. He found himself sitting with two men and a woman, all youngish employees of the Lunar Enterprise System. Bardeen knew enough about LES to make reasonable-sounding comments; the conversation helped keep his mind off the food.

Then, with about ten hours until his departure, Bardeen went to his own assigned cubby. He had a roomie: a Russian who spoke very little English. Making do with gestures, they managed to cope with their gear in the confined space, and settled into the narrow bunks for sleep.

The ride down to Luna, in another skinny-built vehicle, gave Bardeen no jitters: this pilot didn't need to do anything Neil Armstrong hadn't done in 1969, and had a lot more to work with. The landing jarred hardly at all, and after a wait the passengers walked, half-crouching, through a flexible transfer tube and into a groundcrawler.

Here there were windows. Thick and small, dusty and heavily tinted, but windows. Seating himself by one of them, Bardeen peered out. He wasn't impressed; the drab moonscape still looked like TV shots from the later Apollo missions: grey dirt, bright light, harsh shadows. He'd been a kid then, thrilled by the *idea* of being on the moon. Somehow the reality had never measured up. He let his seat-back recline the one notch it would move, and closed his eyes.

What woke him was people saying "Wow!" and "Look at that!" Squinting, he saw a huge downward ramp cut into the terrain. The car passed by it to approach a lesser one, leading to an airlock closer in size to the ones he recalled, and the crawler entered.

The mechanism had grown more complex: three portals and two intermediate chambers. For extra safety, no doubt. Inside, the passengers debarked; attendants checked travel credentials and directed people to one elevator or another. "Your quarters, Mr. Bardeen, are on Level Twelve," and the woman handed him a numbered key. She checked her clipboard. "Oh, yes. Mr. Sutton asked to be notified of your arrival. When you're ready to meet with him, the vidcom directory has his number and location."

Bardeen nodded. "Thanks. I'll take it from here."

Level Twelve, counting downward, covered a much larger area than he'd expected; since his earlier visit, this miniature city had expanded tremendously. His quarters weren't hard to find.

The room-and-a-half certainly wasn't lavish, but compared to the cramped space of shuttles or satellites, he found it roomy enough. Decor was simple: modest furniture, bland colors, flexible lighting.

The door chime brought him prematurely out of the shower, but it was worth it. Luggage, clean clothes, and a well-wrapped flask of bourbon. He had one good shot, then called Sutton.

In lunar gravity, Pidge Sutton's excess weight didn't hamper the practiced grace with which he walked. Showing Bardeen around the proposed lab-expansion area, the man made him feel clumsy. Not on purpose, of course; moon-adapted people couldn't help it that Earthies lacked the proper trained reflexes.

As the tour continued, though, and Bardeen checked what he saw against the proposed plans, he felt a growing irritation. When he'd seen all of it, he rolled the prints up and began to slap the roll against his other palm. "Pidge?"

Blinking, Sutton ran fingers through his short, curly hair. "Does it look fairly good, or will you have to start over?"

Bardeen shook his head. "You really don't know, do you?" He paused; this wasn't being fair. Carefully he said, "Actually, except for a few minor changes, I'm approving your plans."

"You are? But I'm no good at that kind of thing; that's why the Chairman sent you to—"

"Good or not, this time you did it right. But who in hell did up the report for you?" Breathing hard, he let his anger show. "Because of some idiot who can't draw a cat that looks like a cat, I've had to come up here where I didn't want to come, to do a job that doesn't need doing!"

"Kennet? I did that report, all by myself."

"Oh, shit, Pidge!" He put an arm around the other man's shoulder. "Let's go have a drink. To the proposition that nobody's perfect, including me."

The job had been tentatively scheduled for two weeks; Bardeen had the alterations wrapped up in as many days. Pidge Sutton's hurt feelings healed fast; the man had never been one to hold a grudge.

Bardeen's problem was how to get back to Earth ahead of sked; none of his tentative reservations came due for another ten days, and currently the Feen was overdrawn on its priority swaps with other organizations.

Eventually Sutton said, "I called in a debt and got you an off-moon seat three days from now." He shrugged. "I realize it's not what you'd prefer, but it's the best I can do."

Bardeen grinned. "I know. Thanks for trying."

"Well, it's my fault, after all. Tell you what I *can* do, though. How'd you like to walk on the moon? On the surface, outside? Haven't you always wanted to do that?"

Decades ago, *hell yes*! Now? Could he feel anything at all for the concept? Still, Pidge looked as if he wanted to be Santa Claus, so Bardeen said, "Well, sure. Hasn't everybody? But I didn't think much of that was happening lately, for tourists—just people on real projects, is the way I understood it."

Sutton looked happy. "That's right. Except that LES had a red-carpet tour scheduled for some politicians and a few of their own high-mucky-mucks—LES does have to give the civilian brass a little jelly for its bread—and it was postponed a week, until day after tomorrow, because of solar flare activity. So two of the group had to go back to Earth and won't be able to make it." He smiled. "Would you like one of those slots?"

Bardeen didn't have to think. Suddenly he felt the way he had when he was a kid. Walk *outdoors* on the moon?

"Fuckin'-aye, Pidge."

# VIII

Vacuum suits had changed, too, from the bulky units of the Apollo days. Bardeen was issued a snug, flexible garment much like a heavyweight leotard, with airtight and insulating layers alternating. The fit could have been better, but suits for tourists didn't come tailormade. At least the gloves and boots, separate items, were better matched to him.

But he wasn't complaining. As he got into the coverall-like main portion and watched the front seam being sealed, he felt excitement. Next the two-piece helmet, opaque back and darkly tinted front, was placed and sealed. Squinting downward, he could see the air-feed coupling. Two bottles attached to the suit's upper back, with both hoses clamped to a site near the connector. "If you were going to be out more than two hours," an attendant told him, "you'd have to change bottles. The couplings are self-sealing, so you couldn't possibly lose pressure." And an audible alarm would signal the need for changing. Indoors, a pressure-operated valve kept the suit open to outside air. A vacuum environment closed that access, and caused another valve to start the flow of bottled air.

He'd arrived while the first four people, faces hidden by the tinted, reflective plastic of their helmets, completed their ensuitment, and was in the third batch serviced. While he waited for the rest to be finished he emulated others in bending, stretching, sitting and kneeling, then getting up again—testing the limitations on his movements. The suit's resistance made him awkward, and the catheter gave a slight discomfort he couldn't quite ignore, but for the most part he moved well enough. The air bottles were no more burden than a medium-weight backpack.

Eventually the party was led, by three persons in heavier-duty suits, out to the boarding area and a groundcar.

\* \* \*

The airlock and ramp looked the same as the ones Bardeen had entered on arrival. The sun couldn't be seen from the car's small windows; it shone from high to the car's right, making sharply defined shadows leftward of the surface irregularities. He tried to figure what direction they were going, but decided he didn't know enough to make even a horseback guess.

Motion startled him; all around, persons here and there were each raising a hand. He hadn't turned on his suit's comm unit; now he did. "—will be let off at the first hiking area. Now how many of you would prefer the second? There's much to be said for all three, but we simply don't have time to give anyone more than one jaunt. So for Area Two, now?"

Without thinking, Bardeen raised his hand. Hell, he hadn't heard the descriptions, didn't know what he was choosing—but damned if he'd admit to being so inattentive. Besides, it was all the same satellite, wasn't it?

After a few moments, "All right; your suit numbers are now registered for this stop. And I presume the rest choose Area Three, so we won't bother with another call. I—"

Over the channel came a buzzing noise. The tour guide's voice said, "Yes? Somebody have a problem?"

The suits' comm systems must have been ordered from the lowest bidder; words could be recognized, but barely. "—change my mind. That second area sounds better, after all."

"Very well. Your new choice is registered." After a pause, "Anyone else want to make a change? If so, let's do it right now." No more buzzers sounded. "All right. Approaching first area shortly. Those persons, be ready to get out and walk!"

Bardeen chuckled. *I like that man's style.*

Area One looked bland: practically smooth and level, with occasional large boulders providing the only contrast. Of course, looking through the tandem filters of dark-tinted helmet *and* window, one might miss the finer points.

At the stop a guide and nine tour-groupers got out. One at a time, crouching in the car's tiny airlock which was separate from the normal entrance, then stepping awkwardly down to the surface before reaching to extend their helmets' antennae for "outdoor" communication, they made exit into isolation.

Not far away stood a tall, guy-wired mast, topped with a fluorescent-orange globe and some gadgetry that Bardeen guessed to be antennae for line-of-sight comm, and possibly lights. *Right. Just in case anyone gets lost.*

The tourists out on the surface didn't move around much; their steps looked tentative. As the car left Area One, none of them had set out in any definite direction.

Area Two, about thirty minutes farther on, had a different look: choppy ground, with deceptive patches of shadow in sizes up to several meters. And the isolated boulders of Area One were largely replaced by jagged formations, apparently rooted in underlying bedrock.

If someone hadn't been sitting next to the airlock, Bardeen would have been the first tourist out. As it was, with others moving slowly in apparent reluctance, he was an easy second. Once outside, extending his helmet antenna and seeing the others pause and wait, as unwilling to move as the debarkers at Area One, Bardeen laughed inside himself.

Looking around, at a distance he saw a really large extruded crag. *I want a closer look at that.*

No one was watching; the guide was busy. So, cautiously at first, then more quickly as he picked up the rhythm of walking in the suit, he headed toward that crag.

When the distorted, querulous voices of his fellow tourists began to bother him, he turned the comm unit off.

The huge, up-jutting rock fully repaid the walk to get there. It rammed up from a slope. He had no idea how it might look from topside, and he wasn't going to find out, because when he looked at the terrain to either side of the protrusion, *you can't get there from here.* The suits were good, but some of that rock might be sharp enough to slash through. And out on one's own was no place to test the material!

Walking back and forth, looking at the gargoyle-like formation, Bardeen wished he'd thought to rent a camera. Then he shrugged: thousands of people had been here; surely some had made pictures that would be for sale.

Feeling a sudden need to relax, he went to a seat-sized rock and sat facing the scenic feature he'd walked here to see.

The view lulled him into a semidoze. Even a light tug at his helmet didn't break the trance.

What did rouse him, and cause him to lurch upright, was the arm that came around his neck, under the chin-bulge of his helmet, to grip his left shoulder. And the voice that said, helmet-to-helmet, "You want to know why I'm killing you?"

Adrenalin brought Kennet Bardeen fully alert. Not to the point of time-stretch, but totally aware. Did he want to know *why* someone was trying to kill him? Hell, it didn't matter! What did, was the time he could gain if his attacker felt a need to explain things. So, even as he noticed that his antenna, ripped away and with broken wire dangling, lay on the ground a few meters away, he said, "Yes. I want to know."

"Just a minute." The man's other hand moved, and Bardeen saw his air hose disconnected, heard and felt his air bottles torn loose, presumably thrown away; here in vacuum, no way to hear where they might have landed.

So now he had only the limited amount of air left in his helmet and in the suit's bulge just below. The man said, "I know who you are; our people spotted your listing to come here, so I came, too. Cost us a bundle, that did."

*Get* on *with it!* "Whose people?"

"You made that devil's vaccine!"

The AIDS cure? But he'd only been the administrator! No; he shook his head—damned if he'd plead with this bastard. For one thing, there wasn't *time*. "So? Who are you?"

"Name doesn't matter; anyway, you'll get no chance to tell it. But my sainted sister was wife to Jody Jay Tolliver."

*None* of it mattered, only how much air he had left. Moving his feet, trying to get braced, Bardeen said, "He sent you to kill me?"

"Never said that. Just come talk to you; so we're talkin'."

"You'll get caught."

"Huh-uh. Once you're dead I put your bottle back. Nobody figures out how you went. You see, I figured—"

Some learned skills, a man never forgets. The thing was, how would lunar gravity affect the results? Putting both hands to grip the arm across his throat, Bardeen bumped backward with his butt, then abruptly bent over and lunged—mostly straight ahead, only a little bit upward—with the full thrust of both legs. Overbalanced, he fell.

He came to ground quickly; the man flying over his head kept moving. Bardeen held fast to the arm until momentum tore it from his grip; then he scrambled after the man, catching him still trying to get hands and feet under him. The first thing Bardeen did was kick the son of a bitch in the gut. His second and third acts were little more than encores.

After that, there was no problem. He took the man's two air bottles, connected one to breathe from while using the other to beat off his attacker's staggering charges until the man died. Then, once his own breathing was back to normal and he'd stopped shaking, he retrieved his two air bottles so that both suits again carried full complements, and proceeded to make a few improvements to the plan Jody Jay's brother-in-law had specified.

First he carried the body over to a cluster of boulders and let it down into a gap between them; then he found a head-sized rock. After carefully disconnecting the other's antenna and plugging it into his own suit, he placed his broken one alongside the dead man's helmet, then dropped the rock on that helmet. Threw it down hard, in fact, so that it might appear to have fallen from a height; the helmet dented but didn't break.

Before leaving the scene he did peer closely into the dead man's faceplate. And eventually, moving to squint from several angles, dimly made out the features of his early, nosy seatmate. Certainly he hadn't seen the man in the equipment room where everyone suited up—neither when Bardeen arrived there, nor among those who came in later.

Only one answer fit: the man had to be one of the four already helmeted when Bardeen entered. Then another fact meshed; there'd been only two vacant slots. Jody Jay's in-law had somehow snaffled the second one. Bardeen shook his head. A lot of money had been invested in the dead man's try at him. Well, it hadn't worked. Walking away from the corpse, for a moment Bardeen felt almost cheerful. But not quite.

He mussed up the existing footprints as well as he could manage quickly—most of the ground here was bare rock, so it wasn't much of a job—and set out to make a new set of tracks in a different direction.

While he made his false trail he tried the comm unit. It worked, but barely—not even as well as before. Presumably the suits were checked each time before being issued, so he saw no reason to report the malfunction.

By the time he returned to the homing mast—and waited, with three others, for the last of the area's group to assemble—he had most of his adrenaline under control. The chief guide, the car's driver, insisted on looking for the missing tourist, but with time running short, came back without finding him. "Always some damn fool forgets what a tough place this is!" the man fumed. "This is the first we've lost in nearly three years; funny, how that doesn't make me feel any better."

Or me, thought Kennet Bardeen. But he had no urge to say so, out loud.

Underground once more, as the group was being helped to unsuit, the guide announced, "All you Area Two people stick around. I need to interrogate you about the missing man."

Most of those addressed either shrugged or otherwise indicated resignation. Bardeen didn't; as he dressed in normal clothing he said, "Hold that. We've been out there for hours. Personally I'm tired, hungry, and need a shower." He didn't mention that the damned catheter had his urethra burning. "If you want to ask me questions, the name is Kennet Bardeen and I'll be in my quarters. Give it an hour; all right?" Not waiting for an answer, he left.

*To hold your own, sometimes you have to push it to them.*

Fed, cleansed, and partially rested, Bardeen sipped a strong, iced drink and waited for his inquisitor. But when the door chime rang and he answered it, there stood Pidge Sutton.

"Kennet? I heard about it. You must feel awful."

Bardeen shifted mental gears. "Yes. A man lost, out there. It's hard to take." He raised his glass. "Fix you something?"

"Oh, no. I just wanted to make sure you're all right."

"I am. And thanks, Pidge."

Roughly ten minutes after Sutton left, the tour guide came. Bardeen proffered lukewarm welcome, made a mild drink to the man's preferences, and sat to answer questions.

Arvid Thurwald, this man was: a large-framed Viking with a heavy jaw and alert movements. He said, after a minimum of courteous preliminaries, "How well did you know the missing man?"

Avoiding laughter, because once started he might have had trouble stopping, Bardeen said, "You haven't checked the background. Weeks ago, this tour was arranged. Day before yesterday Pidge Sutton set me up for a vacant slot. I didn't know any of the other people on the tour. And still don't."

Thurwald moved muscles in his face. "Amos Calhoun. Ever hear the name?"

"Not to my knowledge. Sorry."

The Viking frowned. "I don't think you're telling me everything you know."

Bardeen shrugged. "What is there I *could* know?" Then, to avert the annoyance he saw building, he said, "I'm not being uncooperative. Ask, and I'll answer." *But damned if I'll provide you with the questions!*

"Are you saying you have no information at all?"

"I know perhaps as much as you do. At Area Two, somebody got lost, and now I learn that his name is Amos Calhoun."

The way Thurwald looked at him, Bardeen had the horrible feeling that this blond Viking could read his mind and see the actual killing.

But he kept his breathing even, *forced* himself to leave his facial muscles loose. And after a few more questions, asked in a rather discouraged tone of voice, Arvid Thurwald took his leave.

It would have been nice, Bardeen thought, if he could have left his tensions—fears and guilts and regrets—out in the lunar waste along with the man he'd killed, then left to rot and fester in the confines of the airtight suit. But it didn't work that way. His restless, intermittent sleep was punctuated by dreams that replayed the deadly combat; in waking periods his mind kept rehashing the same ordeal. He hated to take pills, but after a few hours he gave up and swallowed two. When he woke, he didn't feel particularly rested.

Well before his departure time, Bardeen stopped by to bid farewell to Pidge Sutton. "Like to thank you for everything. And it'll be mostly your credit, not mine, that the lab expansion plans worked out so well."

"Nice of you, Kennet." Sutton nodded. "I got lucky."

"Maybe. Or else you're learning."

Pidge shrugged. "Whatever works." Then he said, "Oh, hey. With all the hassle, losing that guy when you were all out on your outdoor tour, I forgot something."

Bardeen felt one eyebrow rise. "Anything important?"

"Who can tell?" Sutton shrugged. "All I have is the note my secretary took down. It's to you, from Thane Cogdill, and it doesn't seem to make much sense."

Refusing to let his impatience show, Bardeen said, "Maybe it would, to me. Shall we try it?"

From the middle of a stack of papers, Sutton extracted a memo-sized sheet. "Leaving out all the address stuff, here's what it says." He cleared his throat. "The hens are laying. Get back here fast and take charge of the hatchery." Sutton's expression was querulous. "Do you have any idea what it means?"

"Maybe." Bardeen clasped the other man's shoulder. "Pidge, you worry too much. We have time for a drink before I catch the shuttle. So let's have one."

Actually they had two. When Kennet Bardeen climbed aboard, he strapped in feeling rather good.

When his final-leg shuttle touched down on Earth, Bardeen put his worries on hold; the problem, now, was coping with all that damned *gravity*.

But everybody else managed it, so he guessed he could, too.

# IX

Ulla Salich was pregnant. To her relief, Stan seemed more pleased than not. Maybe just glad to have it all settled, no more need to argue. Now she could concentrate on ten-year-old Brad: making sure that he felt like an important part of the family expansion project.

Of course Brad didn't know all the details. At least she certainly hoped not!

On Tri-V the Reverend Jody Jay Tolliver delivered a long and confused sermon, naming space travel as a major source of sin and evil. "When the good Lord put Man on this Earth, He knew what He was doing; who dares to say different? Because out there, my good friends—so far from the Garden of Eden that there's never a whisper of that lost innocence—evil flourishes. *Flourishes*, I tell you. So write your congressman, your senator, even your president. And tell them it's their *duty* to shut down all that evil out there!"

Bardeen turned the sound off. His guess was that Jody Jay had learned of his brother-in-law's disappearance.

Thinking about that episode, Bardeen found he was gradually working free of the recurrent attacks of guilt and horror. It was something he'd had to do, and it was over. Well, almost . . .

The main thing was, nobody like Amos Calhoun could get into the Feen compound.

"Sit down, Kennet." In Cogdill's view the man didn't look too well. Granted, the moon trip was a strain—but after three days' rest, Bardeen still showed undue tension. Reconsidering his impulse to offer a drink, the Chairman said, "You look tired. Is everything all right?"

Bardeen shrugged. "I suppose so." He leaned forward. "Isn't it time you told me what's going on?"

"We'll get to that. First I want to know what's eating on you. Something happen up there?"

A spasm crossed Bardeen's face. "Yes, I suppose I have to tell it." As he did, Cogdill felt wonder at this quiet man.

After a pause, the Chairman said, "It's a good thing you're used to thinking fast."

"Is *that* all you have to say?"

What did the man need? "If you're expecting moral judgments, you won't get them from me. The swine tried to kill you, and it backfired. If your conscience needs scrubbing, we have counseling service available."

"It doesn't. Just some time to let the residue wash away."

Cogdill looked at him. Yes; the words rang true. "All right. Now let me tell you what's been happening."

Bardeen already knew of Singh's hypothesis that specific chromosomes triggered the sperm-immune reaction—and that the Sikh was applying Blixor's pseudogene theory, trying to disguise any offending chromosome. Cogdill went through that part briefly, then said, "Here's the new development. In both rat and human gametes, the sex-determining chromosome is the culprit. Once the X or Y is disguised, conjugation completes itself."

The result wasn't necessarily a viable zygote; pseudogenes came in almost infinite variety. It took considerable cut-and-try before fertilized ova, implanted in surrogate mother rats, produced live, healthy young. "So the next step," Cogdill added, "is to see if we can make it work with humans."

"That's impossible! The government—"

Cogdill shook his head. "The government isn't in this, and it's not going to be."

"But we can't—"

"We *can*. Volunteers, our own people, sworn to secrecy under Feen security." Cogdill permitted himself a grin. "In a way, we can thank Jody Jay Tolliver's reborn redneck terrorists; if it hadn't been for them, we wouldn't have secured our enclave. Wouldn't have the ideal setup for experiments the government can't lay a finger on, so long as we finance them ourselves. But we do have it, Kennet. And we're going to use it."

"The *risks*, Thane."

"What risks? The worst that can happen is a nonviable or adversely mutated infant. Against the possibility of a sound, healthy one. We'll have more volunteers than we can use."

His face showing no expression at all, Bardeen said, "And supposing we succeed. How do we announce it, without becoming liable to prosecution on more charges than I can even *count*?"

Cogdill shrugged. "Oh, the government will mutter; no doubt of that. And grumble, too. But if we beat this thing, public opinion will *crucify* anyone who tries to punish us."

Bardeen stood. "I suppose you're right. Well, thanks for the fill-in; now when I talk to Fallon I'll have some idea of what's going on." He turned to leave.

"My pleasure. And if you don't mind a little advice, why don't you take some more time off, until you get the rest of that moon incident out of your system?"

Stopping, Bardeen looked back. "I think I will. Thanks."

Cogdill waved a hand. "Any time."

As soon as Bardeen left, Cogdill's intercom chimed. Glynnis Payne said, "I held off while you were busy, but a Mr. Schofield, at Gilcorp, wanted to talk with you. Shall I call him back now?"

"Now's as good a time as any."

While he waited, Cogdill looked up his notes on Schofield. When his Line Four signaled, he was ready. The picture showed a man in his forties, wearing standard middle-executive clothes. Blond hair, medium complexion. "Mr. Cogdill? I'm Alex Schofield; I'm the one who called Mr. Bardeen initially, about our security problems."

Right. And Bardeen had played it well. By subcontracting Dlumane's services to Gilcorp, he'd managed to recover a good share of the Feen's earlier development costs. Cogdill said, "Yes, I remember. How's your installation coming along?"

"Very well; I called to thank you."

"My pleasure." Schofield looked ready to end the conversation, but before he could, Cogdill asked, "How's the Sterility project going?" He saw the man's face going deliberately blank, and said, "Oh, not in detail. But do you feel you have any good leads?"

Blank was the word, all right. Maybe Schofield was actually covering something, or maybe the blank-reflex was automatic; Cogdill couldn't know. But after a moment the man said, "If you know any way to tailor an immune-suppressant to work only on haploid cells, we'd pay a lot of money to know about it."

"Afraid not. Too bad. Well, I appreciate your call."

As the screen went dead, Cogdill thought about what he'd heard. Gilcorp was still trying to attack the ovum's defenses; they had no handle at all on the real solution!

No longer directly in charge of the Sterility project, still Bardeen put extra time into overseeing it. After all these years, thought Cogdill, no wonder it's his pet chick. Yet the man certainly wasn't neglecting his other work.

Cogdill had no plans to retire soon. When he did, though, more and more Bardeen looked to be his best bet for a successor.

On a totally confidential basis, the Feen contracted with employees to test pseudogene-treated sperm as the agent in artificial insemination. Ramda Singh was working on a method of getting the pseudogene into the sperm *in vivo* rather than *in vitro*, but with no luck to date.

All volunteers had to be live-in employees, committed to maintaining that status. And while the Foundation stood guarantee for health damage to prospective parents, any liability with regard to possible offspring—miscarriages, stillbirths, or defective infants—was specifically waived. In fact, custody of live-birthed infants was granted to the Foundation; at its discretion and in its sole judgment, such custody could be transferred to the parents or other suitable persons.

The point, of course, was that marginally viable monsters, not detected early enough for routine abortion, could be disposed of—with or without the parents' consent. The rats had borne a few, early on, before the pseudogene structure was fine-tuned. Knowledge gained during that tinkering eliminated some of the false steps when human gametes were researched—but as in all experimental work, Murphy's Law still applied!

Bardeen had asked, "You really think they'll sign that?"

Grinning, saying nothing, Cogdill showed him the stack of signed contracts the Legal Department had already obtained. "Didn't want to bother you with details, Kennet. The report's probably halfway down the stack in your In-basket."

While some volunteers were in it for wholly personal reasons, others were also concerned with society's well-being. The Plague had built a step function into demographics; at any age below eleven, the numbers of children were noticeably fewer than those of greater ages. The early Social Security riots, and analogous disturbances in other countries, had eventually worn themselves out. But in their place, smaller and less coherent upheavals had become increasingly common. "It's not," Cogdill told the Board, "as though we had a lot of stability to spare, *before* this thing hit. The Only Child Syndrome may just bring the imbalance that tears the whole engine apart."

By a slim margin, then, he got his vote—to continue the Feen's attack, using its own money, on the Sterility Plague.

One day, neither of them able to control their obvious excitement, Fallon and Bardeen came to Cogdill's office. Not even the Chairman's best bourbon helped, so he gave up. "All right. Somebody *tell* me."

Bardeen raised his glass. "We didn't want to say anything until we had enough success to be significant. But as of today, six pregnancies have missed two menstrual periods, and five more have made it past one."

The news, Cogdill felt, deserved a second round.

During the next few months, over a hundred artificial insemi-nations were tried with pseudogene-treated sperm. Most of them "took," and the miscarriage rate was phenomenally low. By the time the first pregnancies neared term, Dr. Mareth Fallon was beginning to run short of volunteers.

That shortage wasn't her problem, though, one afternoon when she met with Cogdill and Bardeen in the Chairman's office. Tapping the sheaf of papers she'd brought, she said, "These amniocentesis reports."

"Yes." Cogdill nodded. "I trust the sex-ratio is holding up? Roughly the same number of XYs and XXs?"

"Actually, the modified chromosomes differ enough that we call them XZs and XWs. Still with the same connotations, of course; it's a case of technological purism, I suppose. But yes, the ratio holds close to fifty-fifty."

"Then you have another question."

"That's right. Where do we draw the line on defects?"

Bardeen cleared his throat. "To abort or not, you mean?"

She nodded. "Yes. We'd been having good luck—both in the small percentage of defects and the fact that most cases were clear-cut. But now we have two Down's-syndrome fetuses."

Frowning, Cogdill said, "And you want a policy decision? Whether to bring the fetus to term, abort it, or let the parents decide?" He paused, then nodded. "The latter. We don't play God here; we just spare the parents the really bad cases."

Fallon stood. "That's what I hoped you'd say. But the way some of those directives read, I wasn't sure."


Cogdill was preparing to leave his office early when Bardeen called him. The Chairman sighed. "Sure; come on around. I hope this won't take long." Because for the first time in three months, Laura was arriving.

Bardeen, when he came in, seemed excited. "A breakthrough, Thane."

"Sit down and tell me about it. Drink?"

"No, thanks; I see you're on your way out, so I'll tell it fast." He paused a moment, then said, "Singh thinks he can produce the pseudogene in the male gonads themselves, rather than modifying the sperm in vitro."

"He's found a way to put the stuff into pill form?"

"Not quite that easy; it takes intravenous injection. The chromosome change shows up in sperm samples after about three days—and the effect lasts nearly a month."

"This method will give equivalent results? He's certain?"

"In the lab dishes he gets zygotes. But now—"

"Now what?"

"Singh wants to bypass the testing stage of implanting them in volunteers. He wants to find out, as soon as possible, if females and injected males can conceive normally."

"So? Is there any reason he shouldn't?"

"Only that Fallon feels they shouldn't go ahead so fast without your okay."

"That all?" Cogdill grinned. "Go tell her they have it."

He no longer met Laura at the airport; by riding a cab to the hotel where he kept a suite, she saved time for both of them.

He thought he'd be late, but she was just opening her suitcase. After fourteen years he still thought *How lucky I am!* Not unlined, her face had changed so gradually he'd hardly noticed her aging. A few years ago he'd seen grey threads in her midnight hair, but there was no reason she had to tolerate them!

Throughout their long-established ritual of greeting—shower together, a relaxing drink, then bed—Laura showed no lack of warmth or love, but seemed preoccupied.

Until they'd had dinner, he let it alone. Then, "All right. Something's bothering you. Reassure me that it's not *me*."

Her brief laugh carried a startled sound. "Oh, no! It's job problems." Being second-in-charge under a boss few could get along with. A reduction of staff, and—"Krehbiel won't give me a decent Efficiency Report. When I apply for jobs in other areas, I'll be expertly set up for demotion."

Only three or four times, perhaps, had Cogdill seen tears from Laura Casey. Carefully, he said, "Then this might be a good time to bag government work?"

"And do what?"

"How many times have I told you, the Feen needs liaison coordinators of your caliber? So why not—?"

Her headshake whipped curls across her face. "I'm not taking a job where everyone knows my lover pegged my salary. Nepotism, or whatever, simply isn't worth it."

Leaning over, he kissed her nose. "That's not how it'll be. Put your application in to Personnel. They've never heard of you and I won't tell them. So not only your salary, but whether you get hired at all, rests entirely on your own record."

"And if I'm rejected? Then what will you do?"

"Nothing. I won't have to. You're a shoo-in." He hugged her. "Actually, if you're willing, you're up for *two* positions. Job title of the other one is Wife."

A month later, she was holding down both.

*  *  *

The first volunteer to go into labor was Ilene Hagen; she came to it several weeks early. "I guess," she said between contractions, "the boy's going to be a competitor." Then it was time for the chunky, freckled redhead to bear down again.

Outside the delivery room, Cogdill and Bardeen waited with Ilene's husband, Mike. He'd told how their first baby had miscarried, "—and after that, nothing worked. We didn't know it was the Sterility Plague, of course; nobody did. So for several years we had a lot of strain." He smiled. "Certainly never thought we'd get another chance, like this. Coming to work for the Feen was the best move we ever made!"

"I'm glad you feel that way." Cogdill tried to smile, but other concerns interfered with the effort. When the door opened and the obstetrician came out, Cogdill stared, waiting.

The doctor turned to Hagen first. "The baby's in fine health, and so's Ilene. If you'd rather wait in her room, she'll be there soon. You know where it is?"

The man nodded. "Thanks, Dr. Klein." To Cogdill and Bardeen, "I appreciate your keeping me company." Then he left.

Thane Cogdill said, "All right, doctor. The last sonic scan reports hinted at anomalies. You told Hagen the boy's healthy. Now tell *me*; is that the whole truth?"

Klein's expression wavered between worried and defiant. Finally he said, "The healthy part's true enough. It's the boy part that's a little doubtful."

"You mean, you can't tell? One of those gender confusion cases, with—" He tried to think of the terminology, and got it. "Undifferentiated organs?"

"Nothing like that. He has all the boy equipment."

"Then what—?"

"I don't *know* what, for sure. But unless you believe a pair of matched tumors, the baby also has ovaries.

"I wouldn't recommend surgical interference. Not until we know what we really have here. And to find out for sure may take years."

"I see," Cogdill said. "In the meantime, then, you will classify this development absolutely Top Zip."

# BOOK THREE

"*It is well known that breakthroughs do not always occur solely in the intended direction; as often as not, side effects may result.*"
(From Origins, by Rome dos Caras.)

# X

As far back as I can remember, I knew I was different from most people. And so were the rest of the kids, my age and younger, in the Feen Enclave. What the difference was, I had no idea, because nobody said. And I couldn't ask; the hints gave me nothing solid to go on.

But I knew. Every time I had a physical exam, the doctors and nurses inspected the ultrasonic pictures of my insides and nodded as if everything was all right, or else looked puzzled and said things like, "I don't know; we'll just have to wait and see."

"Wait and see what?" I said, one time. "Whether I've got cancer or something?" The younger doctor, the intern, shook her head and laughed. Oh no, I was perfectly all right: Dr. Gill's voice sounded honest enough, so I believed her when she said these special tests were just part of a project the doctors were working on. And when they had some real answers, they'd tell me all about it.

Except that they never did. But I found out, anyway.

My name then was Troy Hagen. It was only later, when we began to move outside the compound and live among the Mark Ones, that Rome and I took the surname of dos Caras. There's a joke to that; in Spanish it means "Two Faces." Somehow my brother and I thought it most appropriate; I have no idea what the M-ls think.

It may be odd that even now, in phase or out, I still see Rome and me as brothers. But that's what we were during our formative years, and the concept persists.

After ten more Project births, when it developed that all the infants carried anomalies similar or complementary to those of the

73

Hagen baby, Rog Forrest called a staff meeting. The Chairman wasn't there; as his representative, Kennet Bardeen attended.

Mareth Fallon spoke. "What we're faced with is that each of these children—male or female—carries, in rudimentary or vestigial form, the organs of the other sex."

Forrest looked puzzled. "Somebody draw me a picture. Because I don't see how all that plumbing could fit together."

One of Fallon's aides did have sketches, center-line cross sections, of both "normal" and Project children of each sex. Bardeen found the females easier to compare. The modified version varied mostly in routing the urinary tract back almost to the vagina, where an analogue of a prostate gland straddled it. Then it curved forward again to emerge at the normal location, just behind the clitoris. Small ovoid lumps at the bases of the labia majora were, it was postulated, testicular tissue. "No," said Fallon. "We've made no biopsies to check the hypothesis."

The males were a little trickier. The small ovaries weren't sitting in isolation; threadlike structures that certainly routed like Fallopian tubes led to a tiny, barely identifiable uterus; from that, descending to a locus behind the urinary tract and forward of the rectum, a thin tubular shadow appeared. At its exit point there was a kind of dimple but no actual opening; still, it fit the pattern of a vaginal analogue.

When he was through figuring these things out, Bardeen waited for a pause in discussion and then spoke. "All right; this isn't the only instance where organs useful only to one sex appear vestigially in the other."

"Useless as tits on a boar, you mean?" Bardeen didn't know the man who spoke, but nodded to him anyway.

"Good example, yes. But the point I wanted to make is this: would a truly painstaking analysis find some trace of these redundant organs in our own bodies?"

Fallon looked puzzled. "What gave you that idea?"

He cleared his throat. "Without a preexisting basis, how could a pseudogene manage to *pattern* so much detailed structure? Also, acting on two different chromosomes, X and Y, how else could it produce such mirror-image results?"

"That last," said Fallon, "I can answer. On an intuitive level, at least—by which I mean, my idea *feels* right, and nothing disproves it."

Despite himself, Bardeen chuckled. "Would you tell us?"

"Certainly. We thought it would require two separate designs of pseudogenes, to slip X and Y chromosomes past ovum-immunity. But we got lucky." She smiled. "One size fit both, so to speak. And I think that by using the same pseudogene to modify X and Y into what we call W and Z, we simply increased their commonality."

"In other words," Bardeen said, "you don't know, either."

"True enough. But I've given you my best guess."

The meeting shifted from informative to controversial. Dr. Bart Crandall—tall, bony, with black hair and a permanent five-o'clock shadow—demanded a policy decision. "I've said it before, and a number of people back me up: the way to make sure these kids grow up normal, is to excise the anomalous structures and leave nothing to infringe on the dominant gender."

Fallon shook her head. "We don't know yet—and may not know for a long time—what necessary balancing functions these apparent anomalies may serve. Enter your recommendation if you wish, Crandall—but I'll fight it all the way."

Bardeen had heard enough. As he stood, and moved to leave, he gripped Fallon's shoulder; when she looked up, he winked.

After Thane Cogdill took Bardeen's report and addressed the next Board meeting, the vote shot Crandall down in flames.

I was twelve, going on thirteen—sitting on the toilet and long done with any valid reason for being there but still reading—when my penis began doing something strange. At first I didn't really notice, but then there was this good throbbing I'd never felt before; I looked down and saw that part of me growing larger, bobbing higher and straighter with every pulse.

Without thought I set the book aside and watched, as the organ stopped growing but kept bobbing, each throb sending starbursts of pleasure through me—in every direction but mostly up toward my belly. After a time I realized I wasn't breathing, and inhaled a gasp, then more of them.

I suppose every young male has this experience; it's not something you forget.

The surprise had stopped my thinking, but now I realized this had to have to do with Sex. I knew about it, of course, and in a way it had always seemed a little scary. But if *this* was how it felt—well, maybe it was a good thing, after all.

The only trouble was, I had no idea what to do about it. So I sat there, feeling the good throbs and watching as a drop of clear liquid formed at the tip. I might have sat much longer, but the door rattled and my brother said, "Hey! You gonna stay in there all day?" Confused, I shook my head, then stood up to fix my pants and everything. Probably due to the interruption, my penis had gone limp, back to normal, and caused no problems. As I opened the door, though, I felt the slick wetness still oozing into my shorts.

I didn't know how to tell anyone about this new thing, but I knew I had to; the doctors always said we should report any changes. They didn't say why; we figured it was most likely all a part of the special project.

Until my next scheduled physical, though, I kept that new pleasure to myself. I'd go to the toilet when nobody else was likely to need it for a while, and sit there and *think* at my penis. Almost immediately it would start pumping itself up, and I'd just sit there and enjoy it. I had the feeling there should be something more, but nothing else happened; finally I'd think of other things until the throbbing ebbed and ceased, then take a leak to clear out most of the slippery juice before putting my clothes to rights and rejoining my family. At such moments I always felt strange, as if I'd been somewhere that no one else could know about. But after a few minutes, that strangeness always wore off.

When I went to the Test Section for my next physical, Dr. Gill was the only medic on duty. She was taller than I was, thin, with fluffed-out reddish hair and a friendly smile. At that time I believe she was about thirty-five. Her first name was Sharla, but we never called doctors by their first names.

As always happened, she had me go into the examining room, take off my clothes and get up onto the table. While she went through the routine I kept wondering how I could tell her about this new thing. It wasn't just her; the problem was how to explain something I didn't understand.

As things turned out, I didn't have to explain. While Dr. Sharla Gill was moving the ultrasonic "camera" over my belly, her breath came warm near my crotch. Then as she moved away to scan the camera's results, the sidelong view of her lower body triggered something; when the doctor looked back to me, she couldn't miss seeing the throbs begin, and then increase.

Her smile seemed confident; her voice didn't. "Well, Troy. Has this been happening for very long?"

"No. A couple of weeks, maybe. Is anything wrong?"

"Of course not. But excuse me a second? I need to make a call."

"Sure."

She went to the intercom. "Dr. Barnes, please. Gill here." A wait. "Yes, doctor. No, nothing wrong; just puberty." Pause. "Troy Hagen. Of course I'm sure. He's—" She looked back toward me; the throbbing had ebbed. "He was, I mean. And the fluid is there. So—"

With no idea of what the doctors had in mind, I could only wait. She asked more questions, then said, "Certainly, if he's willing. Yes, I agree. It's something we need to know. No, I have no objection. Yes, sir. I'll let you know later."

After shutting down the intercom, she came back over to the table and began taking her clothes off. She was thinner than most of the women I'd seen naked in the Enclave's pool and sauna, but pretty, anyway.

Touching a finger to the tip of my penis, she brought it away with a drop of clear liquid. "Have you had orgasm yet?"

"I don't know. What is it?" Uneasy, I caught myself scratching at the thin line of scab on my cheek, where the nextdoor kitten had objected to being cuddled—but stopped before I might pick it loose and draw blood.

"If you're not sure, then you haven't. The fluid would be milky-colored, and come out in spurts."

"Then I didn't. Just this, is all. It oozes. Tastes okay." Her eyebrows, darker than her hair, raised. "Well, I got some on my finger, and checked. Was that wrong?"

She shook her head. "Why should it be? You have the right to be curious. Now, though—I want you to do something more. To have real sex with me. Do you know what that is? Would you mind doing it?"

I didn't want her to see how nervous I was, so I took a deep breath and hoped she wouldn't notice how it shuddered. "Sure I know; in school we see those tapes. I wouldn't mind—if it's all right to. Is it? Nobody's said."

"This time it is. Dr. Barnes has asked that you do it."

"Then I guess so."

At first I thought I was too scared—everything so new and all at once—but her hand's touch proved that I wasn't. She talked to me, softly, as she moved us both around the way she wanted us. I knew what a vagina was, and its function; I wasn't prepared, though, for the heat and moisture and gripping pressure. I started to move in rapid thrusts, but gauged them wrong and slipped out. As I fumbled to get back, her hands went to my hipbones and steadied me. "Slower, Troy; take your time. You'll be all right." Leaving all guidance to her, I lost track of everything but my own sensations.

Until—my senses peaked, higher and higher—without warning an explosion convulsed me; thought was impossible, and feeling was almost too intense to bear. Over and over again, my belly clenched and erupted; I heard the sounds I made, but they weren't words. *Would this never end?* It was ecstasy, but too much to withstand, for long.

Finally it ebbed, and I could almost think. Panting, I tried for words and found none. After a wait, gently the doctor pushed my upper body to one side, and turned to look at me. "Are you all right, Troy?"

I didn't shake my head to clear it, because she'd take that for a "No." "Mmm." I put a hand to her cheek. Two breaths later, I said, "I will be. Is it *always*—?"

She smiled. "First time, I believe, is apt to be a surprise. Then you learn to enjoy it better."

I thought about it. "Yes. The scary part was, it was all so *new*." I nodded; then an idea came. "I think—I should thank you now, shouldn't I?"

"Only if you feel like doing so."

"Well, I do."

"Then I accept, and you're welcome." Her body nudged at me. "Could we get up now, though, d'you suppose?"

"Oh. Yes, of course." But as I pulled away and moved to stand, on both of us I saw stains of blood. "Oh, no! I've hurt you. How—?"

She looked at me, then at fingers she touched to herself, and shook her head. "There's no hurt, Troy. I've started early, that's all. My period—you know how those things work?"

"Sure. It's just that—" It was different, seeing it, from just reading about it. Confused, I asked if I could go now; she said yes, so I did.

I had the feeling, though, that I was disappointing her. That she expected me to do something else first.

But I didn't know what, and all she said was, "Please come back in a few days, will you?"

"All right." We set the appointment; then I did go home.

The next day, going into the toilet room when no one else was likely to want in there, I decided I'd do a little more than just sit and enjoy the throbbing. Not all the way to that scary "orgasm," but—well, when Dr. Gill used her hand on me, before the "real sex," it felt awfully good. Maybe my own hand would work, too.

So I sat down and began thinking, and then touching myself, but it didn't work. My penis throbbed faintly and grew a little, but it wouldn't come *up*; the sensations I'd had before, simply weren't there. Finally I decided that maybe this orgasm thing took it out of you, that I needed to rest up first.

The next day I tried again. And couldn't even get a throb going. A closer look showed my penis smaller than it had been for years. And my balls, too; instead of hanging loose a little, they were pulled up tight in my crotch. Something was wrong!

I tried to think. Was this what "real sex" did to you? Was it, maybe, why most couples never had more than one kid? No, that couldn't be; all the grown men I'd seen naked had perfectly normal-looking organs.

The trouble was, I didn't know enough. It seemed as though I didn't know *anything*. So I went out of the room and tried not to think about it.

The day after, though, I was hardly a boy at all: penis shrunk to a tiny nubbin, balls shrunk or pulled up inside my body—and behind them, a moist area where there hadn't been any. Dreading, I reached a finger between the rearward fringes of the loose flaps of skin where my balls had always been.

A moist *dent*, an opening; I could feel it clearly.

Right then and there I wanted to die. But I'd made an appointment with Dr. Gill, so I had to keep it.

# XI

Checking her calendar, Sharla Gill smiled. It would be good to see Troy again. Not that she wanted or intended to have sex with him in the future: "Just get a semen sample, for examination," Barnes had said. "The method is up to you."

Never before had Gill faced the raw impact of a young male's first orgasm; for long seconds, she'd been afraid that the boy would go into real convulsions. He'd made it, though, and she supposed they all did. Still it felt good to have seen him through it. She hoped he felt the same way.

When he came in, almost exactly on time, the look on his face lowered her high spirits. "Troy? Is anything wrong?" Dumb question, she thought; he looks like *everything's* wrong.

Standing hangdog, Troy Hagen stared up at her. "I don't know what you did to me. How it happened. Anything." He moved his hands, somehow shrugging off all of existence. "I said I'd be here, so I am. Now make your tests. Because I probably won't be back."

First thing, she tranked her patient: three spansules. Then she made a quick examination. She couldn't believe what she found, because it wasn't possible. There had to be some mistake. A hoax? Another child, pretending to be Troy? But she knew Troy—and there was the pink line on his cheek, most of the scab now shed from it, too slight to leave a permanent scar. So—possible or not, she was seeing what she saw. Taking a deep breath, Sharla Gill accepted what she could not explain. As though a visual record would lend greater reality to her own perceptions, she undressed Troy, moved him (her?) so as to expose the changed areas, and took both sonic-scan prints and several Polaroid shots.

Then she called Barnes.

* * *

At first the man couldn't seem to listen, so eventually she yelled. "He's a *girl* now, for God's sake! Last week he was a young male having his first-ever orgasm, and now the kid is female. No mistake about it."

Shaking her head against the older doctor's disbelief, she cited facts. The retracted testes, leaving the empty scrotum to form labia. The shrunken penis, with the urethra's orifice moving back to leave the miniature penis-head as a clitoris. The small but definite swellings of breast tissue. And most impressive: the tiny dot, the rudimentary vagina, expanding to become a true opening, with mucus-membrane expanding into areas that had been covered with dry skin. "I don't *know* how," she said, not for the first time, "but that's what's there." Impatient with her superior's protests, she shook her head. "I'm not *asking* you to take my word for it. Or even to believe the pictures I've taken." She took a deep breath. "All you need to do is get off your butt and come over here—and see for yourself."

Craig Barnes came, and looked, and asked—and finally had to accept what he saw. First he tried to reassure Troy Hagen, but getting practically no response, he had the youngster put to bed for observation. Then he said, "Is this how it will be with all of them?" He must have seen how that question affected Sharla Gill, because he added, "All right. We can't know yet, can we? Dr. Gill, how do you suggest that we proceed to experiment?"

Looking at the tall, haggard man, she decided he could be worse. She said, "We've known all along that the Mark Two children have both kinds of sex organs; in childhood, one set or the other has predominated: male for our XZs and female for the XWs. But now—"

"Yes, yes." The man waved a hand. "And certainly young Troy's male organs were functional. But why would their first real use compel them to abdicate?"

After a moment's thought, she said, "We have only one example; that's not enough to tell us much. But Troy's not a lot older than several other boys—if they *are* truly boys."

Barnes cleared his throat. "And you suggest—?"

"What any researcher would. Further experimentation, with a variety of subjects. The Foundation's contract with the parents covers practically anything, short of vivisection." She gave Barnes a hard glare. "Yes, I think it's necessary that a few more of the boys, when they're physically ready for it, should be initiated. And some, not. So we can see if Troy's reaction is typical, and whether the sex we had together caused the change."

"If sexual activity causes the reversal, *then* what can we do?"

Gill shrugged. "Let's not assume that unless it happens. But there's something else we need to think about."

He nodded. "I know. Without making a lot of waves, what kind of tests can be made with respect to the *girls*?"

She said, "I don't think that will be our decision to make. When we report this development to Mr. Forrest and Mr. Bardeen, I expect the whole problem will go to a Board vote."

Still doped up more than a little and realizing it, eventually Troy Hagen went home. He couldn't face his parents yet, or his brother, so he stopped by a sprightly-eats place and took a plate-to-go. He entered the family residence by his private door, sat and ate, and then faced up to the fact that he had to think.

He took off his clothes, had a bath and dried off. Looking in a mirror, he felt of himself, especially the parts that worried him. And something he hadn't noticed before: his nipples were larger, and now they stood out, on a distinct layer of breast tissue. Not big, but you couldn't really miss it.

For one insane moment Troy wanted death. Then, drawing breath raggedly, he glared into the mirror. "Well, all right, God damn you, whoever you are." He looked at the crotch, only softly-fuzzy as yet, that three days ago had erupted to thrill him but now showed nothing but a gentle, vertical cleft. He said, with no idea who or what he might be talking to, "I grew up a boy; I figured that's what I was. Then that woman let me be a man. It was almost more than I could take, but I'd have tried it again. Now I'm a girl; I didn't ever figure to be one, or want to, but I heard the doctors say I am." His breath came shuddering. "Well, all *right*, damn you to hell. If I have to, I guess I can do that, too."

And for the first time in several days, Troy had no trouble getting to sleep.

Over the next two weeks, the order-loving mind of Sharla Gill had to face one unsettling shock after another. On Barnes's instructions she sexually initiated Moss Frantz, a boy roughly Troy Hagen's age, and a week later Moss showed no changes. Dale Carson, called in for examination, skipped the appointment; when Gill visited the boy's home and overcame his objections to examination, she found that this one had metamorphosed to female without sexual contact of any kind.

She checked with Craig Barnes, and was told that other volunteers were reporting similar anomalies. Gill shook her head. "Dr. Barnes, where is all this heading? Is the male growing-period merely some kind of larval stage? If *all* the Mark Two boys turn female, where does that leave us?"

"Do you really expect me to have an answer?"

"No, of course not. I wasn't asking a fair question, was I?" She sighed. "I suppose we'll just have to keep observing."

The call ended; Gill sat puzzling, totally frustrated. Troy Hagen was her next appointment; that one, she was not looking forward to. She knew she still had much more to learn, there—but didn't expect to like what she learned.


For a number of days after the change, Troy kept mostly to her own room, "attending" school only via the computer terminal. Skipping family meals would have brought more attention rather than less; Troy ate with the others, right on schedule, but didn't talk much.

There was a *need* to talk, to share this vast shock and maybe get some sympathy and understanding—but no idea of how to open the subject. Or, to whom? Dad? Rather die. Mom? Almost as bad. Rome, the brother, was nearly two years younger; he wouldn't understand, and would blab the secret all over.

Yet it was Rome, always snooping and teasing, who broke things open. Troy came back from the kids' bathroom to find that Rome had sneaked in and was rooting through Troy's belongings.

It was too much. Face suddenly heated, Troy yelled. "All right, you little rat! What do *you* want?"

Caught out, Rome grinned. "Hey, I didn't mean anything, Troy. Just wanted to find out what you got in here, so much fun you don't come out any more, hardly." Backing away, the younger boy stood. "Troy? Don't hit me. I—"

Don't hit? Sure not. Not with fists, anyway. No—hit him with what's going to *happen* to him. Without thought, Troy unfastened and dropped all lower garments. "You want to see what's such fun? Take a good look, Rome. Because in a couple more years, you'll be the same way."

Maybe he would be, maybe not; Troy couldn't know. But for certain, Rome had the hell scared out of him. The boy's knuckles were jammed into his mouth; he was biting on them, while he stared as if at a poisonous snake. Then he jerked his hand free, toothmarks on it but no blood drawn, and gasped. Sidling around Troy toward the door, Rome said, more breath than voice, "I don't know what you did to yourself—but I'm gonna *tell*."

Then he was gone. Troy pulled the clothes back up, and fastened them. One thing sure; now there'd be hell to pay.

Nothing happened the way Troy expected. A knock on the door. Mom, still outside, saying, "Rome, you go to your room and stay there; you hear me?" Then she came in, a look on her face that Troy didn't understand but wanted to comfort away; in seconds they were hugging. "Troy. Troy, honey. Darling, you have to show me."

Not wanting to, Troy finally did. Mom looked, touched a little, and finally nodded. "We never knew what all the possibilities might be. Looks like this is one of them."

Questions wouldn't come together well enough to ask; Mom continued. "As soon as you were born, we knew that you—that all the children from the project—had a full set of rudimentary organs of the other sex. We didn't know what it meant, how it could work. Then you all grew up, through childhood, apparently normal boys and girls. So we hoped the project had beaten the Sterility Plague. But now *this* happens!" She pulled back a little, and looked at him. "Do you know if it's happened to anyone else?"

"No, Mom. But I don't really know what the Sterility Plague is, either."

"Or care much, either, I'd expect. About anything except what's happened to *you*, and how, and maybe why. Well, I can't blame you for that." She pulled Troy up to look at her, face to face, and caressed a tear-streaked cheek. "I wish I could tell you something, but I have nothing to tell. Well, just two things. You're our child and we love you, no matter what. And, none of this is *your* fault."

Troy's held breath shuddered out. "Thanks, Mom."

Whatever Troy's parents said to each other first, when dad came in to talk he seemed pretty calm on the surface—but Troy could sense a tension growing. Dad said, "This has to be one hell of a shock to you; it would be, to anyone. It's something nobody expected—but I guess we should have known that just about anything was possible."

"Sure," said Troy, not understanding even half of it. "But what about *me*?"

"When things change, we have to change with them. Because we don't have any choice. I know this has to be terrible for you. But just don't forget—no matter what, you can always count on your mom and me."

Dad meant it, too, Troy realized. The only trouble was that his voice betrayed how much *work* it was, for him to mean it.

Rome never did mind for long. When Troy saw him peeking in the door, maybe their dad noticed Troy's eye movements; the man turned to his younger son. "And *you*, now."

"Yeah. Am *I* gonna have to be a girl, too?"

"I don't know; maybe so, maybe not. But right now, young man, you keep your mouth shut about this. To everybody. It's— it's a project secret. And you know what that means."

Rome probably didn't know, because Troy certainly didn't, but the boy nodded anyway, and then promised hope-to-die.

So for a few days it was almost all right. Troy still didn't go back to school, but started psyching up for that move, because sooner or later she'd have to. But then it wasn't all right at all: one morning Troy woke up bloody.

Menstruating! And knowing what it was didn't keep it from being just about the last straw. Mom brought out the tampon inserts but they were too big; Troy made do with a folded wad of tissues taped into the cleft, and nothing seeped through.

Late the next day, though, the flow stopped. And the opening had shrunk, along with its area of mucus membrane. The clitoris was expanding, too.

Three days after the period began, Troy was male again.

# XII

The way Sharla Gill's hands were shaking, it was all she could do to hit the right button on the intercom. "Dr. Barnes? Could you come here right away? It's—Troy Hagen's here again."

"So? What's the kid done *now*?"

She shook her head. "I'm not telling you—not one word. You'll have to come see for yourself."

When Barnes saw Troy, his eyes narrowed. "I don't know what's going on here, Gill, but I think someone's playing a practical joke on us." His sigh sounded relieved. "All we have to do, to clear this up, is find the girl who masqueraded as Troy Hagen last month."

As Troy watched, seeming a little nervous, Gill laughed. "You mean the one with fingerprints identical to this boy's? Oh, I thought of that, at the time. The girl's prints match those of baby boy Troy Hagen, and also those I took today."

Barnes frowned. "Plastic appliqués? Criminals have used them; I read about it. So—"

"To *leave* fake prints somewhere, yes. But if you read the entire article, you'd know that the things are quite obviously noticeable. No, it's out of the question."

"Then—" Barnes paused. "*I* know what to do."

"Yes?"

"I'm calling Dr. Fallon. Right now."

Sharla Gill suppressed a grin. *How else?*

Mareth Fallon looked puzzled. After a quick inspection—largely visual, but also touching Troy here and there—she said to him, "How many days between the beginning of the first change and this one; do you know?" As the boy frowned, Fallon said, "Gill? Give me the dates of Troy's previous two visits; they should help him pin the interval down better."

Twenty-eight days at the least, it came out—thirty at the most. And although it was impossible to specify exact timing, each transition lasted somewhere between two and three days.

She looked to Gill and Barnes. "The other two boys who changed. Are they still female? And how long has it been?"

Barnes didn't speak, so Gill did. "Only about two weeks, for the earliest. And no girls have changed, as yet."

Dr. Fallon nodded. "Then I think we'd better—"

Surprisingly, Troy interrupted. "*I'll* tell you what you'd better do. You'd better call in all the kids that're getting old enough for this kind of thing to happen, and *warn* 'em, so they'll be ready for it."

"The shock, you mean." Fallon said it quietly.

"You *bet*, the shock!" The boy looked embarrassed, but he went ahead. "I hadn't wanted to tell anybody, but for a couple of days there, until I got mad enough to figure I could handle it, I—I was awfully close to suicide. And—some other kid might not be lucky enough to get mad."

Fallon nodded. "Yes. I should have thought of that. Thank you, Troy. All right. Barnes, Gill—the three of us will start setting up individual counseling appointments. Immediately."

The two nodded, and Troy said, "Am I through with it now? Or will it—every time I have sex, will I have to be a girl for a month?"

"No." Gill shook her head. "That's not what governs. In the past three weeks, two boys changed without having that experience; three others had it but did not change."

"Then why did *I*—?"

"We don't know yet. This is too new; we don't have enough facts to make a halfway decent guess, one way or another."

The boy's grin was shaky. "Well, at least I know it's not permanent." He stood. "Can I put my clothes on now?"

It was Fallon who answered. "Yes, Troy. If Dr. Gill is finished with you"—the other woman nodded—"then you may go home now. Or wherever you're planning to go next." As he began dressing, she added, "For the time being, none of this is to be discussed with anyone outside your own family. Project security."

*That's foolish*, thought Gill. *But Project security is going to be quite a problem.*

\* \* \*

When Troy had left, Mareth Fallon said, "Cyclic hermaphrodites, or so it would appear. The ones who grew up as boys, at least, since no girls have transformed, to date."

"They will, though, I expect," said Sharla Gill. "And then what?"

"I don't know. One thing, however. Until we have more data, there'll be no report to the Project Director. When we go official with this, I want us to have *some* idea what we're talking about."

"—and so Urban IX, the new Pope, has reversed the policy of his predecessor, Pius XIII, and now approves the practice of artificial insemination without restrictions on the source of sperm. The Pope's statement—"

In his office, with the workday about to start, Bardeen turned the Tri-V off. He thought about the background to this news item. Pius XIII had been besieged by liberal forces, advocating Church policy changes—everything from sanctioning adultery to allowing "serial polygamy" via divorce—in order to circumvent the Sterility Plague. Artificial insemination, by someone other than a lawful spouse, seemed a much lesser deviation, but under pressure the old man had stood fast, giving no concessions whatsoever. The new pontiff, having chosen a name unused for nearly five centuries, clearly had it in mind to still the clamor. Somewhat cynically, Bardeen reflected that this concession would help only a small minority—but it just happened to be the minority with enough clout to make waves.

Kennet Bardeen wasn't especially religious, let alone Roman Catholic, but one of Jenny's sisters had married into and then converted to that faith; he knew how Margaret and her husband had agonized over the conflict between child-wanting and religion. Well, now they had an approved alternative. . . .

His intercom sounded. "Yes? Bardeen here."

"Forrest. You busy?"

"Not this early, Rog. What's up?"

"It's taken enough months, but Dr. Fallon's finally handed in a report she's willing to submit to the Board. I expect you'd like an advance look?"

"Sure would. What format do you have?"

"Only paper, I'm afraid. I'll send somebody up with it."

"That'll be fine. Thanks."

"My pleasure. Watch out, though: you may find some scary stuff in this one."

Considering the inevitable leaks of rumor through the curtain of secrecy Fallon had raised earlier in the year, Bardeen doubted that anything in the report could really startle him.

But he said, "Sure, Rog; thanks again." And ended the call.

"Cyclic, you say? The boys and girls, both?" Thane Cogdill shook his head. "I don't understand how that can be."

Bardeen gestured agreement. "None of us do, Mareth Fallon included. But the fact is that once into puberty, both the XZs and XWs become cyclic hermaphrodites. With transition periods, of something less than three days, between the alternating male and female segments. Average length of the full cycle, which varies between individuals, is not quite sixty days."

"Didn't seem to work that way with young Whatsisname, the first time it happened. Anybody know why?"

"I'm afraid not. Fallon's become cautious about testing; what she's doing now is mostly recording observations."

"Kennet, why did she sit on this information for so long?"

Bardeen shrugged. "She says she didn't want to let the info out, at all, until she knew more."

"And now she's satisfied? Knows what she needs to know?"

"Nowhere near. But the pressure—from you and me and Rog Forrest—forced her hand. I wish it hadn't."

Cogdill's brows raised. "And why is that?"

"Because she's given us enough to enable the Board to go off half-cocked. Before we know anywhere near enough to set any kind of valid policy."

The Chairman's smile had no relationship to humor. "You're wrong, Kennet. One item of policy is mandatory."

"Oh?"

"No word of this development goes outside the Enclave."

Bardeen scowled. "That's desirable, yes. But it might be a little hard to enforce."

"I don't think so. Read your contract."

"What—?"

"The membership trust. Its benefits are not only substantial; outside the Feen they'd be called bountiful. Any breach of contract not only voids the membership but also incurs additional, and severe, financial penalties." The smile again. "In a subtle way, our weekly newsletter keeps such facts in the forefront of everyone's attention."

"And you think that's sufficient precaution?"

The noise Cogdill made was somewhere between snicker and snort. "I've taken other steps, too."

"Such as?"

A headshake. "You don't really want to know. But keep in mind: a frightening rumor doesn't have to be true, to be effective."

"You're using scarehead tactics? Against our own people?"

"If they *are* truly our own people, there's no scare to it. You understand? And if not—well, I'm not above learning a thing or two from the Reverend Jody Jay Tolliver."

*I don't like this!* But Bardeen said only, "How far can you expect this secrecy to hold? We can't keep an ever-growing population here in the Enclave. Not indefinitely."

Cogdill nodded. "I know that. But we have to keep the kids— the first specimens of Humanity, Mark Two—here in secret until they're old enough that no outside authority can force them to undress.

"After that, obviously many of them will need to go outside and live within the framework of the Mark One society."

The Chairman's expression showed concern. "Between now and then, our job and theirs is to figure out how to make that work. Because—Kennet, how do you really feel about these kids?"

"Well, from a scientific viewpoint—"

"Scientific bullshit! I'm talking gut-level reaction."

Bardeen nodded. "I see what you mean. I like young Troy, and of course the entire phenomenon is fascinating. But on some level or other, down where I can barely detect it, there's this sneaky feeling that something's *wrong* about convertible gender."

"At least you're honest enough to admit it. And now do you see some problems the Mark Twos may have to face, outside?"

At the next meeting, the Board of Directors was given perhaps one-fourth of the information Cogdill and Bardeen had discussed. Playing cat's-paw, Bardeen made the proposals, so that the Chairman could sit back and appear to be neutral.

The entire charade, Bardeen thought, might have been unnecessary. With only enough quibbling to allow members to save face, the Board passed every item.

One new public announcement would definitely help the Feen keep a low profile. Secretary Granger, having held her position through two changes of administration, announced that Gilcorp had beaten the Sterility Plague. To a certain extent, at least: using genetically engineered agents not described very well on the Tri-V, Gilcorp's researchers had breached the immunity barriers of human ova and achieved *in vitro* fertilization; a number of the resultant zygotes had been successfully implanted into surrogate mothers, and over the past year, more than two hundred healthy infants had been born.

Well, thought Bardeen, it wasn't exactly a quantum leap. But anything that focused attention away from the Feen, he was glad to see.

Looking back, I find it hard to identify with the fears and uncertainties that plagued my debut into the teens. I except the first trauma of losing my male identity; no one, I feel, could take such a totally unforeseen shock in stride. But later, when the sexually cyclic nature of all the Project children was made clear to us and I'd been the rounds two or three times, still every switch to F-mode threw me into depression. It took several full cycles before I was able to accept it as a natural part of my biological nature, and enjoy life equally well in either mode.

Some of the reasons are now clear to me. We were not, we Mark Twos, encouraged to experiment sexually among ourselves; in fact, any such activity was strictly prohibited. There was, I understand, a strong sentiment among the Board members to the effect that we were not, at such early ages, either to be given contraceptives or, when in F-mode, to risk pregnancy. The second point I fully agree with; the first, I still contend, was more Puritan than practical. The result was a feeling of isolation.

The experience of the Mark Two girls, our XWs, paralleled mine somewhat but not wholly. In their case, growing up female, the change was triggered by menarche; three days later they became, unaccountably, male. Their metamorphosis was not as rapidly complete as ours; the testicular tissue had been kept overly warm for so many years that three or four M-mode periods were required before actual male function became possible.

I remember the day, just as classes let out, that Eden Hale came running after me. "Hey, Troy—wait up!" So I did, and she ran over and grabbed my arm. "I need to talk with you."

"Sure." I'd known Eden all my life; I liked her. She was my favorite partner at the school dances—and playing at grownup romance (I suppose that's what we were doing) we sometimes went to a darker corner of the outdoor terrace and kissed. I'm afraid we didn't do it very well, but at the time I was thrilled.

Now her grey eyes, under well-defined dark eyebrows, looked troubled. She pushed back garishly dyed red hair, growing out from an ill-advised short cut and blatant frizz. I didn't mind the hair; girls did that kind of thing but it wasn't permanent. I said, "What's on your mind, Eden?"

"Not *here*." She was stretched; I could see that.

"Where, then?"

She hesitated. "My house. My room. All right?"

Well, sure. When we got there, nobody else was home; we just went into her room. Since the last time I'd been there, she hadn't changed it much. I said, "All right; tell me."

She put a hand to each side of my neck, her thumbs touching my ears. "Would you like to kiss me?"

Saying nothing, I did that. And again. We were, I thought, doing better at it now. But when I pulled back to look at her, Eden was crying.

"What's the *matter*?"

She didn't answer. All she did was undo her clothing and pull out her penis.

I hugged Eden; I patted Eden's shoulder; I talked without really knowing what I said.

Then I got my thinking together. "Your first time in M-mode, this is?"

Eden nodded. I said, "You think it makes a difference? In whether I *like* you?" Another nod. I said, "I'm in M myself, right now. About halfway along with it, maybe a little more. Now *look*—I've been through this and I know how rough it is. But it doesn't have to be. Just accept that we *all* hit both modes, and since that's true, there can't be anything wrong with it." Eden seemed to be looking a little better. "All right?"

"I guess so."

"Just remember—whichever mode someone is in, it's still the same person."

Eden nodded. "I will." There was a pause, and then, "Hey, Troy—there's cold chicken in the fridge. You hungry? I am."

Not too strangely, perhaps, my words of comfort to Eden had the effect of beginning to reassure *me*. So when I went into F-mode about two weeks later, I waited until the transition was complete and then took Eden to my room and showed him. It was safe enough; Rome was off playing baseball or possibly soccer, and my parents respected my growing need for privacy.

Eden was fascinated; he wanted to touch me, and of course it didn't stop at that. We knew and respected the taboo on real sex, and on his first M-mode segment Eden couldn't have done much of anything, anyway, but—well, we played around with each other a certain amount and enjoyed it quite a lot! It felt very strange, having our sexes reversed from what they'd been all our lives, but oddly enough it seemed to give us both a better grade of confidence than we'd had before.

Then in another fortnight, when Eden went F again, we met and compared notes. But didn't play around, any more than we'd done when we were both M. Eden said, "It's too bad we're so far out of phase. If we were to get married when we grow up, we couldn't be real mates more than about half the time."

I had to agree. Because, when we were both in the same mode, somehow things just weren't the same between us.

When my F-mode ended, I was busy and didn't see Eden immediately. Dr. Gill had talked me into sitting in on her counseling sessions, to prepare the younger kids for their own changes. Earlier I'd refused, because I felt so bad myself that I knew I couldn't help. Now, though, I could.

So it was several days before Eden and I resumed our rather innocent sex play. But then it was fun for both of us, being back in our familiar roles.

It didn't last, though. One afternoon Eden showed signs of the start of menstruation. When we noticed them, we stopped our activity, and after we talked a little longer, she went home.

The next day my M-mode began to end. Nearly two weeks early! When I was certain of what was happening, I knew I had to report the change to Dr. Gill.

And that, of course, gave the doctors most of the answers they'd been looking for.

# XIII

"Pheromones," said Mareth Fallon. "Dollars to doughnuts, it's a pheromonic trigger."

Kennet Bardeen gestured. "How much is that in English?" He'd heard the term and had a vague idea what it meant, but somehow this didn't seem the time for vagueness. Judging by Rog Forrest's expression, the other man wasn't having much luck, either.

Bardeen was smiling; Fallon grinned back. "Pheromones carry chemical communication within a species. Through the sense of smell, ordinarily—although the odor may not be noticed consciously. Moths tend to find their mates that way."

He nodded. "Yes, I see. So *that's* what brings dogs from blocks around, when the puppy has her first heat. Which is all well and good, but what does it have to do with Troy Hagen changing back to female two weeks early?"

"Estrus."

"Some M-Two girl was having her period? I don't see how that would apply. And besides, I thought we'd convinced those kids to use restraint for a while."

Fallon shrugged. "Would it have done much good to tell *you* that, at his age?"

It had, in fact, but he didn't say so. Fallon continued. "He said they weren't copulating, just 'playing around.'"

"And what do you suppose he meant by that?"

"Nothing sophisticated, I'd imagine; probably the usual groping adolescent caresses. I didn't ask for details. But with no clothing in the way, the pheromones could diffuse freely."

Before he could speak, Gill did. "It fits; my own oncoming period must have been what caused him to change, the first time."

Bardeen nodded. "All right, then. How much do we know, and what more can we deduce?"

I'll hand them this much: as soon as they had anything figured out, or thought they did, they told us. Which was a good thing; we all felt insecure enough already, without having our imaginations running riot for want of available facts.

Individual cycles, undisturbed, seemed to run steady; the lengths ranged from fifty-four days to sixty. The two transitions, during which we were effectively neuter, accounted for approximately five of those days; the rest were evenly divided between M and F.

It turned out that for any one person the duration of the F-mode phase was invariant; nothing could change it. But exposure to another person's estrual pheromones would invariably trigger an M-mode person into the M-to-F change. Of course the exposure had to be rather intimate.

What this meant was: well, my cycle was fifty-six days; Eden's was fifty-eight. So later, when we were fully together, I would be in M-mode, with Eden in F, about a day longer than the other way around.

It wasn't a difference that bothered either of us.

At seventy-four, Thane Cogdill was obviously not ready to retire from his chairmanship, but the Foundation's bylaws said he had to. With considerable sympathy for the man who had done so much for his own career, Bardeen in his new role as Chairman pushed through an unprecedented authorization: Cogdill went on salary as a special advisor to the Board, privileged to attend meetings and speak, but not to vote. Once all the moving was done, Bardeen hosted the older man in Cogdill's former office. "Bourbon?"

"Thank you, Kennet. And not only for the drink."

As they lifted glasses, Bardeen smiled. "No thanks needed. I value your advice; I won't willingly do without it."

"Kind of you to say so." Certainly the man was taking the change gracefully. Now Cogdill leaned forward. "I've read Fallon's reports."

"Good. Any suggestions?"

"I'm not sure. Kennet, do you see some of the same problems I do?"

"Such as? I mean, the youngsters seem to be handling their difficulties well. With the help of Fallon and her people."

Cogdill set his glass down hard enough to slosh a few drops onto the desk. "*Now*, sure. I'm talking about later. And about questions I haven't seen raised."

Bardeen spread his hands. "The floor's yours, Thane. What do you see that I don't?"

Looking through his notes, afterward, Bardeen had to admit that Cogdill had come up with some queries everyone else had overlooked. Were the Mark Two kids interfertile or were they "mules"? Of course it was out of the question to impregnate barely pubertal F-mode children—but what about *in vitro* fertilization and then, possibly, implantation within a volunteer surrogate mother?

And would the M-2s breed true? It might pay to find out as soon as possible.

What would happen if or when an M-2 *did* get pregnant? Fallon's logical deduction was that since pregnancy stopped menstruation, which induced the F-to-M transition, the pregnancy would proceed normally. If "normal" could be said to apply, at all, with respect to Humanity, Mark Two.

Could Mark Two males impregnate Mark One females? If so, what kind of offspring would result? Now *that* one, Bardeen decided, could be tested easily; all it needed was volunteers, and he rather thought there'd be no difficulty finding them.

Cogdill had been looking ahead, all right. None of the adolescent Mark Twos had yet shown signs of growing facial hair. But was this condition due merely to their youth? As adults, would they have some sort of whiskers, possibly sparse, *all* the time? Or did the cyclic pattern change so rapidly that in M-mode the growth simply didn't get started?

Either way, the former Chairman felt some precautionary research was in order. "When they're living out in public," he had said, "they'll need to look as much as possible like everybody else." He suggested that the Feen develop and market an inexpensive and convenient facial depilatory. Through a dummy outlet, of course. "We should get on it right now, Kennet. And then back it with an all-out advertising campaign to make the stuff popular. So that when the kids go out to mingle with the Mark Ones, they'll be inconspicuous."

And along those same lines: from the beginning, all the Mark

Two children had been registered in the Feen's membership trust. When they left the Enclave they'd still have the protection of that trust; temporary unemployment would not subject them to the toils of government subsidy, with its attendant red tape and possibly dangerous invasions of privacy.

Keeping Thane Cogdill on the team, Bardeen thought, was one of the best moves he'd ever made.

Now that Eden and I were fully in-phase, the temptations of sex became more urgent. But we accepted Dr. Fallon's advice; at our age, pregnancy for either of us was obviously not a good idea, so we continued to police our own behavior. Fallon was, she said, pushing for relaxation of the ban against contraceptives. So all right, we could wait. I won't say we were happy about it, but we couldn't see any good alternative.

I suppose it was inevitable that someone—or rather, one or more couples—would get carried away and take chances. However many may have done so, I imagine most of them stopped after Dale Carson got pregnant by Moss Frantz.

In his final year at college, running a little late because after high school he'd spent two years working, Brad Salich hoped he'd be able to stay on and graduate. The stroke hadn't damaged his father mentally, and Stan could still get around pretty well and handle most ordinary day-to-day activity, but his right arm no longer had enough strength and coordination for his job in groundcar repair and maintenance.

So Stan had taken early retirement, by way of disability. Between that money and Brad's part-time pay at the same shop where his father had worked, the Saliches were still getting by. But just barely.

Brad's mother Ulla hadn't been employed, full-time for pay, in the nine years since her daughter was born. First, because the infant Cecy was a sickly child and Ulla wouldn't trust her to day-care. And later, because methods changed so fast in her former line of work that when she applied for a job she found she was obsolete. She made a couple of attempts at retraining, but both times Cecy got sick and Ulla had to drop out. Since then she'd held occasional part-time jobs, mostly "temping," but the money she brought in hardly paid for the expenses her out-of-home work incurred. Still, Brad thought, if it made her feel useful, the domestic inconvenience was worth it.

At some point near her sixth birthday, Cecy got a new lease on health; now, three years later, no one would know she'd ever been such a miserable little kid. Like her parents and brother she was fair of hair and skin, but her brown eyes were unique in the family and her current state of growth promised, eventually, to make her the tallest of them.

And possibly, Brad sometimes thought, the smartest. Well, ornery though she might be at times, mostly she was a joy to have around. Now if she would only hold off wanting any more kinds of expensive lessons and school activities, until he had his diploma and could go out and try to make some real money!

The way everybody acted, something had to be wrong, but at first we couldn't find out what it was; all that happened was that Dr. Fallon and all the Project medics seemed preoccupied and spoke in cryptic terms. Then one day Dr. Gill had all of us, the "pubertals," in for a meeting. Except for Dale and Moss; they weren't there.

After nearly a year I still felt embarrassed in Sharla Gill's presence—remembering having sex with her, and then what happened to me afterward. I shouldn't have felt that way, I suppose, but the whole thing jarred me so much that it took a long time to wear off. Standing, she said, "I called this meeting to announce that starting now, contraceptives and instruction in their use will be available to you on request."

Eden and I smiled at each other. We were both in transition, mine going from M to F, so the change in policy wouldn't do *us* any good for another day or two, but still I felt a great sense of relief—not to mention anticipation!

Gill was still talking. "—late, I'm afraid. Two of your group jumped the gun, and one of them is pregnant by the other. It has not yet been decided whether the pregnancy will be allowed to go to term."

I heard a few shocked gasps, including my own. Sure, we knew that in a sense the Feen *owned* us—but never before had our noses been rubbed in the fact quite that hard. It was Eden who said, "What do you mean, *allowed*? You'd kill somebody's baby whether they like it or not?"

The question's phrasing might have been a little unclear, but its meaning wasn't. Gill's face flushed. "*I* wouldn't; no. But I'm not in a position to overrule the Board of Directors."

I wasn't going to let Eden carry all the load; I stood, and said, "If they're going to decide something like this, I think they ought to hear our side of it first."

Trying to absorb what he'd just been told on the phone, Bardeen said, "Dr. Fallon? I don't think a Board meeting is the place to bring the matter up." He interrupted her protest. "No, I'm not stonewalling you. Or the kids, either. What I want you to do is bring some of them—specifically the two who stood up and bucked the abortion option—here to my office." She didn't seem to like the idea; he shook his head, waited for a pause, then said, "Bring Gill, too; she seems to have good rapport with the Mark Twos." He checked his schedule. "How about three o'clock this afternoon?"

Fallon didn't sound placated. Bardeen sighed. "Look. I'm not trying to stifle these kids; I *want* to hear their views. I simply don't think the Board room is the place for it.

"What? No. I mean, the Board would eat them alive; it's the way that group operates. You're much better off having the youngsters present their case to the previous Chairman and myself, only."

She didn't like that, either, but with two other calls waiting, Bardeen didn't have time to soothe her further.

I'd seen Chairman Bardeen in person before, and also his predecessor, Thane Cogdill. But never up close or to speak to. I felt scared, but with a kind of go-to-hell thrill to it. I mean, you can't win if you don't try!

With my hand on Eden's arm, I could feel occasional trembles; sometimes, I have no doubt, they were mine.

In the Chairman's office we all got seats. The place would have impressed me if I'd let it, but I kept my mind on what we were there for. Bardeen was talking about how we had come to exist, all the problems the Feen had with our unexpected differences, and the difficult decisions that needed to be made.

He didn't seem to want to stop talking, ever, but if he didn't, Eden and I were going to lose the steam we needed. So when he stopped to sip some water, I stood. "Sir? Could I tell our side of it now?" I gestured toward Eden. "Both of us, I mean. Could we?"

He nodded. I said, "For years none of us knew what we were, and we hadn't been given any choice about it, either. Then when we get to the age we turn horny and your Board says we can't have any protection, we just have to sit on it." I really had the steam up then; I said, "Well, Eden and I, here, we did that. Not liking it, but we did. I guess Dale and Moss couldn't; we *finally* found out, Dale got pregnant."

Bardeen said, "Correct so far. And so?"

Eden was too mad to talk quietly; she yelled. "So now, we get told, you big wheelers think you have the right to kill her baby. Well, you don't! I—"

It was the old man, Cogdill, who slapped his palm onto the table with a crash that stopped all sound and action. "No such thing, young lady; no such thing. There is, I admit, a move among Board members, to abort the fetus. That move is stupid."

Eden: "I don't understand."

"We would lose," Cogdill said, "an unanticipated opportunity to study and learn the potentials of your group. Whether you are indeed viably interfertile, what the characteristics of your offspring may be. I assure you—Chairman Bardeen and I will not allow this loss to occur."

I said, "You mean, sir, that you've gotten the Board to change its vote?"

The man's laugh sounded like somebody chewing a mouthful of clamshells. "No. But we will. Eh, Kennet?"

Following Doctors Fallon and Gill out of that office, somehow I wasn't anywhere near as scared as I had been, going in.

Though on the face of it, I'd seen plenty of reason to be.


Taking his time, the last to leave the Board room, Thane Cogdill thought: *Kennet's no lion tamer, the way I was. He's a snake charmer.* He shrugged. *It works; that's what counts.* Dominating the session without seeming to, he and Bardeen had whipsawed a divided Board into approving all of Cogdill's proposals with regard to the Mark Twos.

Bardeen's idea, to wear the obstructionists down with a long slate of unimportant questions first, had worked quite well.

Walking to his own office, Cogdill was surprised to find Bardeen there. He grinned. "Run out of bourbon, did you? Came around to mooch some of mine? Well, pour it, then—and one for me, too. All right?" When those tasks were accomplished and both men seated, Cogdill said, "So what's on your mind?"

"When do we first put some of our M-2s to living outside? And how do we set it up?"

Cogdill raised his glass. "You know something? I've been *waiting* for someone to start asking that kind of question."

* * *

Going outside the Enclave now and then was nothing new. The
bad times, when the Feen was under physical attack by people
blaming it for the Sterility Plague, egged on by some Tri-V
preacher, were before any of us Mark Twos were born. And I must
have been at least five years old, maybe six, when I and other
children were taken out into the city for the first times.

It all seemed very strange: this entire huge new world we'd
heard about but never seen. We "got our feet wet" slowly, starting
with mornings of sightseeing, restaurant lunches, maybe a little
shopping in the afternoons.

A few years later we progressed to "outside" vacations: a week or
two of traveling with our parents—to nearby places by groundcar,
flying to more distant locations—and actually living surrounded
by non-Feen people. We didn't go out of the country, though,
except for a few jaunts up into Canada, because passports would
have been a complication our people didn't want to tackle.

To my mind, these things all began at appropriate ages. A six-
year-old in strange territory isn't apt to say anything that can
expose his parents' subterfuges—because no matter what he says,
he's only six years old and "Isn't that cute?" Later, as we came to
know what it meant to keep cover, we were old enough to do it
right. A certain degree of shyness-in-strange-company probably
helped, too.

But when, not quite a year after my traumatic introduction to
puberty, we began to receive training toward the goal of *living*
outside the Feen Enclave, I wasn't sure I liked the idea.

"Well, we have to," said Eden. "Even with all the underground
levels they're building, the compound can't handle all the new
kids being born, and us, too."

What she didn't say, but we both knew, was that much of the
expanded space was needed for medical and educational use. The
lab and Project areas hadn't grown to more than about double
their original size, though residence space had increased greatly.
But the spacing required for care and training of us, the Mark
Twos, was the biggest single factor causing the Enclave to burst at
the seams.

"Right, Eden." I shrugged. "I can't say I'm crazy about the
idea. But I expect we'll manage."

# XIV

HEW Secretary Granger asked for and received approval to license the Gilcorp fertilization system to clinics throughout the United States, and to any foreign medical centers or governments that showed interest. The fees were used to subsidize costs of the process for a number of people who could not otherwise afford it. But as Granger told Roth MacIlwaine, "Despite our bushels of cheery propaganda, all the facilities we've managed to equip aren't making any real dent in the sterility problem. Restricting access, to the well-to-do only, would light off a real powder keg."

The man nodded. "I know. The hell of it is, the entire program is more cosmetic than anything else. How many additional live births did it produce last year? A few thousand, no more. But we don't publicize the totals, do we?" A onesided grin. "No. Two or three times a week we put out warm little human-interest stories on the babies born to the most telegenic parents. I hate it."

"So do I, Roth. But if a boat's taking on water, you don't throw away your bailing bucket. Even if it's only a teacup."

When a second stroke killed Stan Salich, Brad changed his surname back to Szalicz, the original form his father had abandoned. Not without pondering the matter a bit: Brad knew that Ulla, his mother, had disliked the Americanized version, but wasn't sure how his fiancée would react.

Over lunch one day, he asked her. Lyndeen Rohr, fair of skin and dark of hair, didn't blink either of her slate-blue eyes. "Whatever you want, Brad. Just as long as you show me how to spell it."

So that part was all right, too. Feeling good, he went back to work, at the Channel 83 newsroom where he was now two steps above low man on the totem pole in the Text and Printout section.

\* \* \*

When both of us had reached sixteen, the legal and not unusual age for marriage at the time, Eden and I took that step. Since Dale Carson had not married Moss Frantz—first because they were too young and later because they had a serious falling-out that never healed—we were the first of our kind to do so. We were in transition at the time, and thus sexless—but even if we hadn't been, the ceremony's wording would have needed some changes. For instance, "wife" and "husband" were both replaced by "spouse," and the promises were the same from each of us.

Afterward we moved out of our respective homes and set up in quarters of our own. Although we were still students, our basic trust memberships provided living expenses; our situation wasn't exactly lavish, but with a little economizing we got by well enough. It was only the first month, while we were learning how to manage a household, that we had to borrow from our parents.

Between general education, career training, and orientation toward the time we'd go to live Outside, we had very little free time. My chosen field was Systems Design—not merely one aspect, such as electronics, but generalized. Eden concentrated on Statistical Analysis, another area with few limitations of category. The main criterion, besides our personal inclinations, was that both lines of work were expanding, while the work force wasn't; there was plenty of room at the bottom, and good prospects for climbing higher.

Dale Carson's pregnancy produced a lot of new information. First, as long as Moss remained her lover he stayed in M-mode, and for the first time an M-2 grew whiskers—scanty, but unmistakable. Two weeks after he and Dale had their blowup, he went F and fell back into the M-2 normal cycle.

Dale grew real breasts, not to be mistaken for the petite swellings that appeared in the usual month or so of F-mode. And they kept their size, after young Lee was born, until he was weaned; then at her next period, about three weeks later, Dale went into M-mode and back to our usual pattern.

All of us, the first-generation M-2s, had been born after normal nine-month periods of gestation, or else were obvious "preemies." Lee Carson took only a little over six months to hatch, and came into the world fully equipped to survive. Unmistakably an M-2, he was quite small initially (then grew at a phenomenal rate), but began life in perfect working order. Everyone hoped Dale's case was typical; our pelvic girdles are too narrow to birth a child the size of a full-term Mark One, so Caesareans would have been required. And from the standpoint of survival-of-species, that's not a wholly viable option.

As a matter of fact, our Mark Two physiques played a major part in determining how we would and could keep cover, Outside. There was nothing notably betraying about our conformations: the ratio of widths of hips and shoulders could pass for either male or female, Mark One. Androgynous is the term. And for each phase of the cycle, clothing could emphasize or hide the presence of our minimal breast development.

The popularity of Feen-developed facial depilatories gave us, for camouflage, a background pool of people who, like us, were beardless. Shifting emphasis from razors and shaving cream to the newer products, the Tri-V advertising wars between Smooth and Comfort and Ease and Sleek (the same product, but sold in different colors by the various licensed manufacturers) also profited Phoenix Foundation well.

"The trick of it," my father told me once, when Eden and I were having dinner at my parents' home, "is buying celebrities. Elgin Thorndyke, the new Tri-V adventure star smash. Or—" He gestured toward the Tri-V we'd all been ignoring, and turned the noise up, barely enough to be heard. "Look at that."

Eden and I looked. The holo showed four women, faces painted with outré patterns of colors, sitting amid a clutter of strange-looking musical instruments coated with fluorescent paint, while they rubbed Smooth onto their already bare scalps. The artificial tones and levels of their voices made it clear that we were seeing a commercial interlude.

"Sure," I said. "The Bald Eagles. I guess they're the hottest ropdop group around, right now." Seeing dad's eyebrows rise, I said, "Can't stand them, myself. No two of them ever play in the same key, and the skinny one has a voice like a crock of rocks. But they're big on the Tri-V, and as you said, that's what sells products."

Dad grinned. "You've got a good head on you, Troy."

And someday, I thought, he might be able to accept, emotionally, the idiosyncrasies of my body.

I could wait.

\* \* \*

Feen strategy, consensus eventually had it, was that a Mark Two couple living Outside could go either of two routes. One was to "be" two young women sharing residence; the second, to make an arbitrary choice of which was to "be" M at all times, the other posing as full-time F. Either way, the odds were that when the pair decided to conceive a child, they would have to pull up stakes and take new identities in a different place. Because in all but one case, that of an M-F couple with the putative F being the pregnant one, the visible changes would reveal too much.

Eden's and my tentative decision was to appear as two young women. For one thing, the physical camouflage was simpler.

We had nearly two years, though, to consider the matter.

Meanwhile we'd already chosen our Outside names, to be fed clandestinely into the government's computer networks along with all the other invented retroactive "facts" concerning every Mark Two who needed Outside ID. Our given names we would keep; our surname would be dos Caras. In Spanish it's quite appropriate.

As research progressed, more and more information accumulated. Some of it Bardeen found reassuring, but not all.

Mark One women who were inseminated with Mark Two sperm produced Mark Two infants. How it worked the other way around, no one would know until Mark Two females matured, and then only if one or more of them volunteered for the experiment. But Mark Two sperm caused no ova-immune reaction; Lana Craig was into her second pregnancy by the same Mark Two donor.

The facts were all well and good; Bardeen was pleased to learn them. What he didn't like was the effect those facts seemed to be having on some of the Mark Twos.

"Moss Frantz is the leader," Dr. Gill told him, "and out of the sixty or so in the group he's organized, there are at least a half dozen more who echo his ideas. Solidly."

"Which are?"

She set a disk packet on his desk. "I think you'd better see this. It has their last two meetings on it."

He frowned. "You feel we have to spy on them?"

Gill pushed curls back from her forehead. "Spy, nothing! They recorded this themselves; it's the minutes of a meeting. And it's not my fault they put it into the files under that heading, and that Jan Gordon told me maybe I'd better have a scan at it. I did, and I think you should, too."

Nodding in agreement, Bardeen asked, "Who's Jan Gordon? A Mark Two, of course, but anyone special?"

"Just one of Frantz's clique, who's starting to have misgivings."

"I see." He removed the disk from its packet and inserted it into a playing slot. When he pressed the activating key, his screen lit.

After twenty minutes or so, he stopped the play. "How much more of this is there?"

"Two hours, I think."

"All pretty much the same?"

"For a time. The last half of the meeting bogged down into trivial arguments and personality clashes."

"Then I've seen enough, for now. Dr. Gill, I'd like you to arrange a conference, here in my office, with Moss Frantz and not more than two of his closest allies. Tomorrow if possible." He checked his schedule listings. "I'm free for an hour in the afternoon, starting at two. If you can't set it up for that time we can discuss a later appointment. All right?"

"Yes, of course. And—do you wish me to attend, also?"

"If it's convenient, please do."

"What part do you want me to play, Kennet? A credible menace or a stalking horse?" Thane Cogdill snorted. "Against these *children*?"

"Children we don't understand, and can't," Bardeen answered. "Because every month their hormones turn them upside down in ways we've never had to experience."

Restraining an impulse to shrug, Cogdill said, "We've known that for years. What's so different *now*?"

"Some of them are getting tired of playing our game; they want to play their own. The trouble is, Thane, they have no idea how deadly the rules could be."

Moss Frantz, tall with a pale, sallow face under lightish red hair, had a look about him like that of a person up for sentencing: part defiant and part scared. Sloane Klemgard, the heavy one, seemed calm enough, but Jan Gordon—short, slight, and dark-complexioned—was obviously holding down a bad case of the jitters. After introductions, the three took seats.

In a whisper to Bardeen beside him, Cogdill said, "Gill can't be here; she's stuck with a patient, so let's get on with it. Now—isn't Gordon the one who blew the whistle? So why—?"

"Don't know, Thane. Let's listen." He cleared his throat. "Moss, I understand that you and your group disagree with the current plans for the eventual movement of Mark Twos out to function in the M-One society." The youngster nodded. "Like to tell us why?"

"So you can suppress what we have to say?" The words burst forth like bullets. "Or settle for talking us out of it?"

Cogdill let his chuckle get loud. "Maybe we just want to know if you've thought of some problems we haven't. If we don't ask, how can we find out?"

Looking startled, Frantz was silent a few seconds. And then said, "Not problems the way you're probably thinking. I mean, not better ways to hide."

"What, then?" Bardeen said it.

"I don't think we should *have* to hide! We haven't done anything wrong—none of us. Where do *they* come off, so high and mighty, that we should have to pretend to be what we're not?" As Frantz spoke, the face got redder and the voice went higher. "It's not fair, is all we're saying. Not the least bit!" Half-standing, now the youngster sat again. "And what do you have to say about *that*?"

Cogdill touched Bardeen's coatsleeve. *This is* my *kind of argument*. To Frantz he said, "Why, that I agree with you."

"You do?"

"Certainly. *Of course* it's not fair; have we ever claimed otherwise?"

"Then why must we hide? Why can't we just go out there and say what we are? And offer to help with their troubles?"

Bardeen beat Cogdill to the answer. "Because they'd kill you. You'd all be green monkeys."

"I don't understand."

"If you dye a monkey's fur green, the other monkeys will tear him to pieces. People and animals fear what's strange to them—and what they fear, they're likely to kill."

"And in this case," Cogdill said, "the only kind of help you could offer would be to inseminate Mark One women and produce children that would be your kind, not theirs."

"But *our* parents—"

"Volunteers," said Bardeen. "Educated, intelligent Feen personnel, dedicated to solving the Sterility Plague. Hardly the same as your average Mark One out there—as you'll realize if you think about your Outside excursions, or evaluate what the Tri-V ratings say about the Mark One public's taste in entertainment."

Still looking doubtful, finally Moss Frantz nodded. "I guess you're right." Frantz first, then the other two, stood. "Thanks for listening, and explaining. I understand now."

But what was the understanding? Cogdill spoke. "You mean you withdraw your objections to our plans?"

Frantz made a tight smile. "Excuse me, sir, but hell, no!"

"Then—"

"The ideas I had, won't work. So I have to think of some new ones."

"Will you run 'em past us first, before you try them out under field conditions?" Seeing puzzlement, Cogdill added, "Outside, I mean."

Looking defensive again, Frantz said "Maybe."

When the Mark Twos had left, Cogdill said, "That one could be big trouble."

Pouring their ceremonial bourbon, Bardeen replied. "So what do I do? Set up a lot of hotshot high-tech surveillance?"

After sipping, Cogdill said, "That kind of thing wastes more time than it's worth, and we both know it."

"What, then?"

"Jan Gordon talks to Sharla Gill. Frantz doesn't seem to suspect his meeting disks, so check them any time Gill says you should."

"And then?"

Irritated, Thane Cogdill shrugged. "You're letting this fuzz your thinking, Kennet. Keep two points in mind. Frantz can turn into an utter rebel, but still be unable to do much about it until the Mark Twos begin infiltrating, Outside."

"So you're saying, simply keep any rebels inside the Enclave, permanently?"

*The hateful truths a man has to say!* Barely restraining himself from using his "lion tamer" glare, Cogdill stared eye-to-eye with Bardeen. "Exactly, Kennet. Alive, or dead."

Bardeen's face went rigid. "You were the one, earlier, who said I was taking 'these children' too seriously."

"That was before I knew any of our Mark Twos could be foolish enough to go public."

He drained his glass. "Frantz isn't your immediate problem. What is, Kennet, is to get the tooth fairy and the Easter bunny out of the training curriculum we're feeding these kids, and for their own protection, put in some solid healthy paranoia."

# XV

On my birthdays my parents always threw a party for Eden and me; for hers, her folks did it. Not big shebangs, but pleasant and lively: most of our immediate age-mates came, and some of their parents. On the earlier occasions there'd been no alcohol, but starting when I was sixteen, mom's punchbowl acquired a tinge of authority, and dad provided a twenty-liter pressure container of the area's best-tasting beer.

It was my seventeenth birthday, though, that really changed things for me. Dad was hitting the beer a lot more than usual; I began to worry a little.

Needn't have, though. What happened was that after the food was pretty well done in, he gestured for me to join him in his workroom. Once inside, he said, "Troy, there's something I need to tell you."

"Sure." Now what was *this* all about?

It took him some time to get around to it, and I had no idea what he was getting at. Then he said, "I've just come to realize, son. *I* did it."

I felt my eyebrows rise. Son? When I was in F-mode?

He grinned, and his hand made an erasing motion. "That's part of it, you see. For years you *were* my son."

"And now—"

"You're still that, but something more, too. And for a long time it bothered me. But now—it's finally hit home that *I* made that difference in you." He wouldn't let me say anything. "I'm the one who volunteered to have my sperm cells modified to get past the immunity reaction. What you are, comes from me—nobody else." He shook his head. "Don't know why it took me so long to see it."

I hesitated, then said, "Does it make you feel any better? About me?"

He didn't say a word; maybe he couldn't. He came over and hugged me, but not before I saw tears.

We talked a little more, not long. The words didn't really matter; I knew what he meant. Then we went back to the party.

The best birthday I'd ever had. Bar none.


Married only a little over six months, ordinarily Brad Szalicz went directly home from work. But Lyndeen's sister Thea, out west in Tacoma, was having her baby, and Lyndeen had gone to spend a week or two helping out.

So today Brad was in no hurry; he decided to wait out the rush hour at the little street-level bar a few doors down from Channel 83's building.

Catering mostly to the station, and other nearby offices, the Prime Time had only a small sign showing; unless a person knew it was there, the place was easy to miss.

Entering, Brad was met by lighting that was soft but not dim. The bar and the dozen tables were less than half full; Brad's hours ran earlier than average.

Tall, skinny Charlie was working the bar alone, so Brad passed up the tables and hoisted himself onto a stool. "Beer."

"Right with ya." Continuing a running line of sports commentary and including Brad in his audience, Charlie brought the beer. "—keep changin' the rules all'a time, wot the hell's *any* record gonna mean? Am I right, or am I right?"

That last was aimed toward Brad, so he put his thinking into bar-gear. "Fuckin'-aye, Charlie. You tell 'em."

When the barman moved on to harangue other customers, Brad took a couple of healthy swallows and sighed. *Good.* He was setting the mug down when a hand slapped onto his shoulder and gripped it. "Well if it isn't Brad Salich! What have *you* been up to, you old pussy-hound?"

Brad turned around, then reached to shake hands. "Clint! It's certainly been a while!"


Brad had known Clint Haydock at the car-repair shop, where their fathers had worked together for years. Always a lot of fun, Clint was—but sometimes a little too much of a promoter, an angle-shooter, for Brad's taste. Now, though, looking much the same as ever with his thin-faced grin and lively dark eyes, Clint got onto the stool at Brad's right. When he had a beer of his own, he said, "All right, Salich—catch me up on current events."

"Well, you know I quit to go back to school . . ."

Brad had intended to while away perhaps an hour in the Prime Time, but he didn't shake loose from Clint for another three. He wasn't exactly drunk when he rode the tubetrain home, but he was coming close. He heated up one of the dinner packets Lyndeen had frozen for him—chili, this one was—and ate it along with some crackers and a glass of Milque. As he sipped the latter, he grimaced. The ads claimed that you couldn't tell this bean-curd product from the real moo, but Brad Szalicz disagreed.

At the airport, nearly home from vacation and only waiting for her husband to bring their groundcar from the Enclave, Blake Lassiter's mother didn't worry until Blake had been gone for quite a long while. At fifteen, the youngster's cycle was well established; Blake was due to end F-mode any day now. But she was certainly taking her time at the Women's.

An hour later, the Lassiters were getting more and more desperate in their questions to the Airport Security chief, whose people could find no trace of Blake.

The trouble was that the Women's had two sets of doors, facing into different concourses, and somehow Blake got turned around and left by the wrong one. She walked along, taking side corridors now and then, for several minutes before she looked around and realized she had no idea where she was. Like the dreams she had sometimes, where everything got lost without rhyme or reason.

No. Not a dream. After a long flight she was tired, but definitely awake. So there had to be a way to get back to where she was supposed to be.

Fatigue slowed her thinking but didn't blur it. Far along the mall-like area stood a pillar with an enlarged map mounted on it. Blake walked the distance and pondered the location of the "You Are Here" tag. *Oh, hell!* She was in the wrong concourse, and she'd totally lost track, even on the map, of the Women's that had misled her. Also, the only return route she could find, back to where her mother was waiting, looked long and roundabout.

Unless she went down to ground level and took a shortcut to cross the Passenger Pickup lanes . . .

She was nearly across the roadway, staying in the marked crosswalk and squinting against fierce, slanting rain, when sudden headlights obscured her vision. The loudness of a warning horn completed her disorientation; Blake froze in midstep.

She didn't feel the impact; all sensation came through as sheer noise, and then as nothing.

"Oh jeezus, Migg, you *hit* her. Whadda we do now?" Lesa clutched the driver's shoulder. "We gotta get outa here!"

He shrugged her off. "Goddamn electric brakes, Tin Man said he fixed 'em!"

"Hell with that. Go, Migg!"

"No." He was opening the door. "That's hit-run." The old external-combustion engine's sound dropped to an irregular wheezing. "Get out here, Lesa. Help me put her in the back."

"Are you *crazy*?"

"Not half. Leave her here, there's clues, they'd get us. Take her along, nothing for 'em to find." Lifting the girl's shoulders, he turned and said, "Get your ass out here, before some shithead stops to *help* us. Or it's *you* I leave."

"So all *right*!" Grunting with effort, Lesa heaved the girl's feet up. Between them, she and Migg got the limp form into the car's back seat, and moments later the old groundcar chugged its way through and out of the terminal area. "Migg?"

"Don't bother me. Tryin' figure a safe place to dump the body. Not gonna be easy."

"Not a body, Migg. She's breathin'."

His fist pounded the wheel. "Oh, *shit*! You mean I gotta kill her myself?"

"No such a thing, you bastard!"

"What, then?"

"We take her home with us, clean her up, feed her. 'Til she's okay."

"So we can get us locked up?"

Lesa yelled at him. "Shuck the dope outa ya stupid skull!" When he didn't answer, she quieted. "So we can get a reward, maybe."

"Reward?"

"Sure, Migg. Didya look at them clothes? This one's got

squeeze, lives high. You trade cars with Tin Man, like you been wantin' to, no way nobody knows we the ones hit her. We just *found* her, see? Saved her goddamn life."

After a pause, Migg laughed. "Always knew they *some* reason I keep you around, you fat-ass gunch.

"I *like* it."

The bowl was dirty. So were the spoon and the woman who was holding it. Grime showed in the creases of the woman's fat face, and her hair fell forward over her left shoulder in a greasy braid. Literally greasy; Blake caught the stale smell of a sickly-sweet pomade.

But the brown, steaming stew smelled good, and it felt to Blake as if she hadn't eaten in a long time.

She didn't know where she was, nor how long she might have been here. There was the airport, and being lost; after that, nothing much she could remember.

The first of it was blurry, because her head hurt and her eyes would neither focus well nor track together. *Concussion*; she knew that much and still remembered it.

Somewhere along the line she'd been undressed and put into a coarse-textured nightgown. A number of times she'd been hauled out of bed and sat down onto the seat of a very smelly toilet; sometimes she went and sometimes not. Now, able to think a little, she decided that her caretakers—whoever they might be— were simply making sure she didn't foul the bed. Though *its* aroma wasn't exactly the breath of health!

She took a spoonful of stew, then another. The woman was talking; she always was, but for the first time Blake paid attention. "You all right, ain't ya, rich kid? You gonna tell how Migg and Lesa save you fuckin' life, on accounta we *did*. Not for us, you be dead. Hey, here—eat some more!"

So Blake ate, then drank lukewarm water to quench her thirst, and allowed herself to be sat onto the toilet again.

By now she could have handled those matters herself; she could have spoken, too. But she didn't, because dimly she recalled fragments of talk between skinny Migg, also more greasy than not, and hefty Lesa. The recalls weren't all that reassuring; Blake's feeling was that the less these two knew about her, the better.

What Blake was waiting for was a time when she would be able to move fast. Preferably with Migg absent. Lesa didn't worry Blake much; if Blake couldn't get past the woman physically, she figured she could always outtalk her.

The only trouble with Blake's thinking was that her period began, and Lesa saw the beginnings of her change to M-mode.

"Hell only *knows* what it is, Lesa. But we got us something here. Only thing, where we get us the best price?"

"Price for what?" Lesa gestured, toward Blake who lay naked, tied to the dirty cot. The male organs were near to full development; no longer was there any question as to what was happening. "What you mean?"

Migg reached to pat the captive's crotch; if Blake tried to shrink away, the man didn't notice. "Reward, Lesa. Like you said before, so's I don't kill her. Thing is, who pays it?"

Lesa held up some pieces of paper. "This stuff, in her handpurse. Says on it, Phoenix Foundation. They a bunch of rich ones, Migg." Looking to his silence, she said, "We could *try*."

Migg stood. "Got us no phone numbers. I go look it up."

When the chance came, Blake's eyes were still not totally dependable when it came to binocular coordination. But Migg had left and wouldn't be back for several hours. So Blake talked enough to get Lesa to untie him so he could wash himself, and then, without asking, dressed. His F-mode clothes were soiled, and torn a little, but looked only slightly disreputable.

When Blake had put together what he could find of his personal effects, and stuffed the lot into the battered shoulder bag, Lesa looked up from the sponge she'd been sniffing. "You goin' someplace? Just 'cause I be nice and let ya clean up?" Pointing a finger, Lesa yelled. "Set yaself down, there!" Eyes dilated, moving unsteadily, still the woman lunged to grab before Blake could evade her, and pulled them both back. Blake landed sitting on the bed, Lesa half on her chair and half off. "*Now*, by God—!"

Blake's move, then, worked because it wasn't away from Lesa but toward and then past her—to reach the lighter that sat alongside the dope pipe. It caught on the second flick, and a moment later the oily braid became a torch. Screaming, batting at herself with both hands, the woman staggered off toward the nearest faucet.

Before Blake got away—out the door and down three flights of stairs to the street—he took time to retrieve the bag. The money was gone, but when he found a pay phone, he still had a card that let him call the Feen, collect.

"The kid was scared, all right, but no serious injury." Erwin Bennest, newly promoted to Chief of Mark Two Security Planning, felt twinges of stage fright. Reporting to Chairman Bardeen didn't make him nervous, but he kept waiting for Cogdill, the old one, to pounce on some unforeseen discrepancy.

Now Cogdill spoke. "And has *no* idea what happened?"

"No, sir. One minute, planning to take a shortcut through the air terminal. The next thing, prisoner of a couple of slumrats, over in Scum City. I mean, that's what everybody calls—"

"We know," said Cogdill. "The area where most of the Unregistereds hide out. Very little law and less amenities." He shifted in his chair. "Get on with it."

"Blake Lassiter's injuries—bruises, abrasions, and an apparent concussion—fit the pattern of a pedestrian hit by a vehicle. Clothing damage is also consistent. So we surmise—"

"Yes, that's clear," said Kennet Bardeen. "Blake must have cut across traffic lanes—departure or pickup—and been knocked over. Then perhaps, walking around dazed, was picked up by someone so that she could be taken away and robbed at leisure?"

Bennest shrugged. "Just a guess; unless the boy remembers, we'll never know." It was funny, he thought, how here in the Enclave, everybody got used to calling the same M-Two kid he or she every other month. "The Security aspect, though—"

"Precisely," Cogdill said. "There's no doubt whatsoever, I gather, that the slumrat pair saw Blake Lassiter naked in F-mode, in transition, and then in M-mode."

"I'm afraid so. Sir. But—"

"Oh, relax, Bennest." Bardeen waved a hand. "There's nothing *you* could have done to prevent it. Nothing any of us could have. It's a wonder we haven't had more lapses."

"Yes, sir." He remembered the last one, a year ago. Easy enough to fix: an agent slipped the witness a dose of a powerful but harmless hallucinogen; when that party came back to normal, someone else's apparent change of gender was in the *tame* part of the trip. Too bad that solution wasn't feasible now.

"There are factors in our favor," Bennest said. "These people are bottom-drawer. Young Lassiter reports a sloppy, even filthy mode of living. Backstreet speech patterns, all that. Not your most credible witnesses. And the important thing is: whatever they might say, there's only their own word for it."

"Bennest?" said Cogdill. "I do hope to hell you're right."

"Sister," said the preacher. "On your own soul, on your hope of salvation as one of the Reborn Righteous, do you swear you saw this abomination with your own two eyes?"

"If I didn't, I hope to kiss a— I mean, sure did, Reverend. And so'd Migg."

The woman Lesa hadn't been here to the church for over a year. She smelled more like burned feathers than anything else that came to mind, and the bandanna over her head covered a lopsided mass. She was about as righteous as a marked deck of cards, and the man she lived with was even worse. But the thing about doing your stint in Scum City was, you learned a lot. Sometimes it could even pay off: Al Jerdan was up for *bishop*, no less. So push it. "Will Migg witness to that, sister?"

Headshake. "Don'know. 'Spect not. But he seen, same as me. Cunt grew a cock, is what."

"And the kid's papers said Phoenix Foundation on them?" Lesa nodded. "But those papers all got away." Nod again.

Why couldn't this have happened to someone who knew how to use a *camera*? Or even owned one . . .

But the preacher knew what to do next: give her a little money and a lot of bullshit. Once she left, he picked up his phone. "Bishop Crade's office? The Reverend Floyd here. Could you put me through on a trunk straight to the Holy City?" After all these years, calling Cincinnati the Holy City still made Floyd want to laugh—but if that's what the Reverend Jody Jay wanted, that's what the Reverend Jody Jay would get.

"Straight to Headquarters?" The other end sounded skeptical. "What's so important? Maybe I can handle it."

*Oh, no, you don't!* No bishop's flunkey was going to ace Floyd out of *this* one; if need be, he'd get off the church network, go through public channels and pay for the call. But not unless he had to; for private subscribers the rates were pure murder. "Doubt it. I don't think the Reverend Tolliver, when he hears about this item, would want anyone to know, who didn't actually need to." That was smokescreen; the sonofabitch would eavesdrop anyway. What he wouldn't do—not in a month of Sundays!—was muscle Floyd out and take the credit.

When HQ's machine answered, Floyd made his report in full.

# XVI

Eden and I were scheduled to move Outside in June, but the Lassiter incident delayed matters. First, until M-2 Security Planning decided the leak hadn't spread—and probably wouldn't—all moves went on hold. Then when Mr. Bennest approved our release, I'd just begun M-mode; the trouble was that Eden and I had set up to be two female cousins rooming together. PDQ Systems, where I was going to work, was a Feen subsidiary, but still it wouldn't look good for any of us to ask for special treatment. Such as trying to bypass the entrance physicals.

I could have switched back to F-mode, of course. All it would have taken was a little deep breathing of air laden with estrual pheromones—and certainly, at any time, *some* of our people would be emitting those potent agents of change.

But that choice would have put Eden and me out of step, and somehow we didn't want to go through all that reshuffling again.

So we moved Outside on schedule, to the suburban condo we couldn't have afforded without our membership trust cushion, and Eden began work with Prime Analysts, Inc. But for the next two weeks, until my transition to F was complete, someone at the Feen made excuses to PDQ Systems, delaying the start of my employment there. I spent the time unpacking, arranging the place, and buying things we'd need now but hadn't before.

Done, for this day, with the cameras, Jody Jay Tolliver left the studio and walked to his Sanctum. Not until he was inside did he pull off his toupee and scratch his itching scalp. He threw his heavy robe to one side; it landed on a chair and didn't quite fall off. Then he plunked down to sit at a paper-strewn table. "Sanduk! Where in the Lord's mercy *are* you?"

"Right here, sah!" The swarthy midget, robed like a Buddhist

117

monk, carried a tray that held a full pitcher and an empty glass.
"Your tonic nectar, it's right here!"

Well, that was better. Tolliver waited while Sanduk poured the
glass full. Jody Jay's own tonic nectar had a tablespoon of honey
for every two ounces of vodka, all homogenized in a blender and
served lukewarm. He took a sip, then a longer one, and said,
"Blessings. Anything come in, Sanduk, I should know about?"

From his robe Sanduk pulled out a few folds of readout paper.
"Here, sah. From Chicago. Reverend Floyd, I was told."

"All right, all right!" Tolliver's hand signaled dismissal. "I'll
ring when I need you."

Sanduk left. He could scuttle with the best of them.

Reading the Reverend Floyd's report as transcribed by the
receiving operator, at first Jody Jay frowned. How could *this*
crackpot nonsense be worked up into anything useful? On a
second reading, Tolliver's expression smoothed. In his mind a
sermon began to build; then he tried it aloud. "*Monsters* among
us, my dear friends. Monsters—and bearing evidence of an
unholy connection to the Phoenix Foundation. That sinful group
who tried to thwart the Lord's vengeance. I—"

Abruptly, the Reverend Tolliver broke off his tirade. "No point
wasting this." He activated his recorder, took a swallow of his
tonic nectar and then a deep, wheezing breath, punched the
Record button, and began again.

Once Jody Jay had the audio part down pat, the Tri-V version
was always easy. "Like shit through a tin horn," he said.

Erwin Bennest sounded agitated, so Bardeen said, "All right;
come to my office and bring Frantz with you." He hadn't expected
that Moss Frantz would be handcuffed, or that the youth's right
eye would carry a mouse that promised to become a spectacular
shiner. Feeling a faint wonder as to which sex Frantz might be at
the moment, but not really caring, Bardeen shook his head.
"Your story first, Bennest."

Setting a medical sample case on Bardeen's desk, the security
man said, "We caught this skinny bastritch trying to smuggle out
enough oral-effective pseudogene agent to juggle all the sperm in
a fairsized town."

Well! The orally administered form had been developed so
recently that Bardeen wouldn't have expected such a quantity to
exist. Arguing that point, though, was a waste of time; the

Chairman looked past Bennest. "Moss? How you managed this is something I don't need to know until a little later. What I *will* hear, and right now, is just what you thought you were doing."

With a toss of head, trying to get rumpled hair away from the good eye, Frantz said, "If it's not obvious, you Mark Ones are even dumber than I thought you were."

For a moment Bardeen thought Bennest would hit the kid; he gestured for a hold on all action, then said, "Your objective's obvious enough; it's your justification that puzzles me." He waited, but Frantz didn't answer. "All right—Erwin, let's hear what *you* have. From the top."

Gilly Monlux, a young lab tech, was fascinated by the idea of Mark Twos being sometimes one sex and sometimes the other; she'd made passes at several before Moss Frantz responded in kind. "Frantz knew she had access to the storage freezers; that was the reason for playing along with her. Sort of *quid pro quo,* as they say."

The quid was that Gilly could have sex with a Mark Two. When her period began, and put Moss into F-mode, another facet of Gilly's motive emerged: bisexual tendencies, and the lure of having one lover who could satisfy both sides of her nature.

The quo was that Moss Frantz swiped thousands of units of the pseudogene factor, and tried to take them outside the Enclave.

Bennest continued. "But Monlux decided something was wrong, sir. She panicked, and came and told me. So—"

Moss Frantz spat on the floor. "So much for trusting a Mark One bitch!"

Bardeen raised an eyebrow. "Now that's an interesting comment. How about, from the young woman's viewpoint, so much for trusting a Mark Two bastritch?"

"It's not the *same!*"

"Why not? I'd be interested to know."

Frantz strained shoulders against the handcuffs. *Should get those off the kid. But not just yet.* "I was trying to free us all! That bitch Gilly, and all the rest of you, you're determined to keep us slaves. Nonpersons. People who have to hide and can never stand up and be who we *are.*" Glaring, the prisoner shouted, "You can't deny any of this. I dare you to!"

If there were an easy answer, Bardeen couldn't think of it.

*  *  *

In Thane Cogdill's office, Bardeen looked harassed. "So then what did you do, Kennet?"

The Chairman's gesture indicated futility. "Not much. Grounded the kid, of course. Without money cards, or the ID we provide for use on the Outside, a Mark Two wouldn't last long—so I confiscated all that."

Cogdill thought about it. "Given enough anger, young Frantz could run anyway. Nobody needs ID to *leave* the Enclave."

Bardeen's smile had a grim look to it. "They do now."

He sipped the last of his bourbon, but shook his head against Cogdill's gestured offer of a refill. "The hell of it is that in a way, Moss Frantz is right. The M-Twos *have* to keep cover in order to survive in the current paranoiac climate of opinion, and I can see how it makes them feel. But—"

Cogdill nodded. "But there's no choice. The problem seems to be, how to get the Moss Frantz clique to realize the needs of the situation." He leaned forward. "Sometimes, Kennet, problems yield only to cruel solutions. To convince a group, you may have to make an example."

"Such as how?" Bardeen looked skeptical.

"Do you remember that doctor, when Troy Hagen was born and then the next few M-Twos, who wanted to do surgery and turn them all into Mark Ones?"

"Mmm—yes. Don't recall his name, though."

Cogdill let himself chuckle. "That's because I fired him; he wasn't around long enough to make much of an impression. But Kennet, tell me—what would happen to a Mark Two if the organs of either of its optional sexes were removed?"

Bardeen shook his head. "I don't know. Do you?"

"Short of conferring with Fallon's people, no. But my guess is that one way or another, the result would be largely neuter."

He sipped from a glass still half-full. "You might want to find out how many people in the Frantz faction would like to go Outside and blow the whistle about M-Twos, with only one set of organs to demonstrate."

Bardeen's face foreshadowed his words. "I *hate* that idea!"

"Of course you do. So do I. But with any luck at all, Moss Frantz may hate it even worse."

Growing up in the Enclave, once we knew about and eventually accepted our cyclic natures, most of us hadn't paid much heed to conventional appearance as prescribed by gender.

We dressed as we chose—mostly unstressed M-styles—and in general, the same went for haircuts. Though Eden, for one, tended to prefer the longer coiffures of her girlhood.

On our Outside excursions, of course, we followed Mark One conventions. It wasn't all that difficult. For instance, the same as with the facial depilatories, the Feen's advertising subsidiary had done some long-term covert work in the area of makeup usage; nowadays both sexes used it lightly—and not much differently.

So Eden and I had little trouble assuming Mark One appearance; we simply kept in mind that we were Outside, and if one of us forgot the makeup—well, so did M-1s, now and then.

The social part, while it seemed easy at first, sometimes gave us problems. Being young and ostensibly female, we knew we had to expect and deal with attentions from Mark One Ms. What we hadn't realized was how tricky such things might be to cope with.

Tim Cadeland, Dr. Sharla Gill's freemate of several years' standing, had held counseling sessions for our group, the first to be moving Outside. To cope with sociosexual pressures, several strategies had been proposed. For instance, the easy way for two "females" would be to pose as Lesbians. "But that might not be such a good idea," Tim said, talking fast as usual. A tall, skinny beanpole, with sandy hair and an Adam's apple that might make the *Guinness Book of World Records*, even when he stood still he looked to be in a hurry. "These things go in cycles."

"Like us, you mean?" Dale Carson said it deadpan.

Cadeland grinned. "Only not so rapidly." He went on to cite, back in the previous century, the Sexual Revolution of the sixties and seventies, the next decade's backlash, and, "—the pendulum keeps swinging. Right now, with regard to deviant sex we're in a longer-than-average repressive period, due largely to the Sterility Plague. So I wouldn't advise the Lesbian camouflage; among other possible consequences, it might just lose you your jobs." So Eden and I, at least, gave up on the idea.

The trouble was that we'd been planning to use that option, and Cadeland didn't throw the cold water on it until shortly before we moved Outside. Which didn't really give us much time to think of an alternate ruse.

So when in my third week with PDQ Systems, Barry Taylor at work asked me for a date, he caught me flat-footed.

Barry was about twenty-five, I think. Eden and I were eighteen, but in order to make the Enclave's accelerated education program look reasonable to Mark Ones, our IDs added two years to our ages. So the apparent difference wasn't any kind of barrier.

I don't know whether Barry Taylor was naturally pale-blond or if he gave Nature some help. He followed a then-current fad of using Smooth to depilate his temples and the sideburn area; from his forehead, on either side the hairline slanted in a smooth curve to just above the front of each ear. He looked all right, I suppose, but the result struck me as affected.

I wasn't used to the way Mark One males think. Barry's system was to ask in such a way that compliance with his wish was assumed; to say No, you had to *work* at it.

The "trap" aspect angered me, but I knew that showing my reaction would be foolish. So, lacking any clear-cut plan, I said I was busy for the first two dates he proposed, and wasn't sure of anything further ahead.

By the next week, though, Eden and I had figured out a good way to handle all of it.

We got engaged.

Not to each other, of course. Our troths were plighted, if I remember the medieval terms correctly from Fifth Term, to real identifiable persons in the Feen's employ. Their major virtues were that (1) they had reasonable ages, (2) both Craig Merritt and Asa Jerome were on extended-service contracts in overseas locations, and (3) for moderate bonuses they were willing to be officially engaged to a pair of Stateside M-2s they'd probably never meet.

So if Eden and I chose to look a bit prissy, we had the society's unqualified sanction to do just that.

"In their eyes," said Moss Frantz, "I've given in. Totally surrendered. Because I had no choice." Out on the shrub-girded terrace, the group sat in fading twilight, limned against the ghostly luminous blue-green glow that preceded imminent darkness.

"I know they threatened you." Sloane's voice. "You said that much, already. But not how, not the details."

Thinking back, Moss suppressed a shudder. "They tried it on the rats. Produced Mark Twos, then cut them back to Mark Ones, some M and some F. And said, next move we make against the Feen, that's what could happen to *us*."

"And so?" Brook said it. "I could live either way."

"*No!* You don't understand." How to say this? Frantz paused, then said, "In our cycle, the female segment governs. So if they cut out our male parts, we'd be F for half a cycle and neuter for the other half. But if they left us M, only, then when that segment ended we could *go* neuter. And never come back."

Over the next half hour, the cabal rearranged its plans completely. There'd be no more agitation for public recognition of Mark Twos, no bitching about being forced to hide. Oh no; from now on, said Moss Frantz, "—we'll be the nicest little repentant people they ever saw."

Frantz grinned. "So we'll get assigned Outside, just like all the others. And mostly we'll behave ourselves. Of course if we happen, over the next few years, to get horny in M-mode and knock up some Mark One floozies with Mark Two kids—" The gesture swung both arms wide. "It's not easy, my friends, to unhatch an egg!"

At this point, Moss felt no need to mention that the confiscated batch of oral-effective pseudogene was only one of two, nor that the second was safely stowed for later distribution.

Moss Frantz had waited for a long time. The way the situation stood, that wait might need stretching quite a lot longer. But eventually . . .

# XVII

The Tri-V press liked to joke that Uther Stanton Archer became the country's forty-seventh President on the strength of his initials. As Thane Cogdill saw it, there may have been something to that view; certainly the picture of Archer's head peering over an Uncle Sam cardboard cutout, and wearing the appropriate hat, made an effective, good-humored poster.

But "Uncle Sam" had more going for him. The Archer fortune, for one thing; it was both "old money" and impressively large, bearing with it prestige and connections—clout, to be precise—in a degree difficult to overestimate.

Another thing he had was a solid lock on the state of Massachusetts with a gradient of influence through the rest of New England, and resonance well into New York circles. These things accrued to Archer when after he had spent years of dutiful service to his party structure, first at the state level and then in each house of Congress, for the first time in decades the state ran out of politically minded Kennedys.

All in all, Cogdill thought the country could have picked a lot worse than U. S. Archer.

"Sit down, Paige, sit down." Before his new Cabinet secretary for HEW could begin her presentation, Archer said, "Have you ever read much about Winston Churchill?"

Under strong, heavy brows, her hazel eyes blinked once. Paige Barnard, not quite as slim as she once had been but still with the advantages of smooth complexion and coppery hair, looked considerably less than her near-fifty age. After a moment she said, "The novelist or the politician?"

"Novelist?"

Barnard's laugh came briefly. "There was one, really. With a middle initial S. But I knew you meant the bulldog with the cigar. Yes, of course I've read of his life. Just what part do you have in mind?"

"Following War Two, shortly before he lost his post to—oh, whoever it was."

"Clement Attlee. Labor."

"Probably." Archer hoped his growing irritation didn't show; it wasn't Paige's fault that sometimes she knew more than the occasion truly demanded. "At. Any. Rate."

"Yes?"

"At one point, Churchill told the House of Commons that he hadn't become Premier to preside over the dismantling of the British Empire." He shrugged. "Of course, that was exactly what was happening. And so poor old Winston was out on his—"

"Cigar butt?" Archer's grin came despite himself; hell, he could never stay sore at Paigey. She said, "All right, Uther; I think I have the frame. Now what's the picture?"

"Well, I didn't become President to preside over the dismantling of our society, maybe even our pretensions to civilization.

But until I took office, and banged a few heads enough to get some real information out of all the gobbledegook, I had no idea how close my—our—situation is, to old Winnie's."

The population drop showed near-catastrophe postponed but still looming; the work force hadn't dwindled greatly as yet, but changing demographics did not bode well for the future.

The growing schism between the fiction of public morality, and the facts of what people did if they really wanted to have more than one child, were tearing hell out of the social fabric. "You can see it, Paige. Not just the rise in crime, but the *kinds* of crime."

"Against children, yes. Stealing them, mostly, but sometimes hurting or even killing them. And all out of frustration." She spread her hands. "What can be done?"

His fist drummed on the desk. "I wish to hell I knew."

It was Dr. Fallon, now approaching seventy, who asked Eden and me if we'd like to be the first Outside M-2s to essay pregnancy. Well, why not? We were twenty years old and, by that time, earning reasonably good money; even when one of us had to leave work, our membership trust dividends would help enough that we shouldn't have to rely heavily on our credit line.

She left it up to us to choose biological roles; when we got home we flipped a coin. It came up that Eden would beget and I would bear, so we postponed the attempt until our next transition put us both in form for that option. Then we set contraceptives aside. The only problem was that I didn't conceive, but eventually menstruated as usual, initiating another transition.

"It could be," said Eden, "that you're F-sterile, or that I'm M-sterile." Out of the considerable number of M-2 pairs who had tried for children in the Enclave, some few had run into one or the other handicap.

"Or else we just missed, this time," I said. We had finished dinner—a spicy casserole that owed quite a bit to Greek cuisine—and were drinking tea. "Maybe on my next turn at F, it'll take."

Eden gave a headshake. "Let's don't wait for that. As I see it, the coin was for *first* try. When we're through this transition, why not see if we're both fertile the other way?"

After a moment, I nodded. "Sure. We can't let a stupid coin boss us around indefinitely!"

Eden laughed; again it struck me how good it was for us to be together, whichever way our genders were running—or even now, when we were between phases.

Whether our initial miss denoted a problem or was merely a fluke, we didn't find out; Eden conceived. And as soon as that fact was known beyond doubt, the Feen's plans went into action. Because now, of course, our public roles needed to be those of a standard Mark One married couple.

I never did understand the complexities of computer-fiddling that kept our names and track records intact while specifying Troy dos Caras, at my new place of employment, as male. And married to Eden dos Caras, who also switched employers. I went to ALSAB, which was once the name of a racehorse but now meant the American Liaison Systems Associates: Bonded. Eden's new job was with All Your Problems, Inc., a top business analyst firm.

The move took us to the far side of the urban center, some miles north of Scum City. Since we'd done a minimum of socializing with Mark Ones, our fresh start brought few regrets.

My new job was different enough, from the previous one, that learning the fine points kept me both interested and busy. Eden didn't find all that much novelty, except of course in getting acquainted with new people.

Brad Szalicz hadn't really minded Lyndeen's insistence on moving out of the inner city; he was making good money, and the commuting didn't waste too much of his time.

But then the Transit Commission began making "improvements," and the consequent reroutings and reschedulings put Brad to considerable inconvenience. If he couldn't skip out from work at least ten minutes early, he was stuck with nearly an hour's wait for his tubetrain. Sometimes he made it, but more often not. And since the train station was drab, dingy, and the haunt of numerous unsavory-looking characters, Brad hated to wait there.

So when he knew he'd miss his early departure, he spent most of his waiting time in the Prime Time, nursing a drink or two. He always called Lyndeen, to let her know he'd be late, and he never got home drunk. So all in all, they made the best of it.

The first time, sitting at the Prime Time's bar, that he ran into Clint Haydock again, Brad thought his old acquaintance looked distinctly seedy. Clint wasn't broke, though; he insisted on springing for three drinks in a row. Three was more than Brad usually took during his wait, and he never did finish the third before time called him to the station in a breathless hurry. On the train, with time to think, he decided that Clint had been trying to pump him about some of his investigative news work.

Well, no harm in that, surely. His current project was an overview of the ramifications of the Phoenix Foundation's influence throughout the Greater Chicago area. And so far, lacking any inside viewpoint, it was coming out dull as dishwater.

I remember, in my first few postpubertal years, how curious the Mark Ones were about us. The younger ones—and naturally there were a few in our own age group—especially so. "But how does it *feel* to be sometimes a boy and sometimes a girl?" was the basic generic question.

I don't know how other Mark Twos answered. All I could say was that having grown to my teens thinking I was a "normal"— i.e., Mark One—male, those first changes were one hell of a jolt. But once I'd accepted my situation—well (at that point I'd tend to shrug), it soon became natural enough to me; I found it difficult to imagine *not* changing. "So you see," I'd say, "what puzzles me is how *you* feel, being always the same."

I was lying a little; I did remember my unthinking acceptance of maleness before the first change happened. But I wanted them to feel a reciprocity with me and with the other Mark Twos—to draw a parallel to the way Mark Ones could never know the "selfness" of their own kind's opposite sex.

Fuzzy though it may have been, my theorizing wasn't bad for a fifteen-year-old, and in general was accepted by my Mark One contemporaries. What they wanted to know next, of course, was how did being one sex feel different from being the other.

"Mentally, not at all. Emotionally, if there's a difference I haven't noticed it. And physically—" Here again I'd probably shrug. "Physically I know it doesn't feel the same but there's no way to put it into words."

Finally I thought of the analogy of being unable to compare two tunes in your own mind if you couldn't listen to them. "If you have them taped you can switch back and forth, and *hear*. But the trouble is, there's no way to tape physical sensations. I can tell you it's different, a little, but even to myself I can't define just *how*."

These questionings were before I'd had sex, except for the one time with Dr. Gill, which I *wasn't* telling any kids about. So I was spared any querying on that score. But when Eden and I became lovers, we tried to specify for ourselves the differences between sex as M and as F.

There still weren't any words that made much sense.

I suppose it was inevitable that a few of those curious Mark Ones would make sexual overtures. Occasionally I had such— from boys and girls both, depending on my gender at the time; as I recall, the propositions were all heterosexual.

The offers hadn't tempted me. First, what good was a lover who half the time was the wrong sex for me? But more important: those were the times before Dale Carson's pregnancy jolted the Feen's Board into approving contraceptives, and in neither mode was I of any mind to take chances. So I abstained.

Bertie Gables, I learned a few years later, had been more adventurous. Also more imaginative; for contraception, Bertie invented means I'd never heard of. "A good wad of biscuit dough well up the slot," Bertie told me once. "Baking powder type, of course; I'd heard of yeast infections." I was fairly certain that baker's yeast would be innocuous in that way, but one never knew whether Bertie was joking.

At any rate, for some months Bertie maintained a triad liaison with a youthful pair of Mark One lovers. "So the boy would have two girls for a month, then the girl had two boys. But *I*"—and here, Bertie pouted—"all I had, ever, was a half share of either one. Which was why, eventually, I dropped the whole thing."

That was the only time Bertie ever drank enough to talk about such matters; I have no idea what may have happened later. Except that shortly before Eden and I left the Enclave, Bertie, in F-mode, mated with another Mark Two whose name I forget, gave birth to an XW. Who would, like Bertie, begin life female.

For a long time I hadn't thought of those incidents. But when Eden conceived and missed her period, then another, so that for the first time in years our cycles didn't happen, I felt very strange indeed. Almost, I had the illusion of being thrown back in time— for now I was male and *stayed* male. "We knew this had to happen," I told her, "but somehow I keep waiting for the other shoe to drop."

Eden nodded. "I know; I guess I'm having the same problem." We were in bed, just having made love, and finding a certain amount of wonder in our bodies' increasing changes. Already her breasts were more clearly defined, and growing. My face and chest were sprouting hair, sparsely at first but steadily increasing. Since some few Mark One males wore beards, I disdained any variety of Smooth and shaved the whiskers with a blade; when they were plentiful enough to look normal in Mark One terms, I intended to let them grow. Neatly trimmed, of course; it was no part of my plans to look like a refugee from Scum City.

Meanwhile, Eden and I talked and cuddled. As I wondered, what would it have been like for me if I'd been the one to conceive?

Of course, if between us we had that capability, sooner or later I'd find out.


Clint hated it when Olive sulked at him. Even when they screwed, she sulked; in fact, Olive Schweer was the only woman Clint knew, who could bitch and come at the same time.

The hell with it. He'd finished first, but stayed in there with the round-and-round grind until Olive got her jollies. And a fat lot of thanks he got. So he pushed off, reached over, and lit up some of the new dope Grego had brought.

When she was, in turn, holding her own drag, Clint said, "Yeah, look, I know. We have to get something set up."

Olive exhaled; she'd held it until only faint wisps of smoke showed. "You say that. When you gonna *do* it?"

He toked, held, tried to think. Letting his breath out and not liking the taste of it—*this is hog dope!*—he said, "Why me all the time? How about your damn brother? Why can't Grego find us something, for once? Him and that freako cunt-man of his? Do they always get in free, or what?"

Right away, Clint knew he shouldn't have said it. Olive butted the stick out, took enough breath to last her a while, and teed off.

Clint already knew most of it; Olive's spiels didn't change much. "You ever set up a job like Grego Collins pulled off down in Springfield eight years ago—and never caught, by God!—and you can go sit on your ass from then on. Which you're doing already, God knows. And let me tell you something—"

"Aah, I already heard it!" But he had to listen, anyway. It wasn't Amory Neill's fault, she said, that he got stabbed so it put his cock out of business. And wouldn't that make *anybody* a little crazy?

It was God's own mercy, she said, that at least poor Amory could get his rocks off by *being* laid. "Grego never thinks the less of Amory for that. They do each other a favor, is all." She glared at Clint. "Anything wrong with that?"

"Not a thing." Clint meant it. "What's wrong with Amory is his goddamn knife. His nice sharp hard-on that never quits."

"He's never threatened you with it, Clint."

"No, and he'd better not. I'd stick it where the sun don't shine, and spoil *all* his fun."

If looks could be trusted, Olive believed the brag. Clint didn't, though. He knew, for certain sure, that knives scared him shitless.

There was more dope, but somehow he didn't feel like it. To Olive he said, "I admit, I don't have too many leads right now. This one guy I know, though. He's into things, and I've got this hunch, if I stay on him once in a while, I could find something."

Olive looked to him. "You do that." Then she pulled at him. "Hey, you ol' bastard. You ready to go *this* quick?"

Clint wasn't, but his body showed willing so he was stuck with the move. He hung in until Olive made it, but what with the dope and all, he could have stayed for Christmas and still no luck. Finally he gave up. But not soon enough; he was too sore to sleep right away.

A few slugs of Olive's booze helped. It tasted as rotten as you might expect of anything Grego would buy, but after a while Clint's pee-tube quit burning so bad, and he dozed off.

When the Arnolds sold out and left, the condo that was three numbers away from Brad and Lyndeen's sat vacant for several months. Brad was going to miss Sam and Edna; even though they had to be nearly forty-five years older than the Szaliczes, there'd never been any feeling of age gap.

But after deferring his retirement more than once, when Sam hit seventy-five he refused to bite on any more incentives to keep working. "We're buying a place on Pier City," he said. "Oregon coast. A whole town built out into the Pacific; not too high-rise, either. Our condo's on second level; hang a fishpole out the window and catch dinner!"

Not wanting this informal goodbye party to end, Brad nursed his glass of chablis and accepted another cup of Decaf. "Cost a bundle, I imagine."

Lyndeen lowered her brows at Brad, but surely Sam knew him well enough to realize he wasn't angling for exact figures. The older man said, "And a half. But it's a great layout, and near the kids. Well, visiting out there is how we happened to get onto Pier City. Twenty-five minutes to Harry's place, and maybe forty to

Julia's." He laughed. "Not living in their back pockets, you understand. Works better that way."

After that evening, Brad and Lyndeen did see the Arnolds a few times, but never to talk at any length. And then the unit sat vacant; Brad hated to walk past it, to or from the elevator.

So when movers began bringing boxes and furniture to the condo, Brad Szalicz felt relief from tensions he hadn't consciously felt.

The new tenants, when by chance he saw them carrying some things to their door and then inside, looked too young to afford the place. Well, maybe they were rich kids. Or their parents could be subsidizing them. None of Brad's business, anyway.

Except that somehow he felt a proprietary interest in the place where his friends had lived.

# XVIII

In the U.S. Senate a new Social Security tax boost passed. The next day eighty-year-old Senator Layne, the bill's chief sponsor, was killed by a car bomb. Breaking into a Tri-V network satellite feed, a bootleg transmitter showed a ski-masked woman reading a long manifesto. The gist was that a group calling itself Free Youth strongly opposed raising Social Security taxes.

About two dozen armed, masked persons raided Cabrini Hospital in Seattle. When they left, having killed one nurse and wounded two others, they took with them forty-three infants. Dr. Sara Gabriel, head of the hospital's Maternity Division, went on Tri-V news to plead for their return: "Without reasonable care and medical attention, many of those babies will die!" Her plea brought no response.

President Archer confirmed Annek Getzlor to succeed Frank Haines as director of the Federal Bureau of Investigation. Due to Getzlor's sometimes cavalier attitude toward suspects' rights, the appointment drew a certain amount of congressional fire. But her official record was clear, and she'd held the Number Two spot for nearly a decade, so opposition fizzled.

The President also signed a bill making "willful injury to, or endangerment of, a pregnant woman" a capital crime.

Thane Cogdill yawned and stretched. "Want to turn that thing off, Laura? I've had enough news. Time for bed."

"I agree." The image shrank to a bright dot, then vanished. Laura Casey stood, and moved to embrace her husband. "See you in the morning, Thane."

He checked his watch. "That's right. In about fifteen minutes it'll be morning."

"Oh?" He liked it when she pretended surprise.

"Yes. I peg this to be one of our *good* nights." Being eighty-two years old wasn't perfect, but it beat hell out of the alternative.

Eden and I weren't used to being "neighborly" with Mark Ones, so at first the Szaliczes down the hall made us uneasy. Oh, they were all right—more friendly than average, maybe, but not really pushy—it was simply that our *pattern* didn't include so much interaction with people who happened to live nearby.

I guess theirs did. So, without ever discussing the matter, we and they gradually reached a sort of compromise.

Brad and Lyndeen were about ten years older; he mentioned once, early on, being thirty-one. A good-sized man, about my height but built sturdier. Fair complexion and hair, with one of those broad, high-cheekboned faces that locate their ancestry on the map of Europe. Lyndeen was slim, with dark hair worn longish and curly. Hazel eyes, and pale skin with freckles.

Pleasant looking, both of them, and pleasant talking. More given to visiting than we were, though, and that put me on edge sometimes. But after a time we got along all right.

"*That's* your witness?" said Jody Jay Tolliver. "Floyd, I swear by the good Lord, I wouldn't believe that woman if she told me my own name! I mean, *look* at her."

On the phone's screen, the Reverend Floyd looked sheepish. Beside him, Lesa Pfluge looked unappetizing. "Before you show *me* a witness," Tolliver went on, "you could get her washed, put her into clothes somebody hadn't likely died in, cut her hair so it don't look so lopsided—" Surprisingly, the slattern smiled; Tolliver shook his head. "And do something about those *teeth*."

"Well, sure, Your Reverence; certainly." Floyd talked rapidly, as if fearful of interruption. "But that's part of it, you see. To do those things, I'll need some money, and—"

Jody Jay waved a hand. "See Bishop Crade. I'll give him a list, what you're authorized to charge to the Church. Now you read the list careful; anything you go over and above, costs you personal. You got that?"

Floyd nodded. Tolliver said, "What happened to the other one? The man."

The woman spoke. "Migg run out. I knew he would of."

Jody Jay frowned. "The money not good enough? That it?"

"Ain't no money good enough, Reverend. Migg, he—well, he the last man ever should put his face on the *Trivee*." Again, her smile reminded Tolliver of an eroded, gap-ridden rock ridge. "Might's well go right down and tell The Badge, put me in the lineup. Migg's some dumb, but not full crazy."

Tolliver's eyes narrowed. "But you don't have that kind of trouble, do you, uh—?" And couldn't recall her name!

She shook her head, the incredible lopsided mop of hair swinging with the motion. "Oh nos'sir, Your Reverence. Not sayin' I never made no mistakes. But no live warrants out on me. I had a fella check, fella I know. He—"

"All right, all *right*! I'll take your word for it. Now then, Floyd—how soon can you bring Lesa down here, all fixed up and ready to witness for our dear friends we need to warn?"

Floyd scratched at his right cheek. "All depends, Reverend. The teeth—that's an upper plate at the least, and she won't be talking comfortable, the first few days. So to hit a Sunday—"

Six days a week, Jody Jay's program ran thirty minutes, but on Sunday he sprang for ninety. Floyd was thinking fairly well on this, but not perfect. "Bring her down when you figure she'll be ready, and let me know a day ahead. Sunday or not, it makes no mind."

As the call ended, Jody Jay thought: lately, except for the testimony speeches from folks around the country, more often than not he'd been doing his show live. But not this time. No; Lesa Pfluge was going on disk. Until she got it right.

No matter how many takes it needed.

"It's not just you, Szalicz." Greenmain, head of Channel 83 News, looked uncomfortable. But only, Brad realized, because Greenmain had to do his own talking for once. Now he said,

"The station has to cut costs. It can't afford to pay full-time salaries to part-time producers."

With anger rising, Brad leaned forward. "Since when am I part-time, Greenmain?"

"Since you're out doing investigative stuff; it may hit the news next month or next year. Or never. You're not filling news *time*." Hands in front of him, palms out, Greenmain fanned them nervously sidewise, together and apart. "Now don't get us wrong, Brad. When some of your work—anybody's—is part at the desk and part not, we have this plan where the desk work is salary and the outside stuff is sort of commission. I mean, you know that."

"Yeah. But how come all at once you shift the percentages? Practically no salary, and commissions only when the show's aired?" Because Channel 83 had always paid commission on acceptance of a feature; if events aced the item out of its scheduled showing, the reporter still got paid. Not now, though. Brad Szalicz waited for Greenmain's reply.

It didn't surprise him. "Because our accountants say we have to, and our lawyers say we can."

Brad stood. "Want to hear a riddle, Greenmain?"

"Uh—I suppose so. What is it?"

"Why don't you need a dental appointment tomorrow?"

Looking puzzled, "I give up. Why?"

"Because my mother taught me to always count ten first."

But still, on the way out, Brad slammed the door.


For two years now, Moss Frantz had been very careful. Although the dissident group still met, Moss stayed away from the meetings, but kept in touch through Sloane Klemgard who was on the same bowling team.

What Moss did attend were Tim Cadeland's counseling sessions on how to blend into Mark One society. For one thing, the advice was useful; for another, it built up brownie points.

So when the time came, Moss put in an application to live and work Outside. And was relieved, though not greatly surprised, that the bid was approved.

Moss was mated with although not married to Heath Crawford, but Heath wasn't yet of legal age by Mark One standards, and looked even younger. So Moss proposed the option of living alone and taking a male role. Feen security okayed the plan.

Finally Moss Frantz was Outside. To celebrate, he stopped by a sperm bank and made a Mark Two deposit.

* * *

Kennet Bardeen never swore in front of his grandchildren, but when the Sunday afternoon visit ended and Celia took the kids home, he said some words he hadn't used in years. Winding up with "asshole bastard causing trouble *again*! Back the tape up and run it for me, would you please, Jenny? From where he introduces that moronic woman." Shortly after Celia arrived he'd turned the recorder on and the screen off, but not before he saw and heard enough to know that Jody Jay Tolliver had found himself a new monkey wrench to swing at the machinery.

Now he and Jenny watched and listened, as Jody Jay made portentous noises about the new menace he'd discovered. "Monsters among us, my dear friends! Creatures which their very existence defies the laws of God and man." The Reverend still sweat as much as always, Bardeen noted; maybe the man didn't believe in air conditioning. And either he wore a wig or else he'd worked a bona fide miracle since the last time Bardeen had viewed him, and that was some while back. He wouldn't be doing so this day, except that someone on the opinion-checking side of the Feen's PR team had mentioned that Tolliver, all week, had been promising a big revelation and dropping hints about the Foundation.

So now, here it came. After the second commercial break, Tolliver began, "I have here today with me our sister from the Northwest Central Chicago congregation of the Church of the Reborn Righteous—a humble woman who has seen the face of great evil and now is come to tell us what that evil is, so we can all be warned. Here, my dear friends, is Miz Lesa Pfluge."

The first name triggered Bardeen's recalls. Superficially the woman didn't match Blake Lassiter's description: her short hair was smartly and neatly frizzed; her makeup was professional grade, and her teeth as real as Tolliver's hair. Someone had gone overboard on the clothes—too stylish for credibility, but still looking like an *expensive* sack of potatoes.

But her face, or rather its expressions, gave away the whole pitch. As she spoke, answering Tolliver's questions, she had the sneaky look of the petty criminal at bay. "Yeah, Your Reverence. Found her lyin' in the roadway at the airport; took her on home, be sure she awright." But always the sly sidewise glance: *Am I getting away with this? Is he buying it?*

Jody Jay wasn't buying it, exactly; rather, he was selling it on commission. As he led the woman through her story, he looked more and more harassed. Puzzled at first, suddenly Bardeen laughed. "Jenny, you notice the abrupt breaks every now and then?"

"Well, yes. But what—"

"This isn't live. Every time she blows her lines, he cuts and starts up again!"

Now Bardeen leaned forward, watching closely, as Lesa Pfluge finally came to the crucial part, the part Jody Jay hoped would damn the Feen in the public view. She said, "No idea, Migg and me, any such a thing could be. But then we seen it!"

"Tell us now, sister, just what *did* you see?"

"Was a girl, first. A real girl, had the curse, and all. But *then*— done grew a co—"

Tolliver cut in, loudly. "Grew the organs of a man, you mean?" Lesa nodded. "And with your own eyes, you saw that? And the man, the one who helped bring her to your home, he saw it too? You both did? And on the Bible you'll swear that?" After each question, another nod.

Jody Jay spread his arms wide. "We're talking no human person here, my dear friends. We're talking monsters. Demons, maybe. Yes, *demons!* And now just one more thing. Sister Pfluge, that creature had some ID papers with it, am I right?"

"Yeah. I seen 'em."

"And what institution did those papers have to do with?" Lesa looked blank; Tolliver showed irritation. "Didn't they all tie into the Phoenix Foundation?"

"Oh, yeah. Sure, they done."

Now he turned away from Lesa Pfluge. "Well, there you are, my dear friends. The mills of the Lord may grind slow, but they get there. Years ago I told you that Foundation was the hiding place of great sinners; now it turns out worse.

"Demons, my friends. *Demons!*"

"Oh, living *shit!*" said Kennet Bardeen.

Alvin had agreed she could have a second child, so here she was at a matchup bar. Wearing a green triangular pin. Strictly speaking, green meant a woman was looking for blood type AB, but it could be used to include A and B as well: simpler than also bedecking oneself with yellow for A and blue for B. For a new fad, she thought, the pins had caught on fast.

The bar featured soft lights, soft music, and small tables. This early, the place was less than half filled. Looking around, she didn't see anyone she'd want to approach—and besides, the idea embarrassed her. She took a vacant table near the end of the bar, ordered a safe drink, and looked around.

Not very good pickings. The men's diamond-shaped ID pins were mostly orange for O, and her son by Alvin had taken care of that option. Squinting to see farther, she spotted two blues and a yellow, but all three were too dissimilar to Alvin, in looks, to be acceptable. One did have to pretend, after all!

"Excuse me." The tallish man who had bumped her chair, spilling a few drops of her drink, didn't wait for an answer; he moved on to sit at the bar. She looked at him, but the way he faced, she couldn't see a pin. His pale complexion and light reddish hair were no close match to Alvin; not too far out of the ballpark, though. A little tall, maybe, but nothing critical.

The only trouble was, he hadn't given her even one look.

In the bar mirror, Moss could see that the woman he'd bumped was watching him. Three days into M-mode he was ready to find some action—but now that he had her attention, let her wait a little! He took his drink slowly; when he ordered the next, he pointed a thumb back toward her table and said, "One of whatever she's having, too. I'll take it over."

Walking toward her, then, he catalogued her. Brown eyes steady on him, smooth complexion and a heart-shaped face, light brown hair short in front and longer toward the back. Slim, he suspected, though sitting down it was hard to tell.

He reached the table, stood almost touching it. "I was thinking about something else. Finally realized I'd spilled some of your drink. Can I offer you another?"

Saying nothing, she nodded, so he set down the two glasses and then sat, himself. "Moss Frantz."

"Cecy Salich. But where's your pin?"

*What the hell*—? Oh, yes—she was wearing one, and now that he noticed, so was everyone else. "Uh—it must have fallen off."

Cecy smiled. "No hoo-ha. What color is it?"

Colors? Probably they should match. Or be complementary? Before he thought to look at hers, her hand went in front of it. Other people's, though: a quick glance showed mostly orange. He almost named that tint, then had a misgiving; *if she liked orange she'd already have a date. I need to*—

He'd waited too long; she said, "Where've you *been*, anyway? Not to know these things."

Moss had heard enough of Feen strategy to know that when in doubt, always invoke the magic word: Security. "Sorry; I'm not authorized to say. Classified."

"You work for the government?"

"Uh—no." Because he didn't know the jargon for that. "Call it industrial security."

But still he was stuck. He said, "Why don't you pretend I've been on the moon a long time?"

"You were on the moon? But *they* have the pins. So—" *Damn.* "Not there. Farther."

"The asteroids?" She gasped. "What's it *like?*"

Think fast. "Not the asteroids. And I can't tell you."

Smiling, she touched fingers to his cheek. "Were there any women, where you lived? That you could be with?"

"None like you." *And that's the truth!*

Not much later, they left the bar. She'd been drinking some kind of beer he'd never heard of, so he bought a few bottles to take out, along with a small flask of his favorite brandy. He didn't want her to know where he lived, so he took her to a medium-rate hotel.

Except for the breasts, which reminded him of Dale when she got pregnant a few years ago, sex with a Mark One didn't seem much different than with Mark Twos. He managed three times; the first was for fertility, the other two merely for fun.

The next morning he drove her to the street entrance of her residence. "Don't come in. My husband agrees we want a second child; he might not want to see whose it is." Kiss goodbye.

Then, after waiting to see that she did get inside all right, he drove away. In the Feen compound there'd been no need or occasion to learn to drive; so far as Moss knew, he was one of only two or three M-2s Outside who had opted for private transportation.

Moss rather enjoyed the freedom of impromptu movement; it left him less subject to the rules or whims of others. Well, he was certainly breaking rules right and left: for every covey of spermatozoa he donated, in person and with great pleasure, to a Mark One female, he left three or four at various sperm banks.

But even better: all the while since Moss had been caught with a batch of oral-effective pseudogene, he'd kept his own counsel. Gilly Monlux had blabbed all about the stuff she'd helped him steal; what she didn't know was that while she took a needed break, he lifted a fair bundle on his own account.

So, biding his time, Moss had waited for the Feen's permission to live Outside—and then, rather than trying to bring his cache out all at once, was sneaking capsule-sized loads, a few at a time. In with his allergy caps, in fact, and looking much the same as those prescribed remedies. Moss could tell the difference, but anyone else would be hard put to do so.

What he liked to do was drop a capsule or two into the water cooler where he worked, or in any office he visited in the line of business.

For the couples who might benefit from the largesse of Moss Frantz, the problem was not, as Cecy Salich had said, "whose it is." *What* it is, was more like it!

# XIX

I got home tired and would just as soon have spent a short evening relaxing at home. But Brad looked out as I was passing their door, and invited us to come over for a while after dinner.

So we went, Eden and I. It wasn't as if either they or we had in mind to party up, late. For one thing, with pregnancy Eden had dropped booze entirely; somewhere she found a brand of imported nonalcoholic beer that actually tasted better than most of the real stuff. Sometimes I even drank it myself. And Lyndeen had taken to keeping some on hand.

We got there in time to give young Stanislaus a couple of bedtime hugs. A nice kid, Stosh was: going on five, which is always an interesting age.

At this time Eden was naturally fascinated with children, so I wasn't surprised when she went along with Lyndeen, to put Stosh to bed. Brad got out beers for the two of us. "Cheers."

So we talked. He was definitely on the down side. Well, he'd told me the way the station had cut him back. "—and under this setup, I'm not sure how long we can manage." He shrugged. "If I could find a strong handle on my Phoenix story, maybe I could hit Greenmain for an advance. If I don't get a wrapup going pretty soon, I'll have to drop it and go back to straight desk work." Brad made a face. "I'd hate that—but at least we wouldn't lose this condo."

Our wives came back then, so he dropped the subject; the talk turned to Tri-V and then to sports, where I was pretty much at a loss. But Brad, so to speak, carried the ball. "—wish my dad had lived to see the Bears make this big comeback, the past couple of years. He saw their first Super Bowl win, nearly forty years ago, and I don't think he ever forgot a single play!"

The Bears were professional football; I knew that much. I said, since it was a safe enough guess, "They've had some strong years since then, though."

"Oh, sure; the tides come and go. But nothing much good after dad had his stroke."

He stopped there. I was trying to think of a new subject but didn't need one; the door chimed. Brad went to open it. "Cecy! Come on in. Where's Alvin?"

She was about my age, fair-haired and brown-eyed, slim. She looked cheerful and moved well. "Hi, Brad, Lyndeen. His model-car club meets tonight." She looked at Eden and me.

"Troy and Eden dos Caras," Brad said. "Neighbors down the hall." He motioned. "This is my sister Cecy."

Half-sister, that would be, considering their ages. But I knew Mark Ones tended to ignore such distinctions, because of the circumstances that caused them. Or rather, I *thought* I knew those things. Because immediately after the how'd-ye-dos, the newcomer said, "Guess what? I'm pregnant again!"

It was obviously a time for family talk, so as soon as Eden and I could make a polite getaway, we did.

What bothered me was that almost certainly I had information that could help Brad's article and perhaps save his financial neck. But couldn't possibly reveal it to him.

Although there'd been a few more dates with Cecy Salich, and now at his apartment rather than a hotel room, Moss Frantz really liked the matchup bars. Equipped with a full selection of the pins that specified blood types, a person could scout the talent and put on whatever color matched one's first choice. Over a period of nearly three weeks Moss bedded with more women than in all previous M-mode experience to date. Two the same night, sometimes.

The last of the series must have been out strictly for fun, not fertility. Otherwise her premenstrual pheromones wouldn't have put Moss into transition to F-mode a week early.

First move was to phone Cecy and postpone their next date. "A whole month?" she said. "What's going on, Moss?"

A headshake. "Sorry, Cece. Classified. I'll call you, though, when I can."

When she was reasonably well soothed, Moss called Heath. No luck there, either. Heath was only four days into F-mode; her next period, which could shift Moss back to M, was more than three weeks away.

Damn all! M or F, Moss had equal horniness—or maybe, as one counselor had suggested, equal need for sexual reassurance.

So for Moss it looked like a thin month. In the matchup bars *he* was too well recognized for *her* to risk appearing. Also, pregnancy was an unacceptable hazard; Moss had no contraceptives along, and going back for them might prove embarrassing. Here on the Outside, for nearly two decades all such measures had been banned. Unless prescribed for medical reasons.

Just now, there were no good answers. For later, though: *from here on out, I ask those women more questions!*

Cecy's news pleased Brad Szalicz. He knew she'd wanted another kid, but he hadn't been optimistic about Alvin saying it was really okay for her to go out and get one. Well, Cecy didn't seem edgy, so Brad guessed it had all worked out.

If it wasn't for the money thing—Greenmain putting the screws on—Brad would have used this development as leverage on Lyndeen. He knew she'd like a second child, every bit as much as he would. Years ago, Brad had figured out that his folks must have had some tough problems before Stan agreed that Ulla could find somebody to conceive Cecy with. He'd thought about the situation, all of it, and decided that if Lyndeen wanted Stosh to have a sibling, that was fine with him.

The first trouble, though, was that Lyndeen herself had a strong thing against infidelity, even for a good cause.

The other was that now when the example of Alvin and Cecy

could have worked to good effect, Brad couldn't afford another
kid, even if he could have sired it himself.

*I need to get something going. I have to.*

"You'll talk. Oh, *yes*, you'll talk!" As the man moaned and
writhed, FBI Director Annek Getzlor squeezed harder on his
balls.

"Never!" Then his mouth was covered, the words muted.

"They always say that!" Getzlor snarled it, panting. This was
beginning to go really well!

She picked up the whip. Twice, three times, she swung it,
feeling the groans of pain more than hearing them. "Enough?"

His headshake gave her the cue; she squeezed harder. Soon she
felt his surrender, and not long after, her own triumph.

As she took the handcuffs off, Getzlor said, "That was a lot
nicer, Duane. The more you're hurting, the better head you
give." Using a wad of tissues to dry his matted beard, she asked,
"Is there anything you'd like *me* to do differently?"

He frowned. "Well, you might start a little earlier with the
whip."

"Whatever you say. Now why don't you go fix us a drink?"

After this Moss Frantz had done his begetting job, Cecy knew
she shouldn't have gone on seeing him. But he had a type of
appeal she couldn't quite understand, and Alvin was going
through some kind of strange reaction where she was on her own
for a while; he wasn't touching her. *Credibility Zero*, but if that
was the way Alvin wanted it . . .

So when Moss chopped Cecy off for a whole month, she felt
jilted, just the same as in an old-time romance story.

It wasn't anything she could talk about, but she couldn't keep
from worrying the subject around the edges. Over at Brad's place,
with that cute dos Caras couple there, she found herself telling
more of the story than she'd planned to: wine can do it. "Well,
until Alvin gets over being a saint or whatever it is, I might as well
keep seeing Moss. Except that—"

"Who?" Troy dos Caras leaned forward. Not many men wore
beards now; Troy, Cecy thought, looked good with his.

"Moss who?" he said now.

"Moss Frantz."

Troy nodded. "I see. Thank you." His face went tight, and
Eden's, too; the next few minutes until they left, neither of them

had much to say. What their problems might be, Cecy had no idea.

"The crazy *bastard*! Running around, knocking M-One women up with M-Two kids! That kind of irresponsibility could shoot us down, give that imbecilic Jody Jay Tolliver the evidence he needs to give us more trouble than he's done already. Eden, I—!"

"You what?" she said.

"I have to stop Moss Frantz. Even if it means killing."

Of course Eden talked me out of that stupid idea. No; call the Feen. "Let the experts handle this."

So I did; I told them everything I knew.

What I didn't like was that they seemed to know even less.

The Board meeting left Kennet Bardeen feeling totally wrung out. Like playing a game of badminton from both sides. Yes, we need to do something about this. No, we can't do *that*—or that, or that. What *can* we do?

"By next week we hope to have a report from the Interface Committee." (Translation: Thane and I and Fallon and Forrest, plus a few others, are busting our butts to see if there *is* any answer.) The Board bought it, so the meeting finally adjourned.

But during all the talking, Bardeen had figured out what to do. Not how to tell the Board, though. Or whether . . .

He sighed. *Move over, Pandora.*

Brad didn't mean to get nosy, but when he saw the envelope he couldn't resist looking inside. Troy had stopped by on his way to the dos Caras condo; Eden, he said, wouldn't be home yet. So Brad broke out some iced tea and they talked a little. Then the phone chimed; Eden was home now.

So Troy said thanks, and left. But he forgot to take his mail along, that he'd picked up at the lobby box. And one envelope, already opened, caught Brad's eye. Because the return address was Phoenix Foundation.

Feeling guilty, but unable to help himself, Brad read the contents. Then he nodded. Before he took the mail down the hall, he ran the important parts through his copier.

"But this is big, Greenmain! It's what I've been needing, to put a kicker on my report."

"Forget it, Szalicz." As usual, Greenmain's thin red face showed no expression. "The story's killed."

"Killed? Who says so?"

"Front office. Who else?"

With effort, Brad unclenched his fists. "What is this? Those bastards okayed the project; I've put in three months on it; *now* they kill it? What about my time?"

Greenmain shrugged. "It's against the new guidelines, but I'll see if I can get you a little something. For now, though, you're grounded. It's back to straight desk duty." The man spread his hands. "Hell, at least that puts you on full salary."

Brad shook his head. "I can't believe this. Well, I'm not going to put up with it. If this outfit doesn't want the story, I can sure as hell find someone who does!"

He turned to leave; before he took his second step, Greenmain yelled, "Just a minute!" Brad swung back, and the other man said, "Let me do you a favor."

"Such as?"

"Don't try it."

"Why not?"

"Because there's no market; we're not the only outlet to get the word. And, Szalicz—the way it is, either you drop this thing or you're out of here."

"Maybe that's a good idea!" Brad shouted it.

Greenmain shook his head. "Not when there won't be anyplace else to go. And I mean *any*place."

Brad frowned. "You mean that, don't you? What you're saying is, somehow I got caught in the big gears."

"That's about it." Quickly, then, "I don't *know* how."

"And if you did, you couldn't tell it." Brad needed a deep breath, then one more, before he could say, "All right. Log me back to desk, starting today. I know it's not your fault—and any money you can pry out of the Three Scrooges, for the work I put in on the story, I'll appreciate."

As near as Greenmain could show any feeling at all, Brad thought the man looked relieved. As he said, "If you need some time, today, to close out the project, that's all right."

"Matter of fact, I do." But Brad Szalicz had no plans to do either project or desk work, this day. At two hours before noon, he left the building and went to the Prime Time bar.

He did remember, a little late for it, to have lunch.

* * *

The phone woke Moss Frantz. Sleepy, she answered. "Hello? Oh, Heath—how are you?"

"Just fine. I miss you, though. Could you come in this evening, so we could visit a little while?"

"Sure, I guess so. But I'm still F, you know."

"That's because you played around at somebody's wrong time. Don't worry, though; we'll get back in phase."

"Right." The call ended; Moss thought about the reshuffling. When Heath went M they'd have a few days that way; then when Moss's period came, Heath could make early transition.

The main thing was for Moss not to screw up again, this way.

Jeez; Brad was *plowed*; Clint hadn't ever seen him this bad. And here it was only four in the aft—before Brad was supposed to be off work, even; Clint had figured to get here early, and wait.

Now, signing the bartender for two beers, Clint walked over to Brad's table and sat. "Y'awright, ol' buddy?"

Owl-eyed, Brad stared. "Pig's eye! Fucked over is what, Clint. Worst way." In one hand he waved some crumpled sheets of paper. "See this? I didn' tell you, you wouldn' *believe*."

Shit. The way it looked, ol' Brad wasn't going to last long enough to tell anybody anything. Well, there were ways; Clint got out his handy pocket-pharmacy and checked the inventory. Hell, yes; here was the kind that could damn near undrunk a passout case: only three left, but one was plenty. Of course there'd be a real bitch of a headache when the thing wore off, but that was Brad's problem.

The beers arrived; Clint paid, and as the barman walked away he crumbled a tablet between his fingers and dropped the powder into Brad's glass. "Here ya go, buddy!"

The dope didn't work right away, but after a few minutes Brad began to make better sense. What he was so pissed about, Clint kept trying to find out, and after a time it began to come clear. Partly, at least; all the stuff about the different ways Channel 83 had knifed Brad in the back boiled down to two things: Szalicz was hurting for money, and somehow the Phoenix Foundation was to blame.

But how? Maybe the wadded papers held the answer. "Hey, Brad, why'n'cha just show me, let me figure out how to help, maybe?" Because Clint had a hunch something was up, here.

Still bleary but now tracking better, Brad nodded. "Sure." He tried to smooth the sheets out on the table; it was a little wet in spots, but not too bad. He pointed. "Right here; y'see it? Memmership trust, monthly div'dend."

That's what it said, all right. "So?"

More sober by the minute, Brad blinked. "Ever' month, the Foundation credits those kids with a hunk of free money. *That's* how they can afford the condo. And look *there.*"

Clint did, and his brows rose. Because under the entry "Credit Line" the paper stated that Eden and Troy dos Caras, either or both, were entitled to borrow, interest-free, up to a total of a half million dollars from the Membership Trust Fund. "Brad? That mean what it looks like?"

"Why shouldn't it?" But Brad was frowning, and now he reached a hand out. "The Foundation leaned damned hard to kill my story. Clint, for the sake of my own ass I think I'd better destroy those papers."

"Sure, just a minute. All right. Here." But as Brad Szalicz wadded the papers again and shoved them into his jacket pocket, under his breath Clint was saying, "Dos Caras. Dos Caras. In Brad's building." And the address.


"I don't understand. What's going on?" Grabbed by two Security men as soon as she entered the Enclave, hands cuffed behind her back and all her questions ignored, Moss was hustled to Erwin Bennest's office and sat down onto a straight chair. Facing her and also sitting were Bennest, Dr. Mareth Fallon, and Board Chairman Kennet Bardeen.

None of them looked especially pleased to see Moss Frantz.

Fallon spoke. "First, Moss, we want a list of all the Mark One women you've been to bed with. *All* of them."

"But I'm not sure I *remember*—"

"Under hypnosis, with the aid of drugs, you will." Erwin Bennest sounded sure of what he said; already intimidated, Moss made no protest. What were they *after*, anyway?

"But I have to go to work tomorrow." Bardeen shook his head; well, it had been worth a try.

"You'll call in sick," Fallon said. "I'll vouch for you."

"For as long as it takes," said Bardeen.

Nothing to lose, now, so Moss tried a show of outrage. "I just came—Heath called me, to come visit, so I did. Don't we have any rights now, in the Feen? What—"

Bardeen's face could have been carved from granite. "You've

impregnated at least one Mark One woman, maybe more. Possibly a *lot* more. You know what the consequences could be, and yet you did these things deliberately, on purpose."

"You have your ideas; I have mine. What's the difference?"

Bardeen smiled; Moss wished he hadn't. "The difference, my young firebrand, is that *you* don't have to decide whether *I* need to be given a vasectomy. Or perhaps something more. Whereas—"

Oh, *shit*! "Hey, no! Mister Bardeen—Chairman, sir—you don't have to do any of that. I'll tell what you want—and the drugs, hypnotizing, that's all okay too. Just don't—"

"We'll see." Bardeen stood. "When we know everything you've done during the time you were Outside, and determine whether it's still possible to preserve our necessary security—that's soon enough to reconsider your own future."

Damn it! How had they found out?


"Champagne? Wha'd'ya do, Clint? Win a big fat ten-dollar pool?" That was the thing about Olive, Clint thought; she was always such a great cheerleader.

Be fair, though; she had her hair out of curlers and her bod into a dress, not schlepping around in that crummy robe. So give it a chance; Clint put on a grin and said, "You wanted something set up. What I got, it's so good, we're gonna celebrate first, before I even tell you."

All the while they drank the champagne (it was Bulk Process but Olive didn't know the difference and Clint couldn't really tell by the taste), he kept fooling around on her. So that when they got to it, Olive was hot enough and high enough, she forgot to bitch about anything. *Best in a* long *time!*

After, he told her. Not all of it, not enough so her brother Grego could move in and take it away from Clint. Just the numbers, mostly. And then, "I wish it didn't take four; I think it does, though. But does one of 'em have to be Neill?"

"I *told* you it's not his fault."

"And I told *you*—I don't care how Amory Neill fucks, or which way. What worries me is how sometimes he gets too soon with that goddamn knife."

"I'll have Grego talk to him."

Clint nodded. "You do that." Then, maybe because he had to say it or maybe just because the wine made him braver than usual, Clint spoke. "One thing Grego should tell Neill."

"Like what?" The nagging tone again.

"Like, if that knife cuts without I say it should, I erase Amory's share of the job. With a .38-caliber eraser."

"If you say so, Clint." And maybe she even meant it.

The second night Moss was in the infirmary—punchy with the hypno drugs but not forgetting this was a lockup—Heath came to visit. Heath's hugs, and the kissing, made Moss feel better. Then Heath said, "I'm sorry, Moss. When Gilly asked if you were coming in soon, and I told her, I didn't know it was a setup, to grab you. I—"

He put his hand to her cheek. "That's okay, Heath. I know you wouldn't do that. Just bad luck, is all."

Looking relieved, Heath smiled. "Hey, this won't last forever. Either I'll come due and go M first, or you will. Then we can get close, and when the other one changes we'll be back on cycle again. All right?"

"Sure, Heath. Great." *If they leave me the option!*

Which, in Moss's view, wasn't exactly a cinch bet.

# BOOK FOUR

"*Concealment, the refuge of the weak, tends to be a very demanding stratagem. To accept, without careful thought, the premise that it is one's only option, may sometimes turn out to be a costly mistake.*"

(From Origins, by Rome dos Caras.)

# XX

Before I came awake enough to realize the noise was real and not a dream, they had me held down. The lights came on; over by the wall Eden was screaming, clawing at someone. I heard, "Amory! Don't touch her, you insane bastard! And put that knife away! Can't you see she's pregnant?"

There were four, each masked and hooded; I couldn't tell who said what. Except, the one with the knife used it to gesture. "*I* know that, Clint. You just take care of your own part."

Two of them held me pinned in our own bedding. The fourth one, not the one with the knife, came with some kind of sack to pull over my head and down past my waist. I could breathe but couldn't see, and my arms were pinned to my sides.

I tried to say something; whether they could hear me or not, nobody paid any attention. Eden was yelling "What are you doing? Let him go!" Then her voice was muffled, maybe by the same kind of thing they'd used on me.

So we couldn't talk, couldn't ask if the other was unharmed. I was pulled to my feet, the bag confining me above, naked below.

Humiliating, I suppose, if there'd been time to think in such terms. Someone pulled me in one direction; somebody else jerked me the other way. In between, I bumped front-to-front with one of the intruders.

What I did then was stupid—but sometimes you *have* to hit back. I thought I knew where the one in front of me had moved to, so that's where I kicked.

I liked the yell that kick brought. But not the slam to my head. Which is the last I remember until I woke, head hurting like all hell, in one of the crummiest rooms I'd ever seen.

\* \* \*

"Brad! Wake up! Someone's at the door."

He shook himself conscious. Somebody sure as hell *was*—and banging and screaming like crazy. How he'd slept through it . . .

Slippers were too much work, but by the nightlight he found his robe and wrapped it around him. Heading for the front door he paused to turn the living room lights on. "I'm *coming!*" Then as he opened the door, "Eden! Jesus Christ, what's wrong?"

She was a mess, all right. Face smudged and scratched, nightgown torn, hair a tangled mop. At first her screaming babble sounded like nonsense, and Brad wondered if he'd have to slap her out of it. But then Eden shook her head, took a deep breath, and said in almost normal tones, "They took him. They took Troy. Four of them, all in masks." She paused. "I have to make a call, Brad. They tore the phone line out, so could I make it from here, please?"

"The police, sure. Over here; sit right down, now." Then as Lyndeen came out of the bedroom and Brad saw her face take on a shocked look, he said, "Can I get you anything, Eden? Coffee?"

"*Not* the police!" Eden wasn't following along, very well. "They said, keep the police out of it or Troy's dead."

"Who, then?"

She shook her head, and then her eyes looked clearer. "It's the Feen I have to call—the Phoenix Foundation. And—and—the coffee or whatever, you don't need to, thanks."

Eden paused. "Please don't be offended, but would you mind if I make this call privately?"

Considering the time of night, Erwin Bennest was easy to reach and didn't even look sleepy. After Eden's first few sentences, the man's lined face went slack and then, almost immediately, showed tension to the point of pain. "It's ransom, I suppose," he said. "Though I can't see how they'd know enough to expect much money for an ordinary young systems expert. Did they say when they'll make their demands?"

"They've done that. And however it is they know things, they do know them. What they demand just happens to be the full total of Troy's and my lines of credit at the membership trust."

Bennest made a low whistle. "A leak. I'll get my people on it. There aren't too many Feen personnel who have access to that kind of data on any given account. And pinning down the source of a leak usually gives clues to where it went."

"I hope you're right. But don't forget, they still have Troy, and we *can't* go to the police."

For a moment, fatigue and tension and all, the Security Chief seemed almost amused. "Eden—that's one of the biggest folk myths in the entire field of crime. Kidnappers *always* demand no contact with police forces. I suppose the more stupid ones really expect to get their own way, there. But the rest know what really happens: police are briefed, and waiting in the shadows, so to speak, in maybe ninety percent of cases."

"But they'll kill Troy!"

"No they won't. Not for that reason, anyway. Because they'll have no certain clue to police involvement until Troy's free."

"You can guarantee that?"

Bennest nodded. "It's a science, Eden. How to lie back, out of sight, until the hostage is safe, and *then* move in."

He cleared his throat. "Now, then. You told me the gist of what happened. But before we go through the whole event moment by moment, if you're up to that job at this time of night, tell me: is there anything you remember about any of those people? Anything at all?"

Trying to replay what had happened, Eden thought about it, then nodded. "I was trying to fight them. The one—male, I'm pretty sure—had a knife and seemed eager to use it. But another one, sounding like maybe he was the boss, told him to put it away, not to touch me, because I'm pregnant."

In the screen Eden saw Bennest lean forward. "Who did the telling? And to whom?"

Surprisingly, the names came to mind. "Clint told Amory."

Brad hadn't meant to eavesdrop, but once he got up he generally had to take a leak, and now was no exception. So after moving to the bedroom with Lyndeen, almost immediately he went to the bathroom. He was drying his hands when he heard Eden talking, her voice level rising as she spoke, directly across from him on the other side of the wall. Not intending to, he leaned over and put an ear to the surface.

*Oh, shit!* The membership trust, the credit line. *He* was the one who knew about that stuff. But he hadn't thought he'd told anybody. Not until now, he hadn't thought that.

But somebody named Clint was bossing the kidnap gang. And from not too long ago, Brad barely remembered being very drunk before Clint Haydock fed him a headbusting soberizer.

After Eden ended the call, Brad stood for a time, thinking. *Did I set that kid up?* Shaking his head, he came out of the bathroom. Lyndeen seemed to have talked Eden into sharing some herb tea, but Brad begged off and went back to bed.

He couldn't get to sleep, though. He was trying to think whether he had any idea where Clint Haydock lived.

The headache was bad enough, but I also woke to find my right wrist handcuffed to a bedpost. I didn't have any clothes on, of course, but there was a stained sheet over me, pulled up to my chest.

Across the room a woman sat watching Tri-V with the sound off. She was wearing headphones, the kind with small earpieces, but it looked as if they went to the minidisk player beside her chair. The way the Tri-V sat, at quite an angle to me, I could see shapes flickering but couldn't make out what they were.

The place reeked of cannabis, both fresh and stale. Yes, I remembered; my dad had told me that dopers liked to put other sound to Tri-V images. So this woman was probably high. Well, living in this sty, with its stained, cracked plaster walls, she could most likely use it.

My head was feeling better; I looked more closely at her. Not that the scrutiny was any treat, but I wanted to evaluate her before I got her attention. If I cared to do that at all, right away.

She was younger than she looked, I thought; the lines in her face indicated worry and petulance, more than age. Her hair, dark at sides and back where she'd had it sheared rather close, sported a rambling bunch of bleached curls on top; the style, fashionable among Mark One girls in their teens, couldn't have suited her worse. Under a frayed, faded housecoat she appeared to be thin, flat-chested.

On her right hand I saw several rings, the jewels much too large to be genuine. And on that side she wore two small earrings: blinking lights, one red and one green, not at all in synchronism. That particular fad was at least ten years out of date, and if the pair's circuit had been aligned correctly, the lights would have alternated.

I'd seen about all there was to see; besides, I felt a need. "Excuse me," I said. No response. "Hey!" Fairly loud, and then I shouted it, but no luck at all; she must have had those phones turned up all the way.

I grabbed the bedposts and began rocking them forward and

back. For a minute I was afraid I'd pull the shaky bed down before she noticed anything, but then the vibration reached her. Slowly she looked around. "What you want?"

I motioned taking the headphones off; eventually she did, and again asked her question.

"Do you have a bathroom in this place? I have to go."

"Can't let you do that, just here by myself. You could get away. Wait'll somebody comes."

Immediately, by at least one order of magnitude, my bladder became more demanding. "But I *have* to."

She stood; her thinness didn't include her waistline. Not pregnant, just bulgy. "Can't unloose you; don't have the key, come to that. Wait on, a mo. Is this a crap, or just peepee?"

When in Rome, talk pig Latin. "Peepee."

"Awright." She went through the door in the wall facing the foot of the bed, and came back to hand me a small bucket. "Here. Sit up and use this."

Urgent as the matter felt, still as I sat there naked and holding the pail in useful position, the sphincter wouldn't release. "What's the matter? Thought you had to go."

"I did. I do." But damn it, there she stood, watching. "Could— could you go in the other room for a minute or two?"

She laughed—and surprisingly, instead of the raucous cackle I would have expected, it was a pleasant-sounding laugh, that didn't fit her looks at all. "Bashful, are you? Well, I ain't supposed to leave you at all. But already did, to get the bucket, so why not again? What's to hurt?"

Even when she was gone, it took minutes before I could let go. She must have been listening, because not until I was done did she come back in. "Awright now?" I nodded. "Okay, I'll go dump it." This time she used the door in the wall to my right. So that had to be the bathroom; she'd got the pail from somewhere else. How many rooms were there here?

And what difference could it possibly make?


"A half million, Erwin?" Bardeen shook his head. "Do they know something they shouldn't, or is it a coincidence?" As he came awake better, the two men sipping fresh hot coffee, he was getting over the shock of the news Bennest had brought him.

The Security Chief shrugged. "No info as yet. I'd guess they know, all right. Because otherwise, why the half-mil? I mean, who is there, outside of Scum City, who thinks that's still big

money? What *is* the trust's normal credit limit now? Two years'
pay per person? Two and a half?"

"Something like that." Bardeen gave a quick, snorting laugh. "I
remember when a half-mil *was* big money."

"Me, too. And—oh, yes, for what it's worth, the kids don't have
the full amount on tap. Oh, they're not into it much: thirty-forty
thou, maybe. But—"

"Makes no difference; we could stretch it for them. Have to, in
fact. Couldn't expect them to live broke; right?"

"Yes, Mr. Bardeen. But the Board would need to approve that,
wouldn't they?"

"Theoretically, yes. In the Board's own sweet time; I'll try to
jack 'em up a little, tomorrow. But the next question is, how does
the ransom get paid? Because we have to get Troy back before this
turns into another Lassiter case."

"I know. The only trouble is, the bastards haven't said."

The kid was really kind of nice. So shy, and all; imagine,
couldn't even pee while she was there to watch. That was a laugh;
he was hung good, so why hide it?

Olive checked the time-numbers strip just above the Tri-V. An
hour, maybe more, before Clint got home. She looked over to the
kid: Troy-something, his name was. "Hey, Troy."

"Yes?"

"My name's Olive."

"Hello, Olive."

"Sure, hi'ya." She thought how to do this. "Troy, we're gonna
be together for a while, we oughta be friends. But you got to trust
me."

"Trust you how?"

"Well, I'm supposed to have your other hand tied, too, over
here *this* side the bed. But I forgot to while you was asleep, so if
you don't let me now, Clint'll be real mad when he gets home."

She waited, but he didn't say anything. "Well? You gonna?"

The kid's eyes squinched down narrow. "Real mad, you say? If
Clint got real mad, what would he *do*?"

Olive thought that one over, then said, "Beat the shit outa both
of us. What'd you think?"

For a minute she thought he wasn't buying it, but then he
reached his left hand up to the bedpost and let her tie it.

"Now," she said, "on account you're such a good kid and we're
friends, I'm gonna do you over, real nice."

It took some head to get him up, but then, when she straddled him, he stayed just fine. *Plenty* long enough.

And Olive hadn't worked on top since hell and breakfast. That damn *Clint* sure's hell wouldn't let her.

When she was done, Olive leaned down and kissed him. He didn't seem to be ready for that, yet; he tried to duck it. No hoohah; she climbed off and said, "I did shit you a little bit there, Troy. Hope you don't mind."

He looked spooked. As he said, "Shit me, how?"

Olive grinned. "Clint never said tie your other hand; I just made that up." Then she asked, "The main thing is, though—did you like it?"

His eyes blinked; then he said, "Sure. Why?"

"Then I don't need you tied up the next time. Right?"

Like usual, he never said anything right away. When he did, "Oh, I get it. No, of course not. Not either hand."

She laughed. "Don't try to shit *me*, sonny. The one stays cuffed; you have to know that much."

She untied the left, and brought him the bucket again.


Bardeen, Thane Cogdill thought, was handling the Board as well as he himself had ever done. Not necessarily better, mind you, but damned effectively. He hadn't been able to get Board approval to release the full ransom immediately, but a couple more days should take care of it.

Recovering from a mild bout of flu, Cogdill felt rather well. Oh, intellectually he knew that year by year he became less vigorous and more fragile. But the body itself doesn't remember or compare; how it feels today, good or bad, is all that counts. So, like everyone else, to himself Cogdill felt "normal."

After the Board meeting he arrived a little late for the four-person cabal: Bardeen and Fallon and Bennest were already there. Not hurrying, Cogdill poured himself half a shot glass of bourbon, and sat. "I miss anything?"

"Not much," Bardeen said; he looked to be handling the tension well. "Decided we did about the best we could with the Board, for now." A onesided grin. "And, next item—it seems that Moss Frantz was really a *busy* young stud."

"How many?" No need to specify the subject.

Dr. Fallon brandished a paper. "Repeated hypnosis brought the recalled number up. From twenty-nine to forty-three."

"And that's a final figure?" Cogdill asked.

"It's as far as we can take it, I think. The past few sessions, Frantz has been getting more and more suggestible, to the point that some of the data is self-invented." She made a dismissive gesture. "Moss is putting imagined material in with factual information."

"Making up women, to please the questioner?"

"Not yet," Fallon said. "All the ones mentioned so far are real. But starting with number thirty-seven, one of the three governing parameters is sometimes false."

Not bothering to ask out loud, Cogdill raised his brows.

"Oh. Name, description, address. On the last one, only the address was correct. But the woman lives alone, and showed only moderate surprise when she accepted delivery of flowers sent in Moss Frantz's name, so we assume she's legitimately on the list."

"But," said Bardeen, "it may not be worthwhile to push the kid's subconscious recalls any further, when we're already crowding the limits of accuracy."

"Yes," said Mareth Fallon. "We have to face the fact that no matter what we do, some Mark Ones may birth Mark Two babies. And probably will.

"So we'd better start thinking in those terms."

*The damned woman had* raped *me.* But it wasn't outrage that moved me then; it was the need to suppress laughter that might have gotten totally out of hand. I mean, if one were into bondage games, which I've never been, the onslaught of that grubby woman might be the ultimate thrill. And what with the strain and tension of being a captive complete with handcuffs, the "rape" came largely as comic relief.

Not to mention: appearances aside—which is to say that never in this world would I have *volunteered*—Olive gave a highly stimulating fuck.

Belatedly, worry hit: if she got pregnant, what would that do to the already touchy situation? A related thought, but more immediate: how far along in her cycle was she? Which brought up the real problem: even without an estrual nudge off the deep end, how long did I have left, in M-mode?

# XXI

The way Thane Cogdill felt was what he himself would call grumpy. Here the Board was demanding forty-eight hours' notice before giving an okay to pay any ransom over and above the dos Caras credit line. You'd think, Cogdill fumed, that Kennet would speak up and cut through all that red-tape crap. Instead, the man had drawn him aside and said to take it easy, not to worry.

Well, horse puckie! But just now, taking a seat for another four-way skull session, Cogdill resigned himself to paying attention to the Moss Frantz problem.

"Our worst-case plan," Bardeen said, "was to find ways of getting abortifacient drugs into every woman Frantz bedded. But with further thought, that seems like a bad idea."

"As near as we can tell," said Dr. Fallon, "out of his forty-three contacts, Frantz impregnated at least twenty-nine."

That, thought Cogdill, beat the odds a lot. But when he said as much, Fallon answered, "You have to remember—when most women go to those matchup bars, it's during their fertile periods." She shrugged. "Of course, some do go just for fun."

"Twenty-nine, though," Cogdill said. "That many, all in this area, can't help but point to us. Especially with that coprophage Jody Jay Tolliver, witch-hunting every day on Tri-V."

"Now there," said Erwin Bennest, "is where we've all been overreacting." Before anyone could interrupt, he said, "If all those children were born, how many would be seen by anyone given doctor? Damned few. In a city this size, the odds are very much against more than one apiece."

"Another thing," Fallon said. "I've considered the matter, and it strikes me that when the first Mark Twos were born, if we hadn't been *on the lookout* for anomalies, the vestigial, redundant sex organs might not have been noticed at all."

159

"So you're saying," said Thane Cogdill, "that we should let matters take their course?"

"Pretty much," Bardeen said. "Because Fallon's right; the deviancies are almost certain to get past your unwarned obstetrician. So it could be twelve or thirteen years before any Mark Two differences become apparent."

"And by that time, in this mobile culture," said Erwin Bennest, "the families might be scattered widely enough that nothing much will point back to this area, let alone to us."

Bardeen snapped his fingers. "It could help a lot," he said, "if these women or their husbands start getting job leads, from some of our diversified subsidiaries around the country, that could move them out into a widespread pattern. And as soon as possible—so that with luck, by the time the Mark Two kids hit puberty, a lot of the mothers may hardly remember just where they were started. Or attach any significance, at least."

The round of mutual congratulation ceased when Thane Cogdill slapped the table. "All well and good," he said. "But aren't you forgetting something?"

Bennest looked puzzled. "Such as what, sir?"

"At the very worst, we have eight months or so before the Frantz problem hits us. Troy dos Caras has less than one."

It was the third day, I think, before I saw anyone except Olive. Somebody else came in during my first full night there, though, because I woke to find another pair of handcuffs being put on me, this time around my ankles. It happened so fast, I had no chance to kick, or anything.

There was practically no light, and the other person left in a hurry. I tried to ask Olive what was going on, but she said to shut up and go to sleep, that we'd talk in the morning. When I kept asking, she threw cold water on me.

Actually, what with the heat in that place, the cold water felt fine.

In the morning I found that the new handcuffs were modified; the two cuffs were separated by a short length of chain. So that when standing, I could hobble along but only very slowly. What this meant was that now, instead of bringing the pail, Olive could unlock me from the bed and let me go to the bathroom.

Whenever I was unlocked from the bed, Olive had a gun near at hand. I wasn't sure it was loaded, but I didn't want to find out.

In her own way, Olive liked me; I knew that. But not enough to get Clint really mad. At least I assume it was Clint who gave her the spectacular black eye she was sporting, that morning. I had no idea *why* she was hit; she didn't say and I didn't ask.

So for that whole day and part of the next we went along, Olive and I, in a rather quiet routine. The footcuffs did ease the logistics, as Olive fed me, let me watch Tri-V if I chose (for the most part, I didn't), escorted me to the john when necessary—and fucked me more often than I really needed!

She got a great kick out of the new cuffs. When your feet are essentially tied together, positions become possible that you never would have imagined.

Unfortunately, so does the grade of soreness.

Eden had her phone fixed by now, but still she tended to hang out down the hall with Brad and Lyndeen. For comfort, she suspected. And because being pregnant and alone in the condo tended to get her jumpy.

Lyndeen made Eden feel comfortable, very much at home. Brad was all right, too, but he seemed anxious about something, and obviously was drinking more than Lyndeen liked. So the second evening, Eden begged off and went home early. She didn't think she could get to sleep, but come morning, couldn't remember lying awake long.

After Eden left, Lyndeen said, "Should we go to bed now? I'm tired."

Brad shrugged. In his left hand his glass tipped, rattling ice cubes but not spilling. "Pretty soon, yes. You go ahead."

Her eyes narrowed. "You want another drink, is that it? Or maybe two?"

He shook his head. "Half a one. A fill-up, just to sip on." She was glaring; he said, "Don't get on that, honey; it's not worth it. I need some time, is all. To think."

"Yeah? About what?"

Even getting mad, she was so damn *cute*! Brad grinned. "When I figure it out I'll let you know." He set the glass down. "Give us a kiss goodnight?"

"Oh—all right." And the hug was good, too.

Alone then, Brad punched up the phone directory, keyed for first initial H, and ran the list upscreen. He'd already checked, and knew Clint Haydock wasn't listed. But Josh, that was Clint's

dad's name. No Josh or Joshua appeared, but so many J's, singly or
with a second initial, that it would take too long to go through
them.

Besides, hadn't Brad's father told him, one time, that Clint's
had died? So now what?

Maybe the mother was alive. Her name—*Erma*, that was it.
The listing scrolled; no Erma. A lot of E's: *Now, let's see*—Erma
Lou!

There were eight E.L.'s. Brad got a male, a no-answer, an
Eileen Lorraine, then another male, before a crisp, no-nonsense
voice admitted that its owner was indeed Erma Lou Haydock.

"Yes," she said, after names were exchanged, "I remember you.
Your dad and my Josh were the best two on the shop bowling
team." That was nice, but—"No, Clint's not in touch. Six years
now, maybe more. He quit work, started back to school and quit
that, got into some trouble but drew probation." She cleared her
throat. "I'll tell you, Brad Salich. If you want to see Clint, though
I can't see why you would, you might call a man named Grego
Collins." She spelled the first name. "The last I heard, Clint was
living with the man's sister, I don't know her name for certain.
Down around South Eighty-ninth."

"Right. Thanks a lot, Mrs. Haydock."

"Sure. I hope it helps you, but don't bet money."


When I saw the three men walk in, I knew I wasn't going to like
it. The one in front—you can always pick out the sharpies, the
ones who feel they're either smarter than everyone else or less
burdened by scruples, so they own the world.

Even poorly dressed, looking very much down on his luck, the
man flashed arrogance. So that seconds before Olive said "Hello,
Clint," I knew which one of the four he had to be.

The one next behind looked like a copy of Olive, except made
by a sculptor who was falling-down drunk. The eyes were right,
and part of the chin, but none of the rest fit very well. But either
they had to be related, or else the gene pool was playing bad jokes.

So far, oddly enough, I hadn't felt too worried. Then I saw the
third man, and my gut changed my mind for me.

First sight wasn't much: medium-tall, skinny, shambling a little
but moving faster than it looked; big red hands with lumpy broken
knuckles, hanging loose at the sides.

Next, the red face. Hatchet jaw, downcurved mouth with no
lips showing, egg-knobby cheekbones with a raw-looking scar

along the left one, sand-colored hair over a narrow, bulging forehead. And the nose flat-bridged—a boxer's nose, battered enough that the cartilage had to be removed. Well, who says everybody has to look pretty?

Then, gleaming from deep pits under bushy, overhanging brows, I saw those pale eyes. Flicking from side to side, never still. And the right hand, hovering near where common sense said the man would keep a knife, twitched in synchronism.

Sometimes it's plain stupid *not* to be scared.

Clint took the comfortable chair. "How's it hangin', kid? Everything all right? You need anything?"

All right; play it straight. "Some clothes would be nice."

"Oh, yeah?" In a husky whisper, the gargoyle spoke. "You going somewhere?"

"Shut up, Amory." In a calm, weary tone of voice, Clint said it. Then, looking back to me, he nodded. "Clothes. Sure, you'll need some. Stand up."

"What?"

"To guess your sizes, dummy." So I turned the sheet back and left it on the bed. As I stood, Clint looked me eye-to-eye. "My height, or close enough. A little skinnier. Olive, get out some of my old stuff, that doesn't fit so good now."

"Sure, Clint." She went through the door where she'd gone to find the pail.

"Sit down." Clint gestured. "Wrap yourself up if you want." I shook my head; if clothes were coming, I could wait. "All right then, let's talk business."

When I didn't answer, because I had nothing to say, his voice rose. "What's the matter? You want to stay here forever?" I shook my head, and after a moment he said, "That Olive. She didn't tell you any part of it?"

I shook my head; he nodded. "Then I guess it's up to me."

Clint had to repeat himself a few times, because he was talking through Olive's comments as she fitted me with musty items of Clint's outdated clothing. But finally it came clear that these four people wanted five hundred thousand dollars before they'd let me go home.

Put like that, it sounds stupid. And of course it *was* stupid. But nothing to laugh about. Clint Haydock, no matter how virile a woman-beater he might be, didn't really scare me much. But

Amory Neill—I'd once read the perfect description for people like him: crazier'n a peach-orchard hog, and meaner'n a clubfoot wolverine in rut. He made my nape twitch.

Actually, I didn't learn their last names until later.


The young fellow, Troy, didn't faze easy. He didn't bat an eye about standing up naked. Then, with the cuff off one ankle so Olive could get drawers and pants on him, he seemed more interested in how the clothes fit than in what Clint was saying. When the talk came to the half a million, his face took on a funny look for a second, but that was all. Or maybe the look was because of Olive putting the cuff back on.

Here came the part Clint didn't have figured out too well, but he hoped the kid wouldn't notice. He said, "Now you need to tell me how those people are going to pay off, so it'll be safe."

Troy shrugged. "I wouldn't know. Nobody uses actual money these days, in anything like such an amount." At least, now he looked interested. "Why did you pick that particular number?"

Hell, it wasn't the kid's place to be asking questions! But Clint wanted cooperation, so he went along a little. "Because from what I hear, that's all we can get."

Troy nodded. "I think I know where that information came from. But not how."

"Not your business, either!"

Damn it! Clint wished Amory would keep out. This was no time, though, to bang heads. He waved Neill off, and said, "It's not your worry now, he means. What is, is how quick we can get that half-mil, so you go home free."

Troy shrugged. "Naturally I'd like to help, but we're talking about things I simply don't know." He paused, before saying, "Not all that money is available, by the way. Not quite. There have been other requirements."

"Yeah? How much?" Now *Grego* was asking questions. But it was what Clint would have asked, himself, so he let it go.

"I can't say, accurately. Not over fifty thousand, I'd estimate."

Kid so damned rich he didn't even *know* how much! Getting mad, Clint bottled it. "At least four-fifty thou loose, then?"

"Yes." For a moment his face got a stubborn look; then he said, "I don't suppose you care that this would wipe us out. No, I thought not." He shrugged. "I'll worry about that later, if I get the chance. I'd rather be over my head in debt than dead but solvent."

Suddenly his eyes narrowed. "Hasn't the Foundation told you any of this? And why haven't they offered any plan for paying you?"

"Uh—we haven't got back to them yet."

Looking scared for the first time, though Clint couldn't see why, Troy said, "Don't you think you'd better do that?"

"What I think," said Amory, "you better shut up."

When Mareth Fallon called him, it took several seconds for Bardeen to shift mental gears. Then he said, "Oh, Frantz, yes. I'd forgotten about that problem." The woman actually looked amused; what was going on? "Have you had any further thoughts?"

"I think I know how to keep Moss out of trouble. We'll have to wait for a time, of course, but—"

If her solution were one of the more drastic suggestions, she couldn't look so pleased about it. "What's your idea?"

When she told him, for some moments he laughed out loud.

What Clint needed to talk about next, the kid shouldn't hear. So he said, "Let's go," and knew Grego and Amory would follow. Troy wasn't cuffed to the bed, but his hobbles were on, and that should be good enough.

Olive left the damn gun lying loose too much, but that didn't matter either, because what she didn't know was that her loads were fakes: fancy blanks, built to look real. The thing was, give Olive a gun, she couldn't hit a bull in the ass with a shovel; what Clint never wanted was to be in the same place with her doing any shooting.

The fakes were just right for this job; she and Troy, they'd both think it was real loads. But if she screwed up so *he* got hold of the piece, he wouldn't have much.

Sure, you hit somebody in the eye, it's hello, Blinky. But any other place, no big hoohah.

Outside, Clint said, "Hey, Grego. That cousin of yours, the computer sharpo. He still out on the street?"

"Banshuck? Sure. Had to drop outa sight, though. Broke probation; you know how it is."

Clint didn't; he'd drawn probation only once, and lived up to it. And had been loose ever since: no strings, the way he liked it. "Out of sight, you say. Out of *your* sight?"

Grego frowned. "Hey. You wanna talk to Ban, just say so."

"I want to talk to Ban."

*   *   *

When they came back the next day, there were only Clint and Amory. Grego Collins, Olive's brother, wasn't along. By the time they came in I had pants on but no shirt or drawers; my ankles were free but my right wrist wasn't. Olive didn't think too well when the buzzer sounded from down below and she had to tidy up in a hurry; sure as fate, my unrelieved erection was going to seep juice and spot the trousers. Well, let it . . .

Someone had been coaching Clint; he seemed much more confident. When I asked if he'd been in touch with the Foundation, he grinned. "You mean their people? No; don't have to. Their computers, that's what I talk to."

"And did they give you good answers?" It was hard, dealing with this smug oaf, to stay clear of sarcasm; but I knew I had to. "Anything to help us get things moving?"

I'm no computer expert and never have been, but I doubt if Clint Haydock understood half of what he tried to tell me then. I said, "You use my code number to pull out our credit balance, Eden's and mine both?" He nodded. "You put it all into an account that doesn't exist?"

"Well, in a way it does. For a while, anyway."

"And you transfer it again, then cancel the temporary account and throw in a deliberate error that buries *its* name permanently."

He nodded. "Sounds about like what Ban said."

I said, "Then you're all set, are you?"

"Not quite. You need to come with us, now. To where there's a terminal we can use."

Yes. Because remote withdrawals over some figure—ten thousand, maybe?—require a thumbprint image. So they'd need me for that. Well, at least the knife artist hadn't realized how much simpler it would be, just to skin my thumb!

Before they took me out of there I was allowed a few more items of clothing, including undershorts. And to take a leak.

The punk didn't look rich but Clint said he was, so Amory figured to go along and see what dropped. He didn't much like this fancy stuff, all the computer whoop-de-doo; the way to do it was just *take* some pigeon's money. Sometimes they got pigheaded and tried to stop him, but that's what a knife was for, and those were the best times. After one of those, for a few days Amory didn't have the headaches.

Sure, Clint was right about not cutting the punk's slut, back when they made the grab. The way she was, pregnant and all, you really shouldn't. But the headaches were getting worse.

Maybe the punk would get pigheaded. Amory hoped so.

# XXII

Grego always *had* been a crazy sonofabitch, but he was Ban's cousin, and family should stick together. And he had to have something good going for him, because he'd never been tagged for that Springfield job, which had more loose ends on it than a scrunge haircut.

Ban could use some of that kind of luck, himself. He'd thought his data-net dip was airtight, but somehow he wound up doing nearly two years for it. *No damn justice at all!*

Now he was getting mixed up in one of Grego's deals, and even though Ban needed money like a junkie needs skag, he wasn't sure this was such a good idea. Especially when he saw the people Grego brought along. Ban was glad he'd got Ardis to go visit her mother; Ardis wouldn't like this kind of thing.

Grego was all right, of course. And Clint Haydock, the one who lived with Grego's sister, wasn't so bad: a little bossy sometimes, but not mean about it. Neill, though, the other man, didn't look to have all his chips wired in; Ban could have done without Neill for a long, long time.

With Olive staying behind to keep tabs on the door and phone, Ban led the others into the bedroom, where his concealed terminal was. The one he'd had before, the law took for evidence and never gave back. This one he'd put together himself, mostly out of parts from scrapped units. None of that stuff could be traced, which was good because Ban's parole said he'd better not be caught owning a terminal for the next four years.

But nobody scraps a unit with a main chip array that's even

marginally usable; he had to buy that assembly separately and by its right name—from a salvage house, which made it traceable. Ban used a half-assed phony ID that had come in handy before, but when he went back for a few extra minor supplies he'd found he needed, the clerk stalled him. So he figured his cover was shot, and left. He didn't know for sure that anything had been tagged to his real self, so as to blow his probation. But on the other hand he couldn't take the chance of checking in to find out. So one way or the other, now he *had* blown it.

Which was why he needed money. He'd been sent up on a state rap, not Fed. If he could get away from here—out to the coast, maybe, with enough bucks to float him until he found a tie-in someplace—well, technically his name would be on the overall fugitive list, but so far down it they'd never get to him.

He booted the rig up. "Okay, Clint. Tell me what you want, and for a fifth share I'll see if I can do it."

This Ban was a squat, round-shouldered man with mud-colored face and hair, not exactly what I'd call prepossessing. But the more he and Clint talked, Clint putting muscle into his voice and Ban responding always in the same quiet monotone, the more it seemed that the pudgy little man knew his stuff.

First, if I had it straight, he set up an account number with zero balance, the way you'd start any new account. "That's our decoy; the money'll sit there just long enough to confirm. When that happens, it goes to this next one." He programmed a second number, then something more. "Soon as we have *that* transfer, a glitch which I just set up goes into the first one."

"To do what?" I was every bit as puzzled as Clint was, but I stayed quiet; he did the asking.

"I threw in a dumb mistake, like people do every day, so that once the money's been and gone, I can't get to that account until somebody fixes it. But you see, I don't call in for anybody to *do* that. So without a complaint, the account sits there locked off; nobody ever knows it's there at all unless the number's assigned to another customer and a flag comes up; then they'd check, but too late."

Clint leaned forward. "How do you know the number's good?"

Ban gave a wheezy laugh. "Because when I punched it up, the system allowed it. If it hadn't, I'd cancel and try another one."

Amory was getting the fidgets. "Quit the gab and do it."

Ban turned to me. "What's the donor account number?" I must have looked blank; he said, "You and your wife, your number in this membership trust."

I shrugged. "I haven't the faintest idea."

Then I gasped, shrinking back, because Amory had one hand gripping my collar so I couldn't duck away from the knife he had at my throat. The hoarse whisper: "You better had, punk!"

"No, wait a minute!" Scared and trying to think fast, I began to explain. If Eden or I wanted to call in a transaction from our condo, our terminal automatically sent our personal identifying codes, which connected us to one of our own trust accounts: cash balance or credit line, whichever. All we had to do then (I didn't mention), was to feed in a confirmation word. Without that word, the net wouldn't cough up a nickel.

"But," I said, "*I* don't know those codes; I never need to use them." Maybe they were on paper somewhere at home, but I wasn't about to say so. Not to these people.

Amory hadn't relaxed his threat. Now Clint said, "Let the kid loose, Neill. Dead guys aren't much help." So the mad-eyed knifester pushed me away. But not as far as I'd have liked.

Now Clint and I were both stuck, for answers. Then Ban said, "Calling in from some other terminal, though; you must do that sometimes, don't you?"

I nodded. "But not for a long time now. I don't—"

"Relax." Ban didn't look all that relaxed, himself, but he still spoke calmly. "You call the Foundation, right?" On the terminal he did that. "Now you ask for the directory," and those listings scrolled slowly up the screen. "Membership trust, then *its* directory." He nodded. "Do you ask for the credit-line section now, or identify yourself first?"

Vaguely, I remembered. "Either way."

His fingers moved fast; I wasn't sure which move he made in which order. But then the screen read "Troy dos Caras. Joint account with Eden dos Caras. Available credit is now $471,268." I heard some involuntary, sucking gasps; then the screen added, "To initiate transaction, enter thumbscan and confirming code."

Well, this was it. Time for choice: either I gave these bastards every dime I (with Eden off work for a time) could earn over the next several years, or else I bet on Clint keeping Amory from cutting my throat.

It wasn't much of a choice. As Ban pressed my thumb to the

scanner, I said, "Enter Hagen. That's H-a-g-e-n." Picked for this application because I'd hardly forget my original surname.

Ban nodded. Then, as he worked, he began to whistle.

I didn't watch. There's not much, when it comes to causing depression, that beats watching a bunch of slobs take away a big chunk of your future at knifepoint. I felt so low that I even forgot to be scared. All I really noticed was that I wanted to take fluid at one end and needed to jettison some at the other.

Grego was closest; I tapped his arm. "Is there a bathroom around here? I need to go."

"Sure. Come on." So we went out of the room, past Olive who smiled and said hello but asked no questions, to the john. Grego let me go first before he took his own turn; then, moving to the kitchen, we ran the water cold enough to drink.

When we went back to the bedroom, something was going badly wrong there. I had no idea what it was, and before I could find out, I was down flat on my face and the gun went off.

Ban seemed to know what he was doing, so after Grego took the kid out for a leak, Clint didn't say anything; he just watched. When Ban typed in "Hagen" the screen asked what Ban wanted next and Ban poked up whatever it took to borrow $471,268. That's when the screen beeped, and displayed: "This transaction, plus others in process, will incur charges in the amount of $4,825. Available credit line is now $466,443. Do you wish to renegotiate loan (Y/N)?"

"Y, dammit." Ban's voice stepped up some, as he tapped the key then. Especially when the machine made him type the account number out all the way and then showed "Repeat confirm," which had to be stupid because if Ban knew the word once he still did.

Then, though, it looked like the whole thing was set up. The screen read "Loan approved, recipient account approved," and Clint waited for Ban to do the rest of the tricky parts and get all that money off to where nobody could find it in a million years, except Ban and Clint who put it there.

Reaching down to pull out some dope, Clint felt good.

But when Ban slammed his fist against the console, Clint stared up again at the screen. "What—?"

"Look, damn all!" When Banshuck did get around to yell, he was good at it. On the screen, Clint saw "—normal rollover period, dependent on size of loan. For amount specified, period is six days, at which time moneys will be transferred to recipient account." Blink-blink-blink, then: "Closure/acceptance: do you accept the loan as specified (Y/N)?"

Clint shook his head. "We can't. That gives 'em a week to *find* us, Ban, before you can ditch the decoy. We—I dunno—"

Ban looked around. "I just punched Yes. Even if they track us here, who says we have to *be* here?"

"But then how—?" Clint couldn't figure it.

"You all crazy!" Knocked sidewise to the floor by Amory Neill, Clint saw Banshuck's intestines, riding the edge of Amory's knife, slide out of his body, then come apart to gush fetor. A second stab brought blood like water from a hose. Scrabbling up on all fours, trying to get away, Clint heard Amory's feral panting coming at him from behind.

There wasn't any goddamned chance at all! Clint rolled over on his back, contracted his legs to pull his feet up to his chest, and braced to kick.

But a gun crashed. Amory's arms went wide, the knife flying off to one side, and Neill himself landed at an angle.

*Jeez! Grego shot his own cunt-man!*

Scrabbling out from under, giving not one damn whether Amory lived or died, Clint Haydock ran for it.

It was Grego who grabbed my hand and pulled me up standing. "Come on, we gotta get outa here."

My foot slipped, or I wouldn't have pivoted and looked back. There lay little Ban with his guts spread out around him; my own gorge bucked once but didn't spew. Amory had to be the killer, but he lay off to one side, face down. Maybe dead, maybe not.

There wasn't time to worry about it either way; I held to Grego's hand briefly, until we got to the front room. Then, with Olive along, we went downshaft and outside.

That's when I noticed that Grego's other hand still gripped the butt of a revolver. Once we got into Clint's car, the scent of the gun's firing wasn't all that hard to discern, either.

Not that I had it in mind to raise any awkward questions. Hell, we were almost back to Olive's place before I realized that if I'd had my head working even halfway, there had been all kinds of chances for me to get away clean.

My trouble was that although I'd viewed many adventure thrillers on Tri-V, it seemed I wasn't geared for them in real life.

\* \* \*

"Yes, Mr. Bardeen." Before he turned picture-send on, Erwin Bennest wiped sweat from his face. Then, pic activated, he said, "No, we don't have a fix on the terminal. It's an outlaw line, no way to trace it before they cut."

"What *are* you doing?" Bardeen's expression looked like "Get set to get fired."

But he hadn't pulled the trigger yet; Bennest said, "As we'd thought they would, the kidnappers asked for the entire credit balance. We approved, but the automatic rollover delay went into effect, and that's when they cut the circuit. So we don't—"

"You didn't put any holds on those things? Why not?"

*Nobody thinks of everything!* But he couldn't say that. Or maybe he should; there's a limit to how much you should try to cover your ass. Hell with it! "I thought we had. I was wrong."

Bardeen didn't answer immediately, so Bennest brought up his only new item. "About an hour ago, Intercept handed me a call that may give us some help."

"Tell it." Only a little, the Chairman's face relaxed.

"No picture, sir, and the man sounded drunk. He wouldn't give his name, but he said it was his fault that Troy dos Caras is kidnapped. Then there was a lot of talk that doesn't seem to make any sense at all; my people are checking it for leads, but I wouldn't bet much. One thing, though; he did mention a name."

Again, Bardeen looked meaner. "Is this a secret, Bennest, or do I get to hear it, too?"

"He said we should find a man named Clint Haydock."

"Then I suggest you do that. And get back to me."

The screen blanked.

Going through the city, Clint drove with furious efficiency. At first he said nothing; then, "Grego? Did you get Amory cold?"

I saw Grego shudder. "Dead? I dunno; we left too fast. Why, Clint?"

"Why? Comes to why, howcome it took you so long?"

I knew the answer, but it was Grego's place to tell it. "I just got *in* there, saw poor ol' Banshuck, his guts all over the floor. So I—" I could hear Grego almost gag, then swallow. "So the way it was, I had to blow Amory out."

Olive's chuckle sounded mean. "Should of done that a long time back, Grego. Except he was so nice and tight, eh?"

"*Shut up, Olive!* It wasn't like you think." Grego's face stood taut, features standing out; for the first time I saw him as something other than a lumpy caricature.

He said, "Amory and me, kids—you never knew him then."

"Sure didn't, and just as happy."

He struck her on the shoulder, not very hard. "You only saw him—hit in the brains too much, all the fightin'—then stabbed up the crotch." His face hardened. "Olive, don't you ever wish me to apologize for Amory Neill."

Before she could answer, assuming she wanted to, Clint said, "Save the reunions for later. Grego—do you know how to pull a terminal with all the plugs and cords it needs? And the boxes of other stuff, all that loose junk you slip in there?"

"Yeah, sure. But hey, you don't mean—"

"Sure as hell I *do* mean. Grego, once we get to Olive's place, you come up and have a drink, rest a little, get relaxed. But then you go back to Ban's and get us that terminal."

We were back to my prison. Belatedly I wondered why I'd lacked the sense to contemplate a possible escape. No point in belaboring the past, though; I listened as Clint said, "You just go get the terminal, Grego; I'll take it from there."

To my view, Grego had gone lumpy again. The man said, "What the hell you expect me to do about my cousin Banshuck? Or Amory, even. I can't just—"

Clint was pretty good with Loud; he said, "You just get that goddamned terminal out of there, with all its fixings. To bring here, and don't you forget that. *Then* you take care of Ban, which is too bad and I'm sorry, and Amory Neill if he didn't get away after all. What's best, I expect, is that you take along a little fuel and burn the place out."

Squinting, Grego nodded. "I see what you mean, Clint."

# XXIII

Duane Eads couldn't seem to sit still; he kept fidgeting. Not, thought Annek Getzlor, the way the perfect secretary should behave while giving his boss a weekly briefing. Well, if he couldn't handle the consequences, he shouldn't ask her to satisfy his masochism quite so much. Because when Getzlor got really excited, she could sometimes get carried away.

Being Number One in the FBI was the sweetest setup she'd ever had. Almost as good as she'd imagined it would be, which was, she knew, seldom the case. Shit oh dear!—without even working at it, she had nearly *everybody* running scared.

Now and again she found herself regretting the death of her stepfather, the death that put him forever beyond her reach. So that she could never do the things she'd promised herself, back when she was little and he wasn't.

She certainly couldn't do them to Duane. But pretending, occasionally, that an especially loathsome male prisoner under interrogation was Rolf Steig, and doing just a few of the things, helped some.

Now she said, interrupting, "Duane, do you have anything more on that Tri-V Religion Rat? The one in Cincinnati?"

"Tolliver?" She nodded. "Pretty much the same stuff, Annek." He grimaced. "*You* know—monsters, demons, and then his Phoenix Foundation fetish." Duane laughed. "Phoenix Foundation fetish—now wouldn't you say that's truly alliterative?"

She smiled; Duane *was* funny sometimes. "I might. Now then—Duane, have someone look through all of Tolliver's Tri-V stuff since he started that line of talk, and put together a disk for me. Just those things, none of the rest of his crap."

"Yes, of course. But why? Do you really imagine that behind all that paranoid gibberish the man has any facts?"

"I'm convinced he does. But not what he thinks."

Involuntarily, Getzlor shivered. *It's aliens, that's what!*

Moss Frantz menstruated and went M. He and Heath had four fairly sexy days together before she came to the same point and put them both into transition, Heath to M and Moss back to F.

Well, that was fine, too. The thing that worried Moss was waiting to learn what action the Feen was going to take against him, for giving so many Mark One females their very own little bundles from Mark Two heaven.

For several days Moss had no word at all, but then was called to Chairman Bardeen's office, where Dr. Fallon and the Security Chief also waited. After Moss took the offered seat, an older man joined the group; it took a moment, but then Moss recognized the previous Chairman, Thane Cogdill.

Bardeen led off. "We've considered your case, Frantz. You went to great pains to betray the Foundation in as many ways as possible. You—"

Moss interrupted. "No! I didn't *tell* anyone anything."

The old man nodded; when he spoke, his voice had an edge to it. "Right; he has you there, Kennet. Far as we know, the young puke did all his talking with his joystick."

No way to answer that; Moss waited, until Bardeen said, "If you're wondering what we're going to do to you, Moss, the answer is: nothing. Directly, that is."

The Chairman smiled, and in that smile was something Moss distrusted. "We're not letting you out of the Enclave again for a time; that's all. Until we're sure you can be trusted not to repeat your offenses." He stood. "I think we're finished here."

So Moss left, to tell Heath what had happened. Their life together continued in its usual pattern, with Moss now working at a respectable but minor job.

Waiting for the other shoe to drop, Moss was totally surprised by the shape it took. The time for menstruation came and went, but nothing happened; Moss was pregnant. Dr. Gill took the development as a matter of course, so Moss knew the answer: ever since this term of F-mode had begun, the oral contraceptives must have been fakes!

So Moss was cleared to go Outside again—along with Heath, who was now beginning to sprout whiskers.

No point in being angry. Actually, she rather admired the

Feen's trick; certainly it was the simplest way to ensure that Moss would impregnate no more Mark One women for a while.

*You win some, you lose some.*

Bardeen knew he overreacted to Jody Jay Tolliver on Tri-V, that he shouldn't let the man make him so furious. Jenny didn't like it; that was obvious. But he couldn't seem to help himself.

One Sunday he turned Tolliver off in mid-rant. "You know what really bothers me, Jenny?"

"Well, his attacks on the Foundation—"

"Those, of course. But more, that he spouts that crappy venom from behind a mask of false piety."

She frowned a little. "False? How can you be sure of that? Fundamentalists aren't necessarily hypocrites."

"They aren't necessarily vicious bigots, either. But this one is." He spread his hands. "Tolliver almost turns me against *all* religion, and I don't like that."

"Kennet, I didn't know you ever gave a thought to religion one way or the other."

"I don't, usually. And of course I've never been a churchgoer. But I'm not conceited enough to think there isn't Something bigger than we are."

"And if there is? I'm not disagreeing with you; I'm just curious, now you've brought the matter up, what you *do* think."

He felt embarrassed; he hadn't planned to get into his own deeper, seldom-sensed feelings. "Well—whatever it might be, I guess I feel we'd all have to be a *part* of it."

She smiled. "So what's wrong with that?"

"Just that I can't make people like Jody Jay Tolliver fit into the concept." Then he grinned. "Unless, maybe, I cast him as some kind of cosmic retrovirus."

Jenny laughed, and suddenly Bardeen felt much better. "So, what's for dinner?"

Once he got a cloth tied, one hand and his teeth doing the work, to hold a pad over the hole, Amory's wound didn't bleed much. What hurt most was any time his movements jarred the broken collarbone to grate the ends together. And maybe gouge the muscles there; he couldn't tell, but it felt that way.

At least it wasn't his knife hand.

There hadn't been time for Ban to start rotting; when he did, though, how could you tell? Ban wasn't the first one Amory had gutted, just the first he'd had to stay around and smell for such a long time. But his head was clearing now; he stood and took a few steps back and forth, feeling stronger and not so much like falling over.

When he heard somebody at the door, though, Amory wasn't ready for it. He staggered toward the back of the place before he remembered there was only the one way out; he turned, hearing the door open but still out of sight of it. Not for long, though, so where to go? No place left but that damn' bedroom. So stink or no stink, Amory Neill went into the room, stepped over Banshuck, and slid himself under the bed. He couldn't let himself puke at the stink, because that'd make noise. But when he banged his bad shoulder on something as he crawled under, he bit his lip clean through, to keep from yelling.

And then somebody was clumping around the place, doing God only knows what, for hell and forever. There was another smell now, besides the stink from Ban's opened guts; Amory couldn't figure what it was, and that made him even more nervous. It got so bad that if he could have jumped out and stood up to fight, hurt or no hurt he'd've done it. But trying that now, slow and crippled, he'd be cold meat.

So he swallowed blood from his lip, and waited.

Grego didn't want to go back to Ban's place. But Clint said do it, so Grego had to. Nobody said, though, he had to drive fast. Or couldn't stop off for a beer. That's why it took him nearly an hour, brooding on what he'd had to do and how he felt about it, for the twenty-minute trip.

The trouble was, Amory had gone plain nuts—killed Ban, and looked like maybe he wasn't done yet. So Grego shot. But he sure wished he hadn't had to do it. Like he'd told Olive, he and Amory went a long way back. Grego never got it on for men as a regular thing; he liked women and always had. But after Amory got hurt so bad, there was only the one thing would help him come, and Grego was the only one he'd let do it.

Well, either way—Amory dead or Amory alive—that was done with. Because, Amory alive would have just one thing on his mind. Killing Grego Collins. So Grego really hated it when there he sat in the car, and no excuse at all to sit any longer and not go into the building.

After he rode the elevator to the floor he wanted, he found

Ban's door unlocked. He listened—did he hear anything in there, or was it just loose noises from all around the building? Grego wasn't sure he was more scared it could be Amory, or the law.

Hell with it; gun in hand he pushed the door open and went in. Going through every room and seeing nobody except poor dead Ban, he went back into the bedroom and got to work on the terminal and its side gear. With the back of his mind jangling a warning: *where the hell* was Amory?

He felt a little dizzy, because he was using a trick his granddad had told him once, from back when the old geezer was bagging bodies in a two-bit war. You soak a rag in something strong-smelling and tie it around your face. Granddad had used gasoline; what Grego had was some kind of solvent, the stuff he was going to use to torch the place when he was done here. It kept him from smelling Banshuck, all right, but how much longer could he keep from passing out?

There was more of the computer stuff than he thought, too much for one load. Going out with the first one, after hanging the rag over the back of a chair, he pulled the door nearly shut but didn't latch it. Using the fire stairs just along the hall he went down fast. Once he had the box in the car he decided to take the elevator back up; it was only when he was carrying Ban's things that he couldn't afford to let anybody see him.

It looked to him as if maybe Ban's door was open more than he'd left it, so again the gun came out, but still Grego found nobody inside. He didn't seem to need the rag this time; maybe he'd breathed enough fumes to deaden his nose for a while.

Once he had his load together and was pretty sure it was all he needed to take, he carried it out to the elevator and set it down so as to keep its door open. He knew the smart thing was to use the stairs, but he was too pooped to bother. And if anybody tried to brace him, he had the gun, didn't he?

Then, moving fast, he went back into Ban's place, where he slopped the solvent around as far as it lasted, putting plenty onto Banshuck and leaving a damp trail toward the entrance.

One last look inside; then Grego lit a wad of paper, dropped it onto a solvent-soaked patch of carpet, and pulled the door shut. As he moved his booty into the elevator, before its door closed he heard and felt a dull boom; Ban's door shook but didn't blow out.

Once he had everything into the car, Grego drove back to his sister's place. Feeling damn glad the lousy job was over.

*  *  *

When whoever was messing around the bedroom finally left, Amory hauled himself out from under the bed. Grunting, wincing, he got all the way standing up and began moving toward the hall. Outside the door he started to pull it closed, but the move hurt too much. Hell with that; across the hall the light over the elevator lit, and he could hear it coming up. He went for the stairs-exit and got through it, out of sight, before the elevator dinged and stopped. As its door opened he looked back. To see Grego Collins step out and go into Ban's place.

Then Amory remembered. *Damn! it was Grego, shot me. My own fuckin'-buddy done it. Well, don't that beat shit!*

Against a gun, one good arm and a knife wouldn't do it. Amory waited until Grego left. He heard the muffled explosion and saw smoke coming from under Ban's door, so he didn't waste time there. The elevator was gone now; Amory went back to the stairs and made his slow way down them.

Fire stairs, no less. Amory didn't laugh often, but now, hurt or no hurt, he couldn't help it.

Fire in Ban's place. Fire stairs. And he knew where to find Grego. Might take him a while to get there, was all.

At least he wouldn't be having the headaches just yet.

All the time Grego was gone, Clint sat, saying little to Olive and nothing to me, while he smoked dope and drank gin. Not fast, but steadily. He had to be getting planked, but it didn't show on him.

Olive sampled booze and dope both, but lightly. She kept offering them to me, too, but I really didn't want any.

Finally, hoping I could get her to quit pushing, I accepted a glass of gin with orange juice. The gin tasted awful, the juice was going sour, and one ice cube wasn't enough. But now that I sat with a full glass, and had a token sip now and then, Olive had done her duty and was happy.

No one had thought to handcuff me to anything; I wasn't about to remind them.

When Grego came in, carrying a big carton that looked heavy, I glanced up as Clint said, "About time you got here!"

Grego set the load down hard. "Could have used some help, Clint."

"For that?"

"Just the first load. You want the other one, go get it yourself."

"You *left* it?"

"Down in the car. And far as I'm concerned, it can stay there."

"Not doing us much good that way, is it?"

"Too damn bad. I got the stuff over here and I'm pooped."

Haydock stood; if I hadn't seen him put the booze away, I might not have noticed the difference in the way he moved. "Aw, don't worry about it, Grego. Sit yourself down, have a drink. I'll go haul the rest of the junk up here."

While he was gone, and Grego broke out a tray of ice cubes that turned out to be not wholly frozen, I sat there trying to control my growing fear. Which is to say, I'd already survived a scene in which one man was knife-gutted and another shot. Maybe, just maybe, I'd used up the law of averages for that day.

The trouble was: all the while Clint and Grego were making noises at each other, neither could see the other's right hand. But from where I was sitting, I saw both.

And each of those hands was fingering a gun-butt.

Sanduk never did say exactly why he chose to leave Jody Jay Tolliver's service, but the fact was that he went. At first Jody Jay, making do with temporary help, missed him a great deal. For one thing, a part of the little man's job had been to bring in a Fallen Sister once or twice a week, for Jody Jay to bless overnight. Now, with Sanduk gone, the Reverend Tolliver was getting hard up. He was all out of practice at making those arrangements himself, and besides, it wouldn't be dignified.

What he finally decided was that it would be a better idea for him to be served by just one Fallen Sister, full-time. So he put the Reverend Floyd to looking around, among the Unregistereds in Floyd's parish so's there wouldn't be any embarrassing questions, for someone suitable. Being as Floyd had benefited more than not from the Lesa Pfluge episode and might well feel he owed one to the Reverend Jody Jay. Especially when reminded.

Well, blessed be the diligent if Floyd didn't come up with a Fallen Sister named Cora Sue Travis, who was quick to agree that the way to redemption of her misspent life would be to serve and minister to the Reverend Jody Jay Tolliver. Cora Sue wasn't bad looking at all, except for the acne scars which needed planing off, and if things went right, Jody Jay just might take care of that for her. On top of everything else, she had all her spare parts in the right bins. Which was to say, she could talk and make sense.

Cora Sue had a deep, impressive voice which the irreverent

might call a whiskey tenor but what did *they* know? When she stood up in those saffron robes, with the hood over her head and her hands hidden in the wide sleeves, saying *Om!* a lot because it fit good with this ecumenical movement that looked like a good thing, the Reverend Tolliver thought she did really fine.

One problem, though, was that her hair looked like old straw left over from the manger that birthed the baby Jesus, so she didn't look anywhere near her best with that hood turned back. Well, either she could wear a wig when he found a good one cheap, or shave smooth like a good ecumenical Buddhist nun. No hurry.

Because once Cora Sue got down to ministering, she was just the best Jody Jay had ever come across.

Even if she did pray with her mouth full.

One morning, though, she woke him up too early.

"Cora Sue, what is this? Something wrong?"

"It's a phone call, Reverend. Washington, D.C. The FBI wants to talk with you."

By the time Clint packed the other big box upstairs, he'd sweat enough to know he had too much of a load on. Time to bag the booze and dope for a while—until he got Grego squared away, at least. And then maybe he'd straighten Olive out, too, about having to stay moved out of her place until they got rid of this Troy kid. Well, sure; the dump was small and the bed too, but who said they couldn't put the kid in the storeroom, on the floor in a fartsack, and cuff him to the radiator?

Going inside, he used his shoulder to push the door shut, then set the box down beside the first one, out of the way. He caught himself reaching for his drink and instead went to the kitchen and fixed a glass of ice water. Some moron had broken out cubes that were half water, but this wasn't the time to ask who. Going back to the others, Clint sat.

"All right, Grego. How was it at Ban's?"

"Bad." Grego shook his head. "Never before smelt a gut-cut man. Ol' Ban—!"

"Ban, sure. I already said I'm sorry that happened. But how about Amory?"

"Never saw him."

Clint felt his own guts clench and heard Olive gasp, as he said, "He got away alive?"

"Had to've, I'd think."

Trying to figure some sense into things, Clint said, "Did you burn the place, the way I told you?"

"Sure did."

"Then that part's good. Now all we have to do is set this gear up and finish that loan, six days from now."

Olive said, "I thought you said that gives 'em six days to find us."

Clint laughed. "Not if we don't go on line until just when it's time to." His load of booze and dope was easing; he felt better. "No, Olive. Once we plug this setup together and hook it in—"

"*You* hook it in, Clint?"

"I know a guy who can do it. No need to tell him what for, so it's not going to cost us much."

"And that's it?" Grego was breathing hard. "You ain't even scared?"

Clint felt his face tighten up. "Not about that. One thing, though." The hell with ice water; he reached over and took a swig of his real drink. "Amory. When you shot him he was looking right at you. So he's alive and he knows who did it.

"And the crazy sonofabitch has been to this place. He knows how to get here again."

# XXIV

I didn't blame either man for being worried about Amory Neill. My first instinct had been that he had danger written all over him; what he'd be like now, nursing a wound from a man he'd thought he could trust, I didn't care to think about.

Neither, apparently, did Grego. "I *can't* go back to my room, Clint. What if he's there waiting for me?"

Clint, almost sober now, shrugged. "What's your gun for?" So a few minutes later, still protesting, Grego left.

I kept waiting for Clint to go also, but he didn't. He sat there, and talked with Olive about how they'd spend all that money—

Eden's and mine, which they didn't have yet—until she yawned and said, "'s gettin' late, Clint. See you tomorrow?"

He didn't answer; to me he said, "You want to go to the john, while you can? You've run loose long enough for today."

So I went, and when I came out again, he motioned me toward the room I hadn't yet been in. It turned out to be a dingy place used as a catchall, half full of miscellaneous furniture and cardboard boxes, with old clothes littering the floor. Clint rummaged in a closet, and brought out and unrolled a musty sleeping bag. He kicked some clothes aside and said, "Here, spread this fartsack alongside the radiator and lie down. Would you rather be inside it, or on top?"

"On top's fine. But why this?"

He motioned me down; when I complied, he cuffed my right wrist to the radiator pipe and said, "You've been screwing Olive, I expect. The two of you here alone, I'd be surprised if you hadn't. But not tonight, kid. Because I am."

On his way out, he turned the light off. Through the two dirty windows, dusklight left the room dim.

"The *FBI?*" Jody Jay couldn't believe it. "What in the Lord's sweet name could those vultures want with *me?*"

"He didn't say, Reverend. Just sounded in a hurry, like."

So Tolliver went to the phone. On the screen, the man looked like a type Jody Jay knew well: someone who had no real authority of his own, so he'd push his boss's to the limit. Accordingly, Jody Jay put on his best bless-you smile and said, "Good morning, brother. I understand you're calling me on the behalf of a government agency?" *But what does this shitkicker want?*

"FBI, Reverend. I'm Duane Eads, executive secretary to our Director, Annek Getzlor. And Director Getzlor would like to discuss with you your basis for accusing the Phoenix Foundation of consorting with demons." Eads cocked an eyebrow. "That is, I believe, the way you've stated the matter. Or have we misunderstood your statements?"

Oh, sweet Jesus! "What we speak of here, brother, is a question of scriptural interpretation, which in many cases does refer to demons and—"

"And monsters, I believe you've also stated."

"Monsters? Oh yes, monsters. Now you have to keep in mind, brother, that we have here what we call Biblical allegories which

an upright man such as myself believes deeply in one sense and—
well, but yet—"

Eads nodded. "But sometimes you hype it a little. Right?"

"Now I wouldn't say *that*, brother. I—"

"Just what *would* you say?" But a wave of the man's hand cut off
any answer. "Think about it. You have two days. Because that's
when Director Getzlor and I will arrive in Cincinnati to discuss
these matters with you. I suggest you keep all of Wednesday free
for our interview. And meanwhile, put in order what evidence
you may have, that confirms your accusations."

The screen blanked. Wiping sweat from his forehead and the
bare crown of his scalp, Tolliver yelled, "Cora Sue! Bring me
some of my tonic nectar. To my bedroom.

"And you come in there innocent and unrobed. Because I need
some ministering just now. Bless you, sister, I really do."


When Pidge Sutton retired from the Feen, he didn't even
consider returning to Earth. That was two years ago, four years
after his wife died. He hadn't remarried, but maintained an
occasional liaison with one of his former employees, a widowed
woman younger than himself but not embarrassingly so. Tonight,
though, Lyda had some overdue reports to get out, leaving Pidge
at loose ends. He decided to have dinner out.

The Rille Grille was a comfortable, medium-priced place that
drew quite a bit of Feen trade; maybe he'd run into someone to
gab with, have a few drinks. But when he got there, the people he
knew were all in paired groupings. He didn't feel like joining any
of those; he said a few helloes and was escorted alone to a two-
chair table.

Well, all right; company would have been welcome but he
didn't *need* it. He settled down to enjoy his dinner, and did so.
Food preservation methods were so good nowadays that he
wouldn't have known, by taste, what had been frozen (the lobster,
surely) and what hadn't (was the steak from a Feen subsidiary's
recently begun Luna-grown herd, or not?).

Either way, Sutton didn't ask. He'd progressed through the
meal, to the finale of coffee and brandy, when a man stopped to
stand across the table. "Mr. Sutton? Would you mind if I joined
you? There don't seem to be any vacant tables left."

Pidge looked up. The fair-complexioned man, young in
features but mostly balding, seemed familiar somehow, but no

name came to mind. Oh, well . . . gesture of welcome and "Please do, mister, uh—"

"Thurwald. Arv Thurwald, in Security." Sutton accepted the offered handshake. "I used to see you around now and then. But for quite a few years, until just recently, I was based at Farside North and covered half of the Earth-horizon stations."

Memory put blond hair on the man's head; identification clicked. "Oh, sure. Thurwald. Before Security, didn't you do surface tour guiding?"

"That's right." The talk stopped while Thurwald gave his dinner order. Then the man said, "It was an incident on a tour, a man lost out there and never found, that set my mind toward Security work. And about that, a very odd thing, Mr. Sutton."

"Oh. Yes?" Hell, it was going to be Memory Lane!

"Yes. Amos Calhoun, the man I mentioned, was lost back in 'ought-four, roughly twenty-one years ago. All that time the body lay not three hundred meters off the regular tour route, shaded most of the time and hidden among a clump of boulders nobody in his right mind would want to climb over. And just last week—" He paused, as his dinner was set before him. "Just last week," he resumed, "two days before I came back here on transfer, the body was found!"

"Well. Yes. Quite a coincidence." Trying to think of an excuse to leave quickly, Sutton waffled. "Interesting. Yes. But now at least your mystery's solved."

He was ready to make his excuses and get away, but Thurwald said, "Not exactly. You might say it's only begun. Because the man didn't die of accident or misadventure. It was murder."

Grego Collins hadn't had a phone for more than a year because he didn't pay his bill. But a fifty, shaken into the hand of an employee, got Brad Szalicz the latest address at which the local phone company listed him. No soap there; the landlord had no idea where Grego skipped to, also skipping two months' rent. But on the way out Brad met a wino coming in; for a mere ten, the woman gave him his next lead.

That neighborhood was even worse; Brad didn't like going so deep into Scum City, but what else could he do? So when the armed guard let him off the dilapidated bus he walked along blocks with few streetlights working, and pretended not to be scared by all the loitering punks, until he found the place.

It looked bad and sounded worse, but he went in anyway. The

manager was too stoned to make sense right away, but Brad kept asking until he thought he had it straight: third floor, turn right, end of the hall.

He climbed the stairs, walked the hall, and got there. But which *side*? Try the left; he knocked, no answer. Then, from behind he felt a hand on his shoulder. Turning, in the dim light he saw that the hand held a knife.

From the first glimpse he was glad he couldn't see the face better. The man said, "Lookin' for somebody?"

"I was. But I guess he's not here."

Brad moved to turn away; the knife stopped him. "Who?"

"Uh—Grego Collins. You know him?"

"I'm waitin' for him. Come on in; we can both wait." The man escorted him through the right-hand door, and closed it.

Inside, the only light came dimly from the bathroom. The man said, "Siddown, get comfortable. Sorry I can't treat ya; Grego's outa beer."

What surprised Brad was that he didn't feel panic; somehow the knifeman, acting as though this were a perfectly normal social occasion, set the tone. Passively, Brad sat.

The place smelled of staleness compounded over decades. Reflexively, Brad reached for a cigarette; as he got it out, he saw that the knife hand had risen; the weapon hovered. "Oh, sorry." He reached the pack out. "Want one?"

Headshake. "I quit. You go ahead, though."

Nowadays Brad didn't smoke very much. But waiting this way, he kept lighting one after another. It was when he brought out his fifth or sixth, here, that the other man used the knife to gesture. "Don't. Somebody comin'. Grego, maybe."

Brad knew the door wasn't locked, but he heard a key rattle at the slot. Then the door opened. Brad stood, ready to say something, but the other man moved past him, gripped whoever was coming in and slung him across the room to crash against a wall and slump to the floor. "Hello, Grego. Surprise?" He moved to bend over the prostrate man; Brad heard cloth being ripped.

"No, Amory! Don't do it. Please! I didn't mean—"

"You shot me, Grego. Say goodbye to bein' a man."

"No!"

Brad saw the knife arm start to move; without thinking, he grabbed a dimly seen object from a table. It felt heavy enough; he crashed it down on Amory's head. Once, twice, then a third time, until Amory made a coughing groan and went down flat.

Grego was trying to get up; Brad caught a hand and pulled him to his feet. "You all right?"

Fussing at the ripped crotch of his pants, Grego said, "Cut a little; there's blood, but not much. Sonofabitch didn't get the family jewels."

"Then let's get out of here!"

Grego held back. "First I *kill* that shit!"

Before he saw the gun, Brad spun Grego around. But by this time the gun didn't matter. "Like hell you do! I save your balls, and you want to make me a murder accessory? Come *on!*"

After a pause, Grego nodded. "Awright. Where we goin'?"

He sounded punchy. Brad said, "Out of here, catch a bus, get where things are halfway sane."

Out in the hall now, heading for the stairs, Grego said, "Don't need no bus. I got a car."

Having Clint back wasn't too bad. He took longer at it but Troy could do it again quicker; which was best, Olive didn't care because either way it went, she liked it.

Clint had her a little sore, though. Not bad, just enough to get up and use some lotion. And while she was in the john, take a pee so she wouldn't wake up needing to.

Then, when she washed her hands, she saw the trap under the basin was leaking like all hell. Well, the bucket was there, that she'd given Troy for a pottie that first day; she set it under the leak and reminded herself to get Clint to fix the leak pretty soon. Or have Grego do it; Grego was better with tools.

When Eden answered the chime and opened the door she was surprised to see Moss Frantz and Heath Crawford. "Well, how *are* you? Come on in." As she brought out some finger food and set up tea, then offered the choice of brandy or liqueur as accompaniment, she had time to look more closely at her guests. Moss hadn't changed very much—not yet, anyway—but the upper lip of black-haired, blue-eyed Heath showed an appreciably heavy shadow.

Eden giggled. "That can't be a fake mustache, Heath. Moss, you have to be pregnant!"

Moss Frantz grinned. "They sandbagged us, the Feen did. Could have done worse, I suppose; Lord knows, I'd done my best to undercut their secrecy program. But they settled for this."

Leaning forward, Eden said, "Then you've dropped your campaign?"

"Hell, no," said Moss Frantz. "Just postponed it."

But then Moss and Heath put the talk to Eden's own concerns. When they'd left, she did feel somewhat comforted. Nothing had changed about Troy's predicament, but it was nice to have friends who cared.

It wasn't much of a car, but it did start. As it chugged along the street, Grego spoke. "I guess I owe ya. What you doin' there, anyhow?"

"I need to find Clint Haydock. His mother said you might be able to help."

Grego laughed. "You can't find him but you find *me*? Goin' the long way round, man." Pause, while the car's engine made strangling noises. "What for, do you want Clint?"

"Just to talk. We used to work together."

"On one a them *big* jobs he talks about?"

*Now what's that supposed to mean?* "No, just the regular kind of thing." *Don't say any more.*

"Never knew just what that was, with Clint." They were out of Scum City now. Grego said, "What name do I tell Clint?"

"Never mind; he'll recognize me."

"Wrong. First I tell him your name; *then* he decides, meet you or not."

*Damn!* The whole thing was getting away. After he'd done all that tracing, gone deep into Scum City which scared him shitless, abandoned all caution to clobber the crazy knife artist and save Grego's manhood for him, this stubborn moron had his back up and wouldn't play ball.

There had to be a way, and suddenly Brad saw what it might be. Grego's gun, stuck into his belt, was sagging almost out of it. Right where Brad could reach it, so he did. And used it to prod ribs. "Grego?"

"Hey! Wha'cha think you're doin'?"

"Pull over and stop." Done. "Now leave the keys and get out." Grego climbed down and stood there.

"This ain't gonna find you Clint."

"It will if you want your car back. Do you?"

"Well, sure. But how—"

"Either you take me to Clint or you walk."

Shrug. "So I walk."

And he did. *Now* what the hell?

Brad drove Grego's car home. It didn't exactly fit the image of the condo's security parking lot, but so what? Maybe tomorrow he could think of what to do next.

At least Lyndeen seemed happy to see him home sober. He didn't tell her where he'd been, and she didn't ask.

I couldn't sleep very well. I didn't like the room or the sleeping bag or any of it. And counting back, I knew I was several days past normal expectation for transition to F-mode. I knew that sometimes M-mode could be stretched by exposure to non-estrual female pheromones—and with Olive, that was certainly what had been happening. But now I was cut off from those.

So how much more M-time could I possibly count on?

No, sleep wasn't easy to come by.

"Tri-V?" Irritated, Bardeen said, "Thane, we're already working late. Why do you want me to stay longer and watch the Trivia? We could disk it, and then watch some other time."

Thane Cogdill cleared his throat. "Actually, Kennet, this item *is* on disk. Come to my office and give it a try?"

So a few minutes later, seething inwardly but giving the older man his full dues in courtesy, Bardeen watched as one and then a second episode of an unfamiliar Tri-V show came onscreen.

Its title was *Robin's Ways*; the story line, peripatetic as usual on the Trivia these days, featured a character named Robin Winkhood, who—with great charm and whimsey—helped people, redressed injustice, and was in general too good to be true. But that, Bardeen figured, was the kind of crap the public wanted.

He was close to telling Cogdill he'd seen enough, when he realized he wasn't sure whether Robin Winkhood was male or female. Then it hit him: both. In some parts of an episode, male; in others, female: the changes almost subliminally subtle.

The second episode hadn't finished yet, but Bardeen said, "All right; cut!" The screen blanked. "Tell me about it?"

Cogdill gave his shark grin. "You don't read my memos, Kennet. I'm on Paige Barnard's distrib list."

"Who?"

"U. S. Archer's current Cabinet Secretary for HEW. And"— waving off Bardeen's next question—"they're worried, down in DeeCee. More than ever, that is."

The ever-tilting demographics of the Baby Drought, the

increasingly painful economic results and growing resentment of those consequences—none of that was new. But now Cogdill said, "It's half-past scapegoat time; that's what Barnard thinks. And a scapegoat is anyone who's *different*."

Suddenly understanding, Bardeen stood. "*You* set up this show? Who are you going to get to air it? And how?"

"Public Service Cable Net; I bought us a slice of it. With your authorization: a memo you may have initialed without reading it. These pilot episodes—"

"Yes." Bardeen nodded. "Your syrupy, incredibly lovable lead—the writing's godawful but the acting saves it—is basically a Mark Two. Right?"

Cogdill nodded. "Of course. The trouble is, we should have been doing this fifteen years ago. But—"

"I know," said Bardeen. "We didn't think of it, then."

"No." Thane Cogdill nodded. "Because we had no idea how dangerous the climate of opinion would become."

"Yes," Bardeen said. "It's scary as hell. And this propaganda effort is going to take months, maybe years, to defuse all the paranoid intolerance that's going around."

He shook his head. "Troy dos Caras doesn't have that much time."

"Murder?" This could be interesting; Pidge Sutton decided to stay and listen. "What makes you think that?"

After chewing and swallowing a bite, Thurwald answered. "Well, three things. Item: the helmet was dented by a rock, which bears metal traces. I estimate that to make such a dent, the rock would have had to fall more than a hundred meters, not the ten or so that the nearest crag rises. Item: supposedly the rock also tore loose the suit's comm antenna. But the lengths of broken wire don't match; the antenna we found isn't the one that belongs to that suit. Item: it *could* be happenstance, but the body was awfully well hidden. Good enough, so far?"

"So far? Then there's more?"

"Considerable. Amos Calhoun wasn't a nice man. In what was left of a sealed pouch—you don't want to know the condition of the body after twenty-one years in an airtight, moisture-tight suit—we found a notebook. Quite a lot of the notes could be deciphered. Calhoun came here to kill someone." Before Pidge could speak, Thurwald shook his head. "We don't know who; he referred only to 'the target.' But he had a picture of that target.

Unfortunately, exposure to the juices of decomposition have stained and blurred the image. But once we bring the old computer's files back on line, we should get an ID. Because it will have to be one of the people who took that same tour, and also got out at Area Two."

"If the man intended to kill someone, his own death could be a case of self-defense."

Thurwald picked up his fork, then set it down again. "If the other party had reported the matter, rather than trying to hide it, yes. This way, though, a murder charge is automatic." He paused. "Would you like to see the picture?" Sutton nodded, and the Security man brought out a small rectangle of plastic. "The original was coated photofoil, but still it corroded to some extent."

Accepting the picture, Sutton gestured thanks. Then he looked at the blurred, discolored image.

He cleared his throat. "Not much to go on, is it?" Hoping his face showed no reaction, he handed the picture back, then stood. "Well, thanks for all the information. Maybe you could let me know how it comes out." Walking first casually and then faster, he left.

If he hadn't known the timing of Amos Calhoun's being lost on the surface, the picture would have told him nothing. But he remembered, quite clearly, that in a period of several years straddling '04, only Calhoun had gone missing.

Without those facts, Pidge would never have recognized the man in the picture as Kennet Bardeen.

# XXV

From the living room, raised voices woke me. I could hear Grego arguing something and Clint saying "No" a lot; Olive kept trying to get a word in but no one would let her.

I waited for a pause, moments of something approaching quiet, before I rattled the handcuff as hard as I could, against the pipe it encircled. And when that move brought no response, added some yelling.

I hardly expected Clint to come in friendly; he didn't disappoint me. "What the fuck do *you* want?"

"To pee in the john, not on the floor. All right?"

"Yeah, I guess so," and he unlocked the one cuff. That was Clint for you; peeing was something he understood. So he let me go into the bathroom, where I was true to my word. The drip from under the washbasin, into a bucket, made good punctuation.

When I came out, Clint took me to the storeroom and hooked me back onto the radiator pipe. Grego and Olive were there, too—he rummaging into a dusty tool kit and she standing over him. "That damn leak's driving me crazy, Grego. You gotta—"

"All *right*," he said. "This here wrench oughta work, if the pipe ain't ate through and don't bust." Olive was still talking; he turned to her. "Now shut up and let me *do* it."

As they and Clint left the room, I felt like kicking myself. Because the tool kit had been sitting against the wall, half-covered with some old canvas, so close that I could have hooked one foot around behind, and nudged it near enough to open. If only I'd thought to do that.

But with the canvas over the kit, it looked like some dumb tin box, not worth investigating.

The hell of it was: on the radiator pipe, the wrench would have worked just fine. And still could. Except that Grego didn't bring it back.

The kit was farther away now, but it was open. When a good while passed and nobody came in, I hooked the front of my left foot over one side of the kit and began pulling. The thin metal edge hurt my instep, but with little jerks the kit moved across the floor until I could get a hand on it. Then I looked inside.

When Bardeen answered his office phone, no picture appeared. "Bennest, sir. I think you should listen to our friend here who doesn't want to show his face. He's not hearing me now, by the way, and won't know you're on the line unless you tell him."

"All right. This is important, I gather. So go ahead."

"Yes, sir." Then Bennest's voice changed; he'd been talking to his superior and now he wasn't. "Sorry for the delay; you know how it is. Now, you were saying, Mister . . . ?"

"Never mind that." The tone sounded like a man under strain. "I have information about Troy dos Caras."

"And you're asking how much for it, Mister . . . ?"

"Not a damned cent! Now shut up and listen."

Bennest did; the other man said, "Here's what I know. . . ."

"Clint Haydock, yes; he's the leader." As he described Clint, Brad couldn't get his hands to stop shaking. "No, I don't know his address; the only location I have is for one of the others: Grego Collins," and after giving the address he described Grego also. "He carries a gun." Well, maybe Grego had found himself another one by now. "Then there's a hatchet-faced gargoyle with a flat nose; his first name is Amory and he uses a knife. But that's all I can tell you, so—"

"Don't cut this circuit!" A new voice, now. "If your information helps us, you're in line for a reward. But not if we can't find you." Brad tried to talk but the other man overrode him. "I don't care if you're a goddamned *accomplice*; if you help save that kid I guarantee amnesty. So who are you?"

As if they could see him, Brad shook his head. "I can't tell you. And I don't want your reward." *Click.*

The stupid part, he thought, was that he and Lyndeen needed money in the worst way. But not *that* money.

"Well, you gave it the best try," said Erwin Bennest, and now he appeared on the Chairman's screen. "So now—"

"So now," Bardeen said, snapping the words out, "you'll be wanting to get the hell off here, and onto those leads." *Click.*

Bennest was a good Security man, but this wasn't the time to poop around exchanging pats on the back.

From the rumors about Annek Getzlor, Jody Jay Tolliver expected some kind of glowering stereotype of a bull dyke. But as Cora Sue escorted the woman and her attendant into Tolliver's study, Jody Jay caught his breath in surprise. Slender and of medium height, Getzlor gave a first impression of delicacy: her patrician features, arched eyebrows, and short fluffy grey hair (with a dark streak dyed back from one side of the forehead), almost disarmed the Reverend Tolliver.

But then she spoke. "Tolliver? I'm Getzlor, I suppose you know. And this is my secretary, Duane Eads." Inside himself, hoping it didn't show, Jody Jay cringed—for the soft voice held a nascent edge, and facing the stare of those unwinking slate-colored eyes was like looking into two gun barrels.

His voice performed without conscious direction. "Charmed, I'm sure, Madam Director and—uh, sir." Without his boss, that one was no threat; Jody Jay knew a barnacle when he saw one. "Now before we start talking, can I have Cora Sue, here—" She hadn't left yet, though she damn well should've. "—have her get you something? Coffee, like, or whatever?"

"No, thank you." As Getzlor sat in Jody Jay's own chair, leaving him momentarily adrift, she said to Cora Sue, "Go someplace. We'll call you when we need you." And to Jody Jay, "Sit *there*," which was the chair he put other people into when he wanted them to be uncomfortable and have to look up at him.

Well, he already knew, beforehand, this wasn't apt to go good.

When Amory woke up with nearly the worst headache he'd ever had, first he looked through Grego's place for anything he might want to take with him. There wasn't much; a little ol' beatup shoulder bag out of Grego's closet held it all. So then Amory started to fix Grego's rooms and everything in there. He did it first with his knife and then throwing things at other things, but that got to be work and his bad arm started hurting.

Then he remembered how Grego had fixed his own cousin's place. There was some rotgut vodka that Amory had put in the bag, figuring to take it with him. But now he made a grin that hurt the side of his face where the other creep had hit him when he tried to look around, and he poured the vodka all over Grego's bed, and stacked stuff on top and every place else he could.

Then he lit a whole wad of paper until it was burning good, and tossed it right in the middle of the bed, and backed away from the WHOOM when the flame took off, and walked out of there. When he was about two blocks away, the firefighter tank came past him, going hell for spit. *That's right, earn your money.*

Amory felt sad. He was going to have to do Grego, because Grego had it coming. But then Amory wouldn't have nobody. Nobody at all.

On the screen, Pidge Sutton didn't look as much older as Bardeen would have expected. Actually he hadn't thought about Pidge for a long time, probably not since he'd sent a gift in honor of the man's retirement. He did remember that Sutton had opted to stay on the moon, but little more about him. So now he was more surprised than not, to receive a rather expensive call.

Another surprise was Sutton's using 3-A Scramble on a private call to Bardeen's home, not over Feen circuits; maybe the call's content would clarify the reasoning. As the Scramble validated itself, the image said, "Kennet? Take the greetings and good wishes as read, will you? Something's come up."

Wouldn't you know it? In the entire gaggle of miscellaneous tools, the only thing that could handle the coupling on the radiator pipe was the Stillson that Grego Collins had taken. What I found was a few screwdrivers, two pairs of pliers that wouldn't begin to stretch wide enough, a couple of chisels, a ball peen hammer, and a number of wrenches: open ends, box ends, three Crescents—nothing that could grip anything over an inch in diameter, and the coupling's octagonal screwdown collar measured at least an inch and a half.

Oh, I could have opened the coupling, all right—if the three in the other room were stone-deaf or I knew they'd be away for at least an hour. Simple: hold the chisel at a proper angle to any octagonal face and pound with the hammer so as to put some torque to it. The handcuff left enough reach that I could have positioned the chisel, all right. And although I'd have my wrong hand free for the hammer, if I kept at it long enough the thing would unscrew. Or maybe use hammer and chisel to break the collar apart; that could work, too.

Sure. Hey, folks; why don't you all go out for a good long dinner? It's on me . . .

Because even if I got loose from the pipe, I'd have no hope of breaking out past Clint or Grego. Other things being equal we Mark Twos carry more (proportionate) muscle than Mark One females but less than their males; between F and M modes, our muscle tone doesn't vary enough to notice. But whether due to that factor or merely to the overall climate of attitudes in the Feen Enclave, none of us had ever trained, to speak of, in the martial arts.

At the moment, handcuffed to a grimy pipe and sitting on a dirty sleeping bag, I found myself wishing we had. But it was a little late to start over. Hearing noises from the front room, I did a few things rapidly: the hammer and one chisel and two screwdrivers went under the sleeping bag; maybe they'd come in handy and maybe not. Then with both feet I pushed the tool kit as nearly as I could guess to where Grego had left it. When Clint came into the room, I pretended sleep.

First he walked past me and closed the tool kit, then shoved it against the wall—and now it was totally out of reach. Then he came over and nudged me with his foot. "Hey, kid. Do you want something to eat?"

I sat up. "I guess so."

"Then come on."

He unlocked the cuff; I stood. "All right if I hit the john first? It's been a while."

"Sure. But step it up." So I went into the bathroom. The bucket still sat under the trap, but the leak was fixed. Grego must have made quite a mess, though, doing the repair; the bucket was surrounded by a pile of soggy towels.

After I'd urinated and rinsed my hands, I looked for a towel that might be halfway clean. When I picked up my best choice, I saw something that had been hidden under it.

The handle of the Stillson wrench. Without thought, I slid the wrench down inside the front of my borrowed slacks. To keep it from slipping down and away, I hooked the jaw over my belt. And to hide everything, pulled my shirttails out.

Sitting down at table with Clint and Grego and Olive, I wasn't hungry for food of any kind, let alone a plate of greasy fried fish. But as best I could, I faked it.

Rather soon Grego wiped his mouth and stood. "I gotta go check my place out, see if Amory's hanging around there."

"And if he is?" Clint's laugh had a real sneer to it.

Grego cocked a finger. "Hey, I'm no dummy. I'll send up a scout first, some kid from Angelo's on the corner. He comes back, I ask him some stuff." Grego nodded. "Amory's in there, I don't go, is all."

"The gun isn't enough?" Clint was really putting the other man down. I couldn't see why; maybe it went back a way.

"I—" Grego shook his head. "I guess I left it someplace." Then saying nothing more, he walked out.

I'd faked appetite, all right. But what couldn't be faked, I realized a little later when I was once again shackled to my assigned radiator, was that M-mode was starting to phase out. Without the estrual trigger the change would be more gradual, but it had begun; there'd be no stopping it.

And I could *not* let these people learn our secret.

It struck me that if I didn't find a chance to escape, I'd swiped the wrong tools. Because committing suicide with a ball peen hammer might be quite a trick.

\* \* \*

The three-second transmission lag, waiting for Pidge Sutton's answers, stretched Bardeen's nerves to their limits. First he asked, "What's come up?"

Eventually Pidge said, "They found Amos Calhoun."

It took Bardeen a time to recall who Calhoun had been. When he did, he paused. And then decided that if 3-A Scramble couldn't be trusted, he was down the flush anyway. "What else did they find?"

Wait. Then Sutton told him that Calhoun had carried notes detailing plans for committing an assassination. "No name given, but he had your picture. It's stained and corroded, but sooner or later Security will make ID on you." Pause. "You always treated me right, Bardeen. I just wanted to give you warning, for what good it might do."

"Yes. Thanks, Pidge. I appreciate it." He was going to say give his best to—but first he couldn't recall the wife's name and then he remembered that she'd died. So he said, "You ever come down here to Heavy Country, everything's my treat."

After the time lag: "Well, sure; that's why I want to keep you healthy. Right, Kennet?" A laugh. "So long now."

As the screen dimmed, Bardeen thought, *Now that I know, what in hell can I do about it?*

The beatup clunker, out of place in the condo parking area, made waves. Brad saw people looking at it, imagined them making calls to management or even to the police. At first he didn't dare go near the car. But when on the second day he saw a Warning notice on its windshield, late that night he went down to ground level and drove the thing away.

*Now what?* By the flickering dashboard light he checked the indicators. If the fuel gauge was reading straight he could get the damned bucket well away, ditch it and come home by public transport. Or maybe—just wait a minute!—the gun was under the seat where he'd left it. Maybe he should visit Grego. Maybe this time Grego would listen to reason.

Thinking back, Brad thought he could find the place.

When he got there, though, and went inside—leaving the car a block away in an alley—what he found wasn't exactly what he expected.

Angelo's wasn't the same; maybe Grego'd stayed away too long. Used to be, a cap or a load could get you any errand you wanted.

Now, though, Grego offered and the kids couldn't bother. Somethin' wrong here; he looked around, didn't see anything he could use, sat down on a corner stool and went to pop a cap for his own good.

But another hand caught his; he turned to look. The kid was a girl, skinny, maybe fourteen, dark brown paint done in heavy swirls all over her bare scalp to look like some kind of fancy hairdo, but it didn't. She said, "Spare one of those?"

*Now*, maybe! "Depends. You do me somethin'."

"Sure. Any hole I got. All straight though, paisan!—no burns, whips, stuff like that." Her eyes widened. "Deal?"

Feeling pushed offbase, Grego shook his head. "None a that shit, kid. All I want—" He paused: how the hell—? "I just need a message took up to a place, then you come back, tell me was anybody there and what they say. You do that for me?"

Narrowed eyes, then a nod. "Yeh sure. Two caps?"

"Right." He wrote the note, then the address. "Go now."

But on second thought, Grego decided to follow his scout.


Brad shook his head. Someone had trashed this place terminally; the axing of the door was probably the latest and least of it. Looking around behind, in the nervous way this area made him feel, he decided: having come all the way down here, he wasn't leaving before checking the whole thing out.

The gun at his belt helped his confidence, but still when he was checking the grimy, stinking bathroom and heard a noise in the main room behind him, he jumped a little. As he turned around he grabbed the gun; on second thought he held it down at his side and back out of sight. Then, carefully, he peeked around the edge of the doorframe.

*Hell, it was just a kid!* He said, "You want something?"

She shook her painted head. "Not if it bothers you." She looked around. "You do all this yourself, or somebody do it *to* you?" Before he could answer, she held out a piece of paper. "This is for you, I guess." As he took it, she backed away and went out the door.

Unfolded, the paper wasn't easy to decipher. Stumbling over misspellings and barely legible printing, Brad read aloud, "Amory we got to talk I didn't mean to shoot you there's a lot of money in this and part yours so be—" "Reasonable," he guessed the word was supposed to be; then, just "Grego."

"That's me. What *you* here for? Wreck my place, did ya?" And there, just inside the shattered door, stood Grego Collins.

Meaning no threat, Brad gestured with the gun. Toward the mass of soggy, charred rubble where the bed had been. "And put the fire out with piss and a coffee cup? That mess has been there a while." At Grego's nod, Brad said, "I don't know anything about this. I just—"

Grego gestured. "I do. Amory, it must of been. You showing up here, though—"

"I brought your car back. Your gun, too, if we can work a deal." He spread his arms. "I just want to *talk* with Clint."

"Well, I might—" But behind Grego, Brad saw movement; he heard a wet-sounding thud, and watched as blood came from Grego's mouth and the man crumpled to the floor. Without thought the gun moved to cover the man behind Grego.

Amory Neill's knife didn't look as bloody as Brad would have expected. Nonetheless, all the while looking Brad eye-to-eye, Amory stooped to wipe the blade clean on Grego's jacket.

Then he stood. "You conked me, Jojo." Seeing the livid rawboned face, Brad couldn't answer; he tried to hold the gun steady, as Neill said, "I should oughta take you out for that. Except, maybe—" His lopsided smile, then, had an obscene look to it. "You said you got Grego's car here; gimme the keys." Brad hesitated. "You don't wanna make me take 'em."

So Brad handed the keys over. Amory said, "You buddies with that goddamn Clint?" Headshake. "Awright then. Here's where the fucker's been stayin' . . ."

For a time, after Amory left, Brad waited. When he caught a bus some blocks away, he realized he hadn't ditched the gun.


Awakened from an afternoon nap by Bardeen's call, Thane Cogdill adjusted his phone to Scramble 2-B and tried to understand what the man was saying. "Found who? On the moon, you say?"

Kennet looked agitated, but he kept his voice even. "Amos Calhoun, the man I killed there. You remember."

Thought ran slower these days, but memory did come. "Yes, of course. And now, after all this time—?"

"Yes." Then the information came fast; Cogdill nodded, and Bardeen wrapped up with, "So they know he was there to kill somebody, and Pidge says that sooner or later someone will identify my picture that was with Calhoun's notebook."

"The possibility does seem reasonable. In that event, what are your plans?"

Bardeen grimaced. "I thought *you* might have some ideas."

Cogdill thought about it. "Calhoun tried to kill you, didn't he?"

"He sure as hell did! But this late, having run away without reporting the assault, I can hardly plead self-defense."

"Of course you can. And if it comes to that, you must. But first, I think you should have our attorneys prepare a suit—to be brought immediately, if and when you are charged with the man's death—against Calhoun."

"But he's dead! And what's my basis? What would I be suing him for?"

"For his felonious attempt to deprive you of your civil rights, such as continuing to live. In both civil and criminal law there's a great deal of precedent. And since yours would be a civil suit, you file against his estate and/or his heirs."

"That's crazy!"

"No, Kennet. The *law* may well be irrational, but within its context, my suggestion is quite legitimate."

Bardeen paused. "And would that keep me out of jail in the meantime?"

"I rather doubt it; the two processes are independent."

"But everything's coming to a head now. I *can't* allow myself to be locked away, out of action, at this time."

"Then don't." For long moments, Cogdill looked at the other man's screened image. "Kennet, at your disposal lie all the resources of the Feen. Use them. Think, and use them."

As his screen dimmed, Bardeen thought, *That's fine for you to say.* Because, sure, if there were only himself to protect, he could figure ways to do that. But what all those resources were lined up for, just now, was trying to keep the Troy dos Caras situation from getting loose in public, and looking toward protection of all the Mark Twos in case it did.

Bardeen shook his head. Maybe he could handle that task and maybe not; the whole thing scared him.

But he damned well couldn't go on some kind of hideout maneuver, and take care of the main problem at the same time. The logistics simply wouldn't work.

Later, at home, his false cheer didn't fool Jenny a bit.

# XXVI

Trust a masochist to know what hurts! At first Annek Getzlor had thought Jody Jay Tolliver was holding out on her, so she let Duane Eads take over, and Duane hardly had to *touch* the Reverend to put the man's mouth into high gear. Not that there was all that much to tell: a woman named Lesa Pfluge and a man called Migg claimed to have seen a young girl, going under the name of Blake Lassiter, change into a boy. Maybe the Lassiter ID would prove legitimate, but Getzlor wasn't betting on it.

Once Jody Jay had been through the story a couple of times, Duane stuck him with the scop for a double check. Actually the current drug had cards and spades over scopolamine, but old terminology dies hard. At any rate the man's story—what there was of it—stayed the same. The trouble was that no questions Getzlor could think of, and some came from pretty far out in left field, added the slightest bit to that story.

Back at their hotel, after leaving Tolliver to the timid ministrations of Cora Sue, Eads began transcribing and correlating from recorderdisk, while Getzlor put in a call to headquarters. When both were done, and Eads had ordered up dinner for them, Getzlor said, "*He* couldn't find the Pfluge woman or the thing that called itself Lassiter. But when our search team joins us in Chicago, they'll cut trail within a week, maybe less. Then a little hypno, a little needle, and we'll get usable descriptions. That Reverend Floyd will have Pfluge's address for the time in question, and the way those people live, we'll still find prints there. The alien, and the man Migg, too. You'll see."

Eads cleared his throat. "Annek? You're going to be careful, aren't you? You won't reveal your—your *insight* about the aliens from space, until we have solid proof?"

"Of course not." What was Duane so antsy about? Well, she *had* asked Tolliver some questions along those lines, but the man

201

was drugged; even if he understood what she was saying, he wouldn't remember clearly. "Anyway, as soon as we capture one of them, we'll have that proof."

He nodded. "We have to be sure; that's all."

"We will be. Anything that changes sex isn't human." She grinned. "I'm even a little doubtful about transvestites."

Dutifully, Eads chuckled at the feeble joke. "But supposing we do catch it, how do we get it to change?"

"How should I know? How did Pfluge and Migg manage?" Before he could answer she said "Shut up and eat."

All during the meal she smiled to herself, thinking of what she intended to do with Duane tonight. He'd been kept in a half-full bathtub before, wrapped mummy-tight in wet sheets, but the ingenious use of adhesive tape should surprise him.

When Bennest's men got there, the body was still warm and the blood not yet wholly dried. The damage by fire and water was obviously much less recent, maybe connected to the killing and maybe not. Death was due to a deep wound in the back, made by a narrow-bladed knife, just below the left scapula; at least one lung, the medic said, would be full of blood.

The body carried ID in the name of Grego Collins. Its thumbprint was identical to the one on the card, and the address matched, too.

Painstaking study of a soggy mass of half-burned papers, found among the debris on the bed, produced no useful facts. A scribbled notepad, nailed to the wall beside the smashed phoneset, showed better promise but nothing solid. A phone number listed for "Clint" proved to be long out of use, but the operator came up with addresses that matched numbers ascribed to several other names. "We're working on those," Bennest said. "As soon as we have anything at all, I'll get back to you, sir."

"Yes. Thank you, Bennest." Kennet Bardeen cut the circuit. *This could be one hell of a long night.*

At dinnertime it was Olive who came to turn me loose; I followed her into the other room and sat down. Clint looked up but said nothing. He looked tense, fidgety.

Olive said, "Dinner's ready, but Grego ain't back yet. Do we wait?"

"No." Clint shook his head. "Don't you remember? Gacek's

coming over in about an hour and a half. We don't want him to see the kid here, do we?"

From bits and pieces I'd heard, I knew that Gacek was the computer man, the one who was going to hook Banshuck's machine up so that Clint could follow through and collect the ransom. Out of some perverse streak I found myself saying, "Oh, gee! You mean I don't get to meet Mr. Gacek? I was looking forward to it: the social event of the week."

From under lowered brows Clint glared. "In your shoes, kid, I don't think I'd smart off so much." For long seconds, then, thinking I'd gone too far, I felt real fear. I hadn't figured Clint for any kind of killer—but under stress, you never know.

Finally he looked away. "Will you get some *food* on the table, Olive? It's ready, isn't it?"

"Sure, Clint. Comin' right up."

While she busied herself, he looked back to me. "You want to stay more polite, kid; you know that? Because if you think you've had any rough times here, so far, you could learn better than that. In a fat hurry. You understand?"

I couldn't find an answer, so I was lucky that Olive cut in. She was setting dishes onto the table, and said, "Troy, you wanta bring the big platter? It's kind of heavy."

So I did, and then sat again, shucking off the impact of Clint's vague threats in favor of enjoying the pleasure of hunger soon to be appeased. The big platter was spaghetti, and that was one dish Olive did well. The sauce came from a store, but it was a tasty brand. On the side she'd sliced some cabbage and a few tomatoes. Along with my two captors, I dug right in.

Coffee wasn't Olive's best trick, but when we were done eating, in the interests of apparent solidarity I took one cup. Black, because I loathe powdered cream-substitutes, and in that beverage I want no sweeteners. The inky liquid was truly awful stuff—but aside from a few dissimulating sips I didn't have to drink it.

I don't know where Clint bought his neatly-rolled cannabis sticks. I knew he didn't put them together himself because I'd seen him try that once; what he displayed was a case of the terminal clumsies. Now he lit up, took first toke and gave Olive the next turn. I'd made it clear, earlier, that I didn't use the stuff because it gave me unpleasant reactions, so they no longer bothered offering.

Neither of them was talking much, so I said, "Hey, could I have a shower?" My guess was that they wouldn't mind; I'd be out from underfoot, and at the bathroom door this room stood guard.

I got lucky; Olive even found me a dry towel.

Going in, I wanted some uninterrupted time alone, so I took a chance and threw the bolt. I stripped fast, then went for the jar of Smooth, still half full, that I'd spotted in the cluttered medicine cabinet. The thing was that about six years earlier Moss Frantz was the first Mark Two to grow whiskers. But when he and Dale Carson split, and Moss went to F-mode, those whiskers fell out. My own crotch, I could see easily enough, was changing rapidly: still M-mode by appearance but probably not operational.

So very soon *my* beard would begin to shed, and that would be a solid tipoff to Clint and Olive that something strange was going on. That's why I used the Smooth. I tried to be careful at the sideburn areas, getting both sides more or less even and making natural-looking curved hairlines in front of my ears. Of course the results wouldn't be perfect, but on the other hand, people usually aren't.

While I got the shower water up to a good heat I gave the Smooth its eight minutes, then got under the spray and sudsed down. Hot water in the place was a sometime thing and not predictable, so while it lasted I enjoyed it fully. The first warning flick of cold hit just as Olive banged on the door and gave a yell. I cut off the water, shouted "Just a minute!" and did some very fast drying and dressing. Then opened the door.

Olive gasped. "What the hell you do with your beard?"

"Took it off. Hey, I get allergies, it was itching me. That's all." She nodded.

It's a funny thing: when you don't really give a damn whether people believe a lie, they usually do.

Out in the main room again, I could see that Clint's tensions had dissolved in a relaxing high. By contrast, stoned or not, Olive always seemed just the same. Maybe this was because she was stoned more than not. Now, though, as Clint prepared to light a new joint, she gestured a halt. "Clint, I'm worried. I got to call Grego's place."

He shrugged, and we watched her punch the number. Waiting, he said, "You want my opinion, you looked better with the beard. But it's your choice."

Then Olive's call went through. "Hello? Grego?" She looked puzzled. "Who's this? Where's Grego?" The viewing screen was dead; I assumed things were the same at the other end. Olive snarled: "None a your fuckin' business!" She cut the circuit and turned to Clint. "It ain't good. That sumbidge on the phone, sounded like some kinda cop."

When he didn't respond, she yelled, "We gotta get outa here!"

Clint halfway stood, then waved an arm. "Now hold it, hold it! We don't know why cops are there, if it *is* cops. Maybe it's nothing to do with the big job."

"And maybe it is! Clint—"

"Now you shut up! Listen, Olive. All you have is, you don't know who answered Grego's phone. Right? Now even if it's cops, even if they nabbed Grego for something, he swore not to write this number down anyplace, or this address, so—"

"They got us!"

"Will you shut your damn self *off*? What they've got is doodly shit, Olive. No handle on us at all."

She tried to say more; Clint shouted her down. "Look! You always said, the one thing about Grego is he won't *ever* split on a buddy. And you're his own sister. Now stuff it in! Get your shit together, will you? Put the kid to bed, before Gacek gets here. And you—" His index finger simulated a gun barrel. "While that man's here, you make no noise at all. Or you'll be the sorriest son of a bitch you ever heard of."

There was nothing to say. I nodded, and followed Olive into the storeroom, where I lay down and let her do the handcuff bit.

After she left, I eased the Stillson wrench out. In the dark and being cautious about making noise, it took some time to get the wrench adjusted on the coupling collar.

Then came the hard part. I was lying down, one hand cuffed to the vertical pipe and no way to get any real leverage with the other. I thought I remembered which way the coupling unscrewed, but couldn't be sure. Certainly I didn't want to waste time and effort trying to go the wrong way; I felt above and below the octagonal part and detected threads above. So I'd remembered wrong; the sleeve would unscrew to the left.

All right; I had the wrench on backward. I loosened it, moved it to the other side and re-tightened. Then, how to put some force to it? There was no way to get a brace against the wall and make a strong-enough outward pull with my free left hand. Then the idea came. Again, slowly and with effort, I repositioned the wrench: this time, so that its handle stood straight out from the wall rather than parallel to it.

Then I squirmed around a little. For this attempt my left hand was useless; the right arm, handcuffed, would be merely my anchor. I pulled my legs up, doubling them against me with my knees into my belly until I got one foot, then the other, up and toward me, past the wrench's handle.

Then I planted both feet against that handle and pushed. Gently, slowly, ignoring the pain of the pull on my handcuffed wrist and trying to make no sound that could be heard in the other room where someone, probably Mr. Gacek the computer man, was suddenly talking with Clint and Olive.

The handle wouldn't move; I didn't have enough leverage. I arched my back, bringing my butt up off the floor so that my knees, bent too tightly to have any real pushing force, now drove a vector component of my weight against the wrench. I took a deep breath, held it, and pushed with my very guts.

And the damned thing gave! With the paint and rust seals breaking, it moved almost a quarter turn, letting my feet slip free. I had all I could do to get them—let alone the rest of me—down without a telltale thud.

For a time I lay panting, mouth wide open for quiet, before moving to grasp the wrench. It moved easily now; I gave it another quarter turn, all the way to the wall, then disengaged the tool and put it under the sleeping bag.

Because a quick check told me that the rest of the way, I could unscrew the coupling strictly by hand.

But not now. At this point, all I could do was try to get some sleep. Eventually I managed that.

Ed Gacek was a smart old coot, all right; less than an hour it took, before he had Banshuck's rig up and working. And for less money than Clint had expected to pay. Clint felt good.

But not all the way. He thought he remembered most of what Banshuck had done, getting into the Phoenix Foundation's setup to make the dicker, and he'd taken some notes that ought to help, but still there could be holes in what he knew.

So, over a couple of beers after Gacek had the system working, Clint asked a few questions. He tried to keep them general, not give any clues to what was really up. But in his own field, Ed was nobody's easy mark. After fending off several of Clint's queries, finally the little man, bald and wrinkle-faced but still full of energy, shook his head. "It won't work."

"Don't know what you mean, Ed."

"Sure you do. I don't have any details and don't need 'em, but what you're pumping me for is how to accept money in one account and flash to another, bollixing the first one before it can report the second transfer." Bushy eyebrows raised. "Am I right, for twenty percent if I make it work, or do you still want to try it yourself? Either way, Clint, I don't spill on you; you know me better than that."

Olive looked like making a fuss; Clint, frowning, gestured her to silence. Twenty percent? No problem; if Amory wasn't out of the deal yet, he would be when Grego caught up with him. Clint grinned. "Ed—if you don't mind me not telling you any names beforehand, we've got us a deal."

The smaller man nodded. "In things like this, names don't interest me. Numbers do, though."

"Yeah, sure." Rough-guessing from what he remembered, Clint said, "Ninety-K. Minimum. Will that keep you warm and comfy?"

Gacek's mouth twitched. "Nine-zero-zero-zero-zero bucks. It's a friendly number." He leaned forward. "For that kind of money your approach should carry an extra layer of protection. And I'm just the ex-child-prodigy hacker who can give it to you."

Clint frowned. "What's that mean?"

"That trick you have, whoever gave it to you, might fool a bank, okay. But just looking at it, I see how to put in some more confusion. Tie up the security check-codes, and while they're looking for the right error message, slip in a *third* account number to accept the actual transfer." Gacek cocked an eyebrow. "Would you like to try it, Clint? All by yourself?"

A little irritated but not angry, Clint squeezed the older man's shoulder. "Don't rub it in, Ed. I know we need you."

Gacek stood. "When do you want to do it?"

"It's not what *I* want, Ed. I mean, the time's been set. Tomorrow, at noon. You might get here a little early."

"No reason why not; I'll do that." Gacek stood. "See you, Clint. Good night, Olive."

When the door closed after him, Olive said, "You know something? For an old fart he moves good."

Eyes narrowed, Haydock said, "I think his head does, too." Then he shrugged. "For our sake, it damn well better."

From the shoulder down, where Amory's arm wasn't dead it hurt like all shit. What scared him, as he sat in the crummy bar, nursing a shot and a beer, was the dark red streaks down toward his wrist.

No point worrying; he knew that. You do what needs it and that's all. So he'd done Grego, done him proper.

And now, like he already knew beforehand, Amory didn't have nobody at all. If Grego just hadn't of *shot* him!

Because ever since that knife tricker put a blade to Amory's pants, so he was no good up front, only in back, nobody but Grego done him any damn good at all.

And now no more Grego.

Well, maybe them doctors don't know it all. All the parts still there, they say the nerves was cut and you can't you can't you can't you can't but maybe they're fulla shit.

There's other ways. Enough money, he could get better doctors. And no matter what, from that kidnap job, if it was still on, Amory had a share coming.

Yeah. With Grego dead, that made only three shares now. But maybe he shouldn't push that. Maybe he better drive up and have a talk with good ol' Clint *before* him and Olive hear about Grego.

On the way out he met four-five guys crowding in through the door, but none of them bumped his sore arm. Amory didn't notice, because people hardly ever did bump him, if they could help it.


I had no idea how long I'd been asleep when I woke to find somebody feeling me up. There wasn't a great deal of light, but the perfume said Olive, and at first she was whispering. "That ol' Clint got so stoned he's paralyzed, so why don't you and me just—"

Then she gave a shocked gasp. "Goda'mighty, Troy! What the fuck happened to you?"

Even before she pulled my fly apart, so she could see better, there wasn't much question—except, how far along was the change? I braced up on my left elbow; a quick look was enough: my testes had retracted nearly all the way into hiding, and the penis shrunk to little more than an enlarged clitoris. As to the expanse of mucous membrane versus skin, or the condition of the vaginal opening, I couldn't tell except by touch or the use of a mirror; F-mode wasn't likely to be functional as yet, but to Olive's eyes my appearance had to be female.

With those eyes very wide, she started to back away; I grabbed a wrist. "Wait, Olive; don't go. Let me explain." *Explain? How?*

*Fat chance!* But as she paused, not pulling away much, I heard myself saying something like "It's all right, nothing to worry about, just something that happens sometimes."

So far so good, but we weren't all that far yet. She wanted to talk; I overrode. "It's—it's a rare tropical fever. I mean, rare for people up here; the Indians have it all the time."

"What Indians? I never heard of any—"

"Not here. Down in—" *Geography, where are you?* "On the Plata-Paraná, where—"

"Piranha? Those fish that eat a live cow in three minutes?"

"No, Olive. Paraná." I spelled it. "The Plata-Paraná is the longest river system in the world." Was it, really? I couldn't remember. "It starts in the Andes Mountains and goes down through Brazil to Paraguay—" Or did I mean Uruguay? Who the hell cared! "I was down there with my folks when I was just a little kid, and wandered away into the jungle, and before they found me I'd been bitten by these mosquitoes, you see."

She probably didn't know her mouth was open; she nodded, then said, "And it turns you into a *woman*? How often? And how long?"

"No, no, Olive! It may *look* that way, but I'm sure you know that's impossible. I'm still a guy—just shrunk up, and out of business until the attack's over." Wait a minute! Maybe an angle here . . . "But it lasts a lot longer when I don't have the medicine. If I could call in to my doctor—"

It might have worked. I'll never know, because Clint, staggering a little, came in. "Olive? What in hell are you up to? As if I couldn't guess. I thought I told you—"

His raised fist promised Olive at least a fat lip, but jerking free of me she lurched backward, away from him. "No, listen, Clint. And *look* at him. Or her, or whatever. What it is, see—"

She garbled the story even worse than I'd told it. When she ran down, Clint used a hand to violate the privacy of my crotch. He ran a finger around the rim of the developing vaginal opening and then, not at all roughly (which surprised me) pushed the tip in perhaps an inch, maybe a little more. In my mid-condition I felt no pleasure from that touch, but no pain, either. Then he withdrew it, and stood.

Clint wasn't angry now; he wasn't especially stoned, either. Sometimes a good jolt can have that effect. He said, "This guy—this gal—whatever! 'Sbeen snowing all over you, is what." If he'd been a computer I could have heard the moving parts whir. "Right

here, Olive, we have a female person. And a few days ago it was a
male person, as you damn well know better than I do."

I didn't see Olive's reaction, but Clint smiled. "Be easy; I'm not
mad. Because, what we've got here is even bigger than I'd
thought. Something nobody ever heard of before—and tied in,
one way or another, to all that Phoenix Foundation money."

"Clint? I don't get it." She sounded confused.

"That's all right. As a matter of fact I don't have the details
figured out yet, myself."

# XXVII

"But, Reverend—" Cora Sue was fussing around like an old
biddy hen. "You shouldn't try to tape your sermon now. They shot
you full of *drugs*; you're not thinking straight. I—"

"Silence, woman!" Jody Jay had a real buzz on, from all that
dope they'd pranged him with, but now after a couple of solid jolts
of tonic nectar he felt *good*: if things were a little fuzzy around the
edges, maybe they looked better that way. Like his wig; it was
cocked up and sideways a bit. Staring into the mirror, he nodded:
that's how he ought to wear it all the time.

Cora Sue had that hurt look on her face, so he told her, "Now
never you mind. I just have to put me together this ten-minute
spot to head up tonight's program, which I already put on disk in
case all that FBI unconvenience might discommode my aircast
schedule. So this hunk of work shouldn't take long. What you do
is, you go get in that tub so's you come out all warm and pink and
ready to do some real fine ministering; y'hear?"

"Yes, sir, Reverend."

When she had left, he sat at his work console, checked the
indicator lights, and did a quick test replay on the monitor. Yeah,
it was all set right, so he pulled back to start for real. Clearing his
throat, he began:

"The Lord, my dear friends, moves in strange ways and

sometimes talks through people you wouldn't expect. Now just today I found out what *kind* of monsters and demons I been warning you all about so as to keep your immortal souls out of perilous danger, and a little bit about where they come from, only not exactly, just yet. And like I been saying all along, that sinful Phoenix Foundation is in it up to their ears.

"It's not just me that's got this revelation, my dear friends. Why, the FBI its own self knows that here's these demons, which they changes from man to woman or the other way, too—and such creatures never grew up here on the Lord's good Earth, so right there you know what *that* tells you! No souls, is what these alien demons don't have. And another thing . . ."

When he was finished, Jody Jay replayed to make sure he'd said it all the way he wanted, dubbed his instructions onto the leader segment he'd left blank for that purpose, brought his modem on-line, and sent the entire program in to his originating station.

Then he went to join Cora Sue.

The smart thing, Brad knew, would be to pass all the info along to Bennest, the Security man at Phoenix, and then stay the hell out of this hassle. But he didn't have the phone number with him, and was in no mood to stay on a line long enough to go through channels—and get traced, maybe. No, thanks.

So, feeling the weight of the gun under his jacket, Brad Szalicz rode the subway toward the address Amory had given him.

And wondered just what he was going to do when he got there.

After Clint let this Troy-whatever go take a leak, and put the handcuff on again, he came out of the storeroom feeling wide awake. He'd been really laidback-stoned, but the jolt of this crazy morphodite development triggered his energy.

What he had in mind with Olive was taking her to bed, but the Tri-V was on, and when he started to say something, she *shhh'd* him. "You got to see this, Clint!"

So he looked, and tuned in his ears. The picture showed that Cincinnati preacher, Jody Jojo or something. But what the man was *saying*—!

After the commercial break, Jody-whoever changed the subject and talked about his Salvation Through Donation program, so Clint turned the set off. Ideas flashed through his mind; fucking could wait. "That's it, Olive!"

She looked stricken. "Clint, before you moved back in, I was screwin' a goddamn *alien*; I could of up an' delivered some kind of monster *baby*! I—"

Slapping was too much work. Between his thumb and the knuckle of his index finger, Clint gripped the fleshy part of Olive's nose, squeezed hard, and shook her face side-to-side. Dammit— she'd had her period right on schedule, so why all the hysteria? Letting go, he said, "You didn't, though; you're okay, right? So let's talk aliens."

"Like how, Clint?"

"Like we have a space alien in there, Olive. Like the F-B-and-fuggin'-I is after it. And like someway it ties to the Phoenix Foundation. There's only one question."

"Yeah? What?"

A frown tightened Clint's forehead. "Make it two. Who's most likely to pay best for what we've got? And what's the *safest* way to work the whole deal?"

"That cretin!" Annek Getzlor threw her glass at the Tri-V set. "Duane—have Tolliver picked up and held incommunicado. The story will be that he's gone into a sanitorium for drug addiction." She beat her clenched fists together. "How could that cornpone religion-ripper be so shit-simple *stupid*? He—"

She paused. "Yes. I suppose I'd better unwrap you now." She peeled away the wet restraints that sheathed him from shoulders to hips. "All right, Duane; take care of this mess."

"Yes, Annek." He flexed his freed arms. "When I've made a pit stop, and am dressed, I'll get right on it."

Grego's car quit at a bad place—right in the middle of an intersection, with the light changed and traffic coming at Amory from both sides. He got out, and waited for the next change; then, before cars could start moving again, he lumbered across to the far right corner and walked on, still heading north.

He didn't know how much farther it was he had to go, because the street sign was gone; the post was still there, but some dummy must of tore the sign off it.

He wanted to loosen up his bad arm, but when he went to move it, it hurt too damn much. So he gave up and just kept walking.

"He was calling from Chicago, Mr. Dennis. He didn't stay on line long enough to get a trace." Sandy Moran wiped sweat from her forehead; even after two years working here in New York, she wasn't used to talking with network execs. But this time she'd spoken up, so now she had to go for it.

Dennis, bald dome looming over forbidding eyebrows, stared at her. "This Tolliver, the hinterlands messiah. You've checked the tape of *his* show tonight?"

"Yes, sir." She spread her hands. "It sounds idiotic. He claims to have information about aliens from space who can change their sex at will, and says the FBI confirms his story."

"And of course you've contacted the man."

"No, sir." This wasn't going well; she'd known it wouldn't, but she plowed ahead anyway. "He's not there. Some woman is, and she says two people took him away. She thinks it was the FBI, but I wouldn't air *that* over my own name."

Dennis nodded. "It could fit, though. And I won't even ask whether you have any information from the Bureau, because that's not the way they work."

Now he looked interested. "Your caller, though. Who is he, and can you get back to him?"

Sandy consulted her notes. "He gave his name as Clint Haydock; he wouldn't give me a number to call back, just yet. His pitch is that with respect to the Tolliver statements on Tri-V he has a scoop that's worth millions, and—"

Dennis had a really nasty laugh. "They all think that, don't they?" He sobered. "And what else, in particular?"

"He says he can produce one of these sex-changing aliens, and can trace ties to the Phoenix Foundation. In Chicago."

"*I* know where it is!" The nasty side again. Then, "What does he say the creature looks like?"

She made an open-hand gesture. "Except for the sex-changing thing, just like anyone. And he said it's been living among other people, unsuspected, under the name of Troy dos Caras."

She couldn't disguise the frown that came to her; Dennis said, "And? What *haven't* you told me?"

"There's something shady about it; he wants a guarantee of legal amnesty before he gives us the details. I'm not sure, sir, just what we should do here. I—"

Again, the Dennis laugh. "It's simple. You disked the call, of course?" She nodded. "Then this is your big chance. You listen through the dialogue again, carefully. Then, as you present this with your face on-camera, insert your own comments. Tonight, Moran, the eleven-ten newsbreak is all yours."

It was the best real on-camera chance Sandy had ever been granted. "Yes, sir; thank you. I'll do it right."

*If that's possible.* Because whoever this Clint Haydock might be, she was going to have to throw him to the wolves. Not to mention, the same for the hypothetical Troy dos Caras.

*And* the Phoenix people. That's the part that scared her.

One thing I didn't know, and I needed to. If or when I got the opportunity, I'd have to run for it. But could I? The pipe coupling would unscrew, sure. But then, lying sidewise with one hand cuffed, could I lift the radiator enough to separate the two pipe segments and let me slip the cuff through the gap?

It seemed time to find out. From outside the room came sounds of talk, plus the Tri-V a little too loud, the way Olive liked it. So all right . . .

The coupling, no problem; unscrewed all the way, it slipped down to lodge on the elbow just below. Now the radiator: I got my meager leverage in gear and heaved; nothing happened.

The damned thing couldn't be *that* heavy; maybe the four metal legs of this antique monstrosity were merely bonded to the floor by accretions of paint and primordial grime.

So I needed a different line of attack. I put all my leverage to the nearest leg; of course the next wasn't all that distant. I heaved up; one leg broke loose, the second wouldn't quite give. Another effort, and the entire near end came free.

The far end, I didn't need. The gap was wide enough. The question was, did I want to put everything on the line *now*? Or wait, hoping for better odds?

From outside the room I heard voices. They didn't help. I decided to wait.

No I didn't. I was too chicken to decide *anything*. All I did was lie there.

Walking from the subway, Brad didn't meet with any trouble. Clint's apartment wasn't exactly a top-grade address, but it beat hell out of Scum City. The call-in box, that could let people push a button to admit you, was long dead, so Brad figured he could just walk in, and he was right. He had the bad feeling that the elevators might not work, either, so when the lights lit and the car came, he was very glad to be wrong. On the way up, he tried to think what the hell he was going to say.

At the number Amory had told him, the nametag didn't read

Clint Haydock; the scribble spelled Olive Schweer. Brad shrugged and punched the buzzer; he didn't expect it to work, but it was worth a try.

Nothing happened, so he had to knock. No answer; try again. He hadn't quite decided whether to knock a third time when the door opened, just a few inches against a sturdy chain. "Yeah? Whatcha want?"

A plain, sharp-faced woman, dark hair sheared close at the sides but bleached and fluffy on top. With luck she might be the name on the door, so he said, "Hi, Olive. Is Clint here?" *Always act as if you know what you're doing.*

"Who's asking?"

"A friend. His old friend Brad, tell him."

Olive's face jerked away to the side, out of view. Through the narrow opening, Clint Haydock looked out. "Hi, Brad. What you doing all the way down here? I wouldn't've thought you had this address."

Hospitality, no. Now what? *Don't answer his questions.* "I need to get hold of somebody; the word was, look you up first."

"Like who, Brad?"

"Like Troy dos Caras." Bringing the gun out, Brad stuck its barrel through the crack, blocking any chance to close the door. "I want in, Clint."

The way Haydock seemed to move, the thin slice of him that showed at the doorway, probably he was shrugging. "I can see that. You don't usually ask things quite so hard, Brad."

"I don't usually need to. Are you going to let me in?"

Haydock moved away, out of sight; Brad heard low-voiced talk, too faint for understanding. Then Clint said, "Yeah, come on in. Just put the gun away first."

*Oh, sure!* Clint probably had one of his own, out and pointed. How in the name of sanity had Brad gotten himself *into* such a crazy mess?

The hell with this! He'd leave here and call the Phoenix people. Whatever they might do if they nailed him, it still beat getting shot down in this crummy dump. Or, if you really gave thought to the matter, getting shot down anywhere at all.

He was going to say "No sale, Clint," or maybe just sneak away quietly; he hadn't decided. Before he *could* decide, or do more than barely begin to turn away, fingers touched the right side of his neck, and peripheral vision showed him the outline of a knife blade. "Do like Clint says," came the grating whisper. "I'll come up from outside, and cover ya."

Amory Neill! "Well, get yer ass movin'!"

Something had to be wrong. Coming inside now, Brad Salich looked nervous and damn well should, with Clint holding the drop on him and feeling good about it. But nobody with half sense would come in here this way, at all. Had Brad been dumb enough to call in outside help to back him up—dumb enough to think he could save his ass that way, if things went bad?

Motioning Brad farther inside, Clint shook his head. This deal had been planned to go smooth; how had it got so rough?

He'd only let the man come in because if he didn't, Brad could go holler cop; now he had a second prisoner on his hands and no handcuffs for this one. Olive didn't like it; when he'd told her his idea she'd whispered, "You tryin' to start yer own slammer? Son of Joliet, maybe?"

Hell with it; what Clint had to do now was ice Brad down and then get back on the line to that little blond New York Tri-V network ginch; she'd had her pic onscreen until she saw his wasn't. He said, "You like a drink, Brad? Coffee? Some good dope? Might as well relax; then we talk."

Brad waved the offers away. "None of that. Where's Troy dos Caras?"

"Don't know what you're talking about." But before he thought, Clint looked toward the storeroom.

"Well," said Brad, "why don't we find out?" He had his hand to his gun; with a sinking feeling, Clint realized he didn't *want* to test who was faster, or could shoot to hit anything.

"I could make coffee," Olive said, as if anybody cared.

With only one good hand, down a fire escape was easier than up, so Amory walked the stairs to the floor above, and knocked at the apartment over Clint's. "Police business." The old lady let him in, and stayed mostly quiet while he prowled the place and found the room he needed. "Open the window." She tried, but couldn't. "I guess I have to break it; you'll get paid." He looked at her, mean but not *too* mean, and waved his good hand. "Get back in there and don't yell to nobody. You got it?"

"Y-yes, sir. I won't."

"That's good." When she was out of the room he hung a wad of torn, dirty blanket over his bum paw to muffle the noise while with his other fist padded, too, he smashed glass loose all around the frame. Then, taking the blanket with him, he went outside and inched his way down the rickety, rusted ladder. It was a long way down to the street, so he didn't look.

Clint's window, a floor below, wouldn't open either, but the pane was cracked and so was what was left of the putty. Looking at how the busted glass fit together, Amory pushed at where some of the pieces met and got his fingers over the corner of one. Then he wiggled at it, and pretty soon it came loose, so he sailed it off a long way sideways, to hit where the noise wouldn't get back up here much. Two more came out all right, but the next one fell loose and smashed on the ladder. Well, there was room to crawl in now; better do that before somebody maybe heard and came to check up.

Inside, there wasn't hardly no light at all. Amory moved off to one side of the window, so's nobody coming in could spot him easy, and waited to see better.

Before he could, though, he heard some other sonofabitch, breathing all so quiet, but sure as shit *there*.

Crouched to fight, Amory aimed his knife and moved to find out who the hell was in his way.

A brittle crashing sound jarred me out of my half-doze. I looked and saw someone climbing in through the window; whoever it was, seemed to be having a hard time of it.

When your pulse races, you require more oxygen, but I didn't dare breathe as hard as I needed to. Painfully, as the man moved to one side, no longer outlined against the window, I tried to keep my breathing silent.

For an endless-seeming time I couldn't hear him move. Then a foot scraped against something; he was coming toward me. Toward the door, anyway, where a crack of light showed at the bottom—and that would bring him past me at very close range. Lying there, I tried my damnedest, not to be present at all! Childish, yes; but what can you do?

When a foot brushed my knee, for the life of me I couldn't restrain a quick gasp. The man jumped back a little, and again the dim window light outlined him—knife hand and all, now.

"Don't!" Somehow I had sense enough to keep the sound down. "Look—whoever you are—I'm not armed, I couldn't fight you if I wanted to. Please—!"

In the next room, somebody yelled. I couldn't tell what the

noise was about; it tapered off to sounding like three people talking loudly but no longer shouting. Then, from nearer than I liked, came a rasping voice. "Hold still," and white light blinded me. Only a minihandlamp, I realized, but in reflex my dark-adapted eyes clamped shut. "Shit oh dear it's *you*, kid!"

*Whatever that means!* It was hard to tell, but I thought the knifeman sounded more pleased than not. I said, "Yes. Right. Now then—whyever you may be here, I have a deal for you."

Either he cleared his throat or groaned; maybe both. "Tell it fast, kid; I got some shit to do and they ain't much time."

"Get me *out* of here, out that window. I'll make it worth your time; I—"

"Betcher ass you would, if'n I done that. Except I got no way, nohow, to take them cuffs off ya."

A little hope can be a lot of help; in perhaps fifteen seconds I'd gone from craven panic almost to boldness. "I'll handle that part. You just don't let those people, there in that other room where they're talking, stop us. Deal?"

"What the hell for?" In the dimness, I think he shook his head. "Wait a minute; lemme think." Another pause; then he said, "Yeah! Hadn't thought, but that could maybe work out good. So how you gettin' yerself loose?"

I gestured. "Put the light over here." Seconds later, with the coupling unscrewed, I lifted the radiator an inch or so, and had the bloody-bedamned handcuff free!

But while I was doing those things, reflected light showed me the rawboned face of my helper. Amory Neill, the crazy one! Well, the voice had sounded familiar. . . .

With every instinct shrieking at me to get the hell *out*, I forced myself to pause long enough to take inventory. Assets: a pair of pants, no underwear, a shirt, no shoes or socks. Under the sleeping bag some miscellaneous tools: all right, take along a screwdriver and the hammer. And okay, a pair of pliers couldn't hurt.

I stood; the only way to get through this was to pretend it all made sense. "Ready, I guess. Let's go." I moved over to the window.

"You go. Can't make it down, the ladder stops too high. But up, just one floor, they's a window you can get in. Ole lady there thinks I'm police; tell'r yer workin' with me, then wait. I be there purty quick, kid. So don't you go noplace." The knife moved. "Hear me?"

"Right." Reaching over to the rusted ladder, I stepped backward, out the window—and felt the rust flakes, with their sharp edges, cut into my bare soles!

There wasn't any choice, though. Sore feet or not, I had to keep moving, up and away.

Just as I did, the room came alight. Because, from inside Clint and Olive's living room, someone had opened the door.

# XXVIII

Seeing Brad's hand start to close on the gun-butt, Clint yelled, "Don't! We can't afford this shit. Brad—"

Salich glared at him. "Then damn it, put *yours* away!"

"Now come on, boys—"

"Shut up, Olive!" Whether Clint was angrier than scared, he wasn't quite sure himself. "Brad—take my word, you don't belong in this. Why don't you get the hell out?"

"I will, Clint. Once you convince me you don't have Troy dos Caras." Haydock's revolver pointed downward now; as Brad turned away, moved toward the bathroom door but then chose the storeroom's, Clint started to raise the gun.

Then he shrugged, and lowered it again. Hell, he wasn't going to shoot Brad, and now he admitted it to himself. "Look. Don't open that door."

"Why not? What happens if I do?"

"Just don't, huh?"

Taking a step back, Brad shrugged. "All right; you do it."

*Fat chance!* But then from inside the room, Clint heard sounds he didn't like. So he jumped to the door, threw it open.

*Shit!* The kid was gone; the broken window showed how. And all too near, his restless hand moving the lethal blade back and forth, stood Amory Neill. "Amory! What are you doing here? And what in hell have you *done*?"

Neill stepped forward. "We gotta do us some talkin'."

\* \* \*

The kid wouldn't run for it; he was scared shitless. And having him on ice this way gave Amory a better handle on Clint. Still, when the door opened, Amory wasn't ready. Said first thing that come to mind, then waited. Damn' arm pounding his head off with hurt. Clint Haydock was here, all right, and Olive, and the guy as decked Amory at Grego's place so's Grego kept his balls. Well, Amory he'd *told* that one he could come here, so— Now while Amory sorted everybody out, Clint said like, talk about what? "My share," said Amory. "Just went up."

On account of why?—real whiny, Clint asked that. "On account of I got the kid and you don't. So I get half."

All the arm hurt had Amory dizzy; he missed Clint's answer. Lurching away, he said, "Call ya tomorrow, set it all up."

"You crazy bastard, it already *is* tomorrow. In less than eight hours, we have to make the ransom call."

"So make it. They wanna see the kid, ya stall."

"But they won't *pay!*"

"Sure will! They don't wanna, tell'm they can see him a piece at a time." By now, what Amory mostly needed was to get the hell out while he could still walk. Clint looked twitchy with the gun, so Amory said, "Without I tell ya, you *never* find the kid. And don't nobody try an' folla me!" He lunged to the hall door— outside, he slammed it behind him. Along that hall were the two elevators; as Amory passed the stairwell one car's bell dinged and its doors began to open. Ducking back, he peeked around enough to see three men starting to come out. No uniforms, but he smelled cop! So, up the flight of stairs. He found the old lady's door and went in without knocking.

Sure enough, the kid was still there. "C'mon," said Amory.

The tip had come by no simple route—put together from several disparate sources, some being police officers who augmented their salaries with under-the-table Feen money. Bennest wasn't sure he knew all of it; a parole-breaking computer criminal who died of knife wounds was the cousin of Grego Collins, named by Bennest's anonymous informant as one of the Troy dos Caras kidnappers, but also stabbed to death before Bennest reached him. Questioned by one of Bennest's agents, the first man's wife tied the second's sister to another alleged kidnapper—and gave the address which Bennest and four of his men were now approaching. It all made a *certain* amount of sense.

Since the whole operation was illegal, anyway, Bennest saw no reason to bother with being polite. One of his troops kicked the door in.

Furious now, guns forgotten, Brad grabbed Clint's shirtfront and twisted. "You sonofabitch, you had the boy here all along, didn't you?"

Unaccountably, for a moment Clint Haydock made a smartass grin. "The boy? Yeah, Brad. For a while there, we had the boy." He jerked back. "Now let the hell go of me!"

Letting go wasn't Brad's plan at all; instead he shook the lighter man. "And what happened to him? The crazy one—Amory— how did *he* get Troy?"

"I don't *know*! Window in there—fire escape—you know as much as I do. Now let *go*!" Clint's gun came up; he slammed the barrel at Brad's forehead. Ducking away, Brad caught only a glancing blow but felt blood wet his skin. Outraged, he used his grip on the shirt to jerk Clint bruisingly against him and then with a shotputting motion threw him backward, to stagger and fall onto the bed.

Clint still held his gun, but didn't seem to realize he had it until the door crashed inward, to hang aslant by one hinge. Then, as the three men entered, he raised the barrel to aim.

"*No!*" As Brad watched, everything seemed to take many times longer than normal—including his own leap and the movement to bring his gun up—before he fired. His muzzle was less than two feet from Clint's gun, but when Brad saw that revolver spin away, he still couldn't believe he'd made the shot.

He must have said it out loud, because the oldest-looking of the three intruders said, "You didn't, son. Your muzzle blast scared it loose from him. Now why don't you put *yours* down?" He cleared his throat. "It's not as if you had the choice. Help or no help, we're three to one on you, and as one of the kidnappers, you have some hard questions to answer."

Feeling disoriented, Brad let the gun drop. Now he looked more closely at the speaker. "Mr. Bennest!"

"You know me? How? Would you like to make it reciprocal?"

"On the phone. I'm *not* a kidnapper; I'm the one who called and gave you some names, hoping they'd help you. The only thing is, tonight I got here first. But just before I did, somebody else took Troy away. The crazy one, Amory Neill."

"And you don't know where; right? How long ago?"

"Not long. Five minutes? Ten?"

Bennest nodded, then mumbled jargon into a handcomm set. "We're on it. Now," he said to his two men, "let's take this nice bundle home and wring it out."

The woman began screeching that she needed time to pack some clothes to take along, but one of Bennest's men simply crammed a miscellany of garments into a suitcase he found in one of the closets, and that was that. With Brad's left wrist handcuffed to Clint's right, the group went out to wait for an elevator.

The elderly woman's name was Ms. Jennifer Garvin. She looked and moved like a healthy, aware person. She took my entry through her broken window with reasonable aplomb, and offered me a cup of tea "while you wait." I didn't want any, but in the interests of diplomacy I accepted. It wasn't bad, though I wished I could add some lemon. Meanwhile she offered a chair. "No, thanks. I'll stand."

She squinted through bifocals. "Your partner, what's wrong with him?" I wasn't sure what she meant, and answering wasn't a good idea anyway. She said, "He shouldn't be up and working. Anybody can see he's a sick man."

"He'll be all right." But then the door opened, and the way Amory Neill looked, coming in, made a liar out of me.

"C'mon," he said. "We gotta—" From below, from Olive's place, came the sounds of yelling, then a gunshot. Scowling, Amory gestured. "Let's go!"

The cup was still in my hand; I set it down. "Thanks for the tea, ma'am," I said, just as though we'd been having a normal visit. Then I followed Amory, and closed the door behind us.

I don't know why I followed him—or why, when he walked past the stairwell, I didn't bolt down those stairs five or six at a time and escape. Part of it, I suppose, was that I hadn't had control of my own actions for so many days that it took time to mobilize any initiative, let alone make a decision and act on it. Another aspect was that somehow none of the current happenings around me seemed *real*. It was like watching an action show on Tri-V— except that I couldn't change the channel.

So instead of running, I said, "Hey, the stairs are back *there*."

"I know," he said, not looking around. He was leaning a little as he walked, sometimes bracing against the wall with his good hand. "Elevators."

If the indicators could be trusted, one car was at ground level

nd the other had stayed one floor below us. Amory punched the
utton; the nearer car made its noisy, lurching way up to us, then
n the same fashion took us down.

He tried to stop it at the second floor, saying that they could've
eft somebody in the lobby. "They," I decided from other things
e'd muttered on the way down, pretty much had to be police,
vho would be in Olive Schweer's apartment and most likely had
ired the shot we heard. But he hit the button too late; the doors
pened at ground level, and there was the welcoming committee.

Before I could sort it all out, Amory drew the knife and lunged.
did see Clint and Olive, and Brad Szalicz, and Mr. Bennest from
'een Security. But before I could identify the other two, Amory
noved to attack, and guns came up.

The problem was that I stood right behind him, directly in
veryone's line of fire. So I jumped to tackle Amory Neill, and
rought him down flat. Only one gun fired; the bullet whined its
vaspish way past my head. How close? I don't know, but anything
hat loud is *too* close.

I didn't make that move on purpose, you understand. My
ubconscious must have done it, because it purely surprised the
ell out of me. Too confused to realize that with all those guns
ut, probably I should stay flat, I rolled over and sat up. As Mr.
3ennest said, "Is that you, Troy? Are you all right?"

I shrugged. "Mostly."

"Then let's get out of here." Somebody helped me up, and we
ll started moving toward the street entrance.

Except Amory Neill: he just lay there, with his sleeve turned
oack, showing the angry red and black streaks along his wrist. I
topped walking. "Mr. Bennest?"

"What? Come *on*, Troy."

"Sure." I gestured. "But we have to take him along, too."

The Security Chief's face reddened. "In God's name, *why?*"

"Can't you see? He's got blood poisoning; he'll die." I was being
tupid and I knew it; Amory Neill was a killer, not very sane if at
ll, and totally lacking in what used to be called "redeeming social
value."

But for whatever reasons, he had sprung me loose from
:aptivity. So I kept right on being stupid until Mr. Bennest's men
oicked Neill up and carried him outside, first following the rest of
is but then moving up and ahead.

They led us across the street and a half-block to the left, to a
oair of parked cars, and put Neill in the leading one. Bennest

motioned Clint and Brad, still cuffed together, into the back seat
of the second car; I got in on the passenger's side, up front, as
Bennest and Olive, along with one of the men who had carried
Amory, climbed into the vehicle ahead.

But just then, from behind us came a shout. "Police! Hold it
right there!"

Bennest's second man had started to come back, so he could
drive us, but now he stood wavering, then turned and clambered
in beside Olive. I heard Bennest curse; then he shouted, "Troy?
There's no time! Follow me!" And his car revved away.

His impromptu plan contained one major flaw: I had no idea
how to start the car, let alone drive it.

So as the police came running up the sidewalk—shooting in
Bennest's direction, although by then he'd passed a truck and was
out of the line of fire—I eased out through the left door, closed it,
and rolled underneath. When they came rushing to surround and
arrest everybody, I crawled back to hide under another car, parked
just behind. After a long and noisy time they all left, so I got out
from under, brushed myself off for what good *that* would do, and
began walking.

Three hours later, after heated argument with a pair of gate
guards who insisted on seeing the ID I didn't have, I was admitted
to the Phoenix Foundation by Erwin Bennest himself.

"Where the hell have *you* been?"

I showed him the lacerated sole of one foot. "How many
guesses do you need?"


Pain, helplessness and humiliation are a masochist's basic
needs. At sixteen Duane Eads had never heard the psychological
term for his inclinations but he knew what he liked. Now, thirty
years later, he was a happy man. Annek Getzlor's unpredictable
bedroom savagery fulfilled all his fantasies, and more. So far she
hadn't inflicted any permanent damage, and in his saner moments
Duane appreciated her restraint. But sometimes, when she got
carried away, he had no idea what her limits might be; at such
moments the thrill of fear spiced his shuddering ecstasies.

Now, soaking some bruises, along with whip weals and other
minor contusions, in water as hot as he could endure, Duane
relaxed in gratified torpor. So when the bathroom door opened
and Annek, coughing against the thick steam, yelled "Get the hell
out here," he gave a massive start that sent water out to spatter
Getzlor's legs. He grabbed two heavy towels and followed her into

he suite's main room. She waved her drink toward the Tri-V, here a young woman was running segments of a voice-only hone call, apparently between herself and a male caller, and iterspersing her own comments. "Will you *hear* that stuff?"

"—can *show* you this alien," the man was saying. "First it was aale, like I said, and now it's female. So—"

"Now how can we reach you, Mr. Haydock, in order to—"

"Never mind that, just yet. You huddle with your big shots aere and put together an offer for me. A damned big one, ecause I've got a damned big story."

"But how—?"

"I reached you once, didn't I? Stay available tomorrow."

Apparently that remark ended the call; the young woman said, Well, there you have it, ladies and gentlemen. Does Clint Iaydock, calling earlier from a pay phone in Chicago, really have n interstellar alien on hand? For that matter, has the Reverend ody Jay Tolliver, who broadcasts from Cincinnati and whose ecent sermon sparked more calls than merely Mr. Haydock's— aas Tolliver himself any real information on these matters?"

Pausing, she smiled. "Only time will tell, friends. This is Sandy Aoran, wrapping up your latest up-to-the-minute NBS news-reak. And next, following these important announcements, the veather."

Getzlor cut the image. "Now how about *that*, Duane?"

He shook his head. "I didn't hear enough to make an valuation. Did you disk it?"

"No. At the start I was only half-listening; when I finally ealized what they were talking about, it caught me offbase. But aere's the handle." Her smile showed great satisfaction. "Chicago '.D. has a Phoenix Foundation stooge who plays double agent, eeds info both ways. Phoenix has been trying to recover one of heir people who's been kidnapped—but without telling the olice, let alone us. Now, though, Chicago's finest is on the case, nd so are our own people."

Still toweling himself, Duane said, "But what does that have to lo with this telecast?"

"*Dummy!*" She wasn't really angry; she didn't even throw her lass at him. "Phoenix Foundation. Tolliver. Aliens. That turkey alling himself the Reverend Floyd; we still want *his* ass, don't orget! And the kidnapping I just mentioned: one of the suspects is  man named Clint Haydock."

Duane Eads nodded. "So we get on it personally."

"I knew you'd catch it sooner or later. Get us packed, while
work out the fastest plane reservations."

"Wouldn't a government jet be better?"

"Before one could get here, I'll have some poor suckers bumpee
out of first class and we'll be on our way."

Not bothering to clothe himself, Eads left Getzlor to make he
calls, while he himself set to packing.

# XXIX

Whether Police Sergeant Strom Baylor liked it or not, FBI agen
Keith (no first name given) was pretty much taking over the
interrogation of the suspects. More and more, Keith openly
leaned on Baylor, moving in and calling the plays. With Haydock
under scop, the polygraph confirmed that the man had engineered the kidnapping of one Troy dos Caras, and that he truly
believed he had seen the victim—unmistakably male, original
ly—become female. "All right," Keith said. "Now the othe.
one."

Assuming the needles—both hypodermic and recording—
could be trusted,·this Brad Salich or however he spelled it wasn'
implicated in the kidnapping; in fact he'd tried to locate and
rescue dos Caras, his down-the-hall neighbor. So from this one,
after he named the kidnappers—Haydock, the Schweer woman
who'd gotten away, Collins who was dead, and Amory Neill who
apparently was still running loose somewhere—there wasn't any
further handle on the crime itself. And neither of them knew how
Troy dos Caras had escaped, let alone where he or she might be
now. What Keith and Baylor did learn was that freak or no freak,
dos Caras had a wife.

The officers were polite enough, but still the uniformed woman
insisted that Eden pack an overnight bag and come along.

"But what's this all about? I haven't done anything. My

husband's been kidnapped; I can't leave—I have to be here in case anyone tries to get in touch. You see, don't you?"

No matter what she said, none of it helped. An hour later, with her hastily gathered gear deposited in what was essentially a cell though without bars, Eden sat in a drab room and listened to questions. Some she couldn't answer—the rest, she wouldn't.

Until the grey-haired woman, who looked fragile until her voice dispelled that impression, said, "Needle time."

"You can't do that," the police captain said. "This woman's pregnant, and God knows *what* kind of damage the drugs might do."

"The decision's not in your jurisdiction, Captain. Nor God's, for that matter. It's in mine. You do recall who I am, don't you?"

He nodded. "Yes, Madam Director. But authority or not, it's still a capital crime to deliberately harm a pregnant woman."

"Deliberately, yes. But *you* wouldn't do such a thing, would you? And you're nominally in charge of this investigation." She smiled. "Do you understand what I'm saying?"

"You rotten bitch!" Ripping his badge free, the man threw it at her. He missed. "Maybe I can't stop you—but you won't involve *me* in your shitty moves. Because I quit!"

He went out the door. The woman said, "Duane, have him picked up and put on ice." Beside her the pale, sweating man signaled agreement and spoke briefly into a handcomm. Then, not hurrying, he followed the police captain's departure.

The woman—Director, whoever or whatever—spoke to a white-smocked man. "We've wasted enough time. Shoot her up."

Physically, Eden was no match for any one of the police officers. But it took three of them to hold her down.

Before anything else I got to a phone and called the apartment, but Eden didn't answer. Well, maybe she was out for a while; in the meantime I settled for a hot shower. Then a medic picked sand and gravel out of the soles of my feet and applied antibiotic ointment, so that normal footwear felt reasonably okay—except that the borrowed shoes were too big. After that I called again, but still got no response.

Security Chief Bennest had to agree that none of the mess was *my* fault, but still I wasn't exactly in his good books. "One more time, let's run it past," he said. "Of the persons involved in this kidnap mob, which ones actually saw anything important?"

I don't know why he didn't listen better the first time, but I went through it again: the only outsiders who *knew* I'd changed modes were Olive Schweer and Clint Haydock. Of the others who'd been to Olive's place, Banshuck and Collins were dead, Gacek the hacker didn't know I existed—and to the best of my knowledge, neither Brad Szalicz nor Amory Neill suspected me of any differences from the Mark One norm.

Olive was locked up, of course, but her durance wasn't especially vile; she had a Tri-V in the room, and no one had confiscated the cannabis from her purse. Amory, after emergency treatment including surgery on his wound, was in Intensive Care.

What worried Bennest, of course, was that the police had Clint Haydock. From his tone of voice you'd think *I* turned Haydock in; finally I said, "The cops got Clint and Brad because you let *your* man go along in the wrong car."

Bennest spread his hands. "How was I to know you can't drive?" Then he shook his head. "Wrong. If I'd stopped to think . . ."

I knew what he meant. Growing up in the Feen we had no need for cars, no reason to learn to use them. Living Outside now, I couldn't think of more than two or three M-2s who owned their own vehicles. Now, because Bennest had eased off on me, I said, "I guess it wasn't the best possible environment for thinking."

Giving a sheepish grin, he shrugged. "I suppose not. But still—"

The phone chimed. I started toward it but then realized Eden couldn't possibly know where I was. Bennest took it. The picture was streaky but I could tell it was a pay booth. Moss Frantz, mussed-up and looking excited, spoke fast. "They got Heath! And Leslie Cargill, and at least two others; I didn't get a good look. It's a raid, Mr. Bennest! Some kind of police roundup. I don't know how they found out about us, but the FBI's in on it, and—"

"How do you know that?"

"Heard them talking, from where I hid. When I saw they had Leslie I tried to get to our condo and warn Heath, but they were there first. I—"

"All right, Moss—all right! Call every M-Two you can think of; tell them to head for cover. If the wrong person answers, cut the circuit *fast*. You understand?"

"Yes, sir."

"Then get off this line and start doing it!" When the screen cleared he called Security Comm and gave much the same instructions, then shut the phone off and turned to me. "We have only six operators on duty; let's go down there and help."

"Yes, of course. In just a minute." He looked impatient, but I called Eden anyway. With no success at all.

I stood. "They've got her, haven't they?"

"It's a possibility."

"I have to go find out!"

"And run into a trap? No. You'll stay and help work the Comm Room; we have to reach as many as we can."

If he stuck to that, there was no way I could get Outside. I said, "If Eden gets hurt, and I could have saved her, I won't forget who kept me here."

I'd distracted his train of thought; he blinked, and shook his head. "No, I suppose you wouldn't. Let's hope it doesn't come to that. Look, Troy—I'm acting on my best judgment; it's all I *can* do. Now please go to the Comm Room and tell them I'll be along, just as soon as I've reported this development to Chairman Bardeen."

There wasn't much else I could do, so I went.

*Oh, bloody hell!* "And you say the FBI's in it?"

"That's what Moss Frantz claims, Mr. Bardeen," Bennest said. "And yes, I know that kid's given us trouble in the past, but this time I'd swear she was sincere, totally concerned."

"I wasn't arguing." Quickly, Bardeen tried to put his thoughts in some kind of order. "All right, Bennest. We know Getzlor's history with the Bureau: she bulls ahead, ignoring such legal niceties as individual rights, and she gets away with it. So go ahead with your plan to get Outside M-Twos to cover, as many as you can. But at the same time begin preparations to get our own hidden M-Twos—those past puberty or nearing it—*out* of the Feen, into covered situations Outside. Because two gets you ten: once Getzlor's interrogations give her a solid fix on the Foundation, she'll try to mount a raid."

Bennest seemed skeptical. "Using warrants, or force? Chairman Bardeen—which are you asking me to prepare for?"

There wasn't *time* for this kind of quibbling. "Either or both, dammit! We do have contingency plans for dispersion—they're old, though, and need updating. I'll put some people on it, and get back to you. Meanwhile, concentrate on protection for our Outside M-Twos, as many as are still loose."

"Right. I'm on it." The screen darkened; Bardeen turned away, but almost immediately the instrument chimed again. Exasperated, he moved back to activate the circuit and match the code-indicated scramble pattern.

"Kennet? Pidge Sutton here. The poop's hit the filter."

In practically no time at all, Bardeen knew he was in over his head. "Thurwald computer-enhanced the picture and made ID on you," Pidge told him. "He's faxed an emergency warrant down to Justice, direct to the Attorney General. Murder One, though I expect he'll have to settle for second degree. But asking arrest *and* extradition. So you'd better head for a safe hole."

His thoughts bordering on chaos, Bardeen nodded. "Yes. Thanks, Pidge. Look—shouldn't you get off now, before somebody traces this call and tags you for an accessory?"

Sutton chuckled. "Trace it? Not on my private bootleg relay, they won't. But I don't want to hold *you* up. So get moving, and good luck!" The call ended.

So. If he didn't hide, Bardeen would be charged with the murder of Amos Calhoun, locked up and removed from Earth. And nobody could run a complex evacuation program from a jail cell, let alone a jail cell on the moon. He needed another answer.

He called Thane Cogdill, but Laura Casey answered. Bardeen said, "Laura? Terrible thing."

Her eyes widened. "But how did *you* know?"

*Bennest told me, of course!* But suddenly his hunch said they weren't talking about the same problem. He sighed. "Laura, tell me all of it."

Her lip twitched. "They got him on the machines soon enough; the odds are good. But Thane's stroke was really massive. The ultrasonics dissolved the clot, but if he's able to speak within less than a month he'll be lucky. Let alone walk."

Her smile was a good try but it didn't work. "He can hear, though; you can tell he understands. Do you want to give him a message?"

It was odd, he thought, how hopes could crash to ruin, shake a man's whole world, and still make no sound. "Just tell him to stay tough and get well."

"I will. Thank you."

When the screen cleared, Bardeen tried to think what to do. He needed to improvise a crash program, some way to hide out from the lunar warrant and still stay in touch to guide the Mark Two evacuation measures. Because while Erwin Bennest was very good at following instructions, making plans on his own initiative was no great part of his talents.

Breathing deeply, Bardeen thought back to earlier times, willing his subconscious to come up with something useful.

And it did. He punched up an old computer file—yes, the phony ID from his *first* moon trip, so long ago, was still listed as valid. Quickly he created and inserted a factitious skeleton of the intervening years of "Barrett Kendall's" life. The pseudo was rather obvious; he realized as much. But he didn't have *time* to build a new one. Now then—

Did the St. Louis Hilton's executive suites have lines that bypassed the hotel switchboard, and terminals that could handle 3-A Scramble? Yes, he learned; they did. So he made his reservation, with the suite number confirmed. Saint Louis, he thought, was definitely his best choice: relatively near, and he could get there via the tubetrain system. Starting from the station here in Feen territory, and reaching the hotel without ever surfacing Outside. Perfect? Maybe not, but close to it.

He called Jenny, told her he'd have to be away for a time. "It's hush-hush, so if anyone asks questions—and I mean *anyone*— this call didn't happen; you don't know anything at all."

"Actually, that's true enough." Her voice sounded concerned. "Can't you tell me anything?"

"Best not. Except—I love you, and I'll be in touch when I can. And whatever they say, it's not as bad as they'll try to make you think it is."

*Some reassurance!* Why hadn't he ever let her know this problem existed? Because he hadn't thought it would ever catch up to him. Now, turning away from the phone, he concluded that there wasn't time to set up the M-2-evacuation staff from here; he'd have to do that from his St. Louis hideaway. So instead he began looking through the travel gear he kept at his office, and in a short time put an adequate kit together.

He punched up a call to Bennest's office, to the special line that no one else answered, but got the machine instead. All right; he said, "Erwin? I need to be out of town for a while; I'll be in touch with you via this number. Meanwhile you will serve as my proxy at Board meetings; this call authorizes the appointment, on the basis that you and I will confer on all matters that aren't purely routine, and you will then pass my recommendations along to the Board and exercise my vote as I specify. If anyone questions the arrangement, remind them that Thane had me do the same for him a few times. Good luck, now."

Was there anything else? Yes, the security of calls he'd be making from the hotel. Remembering what Pidge had said, Bardeen set to work arranging a traceproof relay route.

All right. Using first his private elevator and then an underground moveway carrying enough people that he didn't worry about being conspicuous, he headed for the tube station.

"Nearly sixty names, we got from that pregnant freak before she passed out!" Pacing the hotel room, Getzlor raged. "And how many did we net? How many, Duane?"

Duane Eads was, in the vernacular, sweating bullets. He'd *never* seen Annek in such a fury. He hoped she wouldn't want to take her frustrations out with sex; in this frame of mind, God only knew where her tendencies might lead.

"Well, only four. And then, of course—"

She pivoted to turn on him. Finger pointed like a gun, she yelled, "*And then of course* every damned one of the inhuman alien monsters tried to kill themselves, and three came so close that they can't be questioned for at least a day." She lowered her voice a little. "But with all four, plus what we found in the living quarters of the ones who got away, we can show ties to the Phoenix Foundation." Now her hand made chopping gestures. "This is all we have, Duane. That mudhead Reverend Floyd seems to have disappeared off the face of the earth, and with him goes *that* batch of leads. So I say we mount a raid on Phoenix, and take the goddamn place apart!"

"Well, it's definitely one possibility." Stalling, Eads realized there were at least three points here: first, the captives couldn't be aliens because when it came to treating them, their blood matched that of human donors. Second, it seemed that the sex-changing rumors were true: one comatose prisoner combined very small, rudimentary male organs with a patch of mucous membrane—surrounding a dimple that might or might not be an incipient vaginal opening—behind the shrunken scrotum. Duane wasn't sure why the ambiguity made his crotch tingle, but this was no time for dalliance. Not even mentally.

Because the main point needed a lot of pushing. "Annek, *listen*! You may be right about the Foundation. But we mustn't move without full authorization." Getzlor probably neither knew nor cared that a sizable part of the original Phoenix endowment came from the Archer family, the very same that had produced President U. S. Archer. But Duane knew. He said, "Call the Atty-Gen first; that's all."

Snorting like Toro after a nasty bout with the picadors, Getzlor said, "Oh, all right! I'll call the sneaky little mooch. Or rather, you will." She swung around toward the bathroom. "I'm going to take a shower. You get that business done in time for dinner. Which I want in exactly half an hour."

Behind her the door slammed. Eads sighed. Attorney General Asa "Ace" Ritter would either say Yes or say No, or refuse to make up his mind, putting the question on hold; that made two cases out of three in which all hell would break loose. Well, no help for it; he punched up the number.

Thinking all the while: the *real* problem was that Annek hadn't given any hint as to what she wanted for dinner. So whatever he ordered, he would be wrong.

# XXX

Nobody pushed Ace Ritter around; if you didn't believe that, you could ask him. When he took the call from Getzlor's tame pussyhound, Ace said, "How they hanging, Duane? Or has Big Mama bit 'em off yet?" As usual, Ace laughed at his own quip. "Well then, boy; what's on your mind?"

When Eads told him, laughter was the farthest thing from Ace's thoughts. "Raid the Feen? Is the woman crazy, or what?"

Looking pale and sweaty, the secretary said, "She thinks she has cause: proof that something on the order of treason has been going on under Foundation auspices. Some of it I'd rather not discuss except in person, and preferably within shielded premises. But I don't think this is a good move, or a safe one. Of course I've been told to convince you otherwise, but—"

"But you better hope she's not taping calls on that phone, boy, or you just kissed your ass goodbye." Eads looked, then, as though he'd been struck; Ritter said, "Aw, don't worry. You folks just got there; couldn't've been time to put in bugs. And anyway—doesn't matter *which* side of your mouth you talk out of, the orders won't change."

"Orders from whom? Yourself, or—"

"From Uncle Sam Archer *his* very self." Ace wasn't about to tell this wimp the circumstances—that Archer was even stalling around on the matter of letting Ace serve the Feen with a perfectly legitimate murder warrant, issued by a Lunar court.

Eads licked his lips. "And those orders are?"

"Hands off the Feen. No raid, anyway. Whatever you and Getzlor and your troops can investigate by normal means, go to it. But the Foundation's charter has some real funny stuff in it; without you have some reasonable suspicion of a crime or criminal right there on the premises, I don't think a regular warrant'll get you in."

Getzlor's secretary shook his head: sweating like a horse and smelling about the same, Ace guessed. "But what can I tell Annek?"

Ace shrugged. "Tell her your hands are tied; so are hers, and maybe even mine. Maybe she better talk direct to Uncle Sam."

Eads shook his head. "No. That's your job, Mr. Ritter. I've given you the Director's request; now you pass it along. Or else give her your orders personally."

Ace scowled; who did this crotchmonkey figure he was talking to? "I'll think about it."

The other man's voice rose. "*Think* about it? Do you realize that without a direct order to the contrary, she's more likely than not to go right ahead with this raid?"

Ace grinned. "Wouldn't hurt my feelings a whole bunch, if that boss of yours got her ass in a sling."

"Right alongside yours, Ace. You say this line isn't bugged and you may be right—but I have *you* on disk, refusing right out loud to consult the President *or* to give or forward direct orders to my superior."

*What the hell?* "Now just you wait a minute, there—!"

"For what? Either you'll take action or you won't. You have the information, and you have our number here. Goodbye."

The screen blanked. Ace Ritter scratched his head. "What in hell got *into* that bleached-out pansy?"

Ace figured he'd better do *something*. But the lines to Uncle Sam Archer's answering machines were all busy—and when Ace finally swallowed his pride and tried to call back to Eads, he found he had the number wrong.

Eddie Losch was a police clerk; he also took side money from Erwin Bennest. So when Eddie overheard the FBI woman cussing about some suicide-prone prisoners, and mentioning the Phoenix Foundation in derogatory terms, he took his coffee break early.

But not for coffee. Eddie went down to the lobby; from a pay phone there, he called Bennest.

"Yes. Thanks, Eddie, and the tip's worth a bonus. Keep in touch." As he ended the call, Bennest considered what he needed to do next.

It didn't take him long. There were Mark Twos working in the news-copy sections of Chicago's five major Tri-V stations. Within fifteen minutes he arranged that each of those outlets would carry brief announcements, innocuous to the general public but telling Mark Two viewers a very simple message:

*They've taken some of us alive, so the suicide imperative no longer applies.*

Duane Eads found his hands were shaking. Why, he'd actually yelled at the Attorney General! Maybe it had done some good, maybe not. But right now, a glance at his watch showed that never in this world would he have dinner served up here on time.

So the hell with it. Regardless of what Annek might have preferred, he ordered one of his own favorites: shrimp creole.

No doubt of it, he could be in for a rough evening. But now if Ace Ritter would only believe in the nonexistent record of their recent conversation. . . .

Half-awake, Eden felt sore all over—as if she'd been doing strenuous exercise without warming up first or cooling down afterward. She felt sweaty, too, and itchy; all in all, she needed a good hot shower.

She sat up to look around, and—*oh, shit!*—it came to her, where she was and what had happened.

This crummy little room, hardly more than a cell: after the drug part and the questioning, while she was still punchy as a peach-orchard boar, they'd put her in here.

And now where were they? She couldn't hear anyone nearby, but that didn't prove anything. She eased her heavy pregnancy off the cot and up to standing, trying to assess how she felt. Not too bad; her head felt too big and her ears were ringing a little, but otherwise the drugs had worn off. Mostly she was thirsty, and at the same time needed to take a leak: *well, that's balance for you.* The room had a cubby with lav and toity, so everything worked out fine.

Except for the goosebumps. It was chilly in here; she needed some clothes. Nothing in this room—so, first peeking around the door into a larger place and seeing no one there—she went past that door and began looking through a row of lockers.

Most of them held, among other items, dull-green clothing: janitors' uniforms. She checked several of those, but nothing anywhere near the right length would close over her big gut. So she put on some Fat Clothes and rolled up the wide pantlegs. In a mirror she looked like some kind of clown, but since when was *that* against the law? A round, rollbrim denim cap matched the rest of the ensemble.

Eden's perceptions weren't entirely solid, but she knew she wanted clear of this place. She could see the hall leading to the main way out, but probably there'd be a bunch of cops there, ready to stick needles in her again.

It struck her as some kind of miracle that her captors had misjudged how long the interrogative dope would keep her out, and left her alone here. Maybe when it came to tolerance for that kind of drug, Mark Twos were different; *she* didn't know.

Her gut twitched hard, and then again—for long moments Eden feared she might be losing the baby. But then she recognized a combination of hunger and flatulence; the sudden relief almost made her laugh.

*No time for this stuff!* How to get out of here? But as Eden looked around, a door opened and a darkskinned man—wearing an outfit similar to her own—came in. "Hey, you!"

Panic froze her, until he said, "Need some help. C'mon."

So, "Sure," and she followed him through the door and down a hall to where a container cart waited by an elevator.

"Help me get this mutha in, ride on down, we put it out in the alley." The help part was holding the door because it tried to close too fast. On the way down he said, "You're new?"

She thought; yesterday had been Monday. "First week, yeah."

"Not much of a job, but better'n nothing." The car stopped and its door opened; outside the sky was grey, the wind chilly.

When the cart was out, then pushed to the marked pickup area, the man looked back to the closed elevator door and said, "Bar across the street, just off thisyere alley. You been there?" She shook her head. "Time enough we could have a drink; that quick they won't miss us."

A bar would be closer to out of this mess, but one thing might be a hassle. "I don't have any money."

"Left it in your locker, huh? Okay—I'll spring. You can pay me later."

"Right."

Down the alley, across the street at mid-block to the garish dingy tavern. His name, he said while they walked, was Darnold. Her mind stalled; after too long a pause she said, "Edna. Edna Rose," and as he held the door open, hoped she could remember what she'd said.

Inside, the place was pretty bad; its saving grace was a lack of blaring music. Darnold went to the bar itself. "Let's sit right up here." But as she clambered aboard a bar stool he put a tenspot on the counter. "Get me a bourbon rocks—for you, whatever you like. Gotta go see a man about a dog," and he walked away, toward the door that read "Studs."

If the tall, unshaven bartender had come immediately to take her order, Eden wouldn't have made her move. Instead the man gave her one look, then apparently dismissed any importance she might have and turned back to talk with another customer. So after a few seconds, or perhaps half a lifetime, Eden picked up Darnold's ten dollars. Taking care not to hurry, she walked out.

She was tempted by the two restaurants she passed before coming to a tube station, but first things first.

Once this was over, she thought while the train took her nearer to safety, she'd have to pay Darnold's money back.

When Cogdill fell—and couldn't get up or even yell for help—the panic was the worst thing he'd ever had in his life. When Laura walked in and found him she called the emergency number first of all, and only then came to sit and hold him.

After two or three tries at making words and listening to the animallike sounds that came out, he gave up on speech. He couldn't smile, either; the right side of his face felt dead, along with the arm and leg on that side, and he felt drool oozing down the side of his neck. The dying didn't bother him so much as not being able to tell Laura goodbye, and that he loved her.

What the medic jabbed into him was probably a trank, not a

sedative; he was still aware, more or less, but just didn't give much of a damn about anything. At the hospital, when they'd done all the things he supposed were standard practice to hospitals, Laura sat and held his good hand until he went to sleep.

They must have put him out for some of the treatment, because he didn't remember his head undergoing anything that would cause it to need a bandage. Although he was still a bit fuzzy when the taller doctor gave him the pep talk, he took it to heart: he could expect to make a considerable recovery, though probably not total, but he'd have to work at it like all hell.

So then, answering, from his left hand as it lay across his chest he put out one finger. They'd wanted him to blink once for yes and twice for no, but his right eyelid's response lagged and the discrepancy bothered him. So, one finger or two; after a few minutes they caught on and accepted the change.

The medical troops had left. Now, waiting for Laura to arrive, Cogdill tried to think of a more flexible means of communication. Yes and no didn't quite fill the bill, because he had no way to tell people what questions to ask!

In his teens, Thane Cogdill had worked the ham bands with his own licensed amateur radio transmitter; when it came to Morse Code—Continental, actually—he'd been expert. But now— mentally he shrugged—even if he could remember the code and indicate its units by finger motions, who else would know it? (Through his mind ran the arcanely scatological yell his school's cheerleaders had used to mystify opponents: "Three Dits, Four Dits, Two Dits, Dah. Midville High School, Rah Rah Rah!" Or, how to get away with saying "S, H, I, T," right in front of the faculty. *I guess it wasn't really all that funny.*)

He squinted, sidelong, to read the digital wall clock. *Laura should be here soon.* Well, if he wanted recovery he'd better start working at it, so Cogdill visualized his right hand moving its fingers and made the mental effort that ordinarily produced that result. No matter how long he tried, he couldn't feel whether he was succeeding. But the concentration on pure effort did something else for him: an idea came. He could *write*, couldn't he? Not well; he'd always been incorrigibly right-handed. Large block letters, though, he could probably manage. Slowly and awkwardly, but better than nothing.

So when Laura came in he held his left hand up, fingers bent to simulate holding a pencil, and made scribbling motions.

She bent to kiss him. "We can do better than that." She turned back to say to the woman following her, "Let me put the goojie on the bed first—the thing you set trays on. Then we can place the terminal so he can use it."

It was that simple; once the thing was plugged in, turned on, and set to print onscreen, Cogdill reached his index finger to touch the keyboard. First, thank her: TNX LAURA (spacespacespacespace) IM OK IN HR          JST CNT TLK N ALL

She looked puzzled; he realized he was condensing words in the fashion of the old Phillips cable code he'd learned on his first or second job. EEE       he typed—meaning Error, but she wouldn't know that, either! So: WRITING SHORT FORM        OK QQ

Would she understand that QQ meant ?? which was uppercase so he couldn't do it easily with one hand? Close enough, apparently, because she nodded. All right: U OK QQ

Again she nodded. TTS GD          LUV U          SRY ABT THS        CLDNT HLP IT U NO

"Yes, I know. Oh, Thane!" She leaned over and hugged him. "I'm so glad you can *talk* to me!" Then, sitting up again, she said, "Now you just rest, and work at getting well. All right?"

It wasn't all right; there was too much he needed to know. WHR KENNET QQ        WHR HE RT NW QQ

"Right now?" Laura made a puzzled frown. "Why, I'm not sure. I told him about—about what's happened, and—"

WOT HE SAY QQ        "Just, tell you to stay tough and get well. He sounded rather distracted, I thought, but—"

*It's happened*, Cogdill decided. *That moon thing caught up with him, and he's had to run for it.*

So now who was going to handle the whole mess? *Me, I guess.*

No way to condense these next questions; Cogdill's hand was beginning to ache, but he typed THIS RIG PATCH IN TO FEEN QQ

"I don't know, Thane; I'll find out."

Not good enough. No point in sketching alternatives: GET ONE TT WILL        Then: SCRTY BENNEST        OK QQ

She nodded and said, "I'll try, Thane," but before he could type anything more, the nurse was there to stick a needle in him.

"It's a damn *fortress*, Ms. Getzlor," said agent Keith. "Physically and procedurally, both. Eccles and Kincaid played salesmen— manufacturers' reps—and tried the street entrance. They say it

opens into a concrete labyrinth an Army assault platoon would
have a hard time cracking, and at the second check point their
credentials were turned down. Jennings and I went in through one
of their private tube stations, as part of a crew delivering supplies
from Unicorp. Our IDs were good enough for that company, but
the Phoenix security people practically laughed in our faces.
Before they showed us out, though, I saw enough to know it
wouldn't pay to try to force entrance there, either."

He shrugged. "I'm sorry; we gave it our best try. But my
professional opinion is that no quickie raid could possibly work.
The only politically feasible way to open that place up is by *legal*
clout."

Getzlor nodded. "Thank you, Keith." He had a hangdog look
to him, so because his implacable, somewhat blank expression
stirred vague sparks within her, she said, "Nobody likes to get bad
news, or bring it, either. But good or bad, more important is to tell
it *right*. You've done a good job for me."

*Time to wrap this up.* "I'll want your group's combined written
report—and I assume you'll have pictures?" He nodded. "By
noon tomorrow, then." The man left; Getzlor put her mind to
what her next move should be, and a thought came.

Since the raid idea was out, no point in staying pissed with Eads
for bucking her on that subject. And for that matter: although
shrimp creole wasn't one of her usual favorites, the meal he'd
ordered had been surprisingly good. "Duane?"

"Yes?" How could such a limp-minded man have such a stiff-
sounding voice? "Is there something you want me to do?"

*Not what you're thinking.* "Steive Dilmarr. Is that old fart still
hot in Tri-V, anyplace I could get some real action out of him? If
he is, tell me where. Because he owes me."

Not much later the answers came: NBS, the New York HQ, a
sort of side-desk exec. Getzlor was impressed; she hadn't thought
Dilmarr could get that far up the corporate ladder. He wouldn't be
there long, of course; sooner or later he'd fuck up the way he
always had, all his life. So use him right now!

Duane put the call through; then she took over. "Steive? Annek
Getzlor. I'm calling in a few on you, so listen. And make notes.
Damned *good* notes."

There's no reason to think your average Mark Two is any
smarter than other people, so the result of Bennest's warning alert
surprised me: of the ones the Comm Room reached, nearly all

called in to report successful escapes. I suppose it was because we'd always lived, Outside, under constant threat of exposure.

Later, though, one of our police moles phoned in bad news: four M-2s had been taken alive. So suicide on capture was now pointless; Bennest took action to cancel that directive and spread the word as best he could. Well, I'd never thought the suicide idea had a great deal to recommend it.

One equation nagged me. This raid/roundup thing developed soon after Eden disappeared; cause-and-effect said the police got the list of names by shooting her full of dope.

But how and why did they pick her up in the first place? Only one answer: Clint Haydock—an incompetent petty criminal, whose stupid mistakes were wrecking a very important plan and a lot of lives.

Including mine. But there was no point in blaming Clint; I might as well finger Bennest's man, whose failure to come back and drive the car had led to Haydock's capture.

Or Bennest himself. Or me, maybe? Because sometime, somewhere, there must have been something I could have done, to make things come out different.

I just wished to hell I could think what it might have been. Or better yet, something that would help *now*.

But what? Even if I got past Security and made it to Outside, and assuming I had it right that Eden was in custody, how could I get her out?

I'd seldom been much of a drinker, except for taste and the occasional mild social glow, but just then I saw how other people could really want a few solid belts of the stuff.

For me, though, it probably wouldn't work. I went down to the Executive Cafeteria and settled for a medium pizza.

I didn't even complain when it came with anchovies.

# XXXI

"I can't believe this! Travers—don't any of your people know where the brakes are? Or low gear, anyway? You let this get so far out of hand you have to bring it to *me* to fix?"

In a hectic period of nearly three years on the presidential staff, L. Travers Munro had never seen Uncle Sam Archer blow his containment housing this high or wide. Hastily he cleared his throat. "Sir, some of the material reached me only this afternoon. And the earlier items, in themselves, pointed to no definite conclusion. So we—"

"So you need me to kiss it and make it well." Sigh. "All right. Run it all through again, so I don't miss anything."

"Yes, sir." To his chief, Munro detailed the fragmentary, apparently harmless ingredients that now, somehow coalescing, seemed to be coming to a boil. The ludicrous claims of the dressed-up hillbilly messiah, Jody Jay Tolliver ("demons and monsters, my dear friends"), would gain considerable credence if he could really tie an FBI spokesman to his stories of invading aliens and their supposed connections to the Phoenix Foundation. Then the network Tri-V 'cast, with the newswoman Sandy Moran quoting someone in Chicago to the effect that he had physical *custody* of an inhuman monster. That claim, of course, remained to be proved. But still, with a jittery populace verging on paranoia and looking for scapegoats . . . ?

"And now, sir," Munro continued, "Ace Ritter says he's been warned that our FBI Director wants to raid the Phoenix Foundation for evidence, even if it takes pure force—up to and including the threat of martial law. He hasn't come up with any solid facts, though, and doesn't show much sign of trying. I wonder—"

Archer waved a hand. "Don't tell me about Ace; I know already, but we still have to put up with him because I promised I would. If I ever get inaugurated a second time, remind me to stay sober." The President's glare precluded any comment, so Travers Munro reclosed his mouth, as Archer said, "Annek Getzlor was a mistake. I knew she was roughshod but I thought the times called for it. Population riots because the count was *dropping* too fast. And of course I never thought she'd get this far out of hand." He shook his head. "Well, I guessed wrong."

Munro waited, reconsidered his first thought and then said, "What's to be done, sir?"

"Bypass Ace; call Getzlor direct. Tell her to report to me personally—by phone, that is—for orders."

"And—" This was shaky ground. "And if she doesn't?"

When he wanted to, Uther Stanton Archer could make a very mean grin. "Then she'll be fired. And if there's trouble—well, Federal marshals, with proper warrants, can arrest *anyone*. We might want about three, out there. See to it."

Leaving the President's office, L. Travers Munro wondered whether he might not be in the wrong line of work.

It had been a long time, Steive Dilmarr thought—but now maybe he was going to get a little of his own back. He looked through the notes he'd made: the things Annek Getzlor had told him, and what he'd found among the references she'd passed along. Yes—this could make the biggest splash he'd ever tried for.

Whether or not Getzlor's accusations held water, the airing of them should make the Phoenix Foundation squirm; if her claims did stand scrutiny, squirming might be the least of the Feen's troubles. And just in case anything backfired, her name on the entire package made great cover for Steive Dilmarr's ass.

Without explanation, let alone apology, they turned Brad Szalicz loose. Head still buzzing from a drug hangover, he heard the grey-haired woman say that this one doesn't know anything and with any luck we'll need the space. So one of the uniforms gave him, in a plastic bag, the personal effects they'd taken when they brought him in; with no belt to his trousers, nor laces in his shoes, he was escorted outside. He sat on their front steps to correct those items of dress, then checked the rest of his stuff. He was pretty sure somebody'd lifted at least fifty bucks, maybe more, but he wasn't stupid enough to go back inside and make a complaint. *Hell—they could have taken all of it.*

On the tubetrain rides home and while he waited for his transfer, Brad tried to put together his memories of what had happened. Some of it, especially the parts when he was doped, didn't fit too well: how could Troy and Eden dos Caras, a bearded man and a pregnant woman, be hermaphrodites? Of course Troy wore no beard when the Feen's Security Chief nailed him along with crazy Amory, but for months he'd had one—and not phony, because Brad had seen it grow from scratch, nearly. If anybody was haywire here, Brad's hunch said it wasn't Troy dos Caras.

When he got home he didn't expect to find Lyndeen or Stosh there, but he'd lost track of a day or two. "Brad! Where have you been? What's happened?"

"Just a minute." He kissed her as if he'd been gone a very long time, greeted the little boy in much the same way, then went to get himself a beer, and sat down.

"This could take some time. If you understand it, you're doing better than I am."

Like a rimshot on the drums, the judge bounced his gavel across the bench. "Would the witness stop crying long enough to restate her answer so that the court may hear it?"

In the stand, Elli Sugarman wiped her eyes. "I'm sorry. All right, what I said is that I haven't ever gone to bed with anyone except my husband. Ever!"

The husband's lawyer, attorney for the plaintiff in the divorce suit, said, "But you don't deny that you're pregnant."

With a hand to her bulging belly, the woman said, "How could I? Even if I wanted to. But—"

"But," said the attorney, "you've already had one child by my client, and we all know that the Sterility Plague precludes a second pregnancy by the same father. Therefore—"

The gavel. "Objection from the bench. Counselor, you're repeating yourself. Do you have a further point here?"

"I am merely making certain that known facts are stated clearly on the record. The matter of adultery is now established. No further cross-examination."

Only lightly now, the gavel tapped. "Opposing counsel: do you have anything to add, before recess and decision?"

Black and slim, the woman stood. "I do, your honor. I protest the arbitrary prior exclusion of blood-type evidence."

"On what grounds?"

"The amniocentesis results." Speaking quickly, she allowed minimum opportunity for interruption. "Those data prove that the fetus has the same blood type as the couple's first child *and* its father, and Ms. Sugarman's blood type is *not* the same. If there is one *known fact* about the Sterility Plague, it is that for many years no woman has given birth to more than one child sired by men of the same blood type. So—"

The opposing lawyer's cries of "Objection!" drowned out whatever else the woman tried to say; finally the gavel silenced both parties. Nodding toward the respondent's counsel, the judge said, "Are you saying then, counselor, that a miracle has occurred? Is that your explanation?"

She shook her head. "Explanation? I don't have one. Except that perhaps the Sterility Plague is beginning to run its course. All I'm *saying* is that no medical data whatsoever gives any indication that Mr. Sugarman is not the father of his wife's imminent child. So I move that the previously excluded evidence be admitted and considered, to the effect that this divorce action be dismissed."

Tearful and disheveled, still in the witness seat, Elli Sugarman stood. "Sure! Go ahead! And then, Ray Sugarman you self-righteous sonofabitch, *I'm* filing for divorce. For mental cruelty, calling me a liar and putting me on trial. You—"

The gavel. "*Sit down!* Now then—"

"Elli baby, I'm sorry!" Redfaced and sweating, the husband came over the railing and rushed to his wife's side. "If *we* have another baby coming, I take it all back, I really do. Elli—"

The gavel wasn't helping much; the judge motioned for the bailiff to take action. Before that worthy quieted the two, Elli Sugarman said, rather loudly, "—and fire that asshole lawyer of yours, and pay *my* costs!

"And I get to name the baby!"

Eventually the court was cleared. Then, back in his chambers the judge treated himself to a doublesized drink.

With Heath in police custody and the alarm out for however many Mark Twos had been fingered, Moss Frantz saw no point in sneaking back to the Feen for refuge. Particularly when she knew that dispersal *from* the Feen might be the next step. So Moss, after tapping her membership trust credit for comfortable hideout money, was living a fugitive's existence. And except for worry about Heath, was enjoying it more than not.

Ray Sugarman had been a business contact; that's why Moss was in the courtroom to observe the divorce trial. Leaving, she found it hard to keep a straight face. Because, quite obviously, Ray

had benefited from the pseudogene powder Moss had put into the
water cooler just outside the man's office.

Among others—*many* others, Moss hoped—Elli Sugarman
was carrying a Mark Two fetus.

Whether the agencies hunting him had saturation coverage on
his possible exit routes or just got lucky, Bardeen never knew. But
a few minutes out of the station he saw a man coming along the
car toward him, and he smelled cop.

Luckily the aisle was full of people standing. Before the man
could reach him, Bardeen made his way to the exit door; seconds
later, the train stopped and he got off. Moving quickly across the
platform he was barely in time to board a train going the other
way, which he rode through two stops and left at the third. Then,
arbitrarily, he chose to wait while three southbound trains came
through, and got on the fourth.

Without further incident he rode to St. Louis and took a cab to
the Hilton, where he checked in as Barrett Kendall.

He found his suite quite satisfactory. After letting Jenny know
he was safely where he'd planned to go, and then calling Erwin
Bennest's covert phone to leave a message on the answering
gadget, Bardeen settled into the solace of a hot bath, where he
read news printouts and sipped bourbon.

If you do it right, he thought, the life of a fugitive doesn't have
to be all bad.

But neither present comfort nor relief for his clean escape could
keep the worries away indefinitely.

*So now what can I do?*

Rabble-rousing had always been Steive Dilmarr's major forte;
from what Thane Cogdill saw on the small Tri-V Laura had
brought in for him, the passage of years hadn't improved the man's
character. Pouchy-faced now, Dilmarr the executive limited
himself to the anchor role, leaving his younger colleagues to
deliver most of the text.

Which was, with respect to the Foundation, a damned skillful
job of "Heads I win, tails you lose." You had to hand it to the
sonofabitch: if Dilmarr's allegations didn't prove out, his sources
took the rap; if they did, he got the credit. And either way, his
smears put the Feen in deep horse puckie.

Motioning for Laura to turn the set off, briefly wishing these
smaller units had recording capability, he switched up his new

terminal and punched access to the secure line in Erwin Bennest's office.

BNNST V CGDLL        Would Bennest know that V meant "from"? Oh, hell; assume he'd figure it out. U THR QQ CUM IN PSE        No answer. OK I LV MSG        CALL BK ASAP        All right; what was his first priority? Oh, yes— U FIND KNNT YET QQ        I NEED TALK HIM        RE DLMRR MESS N WOT TO DO ABT IT

He was trying to think what to say next, when new words began to flow across the screen. TC V EB. So Bennest did know teleprinter protocol. CHRMN BARDEEN LEFT A VOICE CALL ON THIS LINE, WHICH HE WILL USE FOR FURTHER CONTACT. HE SAID HE HAS REACHED A SAFE BASE FROM WHICH TO OPERATE. HE WAN

Cogdill hit the "break" signal key. WOT HIS NBR QQ

HE DIDN'T GIVE IT. I ASSUME HE'S SET UP A CHAIN OF BLIND RELAY LEGS TO BLOCK TRACING. GA.

Go Ahead, huh? All right. HR MY NBR Carefully, Cogdill punched it up. GIV IT HIM N SAY I WANT TALK HIM        OK QQ

YES, SIR. WILL DO. AND IF THERE'S NOTHING MORE JUST NOW, LET ME SAY THAT I'M GLAD YOU'RE SO MUCH BETTER, SIR, AND ·

Break key! NOT        RPT NOT        BTR        MIND OK        BODY SHITCITY        Laura's hand on his shoulder reminded him not to excite himself; he tilted his head and winked the good eyelid at her. VY GD THEN EB        TLK U LTR N TNX        TC OUT

CALL AT ANY TIME, SIR. I'LL GET BACK TO YOU ASAP. EB OUT.

The modem beeped; its on-line light went out. To Laura now, Cogdill typed NW WE GG GET TIS TING MVG

Frowning at first, she said, "Going to get—?" Then, "Oh, sure—get this thing moving." She made a puzzled-looking grin. "I know the typing's a lot of work for you, Thane, but do you have to be *quite* so damn cryptic?"

He intended to poke up "Live and learn, woman," but the entry of a nurse bringing his dinner tray distracted him; the phrase came out LUV N LRN instead. Laughing, Laura Casey kissed him, moved his terminal off the bed, and sat to feed him.

*One thing I always dreaded was being helpless like this. But by damn!—it could be a helluva lot worse.*

\* \* \*

Whatever Annek's faults, Duane thought, she was strong on pragmatism. The captive with the scanty whiskers was in good enough shape for interrogation under drugs, so she put him to it.

Heath Crawford was the name. Not a bad-looking kid, with his dark hair and eyes, and the olive skin. Too young to be caught in this kind of bind—but whoever said life was fair?

To give Annek credit, she brought the drug dosage up slowly; when Crawford began to respond, she leveled it off. That's when the answers got interesting.

Afterward, with the Crawford kid trundled away to sleep the drugs out of his system while Getzlor and Eads used her commandeered office for private talk, she said, "If they're aliens, they're hypnotized not to know it." Her hand chopped air. "For now, it doesn't matter. Duane, while I run through what we learned here, check me on it."

He nodded, and she continued, "Crawford says they switch sex back and forth naturally, not on purpose. Periodic unless something sparks an early shift. I didn't understand quite all of that, but apparently if someone *anywhere* along the male phase breathes in pheromones from a woman who's having her period, within the next two or three days he turns female." She scowled. "Do I have it right, so far?"

"That's roughly what Crawford said; yes."

"All right then; we'll set up a test case."

His brows raised. "How—?"

"Oh for God's sake, Duane! *Somebody* around this place has to be menstruating. Find me one."

"Me? I'd be embarrassed." But the way she frowned then, he waved a hand and said, "All right! I'll tell that police lieutenant, the older one, and leave it up to her to find a volunteer. I suppose I can say it's a medical experiment." He paused. "By the way, what *are* you going to do?"

With an impatient snort, Getzlor said, "Nothing as kinky as you're probably imagining; all the woman has to do is change her sanitary device and give us the used one. We put that alongside Crawford so he can't help but get a good sniff, and then we wait. Taking pictures every hour or two, with a date-time group in the corner of each shot."

She paused. "We need the hair taken off the crotch, to give the camera a clearer view. So that whatever does happen, when we

take our case to Ace Ritter—and maybe we'll get Uncle Sam
Archer in on the action, too—we'll have good solid proof!"
   "Proof? Proof of what, Annek?"
   "How the hell do I know? We haven't *done* it yet!"

# BOOK
# FIVE

*"Secrets can be two-edged swords; always be sure which edge you face—and don't trust the flat sides, either."*
(*From Origins, by Rome dos Caras.*)

# XXXII

Eden's feet hurt, her back ached, her stomach burned, and this stupid gate guard wouldn't let her inside! "I'm sorry, ma'am, but I have to see some ID. That's my orders."

He was young—younger than herself—and probably new at the job. A Mark One, since Mark Twos seldom wore stubble haircuts. Squinting to read his nametag, she said, "Crayton! Call Erwin Bennest and tell him Eden dos Caras is here."

He shook his head. "I can't do that. His office isn't taking any calls right now. Some kind of emergency."

"I know; I'm part of it. You—" There was no point in getting mad at the kid; she said, "All right, forget that. But I think I'm going to have the baby, so you'd better get me in to the hospital. Because yours is the only place close enough." And if only by power of suggestion, she did feel a cramp!

That claim got to him; Miles Crayton called for a pair of medical orderlies and a stretcher.

When I went back to the Comm Room, still eating on my last quarter-wedge of pizza, one of the techs said, "Troy? There's a call for you." Mouth full, I nodded my thanks. Then she said, "It's Eden, at the hospital," and I dropped the pizza. Naturally it landed gooey-side down.

I don't remember what we said; once I knew she wasn't sick or hurt, I took off for the place on the high lope. How I got there is another blank; running the way I did, I was lucky not to have a fatal crash.

I do recall, vaguely, that the hospital people must have known I was coming, because nobody tried to slow me down. Then I found her room, and didn't quite spill her dinner tray when we hugged and kissed, and over the next hour or so we told each other everything that had happened lately. I even confessed bedding with Olive Schweer. I don't know why, but somehow my being in F-mode for the telling made the episodes seem more innocent.

Eden talked me out of my uncharacteristic urge to put a few lumps on Crayton, the gate guard. All else aside, "It wouldn't be fair, Troy. Not now. I'm sure he's one who's always been taught never to hit a woman." Since I didn't know little blue beans about physical combat, Crayton and I were both in luck.

Most of the next few days I spent in that room with Eden. Because our baby's advent seemed quite imminent.

But the little rascal stalled us for nearly seventy-two hours, and then required a Caesarean. She was XW, ostensibly female until puberty. We named her Hill.

Except for being near Alaska's Arctic coast, the Sand Bar wasn't much different from any other booze joint. When the Tri-V news took off into commercials, the big guy at the end of the bar went back to being loud. "I don't *believe* that crap. We got all kinds of weird critters running around here pretending to be just like us? And we can't tell the difference? This Steve Dilbers guy—"

"Dilmarr," the bartender said, pushing her hair back from one shoulder. "He's been around quite a while, Jimbo. Maybe he's right this time or maybe not." Hoping to shut him up, she said, "Hey, you're dry."

"Sure's hell am, Lucile." So she poured him a shot.

It didn't even slow him down. "Helluva note, if you don't know who's real people and who's not. Oughta be a law, get all those freaks locked up. What the gover'ment oughta do, if you ask me—"

By turning the Tri-V sound up louder than she really liked it, Lucile managed not to hear the rest.

When word came that Eden dos Caras had escaped, Getzlor was too tired to get angry. She put stakeouts on the dos Caras apartment and on the Phoenix Foundation's street-level gates. The Foundation's guards wouldn't let unauthorized personnel off the tube at their major station—and who knew how many other trick accesses there might be? So, since she simply didn't have enough agents to monitor passengers on the trains themselves, after two days she cut back on her surveillance efforts and decided to try another approach.

Heath Crawford wasn't female yet, but by this time he hardly fit Getzlor's idea of a male. He probably didn't know how they'd done it, because at Duane's suggestion Crawford's sense of smell had been knocked out by fumes from a strong room deodorant, before exposure to the menstrual pheromones.

Right now the kid looked scared, and that was exactly what Annek Getzlor wanted. His depilated nudity, as he sat on a cold metal chair with his hands cuffed behind his back, obviously embarrassed him. Getzlor pulled another chair over, swung it around and sat to straddle it backward, facing her prisoner at close range. "Well?"

"Well, what? Why do you have me here? I haven't done anything. You—"

She touched his crotch with the cattle prod, and he screamed. "You're not here to ask questions, Crawford. Only to answer them."

But even when the youngster began blabbing his guts out, the answers weren't a great deal of help.

Watching Annek use the prod, Eads felt his testes try to pull themselves up inside the body cavity. She'd used the thing on *him* once, a long time ago, and it put him out of commission for more than a month. After a time, now, she didn't even have to touch Crawford; a mere gesture brought the flow of words.

It wasn't productive, though; obviously this kid had no idea where the pregnant woman, Eden dos Caras, had gone to ground. Taking a chance, Eads tapped Getzlor on the shoulder.

"Yes, Duane?"

"Why can't our young friend call the Foundation and ask to speak with the dos Caras person? That way—"

"I won't!"

The prod twitched, but Getzlor stopped short of using it. "Oh, but you will."

As usual, she was right.

It was all *crazy*! Heath hadn't done anything wrong, but this woman who looked like somebody's sweet not-so-old grandmother had him here and kept *hurting* him.

Heath was no good with pain—never had been. So when the pale man handed him the phone, he did exactly what the woman told him to do. Knew it was wrong but obeyed anyway, because of what she could do with that damned *stick*.

"I'd like to—to speak with Eden dos Caras. Tell her it's Heath Crawford."

"I'll see if I can locate her." As the voice answered from the Feen's switchboard, the grey-haired woman, listening on another phone, nodded. There was a wait, and then, "I'm afraid she's not available just now, Crawford. She's in the hospital section, having her baby. Would you like to leave a message?"

The woman shook her head, so Heath said, "Uh—no, thanks. I'll—" But the pale man reached over and cut the circuit.

When the Crawford kid was taken away again, Annek Getzlor said, "All right, Duane; now we can move. Call a Federal judge and get a warrant out on Eden dos Caras. For escaping from custody. That gives us legitimate entry to the Foundation."

"But the original arrest wasn't legal!"

She suppressed her impulse to use the prod. "Unless you shoot your mouth off, the judge doesn't have to know that."

And on second thought, "While you're at it, Duane, I want a warrant for the other dos Caras, too. Troy, I think? Female, the last we heard. Might as well wrap up the whole package."

"But that one was the *victim*, not a criminal."

"Material witness, Duane. That's the catch-all term you can't seem to understand." She scowled. "Get cracking!"

Twenty minutes later, she had printouts of both warrants. "Now the next thing is, we seal the place."

After two days Bardeen reached Erwin Bennest directly; the man looked close to exhaustion but gave a concise report. "Now let's see if I can get Mr. Cogdill on here, too. If so, your screen will go to print mode, because that's the only way he can communicate. Now if you'll hold on a mo, please?"

Given no alternative, Kennet Bardeen held on, thinking about what he'd just been told—and how it fit with the Tri-V news.

Items: first Tolliver and now Dilmarr were talking interstellar aliens and putting them in the Feen's lunchbucket. The network newsie, Sandy Moran, was taking a more cautious stance: she told what she'd heard but didn't claim to believe it.

Closer to home, things were better than Bardeen had feared. For instance, both the dos Caras kids were back home safely. Some others had been captured, though, which certainly wasn't good news—but fewer than he'd have expected, once the balloon went up. Now if only—

But his screen went to print. KB V TC     U THR QQQ

Memory reaching back through decades (*I still know how to*

*talk this kind of shorthand!)*, Bardeen tapped at his keyboard. KB
HR     GD TO TLK U TC     HW U QQ

After a moment the screen added: FLAT OUT BUT HEAD
OK     SKIPIT FR NW     GD TLK U TOO     U HID
SAFE QQ

Bardeen punched TINK SO     WY U ASK QQ

The answer came: ON ACCT MOON TING CAUT UP
U     RITE QQ

Definitely. RITE     MAXE TINGS RUF     UNO QQ

Cogdill made no immediate answer. Then TIS TRI VEE SHIT
MAXE ME TINK WE DID IT ALL RONG     NEED TO
RVRS R FLD     UNO KNT QQ

Wrong, all this time? Bardeen wasn't sure; he couldn't change
his mind that fast but he gave it his best try. And now somebody
was pounding on his suite's door. He punched out PUT A MK
TWO ON FEEN BOARD     TROY DOS C MBY QQ     N
THEN FGUR GO PUBLIC OR NOT     GOT GO NW
KB OUT

Because the door wasn't going to last much longer, and it
didn't. Following the people who broke the panels away, a balding
man came in, wearing the uniform of Lunar Security. "Kennet
Bardeen, I arrest you for the murder of Amos Calhoun."


When the orderly came and took him to the room where they'd
asked him all those questions, Jody Jay got so scared he thought he
was going to wet his pants. But this time the woman wasn't
there—just the pantywaist secretary and a younger, skinny man
wearing glasses. And no cattle prod.

"Sit down, Tolliver."

"Yes, sir." Well, a few polites never hurt. But *now* what did the
man want?

He didn't ask; he waited, until Eads said, "How would you like
to go back to work?"

"Just fine. But—"

The man gave a thin smile. "There's been a policy change. We
*want* you to get people beating the bushes for those freaks."

"You mean the aliens?"

"You won't use that term, for now. Nor demons, either.
Unnatural monsters, yes, and with a connection to the Phoenix
Foundation. But none to the Bureau; you'll disavow your earlier
mention of the FBI as an information source."

Puzzled, Jody Jay leaned forward. "Could you write this stuff down for me? So I don't get mixed up?"

The skinny one cleared his throat. "That won't be necessary. I am Agent Gipson, and I'll be going along with you, to supervise your scripts and make sure, before the recordings are aired, that everything is stated properly."

Tolliver slumped. "No more live shows?"

Shrugging, Eads said, "Your other material, do it however you choose. But anything relating to this one critical subject, you'll put on disk. To Gipson's satisfaction. Aside from that, Tolliver, you'll have everything back just the way it was."

He thought about it. "Not hardly. That damn cattle prod of hers, I think it killed me, down there."

For a moment the secretary looked startled. Then he said, "Only for a time—or so I hear. Not permanently."

In a hurry then, they got Jody Jay back in his own clothes and flew him to Cincinnati in a pokey little unmarked six-seat jet. The only other passenger was Gipson, who didn't say much.

When the airport cab dropped the two men off, Jody Jay was glad to see Cora Sue. While he steeped himself in a hot bathtub she helped Gipson settle into the spare room—at least the government man hadn't usurped the master bedroom. Then she came to share the tub.

But all the best ministering Cora Sue could manage didn't do anything at all for Jody Jay Tolliver. After a while, because she was looking like to cry, he said, "You're doin' fine, Cora Sue, but I had me some bad things happen. So you can stop for now. And figure it may take a time yet."

When Annek Getzlor sealed an area off, she didn't fool around. Early one morning the Phoenix Foundation's street entrances were blocked by rows of abandoned, heavily loaded trailers; Getzlor's Tri-V monitors showed how smoothly *that* maneuver had gone. Since tubetrain access was difficult to monitor or control, she sent armed agents to shut down the entire route. Then, electronically from her improvised command post in the drab Fed Building she slapped emergency status to both the dos Caras warrants previously served on Erwin Bennest—or rather, she knew, entered into his computer terminal. But this move would force a quicker response.

"All right, Duane," she said. "Now we'll see what the bastards do."

He'd told her, and she'd been pleased to hear, that the Reverend Tolliver was being put back to work under close supervision. But now that subject lost interest, as Getzlor waited for a response from the Foundation. And waited . . .

The hell of it was that when her patience flagged and she tried calling Bennest direct, his machine promised a return call but no such thing happened. "What's he *doing?*"

Roughly two hours later, one of her monitor screens gave the answer. It showed eight large heelies converging on the Foundation's recalcitrant compound, feathering and extending their variable rotor members, then settling to earth.

Her camera view didn't cover the landing areas. She ordered a plane in the air, to correct the omission—but before she could complete her arrangements, let alone before the aircraft could reach station, the heelies had lifted away and a second group was coming in.

"Damn!" and then "Ooow!" as her fist hit the desk hard enough to hurt badly. Sucking on a sore knuckle, suddenly she knew her next move. "Duane! Why have we been farting around with *surface* access?"

First making sure the screen was blanked, Bardeen turned to face his accuser—and was almost stunned to find that over the decades he remembered the tour guide who had interrogated him.

By face only, not by name. Well, it didn't matter now; Bardeen thought of all the possible answers he might make, and settled for "I beg your pardon; *who* did you say?"

That ploy got him no points at all. "If you are not Mr. Kennet Bardeen of the Phoenix Foundation, please show proof."

Oh, the hell with it! "All right; let's see your papers."

He couldn't pay much attention to the mechanics of getting his gear out of the hotel—or, later, to being checked into detention. He was too busy worrying whether Cogdill and Bennest could handle the crap that would surely be coming down.

And how he might possibly get in touch with them, and help.

# XXXIII

Information arriving out of logical sequence always confuses me. First, Dr. Sharla Gill woke me up—I was sleeping in a bed alongside the one where Eden lay nestled with baby Hill—and said she had to give me a shot.

"For what?" Except that my feet were still sore, from walking half the latitudinal stretch of metropolitan Chicago (well, not *quite*, probably), I felt more good than not.

But she just pulled my sleeve up and shot it to me. "Tell you later, Troy. It *is* important." I was still tired enough that I could ignore the slight sting and ache of my injected shoulder; after a few minutes of feeling irritated, I dozed off.

Later that day, Security Chief Bennest told me the FBI had a warrant out for me. As a material witness in my own kidnapping, which by my lights was a pretty sneaky excuse for having somebody locked up.

The catch was that the warrant listed me as female, and at the moment I *was* in F-mode. So Gill's hypo, it turned out, was a hormone shot used by Mark One females to induce menstruation. It had been her idea to try it on Mark Twos, and sure enough the shot brought on the F-to-M transition. So in three days I'd go male, and then the FBI's warrant wouldn't be worth wiping with. 

That part was fine. But still I thought they could have *asked* me first.

Nearing the end of six months of pregnancy, Moss Frantz was having symptoms she didn't like: brief, unexpected cramps, occasional recurrence of morning sickness—and a certain feeling of puffiness, which sodium restriction didn't entirely correct. Well, she was overdue for a prenatal checkup, and by now it should be safe to go to the Feen and get it. For sure, there was no Mark One facility she'd feel safe in consulting.

So she called for an appointment. But the M-2 on the other end said, "Where've you *been*? We're bottled up in here; the tubetrains don't run and the gates are blockaded. I'm sorry, but you'll have to go somewhere else."

Fat chance! Unless—"Can I talk with Bennest?"

Looking harassed but apparently holding no grudges for past antagonisms, the Security Chief shook his head. "—nothing we can do, Moss; we're literally under siege. The details aren't clear, but we do know it's an FBI operation."

"And you're resisting?" It didn't make sense.

"Not exactly. We've ignored a couple of arrest warrants, is about the size of it. Their next move, with neither threat nor warning, was to interdict the compound."

*Curiouser and curiouser.* "There hasn't been anything on the news about this."

"No, there wouldn't be. Our consensus is that the Bureau wants to force *us* to holler first."

"So why don't you? What's to lose?"

Bennest shook his head. "Policy matters, Moss."

"In other words, Chief, either you don't know or you're not telling. Well, thanks for the update."

"Quite welcome. But on your own problem: what do you intend to do?"

"I guess I'll have to think of something." Moss cut the circuit; the screen dimmed. "I'd damn well *better.*"

Opening and pouring some "fruit juice" that might or might not have any real fruit component, she thought about it. Why *not* blow the lid off?

The gate to an audience was Tri-V. Now who was that woman at the NBS headquarters station in New York—the one who'd interviewed the Haydock character?

Looking back, it's hard to pinpoint when the government's alarm went off, let alone what triggered it. I gather that the weird leaks on Tri-V led to covert moves by Federal agencies. But a lot of the crucial events happened while I was still kidnapped, so timewise I can't nail the trends down.

After I was free, though, I know which statistics may have tipped off the Feen's efforts to scatter us all to best available safety. For instance, the upsurge of business for moving companies in the Chicago area. Concentrating on Mark Two adults and the children who were into puberty or near it, before the FBI closed off our tubetrain access we had nearly half our vulnerable Inside people scattered, plus a good start on those living Outside. And when the shutdown came, the helicopter groups did a good job.

The establishment of new IDs had been in the mill all along; Dr. Gill's developments put some new twists to the plans. For instance, any M-2 with supplies of Gill's period-inducing hormone *and* stabilized menstrual pheromone could pretty much change gender at will, and carry IDs for both modes; the only real danger would be during the two-to-three-day transition period.

My own problems were different. For one thing, Eden and little Hill weren't in condition, just yet, to go on the run with me. And even if they were, my being named to a position on the Feen's Board had me tied up.

The other members were all Mark Ones, and considerably older. The only one I knew was Erwin Bennest, who wasn't really on the Board at all; he was sitting in as proxy for Chairman Bardeen. And no one seemed to know where *he* was, or why. Of course I remembered the Chairman Emeritus, Thane Cogdill, who for some reason addressed the meetings only in print on a computer screen. During my brief tenure I did pin down a few more names: the tallish black man with the glasses was Rory Livingston, the Asian woman was Leona Kim. The sexy, deep-voiced woman with the young face framed by white hair: Elyene Marriott. But the other four, who seldom had much to say, don't stand out in recall. I suppose I have the names written down somewhere . . .

The Board meetings were all much the same. Bennest relayed communications from the absent Chairman, Board members came back with answers or objections or return queries or totally offtrack arguments; it makes you wonder how our remote ancestors ever managed to agree to come down out of the trees. Erwin Bennest, though, somehow held things together.

The man had always struck me as being rather stodgy. But it says something for him, that being stuck as a relay-point operator with all the delays that situation implies, still he got most of our M-2s away relatively free-and-clear—not totally untraceable, perhaps, but certainly not easy to find.

Luckily, he managed most of this *before* the Federals replayed D-Day on us.

*   *   *

Rome Hagen didn't want to leave the Feen. Rome had been working on a history of the Mark Twos—tentative title, *How We Began*—and felt need to research the Foundation's files a lot more. It hadn't helped that he'd been worried crazy while Troy was being held somewhere by unknown kidnappers. Also, Rome's liaison with Burke Kramer hadn't yet jelled, because the sexual part was still mostly in future tense and just now their modes were not at all in proper phase for it.

But now that the exodus was on, Erwin Bennest had no time for such individual foibles—so Rome found his M-mode self, carrying ID for both possibilities, packed off to Sweden. He did insist on changing his ID-surname to dos Caras, the same as Troy's. And got a half-promise from Burke, to join him later.

The M-2s scattered—most to various parts of the U.S., a number to Canada, and some to other continents. As well as could be done by fudging computer records, the destinations had been set up as safe havens, niches that the manufactured identities could fill. Indeed, most of the refugees "landed soft" and settled in without too much difficulty.

With all the dope to keep his hurt down, Amory Neill lost him some days. But come a time he close to woke up and damn if his arm didn't feel like it could stay home. Tubes in the other one; hospitals feed you that way when you can't eat.

Mostly he felt blurred, but sometimes not so much. Like when this cunt in the doctor suit poked a finger on him down where she got no business to. What she said was he'd been cut bad and sewed up worse. "According to the scan, the severed nerve ends don't meet. Crockett, why don't you have a try at fixing it? And I spotted an old depressed skull fracture that needs trepanning; it *has* to be causing seizures."

Crockett was some kind of pisser. "Why bother? This man's a killer; if he isn't executed he'll be sent up for life."

The doctor cunt sounded mad. "The point, Crockett, is that if you attempt these operations, you may learn something."

Then somebody gave Amory another shot so he blanked. But next time he woke up for real, he had his first hard-on in three years. And no headaches.

What that did was put him in mind, he needed to get clear of this dump.

Except, where was he gonna find him a knife?

* * *

"The reason I came Earthside myself," said Arvid Thurwald, "is that you're too big a fish. If I sent a flunkey, you might pull strings and tie him up in knots."

The metaphor didn't work, but Bardeen nodded; he was trying to decide what to try here, and how to do it.

The Feen was under Tri-V pressure—Tolliver, Dilmarr, possibly Moran—and with Getzlor's people on the move, a physical attack wasn't precluded. What Bardeen needed, at the moment, was time. But how to buy some?

Across the table, Thurwald leaned forward. It was considerate of him, Bardeen thought, to conduct this session in the not-so-Spartan detention quarters, rather than in a wholly impersonal interrogation room. The man said, "Extradition. Do you intend to fight it, or will you waive the hearing?"

Maybe there was a handle here. "I'd have to consult with my attorney." He remembered a time when suspects could not be interrogated without legal representation. "When will I be allowed access to counsel?"

"Is that really a major problem, Chairman? Or merely a bargaining point?"

Bardeen shrugged. "As long as I'm *making* the point, what's the difference? I still want an answer."

Unexpectedly, Thurwald grinned. "So you say. But what is it that you really want?"

"Bail." Likely it was too soon to show his cards, but urgency rendered Bardeen impatient. "For—" How long? Oh, make a guess! "Thirty days. Give me that, and I'll waive extradition."

"I don't understand."

"You don't have to. Just grant it." Because with things coming to a head, he *needed* to be at Feen headquarters. Or at least, with his St. Louis base gone, free of detention.

"I'm not at all sure—" Thurwald looked confused. "There's a trick here; there must be. Perhaps—"

*No perhapses!* Bardeen took a deep breath. "That's the deal; take it or leave it."

As he waited, he thought: if he had to, he'd back off a little. Possibly offer, even, to make a confession; in the trial itself he could claim duress and retract it. But Thurwald nodded. "The deal, I accept."

* * *

The only trouble was that when the authorities released Bardeen and he tried to hire transport home, he found the Feen compound interdicted by Federal personnel.

Whether an actual attack had been mounted, he couldn't find out. Stymied, he went to a hotel where computer terminal access was available with scramble, and left a call for Thane Cogdill.

In compliance with a Federal court order, all trunks between the local telephone exchange office and the Phoenix Foundation were being monitored by FBI operators. Since the order specified nothing to the contrary, Lynette Corbin, in charge of the exchange, duly informed Erwin Bennest of the installations—and hugely enjoyed Annek Getzlor's frustration when her snoops reported only routine calls. What Getzlor apparently didn't know, and Corbin did, was that by way of some disguised microwave dishes in the Phoenix compound, a separate set of backup trunks terminated in a different exchange, some distance away.

It wasn't that Corbin had any special reason to favor the Foundation. The fact was, she totally detested Annek Getzlor.

When the Haydock connection fizzled, Sandy Moran lost whatever favor she'd held in the eyes of Oswald Dennis. Her first aircast had brought enough viewer response and ratings to give her a temporary lock on the evening spot, but that perk was hanging by a thread and she knew it.

For tonight, she didn't have much on the docket. Some pervert was still slipping human body parts into shipments from a mail order novelty house in Schenectady, but although some of the customers might be getting a jolt out of it, newswise the novelty was wearing off. A woman in Atlanta claimed her three-year-old daughter was pregnant; okay, it could be worth a mention. But what can you do with a guy threatening to sue the zoo because he'd been run over by a hit-and-run ostrich?

At her dressing table, Sandy looked in the mirror. Hell, even her new hairstyle was a disaster. The ringlets over the ears were fine, but the color combo sucked, and she had *not* given Mr. Emile any okay to shave farther back at the left temple.

As she turned away from her unsatisfactory image, the phone chimed. "Moran here."

The picture wavered and the color was lousy; all she could tell for sure was that the other party looked reasonably young. "Hello,

Ms. Moran. You once ran an interview with someone named
Clint Haydock; am I right?"

*Either you know that or you don't!* "What's your point?"

"The subject matter. The people who could change their sex.
Do you have any further input on that possibility?"

*Damn you!* "Look, whatever your name is—tell me one thing.
Are you just asking questions, or do you have some answers for a
change?"

Maybe the wavering face smiled. "I have *lots* of answers. I'm
one of the freaky people Haydock told you about. At the moment
I'm female and nearly six months pregnant. That's why I'm
calling."

"I don't understand—but don't let that stop you. Why *are* you
calling?"

"Because the FBI has the Phoenix Foundation's compound
blockaded, and I can't get in for my prenatal checkup."

This far, it didn't compute; she went ahead anyway. "But even
in these days, with the low birthrate, there are all kinds of clinics
available. Can't you—?"

"Not really. You see, we freakos can't take the chance that an
M-One doctor would notice our differences."

"I don't—could you explain to me, a little more?"

Headshake. "Not here, not now." To her next question the
caller answered, "On your program, in person. Fly me there
tomorrow, and make me an appointment for my checkup with a
guarantee of *no questions asked*. Can you do that?"

Sandy thought about it. Dennis wouldn't give her that much
budget, but if she simply put the requisition in without comment,
it would go through on the assumption that he'd approved it.

And maybe she really had a handle on something big, here.

So she said, "Agreed. Now then—your name? Address?" And
checked to be certain she had it all straight, including setting up
the travel vouchers and making sure that this Moss Frantz knew
how to utilize them, before ending the call.

Sandy Moran felt good. She could fake tonight's news spot—
piece of cake!

And just wait until tomorrow night!

When a surveillance operator called to tell Bennest at the
Comm Room that the next flight of heelies was arriving nearly an
hour early, the Security Chief asked for a visual on it.

One look was enough. The Feen's copters carried neither armor nor guns; this group was playing hardball.

Bennest wished he could be wrong, that it wasn't Getzlor's troops—but he knew better.

*All right; now what?* He stood, then sat again and flipped a switch. "All-points alert; Bennest speaking. The invaders are armed; don't try to fight them.

"But don't answer any more questions than you have to."

He thought he'd finalized his meager instructions, but in a few minutes the newest Board member came in. When the two of them were done talking, Bennest added quite a lot to the orders he'd set out for his own Security people.

Then he faced his visitor. "We'd both better hope this works out."

A shrug. "It can't make things any worse."

# XXXIV

When Lyndeen told Brad Szalicz that Eden, about as pregnant as she could get, had been hauled away by some kind of cops, he felt his temper rise toward the breaking point. The worst part was that once again it was *his* fault. This time he could blame the interrogation drugs, but that didn't help a whole lot.

Cursing was no help at all, so after his first brief explosion he stopped. Looking scared, Lyndeen asked, "Brad? You know you can't do any of those things you just said. But what *are* you going to do?"

He thought. "Troy got away from them. Maybe back to the Foundation. The least I can do is let him know where she is."

The Phoenix operator said Troy dos Caras was definitely present in the compound, but she couldn't locate him. Having missed work at Channel 83—and missed it by being arrested, at that— Brad didn't dare ask for more time off. So it was the next day, still unable to reach dos Caras by phone, that he decided to visit him in person.

And found he couldn't get there from here, because those particular tubetrain stops weren't open for business.

Brad decided he had a story for his evening news: "Scientific foundation barricaded, under siege," the story could begin. Except that on his way out of the area Brad heard a lot of noise, looked up to see the armed heelies go in, and realized that no matter what he might say on his newsbreak, by that time some sonofabitch would have scooped him.

But at work that evening, Greenmain wouldn't let him use *any* of the Phoenix stuff in his late-night spot. "There's a lid on, Szalicz. So tight, we don't even ask who put it there."

After his shift, walking to his tube station, Brad learned what Jody Jay Tolliver and Steive Dilmarr were doing to the minds, to use the term loosely, of the Man in the Street. Horrified, he saw four men grab a rather effeminate-looking young fellow, strip him, and proceed to beat him senseless.

There was no point in trying to call the police; the men did their nasty work quickly, then ran to the next corner and out of sight. But on the hunch that they were waiting there, watching their victim, Brad was ashamed to find himself afraid to go to the injured man's aid.

At the next pay phone he came to, he settled for calling the Fire Department's ambulance service.

What with the comm-set network to her squad leaders and the bullhorn for any civilians within range of it, Getzlor had a fine time giving orders. Much sooner than she'd expected, her FBI and police troops secured the main building group and controlled all access to other areas.

To her surprise, the Foundation's Security people seemed to be fully cooperative. They hadn't surrendered, exactly; their Chief, a man named Bennest, behaved as though he and she were equal partners—almost as if he'd asked her for help and she was complying. Everything was happening too fast for Getzlor to take time and straighten the man out; for the moment it was easier to let him think whatever he wanted to.

Especially since her freely given access to the Foundation's computer net wasn't producing any useful info. The thing hadn't totally crashed, but all she and Duane could get out of it was a mass of boring routine data concerning the financial side of project proposals. It didn't take much brains to guess that Phoenix had their real stuff code-protected and were playing dumb about it, so she'd told Eads to call D.C. and get Harry Meinster here "—two hours ago, if not sooner!" Because if anybody in this world could break an industrial coding, Harry was the one.

Enough of that! Bennest was present so she decided to lean on him. "All right; where's the stuff on the two-sex freaks? And where are they? We can check them out, you know; we've done it."

He was nervous; she could see his gaze flicker. But he said, "Then I'm afraid you know more than I do. My work is Security; if there were anything like what you're saying—and I must apologize for doubting that there is, or could be—quite likely my division wouldn't have been informed."

Maybe so, maybe not. Anyway, try the easier ways first. "You have a hospital here. I want to see it." As Bennest nodded, Getzlor motioned for her squad of six picked agents to follow. And Duane, of course.

Bennest couldn't believe how well the plan was working—so far, at least. It hadn't been his own idea; young Troy had convinced him to try it. "They use drugs for interrogation; Eden told me. And they will, on some of our people. But they mustn't do it to *you*; they'd learn too much."

"But how—?"

"The odds are," Troy said, "that if this Getzlor woman sees you as an antagonist, you'll get the needle. But who treats their *allies* that way?"

It made sense, so he'd changed his instructions to the Security force. And damned if it wasn't paying off!

But as he accompanied the armed group into the hospital area, Erwin Bennest's digestion had a bad case of butterflies.

When this Crockett guy's beeper went off and he talked on the phone maybe a minute, he took out like a striped-ass ape, and his nurse with him. By then he had most of the stitches out of Amory Neill's arm, so Amory picked up the little-bitty knife—mostly handle, not much blade—and sliced the last three himself, so he could pull 'em out by the knots.

The tubes, Crockett already took loose and taped the places. So there Amory was, set to move and nobody in the way. No clothes either, was the problem—just the coldass white skivvy. But *somebody* had to have clothes a man could take.

Somebody might argue, though, and the little knife wasn't much. So look around. The shelf, over there, had a tray on it. Hey, *lots* of little knives. Only a couple inches worth of blade, but—*ow, goddamn it!*—sharper'n all bloody hell!

No pockets in the dumb skivvy. For now, he had to hold the whole bunch in one bundle, by the handles. Except for the one in his good hand, in case he met some fool as needed it.

Ready as he could get, Amory Neill headed out down the hall.

Bennest playing footsie with the invaders was probably the best idea I'd had all year; even so, I was surprised that he bought it. Once he did, I wasn't needed there any longer. Where I had to be was with Eden, getting her and Hill to a safe place.

A little checking of outside monitors showed me that I couldn't reach the hospital by normal routes. But the Comm Room elevator, among others, had some tricks to it, which I'd been told during my first days on the Board. Pushing certain combinations of buttons let you go past the supposed bottom level, to floors that didn't show on the display—and the outside indicators at each floor would show no movement. Since it was fairly certain the ground-level entry would be guarded by now, I especially appreciated the latter feature.

So I rode the car down to the undesignated Tunnel level and walked to the area below the hospital. There I ran into a problem: in that building only the freight elevators came down so far, and punching their buttons brought no action. All right; somebody upside was keeping the doors open, which was a good move if you were on the invading team.

Stairs, then. I racked my memory to pick a set that didn't open onto the ground floor or administrative levels, and climbed. Eight flights, to Eden's floor; when I got there, my legs and lungs wanted to quit and go home.

The floor's nursing supervisor, a blond, florid-faced butterball named Preston, not much older than I was, tried to get officious with me. "You can't just come barging in here!"

Adrenalin turned me quirky; for a moment I thought of hooking fingers into his nostrils and shaking some sense into him the hard way. But I had to have this man's full cooperation, not mere compliance; I said, "I'm sorry, but there's a problem that won't wait. Anybody in the Plague Ward just now?" Its real name was different; what it had that I liked was a big sign: "DANGER!

Contagion Hazard Area. No Admittance Without Full Protective Procedures And Signed Waivers."

He shook his head; I said, "That's good. But if the invaders should ask you, you have a patient in there with a truly deadly contagion, the worst you can think of. Okay?" Now he nodded. "Good. All right then: time's short, so let's move."

Once he saw what I was after, Preston wasn't a bad chap at all. He followed me to Eden's room and assembled the necessary supplies for her and Hill, while I got their belongings together and tried to explain what was happening.

Even disheveled and confused, Eden had seldom looked more attractive; I'd have loved to spend an hour or so just making over her until she purred like a kitten. But after our hug and kiss and a few murmured endearments, I had to make the situation march. Because we were running out of time. "So I want you protected, you and Hill. The Plague Ward—it's empty now, and totally safe—is our best bet. So let's get you there. And then I'll have to go back out and be a Board member for a while."

The Ward, when we all got up to that level, had more facilities than I'd known about. The Pest Hole (Extreme Isolation Unit, actually) turned out to be our best bet—because it provided for total protection both ways, plus automated supply and remote care functions. So we got mother and child settled in; Preston tactfully went outside while Eden and I said our goodbyes.

Well and good, then; Preston and I went back to his floor. Near his station I found an elevator that responded to summons. But I didn't have time to learn whether it went down to Tunnel level. Because when the door opened, inside were two armed cops.

Sometimes my mind does the right thing without telling me first. "Everything under control? Good. Before you do anything else, this floor is to be checked out thoroughly. I'll go down and report that you may be delayed a little."

Because I walked straight in, taking it for granted that they'd do what I told them, they did just that.

So I rode the elevator down to Tunnel level, walked a distance that seemed much longer than I knew it had to be, and climbed stairs to a small power substation building located in one of the compound's residential areas. By the time I got there, my pulse was nearly back to normal; only the drying sweat reminded me how nervous I'd been.

*   *   *

Now, for a change, I had a choice. Although the Feen was virtually sealed off, there remained access/escape routes our assailants wouldn't likely know about. Not many, and unknown to most of our people—my Board briefing had told me of the "wormholes," ways designed for individuals, not groups. So if I wished, I could exit via one of those—but Eden and Hill were hardly in condition to travel.

Just now, though, I needed more information, so I looked out through the shrubbery surrounding the substation and checked the terrain. No assault troops in sight, and as I'd hoped and expected, a little way down the man-made hill lay the quarters I'd been assigned. So, feeling foolish, I skulked down and entered the place.

As yet it was pretty bare. I'd ordered out minimal furnishings, since our Outside apartment with all our belongings was probably under police scrutiny. Two things I did have were a phone set and a computer terminal.

I thought I'd better call Bennest. But an unfamiliar voice answered his personal office phone. Since no one who worked there would do that, I hung up.

I had no real plan at all; it was time to start improvising. So I booted up the computer and asked for Thane Cogdill.

Waiting for the New York flight to be announced, Moss Frantz began premature labor. Not too unexpectedly premature, really, because Mark Twos always delivered early by M-1 standards—but these pangs had a nasty urgent feel to them.

She had some pills that were supposed to delay and stabilize matters; disregarding the instructions, she took two at once—and later, on the plane, another.

Which may have been the reason that when the flight ended, she was too groggy to disembark under her own power.

The airport had its own emergency medical facility, and although births, these days, weren't among the most common types of emergencies, Moss delivered safely within an hour of arrival. An XZ, the baby was, because the doctor said, "It's a boy."

For a time, then, her cognizance was more or less blurred. She came the nearest to full waking late that evening, just as her roommate's small Tri-V announced "the news, with Sandy Moran."

Moran, when she came onscreen, seemed considerably displeased about something. After a few moments, Moss realized what it was. But there wasn't anything she could do about it.

Or about the disturbing news Moran *did* report.

Well before program time, Sandy gave up on her mystery caller. A check with the airline confirmed that a Moss Frantz had flown from Chicago to New York, but nothing more; at the airport the woman's trail seemed to end.

Moran had held most of her air time open for this story; dammit, there had to be *something* she could salvage. She punched up the recording of the call, leaving the picture off, and listened. And after a few moments, "Well, all *right!*" She could use the part about the FBI blockading the Phoenix Foundation.

Better check first, though: Sandy put a call through to the Foundation. On a hunch she made it voice only, no outgoing visual—and sure enough, the other end did the same. A man's voice said, "Keith here."

"Keith who?" Or maybe, Who Keith?

The voice sharpened. "Who's that? What's your badge number? Are you Bureau, or local PD? Speak up!"

Lacking any real cause to resent the man's take-charge manner, somehow she felt the impish urge to hang one on him. *"You're not the man who ordered the pizzas."* While he was still sputtering, she cut the circuit.

Now to confirm. Another try at Phoenix got her "Agent Greene, Liaison"; she hung up. At Chicago's Channel 83, as soon as she mentioned the Foundation she was connected to a man named Greenmain, who immediately said they had a bad connection, he couldn't hear her. A stall is a stall is a stall; she didn't bother to call back.

Over coffee she tried to figure an angle; after her second cup she thought she might have one. The Chicago police operator didn't mind naming the three most recent medal-winning sergeants: "Any extra publicity those guys get, it's good for the whole department."

Right, and thanks. On her next call she got a different voice at CPD. "Could I speak to Sergeant Williams, please?" Pause. "Oh—if he's on the Phoenix raid, with the FBI people, I could try again tomorrow. Or maybe—?" She let it hang there.

"Well, he's—uh, we're not supposed to—now wait a minute! How do you know about that?"

*Just lucky, I guess!* But not to get a perfectly innocent sergeant in trouble, "Not from him." Sandy hung up.

When her air spot came on, she hit it with everything she had. Except, of course, no names; "FBI sources" and "Chicago police sources" were good enough tags, she thought, to get this whole mess out in the open.

And just in case Moss Frantz might turn up later, no point in scaring *her* off, either.

Working hard at it, Cogdill could now talk a little. Too slow and slurred, though, for anyone but Laura and the doctors to cope with; now, accepting Bardeen's phone call, he stayed at the keyboard. He was almost done explaining why the Feen had to go public about the Mark Twos, plus the rationale to be used in that disclosure, when two things happened.

First his screen signaled another incoming call and split off a "window" to display greetings from Troy dos Caras. He punched to make the call a three-way, then typed HI TROY    KNT BRDN ON HR TOO SO LTS TLK FST    KNT I

But then Laura ran in. "Thane, the police and FBI are on their way up here, any second now! You—"

He waved her to silence. "Lorrruh. Waaait miiinn." On the keyboard he punched TROY N KNT I GOT FUZZ CMNG    HV TO CUT FM HR SO U WRK TINGS OUT BTN U    OK QQQ

He took his terminal out of the circuit, leaving the other two connected, then blanked all text from his screen and punched LAURA DONT LET M KNO I CAN TALK    N TAKE TIS TING AWAY SO TY DONT KNO I TLK TIS WAY EITHER    OK QQQ    And again blanked it.

When the FBI group came in, the terminal was out of sight. Cogdill lay, deliberately slackfaced and trying to induce a bit of drool for best effect, while Laura sat alongside him, looking worried. *Doing great, kid!* He squeezed her hand.

The little greyhaired dynamo was Annek Getzlor; the pale man bird-dogging for her was some kind of flunkey. Given normal circumstances, those people might have actually scared Thane Cogdill. As things were, he "answered" their questions with raucous, uncouth sounds and hyped his breathing up, until Laura got one of his doctors in to tell them to leave him alone.

As Getzlor and Company left, Cogdill was hard put to keep

from laughing. Even though, in the larger sense, nothing about the situation was even remotely funny.

It wasn't that the President yelled very often, but when he did, L. Travers Munro truly hated to be within range.

"Did you *see* this?" Once again Uther Stanton Archer replayed the NBS late newsbreak, with the Moran woman blowing a whistle on the Federal Bureau of Investigation.

"Yes, sir, I did. I came up to tell you, but you'd already—"

"I'd already decided to have Annek Getzlor relieved of duty, arrested, and brought up on charges!" Archer threw a bowl of candy across the room; the pieces were hard-surfaced, Munro noted, and wouldn't stain the carpet. "I have three perfectly good U.S. Marshals in that city, including Hayes Tedrow who's probably the best in the business. But billy-bedamn if even *one* of them can find a way into the Phoenix compound. All routes are blockaded."

"Not all, sir. Getzlor got in."

"Tell me something I don't know. *How* did she do it?"

Out of a total blank, the idea came. Munro said, "Sir, may I make a call from here? Right now?"

"To whom?"

"FAA, Chicago regional office." *One if by land, two if by sea.* But with land interdicted and no sea available, only air was left.

In less than ten minutes Munro had his answers. "After a number of recent authorized copter flights into and out of the Phoenix compound, a rather large unauthorized flight went in. Inquiries, up to now, have been fruitless."

"Getzlor." Archer's clenched fist swept down toward his desk but stopped short of striking it. "So?"

"With your personal authorization, Marshal Tedrow and his colleagues might take the same option. Would you like—?"

Headshake. "You make the call, Travers; it's your idea." And a few minutes later, "Well, we'll see how it goes."

"Yes, sir. Would that be all, for now?"

"Not quite," as Archer stood. "Unless you're in one hell of a hurry, Travers, keep your seat. Because you've earned yourself a drink out of my favorite barrel."

Sometimes, Munro thought, it paid to put up with the yelling.

Going by Bennest's advice I called the Chairman Emeritus in keyboard mode. He'd barely acknowledged when some intrusion (the invaders, I assumed) impelled him to leave the circuit and turn me over to Chairman Bardeen who was also in on the call.

CUT TO VOICE N PIC So I did, and Mr. Bardeen's image on the screen made everything more real to me. He said, "Troy, the entire picture has changed. Partly because of you."

"Hey, I'm sorry—"

"Don't be; I did *not* mean to imply any fault on your part. Now here's what the Feen has to do, so listen fast."

I paid attention the best I could, but some of what he said didn't seem really workable. "Mr. Bardeen, I don't see how I could take over your proxy on the Board. Sit there as *Chairman?* For one thing, how's Mr. Bennest going to believe it?"

"My confirming message on his own phone machine should take care of that part. Now will you tell me your understanding of what we've discussed, to make sure you have it straight?"

So I did. Then, sounding as though he were being more patient than he really felt, he fed me some corrections.

The scheme still didn't quite make sense, and although Bardeen had been around a long time and certainly was nobody's dummy, I wasn't at all sure his idea had any chance of working.

On the other hand, it was the only game in town.

Brad Szalicz was back to work now, and doing broadcast; I'd seen his spot the night before. He could be a good place to start. All right; I decided to give Channel 83 a call.

# XXXV

"Look, Getzlor!" Irritated, she glared at the man, as he said, "You wanted their secrecy codes broken; I've done that. Figuring the jargon they use in clear text, that's something else. Not my piece of meat, lady; you could try a mind reader."

People might expect a computer genius to be some little wimpy-looking guy, but Harry Meinster was built like a bear, and right now he sounded like one. Putting a lid on her growing annoyance, Getzlor said, "You've done very well, Harry. It's only that I hoped for more specific data."

"That's your department, not mine." The man was sweating heavily; to Annek Getzlor's imagination he smelled like a satyr in heat. How she'd love to have *this* one tied up—! But it wouldn't happen; she came back to listening, as Meinster said, "You're good at leaning on people. Go do it." With all his test instruments back in his kit, he sealed the case and turned to Duane Eads. "In case you need anything more, that I *can* do, I'm staying over until tomorrow. You said I have quarters assigned here. Somebody show me where they are."

Duane led him out of the computer center but came back soon. "I found him a guide, Annek. Now what's next?"

"What Harry said." She handed him a printout sheet. "Their Records people. Have Keith bring me in two or three." She smiled. "Young ones. They scare easier."

Some hours later, Annek Getzlor had a partial listing of what Phoenix called "Mark Two humans," and where some of them had fled or been sent to.

"Now, Duane, let's split this list up by areas and get the info to the appropriate field agents. And then we'll be set to pull in a bunch of those goddamn monsters!"

There was hardly nobody around, so Amory didn't get stopped. Didn't have no luck with clothes, neither, 'til he looked in a closet and found some of them doctor robes and cloth masks, and the other cloth stuff they put over their heads on Tri-V, to operate on people and it always works. He changed clothes in a john; with the mirror in there he got the head stuff looking mostly right, so his bandages didn't show.

The robe had pockets, so he stashed the little knives—scalpels, they was called. All but one, that is. Like before.

Going outside he saw these two cops on guard. One looked at him funny, so Amory said "Doctor Neill" and kept walking. The cop let him, so the little knife stayed out of sight.

A piece uphill from there he met somebody else wearing the same kind of duds, so Amory said "Hi" and went along. Just in case the other one might be heading out of here.

When Brad at his work desk answered the phone and saw Troy on the screen, he felt a heavy load go off his mind. "Troy! You're okay? Did you know Eden's been arrested?"

"She's out now."

"They let you post bond?"

"Not exactly." Troy's grin had a wry look to it. "She's had the baby, by the way. We named her Hill."

"Where are you?"

"At the—here at Phoenix. And we're in trouble. I need you to put some material on the air for us, right now if not sooner."

Part of the load came back. "I can't, Troy. I just can't."

"But this is *big*! You'll be *famous*, Brad, and I'm not kidding that we're in a bad jam and really need your help. I—"

Oh, damn all! Brad's fist hit the desk. "Troy, the station won't let me air *anything* about the Foundation. I tried yesterday, after I saw the armed heelies go in. No dice. You—"

Dos Caras waved a hand. "Wait a minute. Let's try it another way. Can you reach NBS News in New York? Set up a conference call, split-screen and full vision? And either get Sandy Moran on, there, or someone who can record for her?"

"Sure, Troy; I can do that." But when Greenmain got the bill he'd have Brad's ass, fried, on toast for breakfast!

Troy must have understood the hesitation; he said, "I'm the originator, so bill it to here."

Sooner than Brad would have expected, Troy was saying to the woman with the weird haircut, "Ms. Moran, my name is Troy dos Caras and I'm calling on behalf of the Phoenix Foundation. Along with me is Brad Szalicz." He spelled the surname. "He gets a byline."

The woman frowned. "Hold it a min. Dos Caras, do you happen to know anyone named Moss Frantz?"

"For years. Why?"

"She called, claiming to be one of the sex-changers we've been hearing about, and offered to appear on my program. I sent authorization for air tickets and she flew to New York. Then she vanished. Do you know—?"

Troy nodded. "It computes; the FBI's on our butts here. That's why I want you to disk some info, fast."

"One mo. All right; I'm recording. Take it from the top."

"To begin with," said Troy dos Caras, "Moss Frantz and I are two of many people known as Humanity, Mark Two. We are all cyclic hermaphrodites, in a manner I'll explain later. We are the result of the Phoenix Foundation's research into the Sterility Plague; in fact we're the solution to it."

Troy cleared his throat. "The story goes back a long way. For now, I'll try to keep it brief."

Listening, Brad found it hard to believe what Troy was saying. For one thing, *Cecy got pregnant by Moss Frantz. My sister's baby could turn out to be one of these Mark Twos.*

"Hold it, Annek," Duane said. He turned away from his terminal, where he'd been feeding data to various field agents. "One of our monitor ops on the line. You'd better hear this."

"If you say so." Getzlor finished reading an address to her Nova Scotia agent. "Getzlor out." Then, to Eads, "What the hell's wrong *now*?"

"Just listen."

So she did, as the operator said, "There's an outgoing call from a residence building here, to NBS News HQ in New York. I think you'll want to stop it."

"Cut the goddamned circuit, you idiot!"

"I tried that, ma'am. We have access, but on that group of lines, no control."

"All right—where's the fucking building?"

"Right here." On Duane's screen a map appeared, with the symbol for one structure outlined in red. Below it, a little to the right, a red "X" flashed. "That's your own location."

"Okay, you've done your part. Just keep monitoring." Trying to get her thoughts in order, Getzlor said, "Duane? To go with us, two good agents, no local police. Do it."

While he got the manpower for her she studied the map. All right, she could get there from here. In less than five minutes the group was on its way.

Partway up the artificial hill and running short of wind, Getzlor realized she hadn't brought along a needle artist. But off to one side, meandering along like a pair of absent-minded professors, came two people in surgical garb.

"You two!" They turned to look at her. Getzlor motioned. "Come with us."

One said, "But I'm on my way to—"

"Later," Annek said. "Right now you're drafted. FBI."

"Set the bird down over there," Hayes Tedrow yelled. "Away from the armed choppers, with that building in between us so they don't see where we go when we debark." What he didn't say was that not far from the landing spot he'd designated he saw some rather purposeful-looking people walking uphill. Even if they weren't Getzlor's troops they might have some helpful info.

As the heelie dropped, Tedrow's fellow marshals said nothing. Well, Ed Morris had never been much of a talker, but Enid Clare was young; in this kind of action, it surprised Tedrow that she kept such a calm front.

The heelie grounded. When the rotors slowed to idle and the dust began to settle, Tedrow led the way out.

Now Clare spoke. "What do we do next?"

Tedrow nodded toward the rise of ground. "For starters, I think we follow that bunch."

More excited than she could remember being in a long, long time, Sandy Moran listened. "—a mistake, probably," dos Caras was saying. "But the Sterility Plague, most likely a delayed result of our AIDS vaccine though our people couldn't actually prove it, wasn't recognized as such for several years. So the Foundation kept its experiments with the pseudogene strictly in-house, using only volunteers and maintaining secrecy while watching for possible side effects." He smiled. "Which, when they hit us at puberty, were quite a shock to all concerned."

Moran leaned forward. "As children you all appeared to be perfectly normal boys and girls?" After a pause, dos Caras nodded. "Then how long has the Foundation known the extent of your differences?"

"Uh, let me think—eight years, close to nine."

"And all this time you've kept the lid on? Why?"

He shrugged. "I was just a kid, not a policy maker. Part of it may have been that until some Mark Twos did grow to maturity, the Board wanted us kept hidden and protected. I do know there was disagreement. Moss Frantz, for instance, led a young group that favored going public several years ago. But Phoenix had been hurt by bad publicity more than once, and the consensus in top management was to keep our heads down and wait for a favorable moment. The problem is, there's never been one. Some people in the media—Jody Jay Tolliver and Steive Dilmarr, just to name two—make a business of stirring up fear of differences in the public mind."

"Then why are you telling it all *now*?"

"Because we're under direct physical attack, by the FBI with local police support. They began with illegal arrests of our Outside people, then interdicted our compound here, and a few hours ago they came in with armed helicopters. And slapped a secrecy lid on every bit of it. So we *have* to get the word out."

"Let's see if I have this straight now." Sandy tried to get her thoughts together. So *much* strange, new information! "With this pseudogene treatment, *any* woman could have more children?"

"Well, she'd have to be fertile in other respects. And it's the man who needs the pseudogene."

"And all those children would grow up to be like you?"

"Mark Twos, yes."

"Tell me. What's it *like* to change sex every month?"

He shook his head. "Could you explain to a man how it feels to be female rather than male? Same problem."

"Yes, I can see that. Well, then——"

But dos Caras was turning away, looking behind him, as a woman's voice shouted, "Hold it right there, you damned alien freak!"

He'd been talking on the phone, all right—to two people on a split screen. The woman looked familiar but Annek couldn't quite place her. The man, though: he said, "Look out, Troy! That's Annek Getzlor!" and she recognized the man Salich. *Never should have turned the bastard loose!*

She said "Shut that thing off!" but the freak didn't obey, and when she moved to do it herself he stood there, barring her way. So she pulled out her miniaturized version of a cattle prod, and swung it.

There were six of them, all told, but the woman led the way and did the yelling. I heard Brad say she was Getzlor, the FBI Director, but no matter who she was I couldn't let her cut the phone; Sandy Moran had to get this outrage on disk!

The trouble was that Getzlor knew combat and I didn't. I tried to block the stick she swung but I was too slow; the side of my neck seemed to explode and I fell.

But through the bright haze of pain, when I hit the floor I couldn't really feel it.

Next to last, Amory went in. For a sec there he could have ducked back and run off. But then he seen the kid Troy; hadn't been for him, Amory'd be dead meat now. And on the phone thing, one of 'em was this guy Brad, that slugged Amory at Grego's place. But all that was, it shook the guy up that Amory was gonna nut Grego.

So no grudge there. And right now, it looked like maybe they was all on the same side.

He still ought to of run, though, and he knew it. But then the ditzy cunt knocked Troy over and went to hit him some more. So Amory hollered, "Cut that shit!"

When the gunch dropped whatever she hit Troy with, she came up with a gun. All Amory had was the little knives, no good from this far. Except he used to play darts, used to win good bucks when the suckers gave him odds on throwing southpaw.

And right now south was his good hand. Amory pulled out a little knife. Took him a sec to get the balance right, so the cunt got her shot off, right when Amory threw. And hit him.

Didn't make him miss, though.

*Sweet screaming Jesus, this is Pulitzer stuff and I'm getting it live!* Sandy Moran's hands were shaking, as part of her mind paid heed to the phone screen while the rest of it helped her punch her boss's number on another line.

When he answered, she said, "Mr. Dennis, I want a live newsbreak. Right now. I—"

"Are you crazy?" The pained, patented Dennis sigh. "All right, tell me in ten words or less."

"FBI Director Annek Getzlor killed. Camera footage."

"Moran, what kind of drugs are you into?"

*Enough of this!* "Suit yourself. This live shot might get me an award, sure. But *not* giving it to me—running this footage late rather than live—could put you out on your ass."

Pause. Then, "You have a deal, Moran. Who owes who, we'll work out later. Gimme two-three minutes. When you get the green light, spin your disk."

*I finally told that bastard off and got away with it!* Moran was so wrapped up in having won the job hassle that when the light came on she hadn't thought to scan the disk forward, on her monitor, to the killing itself. So to avoid dead air time she had to run the interview from the beginning.

Dennis would hate it. But maybe it was something the viewing public could use.

Only a few feet short of the building the six people had gone into, Hayes Tedrow heard the shot. "Come on!" Running, gun in hand he knocked the door open and went in, low and jumping to the side. "Federal marshal! Freeze!"

For long seconds he thought the two armed men would shoot, but then one said, "Stay calm, Marshal; we're FBI; I'm Agent Corson. But Ms. Getzlor—" He motioned, and then Tedrow had time to notice the small woman crumpled on the floor, the large pale man crouched over her, weeping, and the two people in surgical garb—one standing back against a wall, and the big one down on his knees, bent over and holding his gut.

Another man, beginning to sit up and looking dazed, wasn't holding a weapon so Tedrow ignored him—as well as a videoscreen showing a pair of talking heads. "Getzlor's relieved of duty and under arrest. By presidential order, I'm your Acting Director. My name is Hayes Tedrow. Now let's put these guns away."

His was the last one sheathed, as the second FBI man said, "Agent Hansen. I'll accept your authority when you show me something on paper, which I'm sure you can. But the arrest comes a little late." He gestured. "I'm afraid Ms. Getzlor's dead."

Tedrow looked. "Yes." Because for the object sticking out of Getzlor's left eye to stand supported at such an angle, the other end had to be driven well into her brain.

The kneeling man fell over on his side; Tedrow said, "*He* did it?" Hansen nodded. "And which of you shot him?"

"Ms. Getzlor did, but not soon enough. Marshal, we'd better get him to their hospital here."

"Oh? I'd have expected you to finish him off."

"And not find out his reasons? Or who sent him?" Hansen turned to the other surgical-garbed figure. "Get that mask off and tell us who you two are!"

The removal of mask and hood revealed a woman's head and face. "I'm Dr. Sharla Gill. I have no idea who that person is; I was on my way back to Surgery when he came and walked with me, and then that woman"—she gestured toward the corpse—"she told us to come along with her. FBI, she said. So we did."

Tedrow nodded. "All right; see what you can do for him, and call for help if you need it."

Gill bent over the wounded man. "Save him to stand trial for aggravated murder; right? Not much of a favor, is it?"

Moving aside, the pale man wiped his eyes. "Regardless of her faults, I loved Annek. But the truth is that when she aimed to shoot that man, his hands were empty, and I will so testify. As Hansen said, she simply didn't fire in time."

"Will somebody tell the viewing public what's going on here?"
The woman's voice came from the videoscreen, and now Tedrow
realized it was a goddamned *phone*, and those two people on the
split screen were privy to the whole frinking mess! The man who'd
been sitting on the floor was up now, standing near the phone
console and looking a little shaky. Tedrow yelled, "Shut that thing
*off!*"

From the screen the woman yelled, "Don't you do it, Troy!"
Then, "Mr. Federal Marshal Hayes Tedrow, before you do
something really stupid, you'd better hear what the situation is."

"Young woman, the situation has to do with national security."

"Oh, sure! The magic words. Well, listen once! For the past
twenty minutes, everything from your phone terminal has been
going out to umpty million people on a live NBS newsbreak.
These viewers *saw* your FBI Director assassinated, and I rather
doubt that they've turned their sets off. Do you really want to tell
them, hey, sorry folks but we're pulling down the shades now?"

The young man by the phone terminal—Troy, the woman had
called him—was the only one in the room who didn't look totally
confused. So Tedrow said, "Troy? Is she telling the truth?"

"Yes, Marshal. But we didn't expect—"

"I'm sure you didn't." Tedrow felt himself sweating; there was
no easy decision here. Finally, *What the hell? If I guess wrong it's
my job either way. But if I need a new one, I'll be a lot better off
getting canned for taking the* public's *side.* So he said, "Then let's
don't stop now. What's next?"

The young man frowned. "Well, shouldn't we see who it is that
killed Getzlor?"

They went to peel the cloth stuff off. No chance Amory could
fight, and the cough hurt him a lot. He said, "Troy kid, you went
and saved my ass, so I give it a try for you. But—"

"We'll get help. Take it easy now."

For certain, no way else. Amory felt it all come black.

I couldn't believe it. *Amory Neill?*

A couple of medics came with a stretcher; Gill went with them,
of course. The way she was paying attention to Neill, I guessed he
was still alive. I hoped so: killer or no killer, I owed him.

But at the moment I had wider concerns. I said, "Marshal
Tedrow? As the Feen's—Phoenix Foundation's—Acting Chair-

man, I have a very important statement to make. Live coverage is more than we expected, but since we do have it, may I proceed?"

I held my breath until he nodded. "Speak your piece, son."

So I began.

# XXXVI

"In case you tuned in late, my name is Troy dos Caras. I'm one of the people that some of your friendly neighborhood rabble-rousers have been calling monsters. But don't *be* rabble; don't let them rouse you." A little close to the bone, maybe, but it was time for push.

"We've even been accused of being interstellar aliens. We're not, of course, and we can prove it. My parents, and the parents of those like me, are people just like yourselves. Except for one thing. In a research program at the Phoenix Foundation, they volunteered for experimental treatment to combat the Sterility Plague, to try to beat the Only Child Syndrome.

"And it worked. But something unexpected happened, so that the resulting children differ from you in some ways." I paused; had Moran aired my earlier explanation of the physical part? I asked; she said yes she had, but it couldn't hurt to run through all of that again, because she'd thought of some questions.

So we went ahead; this time, using proper scientific terminology, I gave more specific details of the bodily changes at transitions. I couldn't explain, because I didn't know, why an F-mode person's menstrual hormones triggered her F-to-M change, while exposure to the accompanying pheromones did exactly the opposite to a Mark Two in the male phase.

I tried to get through the anatomy lesson rapidly, because if Moran's boss got bored he'd pull the chain on me; I'd lose this heaven-sent chance to make the *pitch*. When Bardeen had fed me the idea, we hadn't guessed there could be *this* opportunity!

But Moran came up with a new query. "Then after menopause,

when you no longer have the internal factor to trigger the change
to male, you'll all *stay* female?"

I'd never thought about it, but she was right! Or would have
been, before Gill's recent achievement that had given me an early
switch to M. I didn't mention that; I said only, "None of us are old
enough, yet, for the situation to arise. But—" A new idea came to
mind. "With a person ovulating only every second month,
menopause might well come much later in life."

"That's interesting." Her gaze strayed to something out of my
view; I felt she was getting ready to chop us off.

I said, "Before we end this, may I finish my statement? Marshal
Tedrow said I could." She nodded, so with an effort to get my
thoughts organized, I continued.

President Archer didn't see Annek Getzlor die. Travers Munro
did, though, and called Archer to the Tri-V. The trouble was that
Munro kept telling what had happened, so Archer had a problem
following the discussion between the newswoman and this young
man who claimed that half the time he was a young woman.

Finally, "Travers? Either shut up or get out." So with the sulky
look of a puppy whose housebreaking had lapsed, Munro fell
silent.

Now then; the young man was saying, "We differ from you in
only the one respect. In M-mode I'm a totally human male, and
in F-mode a perfectly normal female. At the transitions, when we
pass through a neuter stage, it's like reverting, briefly, to the
essential sexlessness of early childhood. It's not disturbing because
we know from experience that it doesn't last."

"So *that's* what those Tri-V hyenas have been raising hell
about," said Uncle Sam Archer. He hushed Munro's attempt to
answer. "Listen some more, Travers."

"—important to keep in mind that we didn't *ask* to be different.
We didn't create or design ourselves. How could we? We weren't
here; we didn't exist. People like yourselves tried to counteract the
Sterility Plague. In that, they succeeded; we are their children.
Yet if any one thing is certain, it's that we're not precisely what
they intended to produce!"

As he leaned forward, his momentary smile tightened to
seriousness. "There's something else, something important. If any
of you are childless now and don't want to be, the same treatment
can be made available to you." Again he smiled. "All you have to

do is accept the fact that after puberty your sons will, on alternate months, be your daughters—and vice versa."

On the other half of the split screen the newswoman asked a question. The young man said, "Yes, you and we are interfertile. In our male phase, the Sterility Plague blood-type limitations don't apply. In our female phase they do—because it's only the sperm that can be altered to avoid the immune reaction."

The woman paused, frowning, and said, "Then ultimately your new race will take over; right?"

"We're *not* a new race, merely a variation. And consider that for years the Phoenix Foundation has used much of its research effort to maximize *your* reproduction—prenatal care, every possible kind of aid toward conception—I don't have the budget figures at hand, but I can get them.

"Does that sound as if we're trying to take over? We're not. We didn't ask to be produced, but here we are; all we want from you is acceptance—to be your friends, your partners.

"Can we be? Will you let us? It's up to you. And thanks for hearing me." He didn't shrug, but his face gave that impression.

"And that's it, viewers! You've just heard Troy dos Caras, speaking from the Phoenix Foundation in Chicago. This is Sandy Moran for NBS, and after these messages we'll bring you up to date on the assassination of FBI Director Annek Getzlor—whose killer, by the way, is *not* one of these surprising new people."

Archer flicked the remote and cut the sound. "Travers, place a call for me. To the Phoenix Foundation."

Troy made a good pitch, Bardeen thought. Missed a few minor points, but got most of it in. So now everything was out in the open and up for grabs.

So that now Bardeen had no more excuse, of any kind, to avoid going back to the moon. To face the music—the murder charge.

Jody Jay couldn't believe it. With the Tri-V giving just background noise, Cora Sue's ministering had come up with real fine results for a change, but when all the hollering started and Tolliver looked up to see that devil woman Annek Getzlor go down stone-dead, it went all floppy again, so he pushed Cora Sue away and watched to see what under heaven was going on.

So he saw this two-sex monster admit what it was but somehow claim to be just an innocent child anyways, and the woman on network news didn't even argue.

He turned the set off. Cora Sue said, "You want some more, Reverend?"

The way Jody Jay felt, right then, he didn't want diddly.

*That should've been me. I wanted to; I tried to get there and do it.* But when Moss Frantz's roommate turned off her Tri-V, Moss had to admit to herself that Troy had done a better job than she could have managed.

The hell with it. Just so *somebody* did.

When Moran ended our session, her half of the screen blanked; Brad's side expanded to take all of it. He said, "Oh, hey, Troy! I hope this works out okay. For you, I mean. I—"

"You'll be all right, Brad." He looked as if he felt guilty about something, but I didn't have time for anything like that. "I gave you the byline up front; remember?"

So he signed off, as the marshal said, "Do I understand it correctly, that you're in temporary charge of this compound?"

"More or less. Why?"

"Then for now, you're the one I report to." His expression puzzled me; he was working hard at being deadly serious, yet somehow I knew he was enjoying himself but wouldn't let it show. He said, "I gather that in our own ways, you and I are each Acting Directors?" I supposed so; the titles weren't quite the same, but I nodded anyway. "Good. My report is that I'm taking the agents and police and armed heelies out of here, soonest. And lifting the surface blockades." He raised an eyebrow. "Unless you want some security protection. With all that went out on the Tri-V just now, you might well need it."

I didn't need any patronizing; I said, "Thanks. But this armed air raid, the FBI and backed by Chicago P.D., is the first time anyone ever broke our own security. I don't think—"

He shrugged. "Whatever you say; I was only offering."

So we shook hands; he motioned for his aides to leave with him. Then the phone chimed—and with no signal from me, its screen lit. Obviously, my caller had heavy priority codes. Looking past me, Tedrow whistled. "Whoop-de-do. The *President*."

As the marshal and his people moved out of the screen's view, all by myself I turned to face none other than "Uncle Sam" Archer.

*      *      *

Without preliminaries he said, "Dos Caras?" I nodded. "What's your job title?"

"Acting Chairman of the Foundation's Board of Directors, temporarily speaking for the permanent Chairman."

He showed a tightlipped grin. "Any commitment you make to me on behalf of Phoenix—would it be binding?"

"Yes sir. But—" This was getting out of hand! "Mr. President, you have to understand that basically I'm in a caretaker situation. On my own authority I'm not *supposed* to commit the Foundation to much of anything. You see—"

My spring ran down; I waited, until he said, "All right; I'll show my cards first. I want this pseudogene thing made available throughout this country and to any other nation that wants it. I haven't decided, yet, whether just free on demand, or maybe put in the groceries the way the AIDS cure was; we can figure that stuff out later. All right so far?"

"It sounds good, sir, but the Board—"

"Never mind that, just now. In return for the Foundation's cooperation in this effort, your government—headed by me personally—will mount a PR push in your favor, such as nobody's seen since the last two elections."

He shook his head. "I don't guarantee it'll keep you people free of trouble; the general public's been on a paranoid swing for at least two decades, and that nuthouse crap won't stop immediately. But this thing—our chance to beat the Sterility Plague before America's population falls below the break-point for maintaining our industrial base—" The President heaved a sigh that left him coughing. Not for long, though; it sounded more like postnasal drip than anything serious. "You offer a hope, son, that I'm willing to put a big bundle on. Can we have ourselves a deal?"

"I can't—I don't really have the authority. I—" *Think fast, damn it!* "Sir, if you'll do just one thing, I can put you in touch with our permanent Chairman, who *can* conclude a valid agreement."

When Bardeen had suggested, on the phone, that there might be some way to manage this ploy, we both knew it was a cobweb chance. But to my total surprise, Uther Archer agreed.

Without a trial, extradition, or even any kind of official arrest, Kennet Bardeen would receive a full pardon. So that he could negotiate the Feen's end of the deal, with no strings.

Somehow, when the call ended, I had the feeling that Archer had let me quit while I was still ahead.

# AFTERWARD . . .

*"We are, all of us, lucky that the future is normally opaque. Had the primordial amoeba been gifted with foresight, that tiny blob might have eschewed fission in the first place."*
*(From Origins, by Rome dos Caras.)*

"Nobody ever claimed it was easy." That's also my brother and sister Rome speaking. I don't know where the line originated; Rome cribs a lot. In some circles this is called research, and pays nicely. In Rome's case I don't mind.

Archer kept his word; he did well by us. The Feen compound itself had all the protection it needed, and for those of us who went Outside—some in exposed identities and others keeping cover—I suspect it was much like the racial problems a few decades earlier. Always there are a great many nice people but also a sprinkling of dedicated shitheads; what else is new?

Eden and Hill and I couldn't move Out until Kennet Bardeen returned to serve as Chairman. He held that post until his sudden, unexpected death a year or two ago. The new Chair is Lana Pendleton; judging by the quarterly reports she does a capable job.

We Mark Twos weren't the only ones with problems; Mark Ones had their own difficulties. In the early years, especially, an alarming number of families broke up because some members opted for Mark Two children while others couldn't stand the idea. And naturally the ones who—for whatever reasons—refused to buck the Sterility Plague in that somehow daunting way, held grudges: against people who used the pseudogene to *choose* how many kids they wanted, against the Feen for providing that option, and of course against M-2s in general. For one thing, the holdouts were being outbred by quite a margin, and knew it.

It takes a combination of fear and envy to make a hate group, and the Human Purity League certainly qualified. Its message didn't *quite* give open encouragement to violence—but nonetheless, sometimes produced it. Shades of the late Reverend Jody Jay Tolliver!

A local event, the beating of a Mark Two child by Mark One adults, triggered Moss Frantz. She hormoned herself to M-mode and pulled a one-man night raid on the nearest League headquarters. He blew most of it up, torched the rest, and put both inside guards to hospital; furious though he was, killing wasn't in his pattern.

Once he'd got away free and clear, Moss began watching the news for other outrages to avenge. On his third try he ran afoul of a police trap and was gunned down. His strikes ruined our M-2 record of nonviolence; certainly they were no help in working toward peace.

But still, knowing the demons that drove Moss, I couldn't help but grieve. Neither could Thane Cogdill; largely recovered from his stroke by then and able to speak more clearly than not, he called me, and we talked of Moss. "A rebel from the word go," the old man said. "Born the wrong time, wrong place." I heard his sigh. "But he always had a lot of spunk, that kid."

Cogdill was my idea of a true tiger; he lasted past ninety, and when he went, he went fast. His widow moved away; in the press of events I'm afraid I lost track of her.

As time passes, life seems to get easier. Not that everything's perfect; ugly incidents still occur, but in these times it's only the fringiest of fanatics who try to cause us trouble. And your average cop doesn't look the other way any more. It does make a difference.

Eden and I haven't had that kind of problem. Considering who we have working for us as Security people, I can see why. Nobody in his right mind is going to challenge Amory Neill; sane now, in case of need Amory might well be even more deadly than before. And the woman he brought with him—they met at their parole office—seems to be a fitting match.

Our young Hill seems well-prepared for the onset of Mark Two puberty; likely she'll set a good example to her three siblings. I gave birth to Jan and then Dana, both XZs; Eden bore Lane, who is XW and adored by her older "sister." As far as planning goes, our family is complete, but (as in the case of our beloved Dana) sometimes planning doesn't go as far as expected.

For some years to come, I suppose, Mark Two children may suffer from residual antagonisms. But the next generation, given any reasonable luck, should face a more accepting culture.

Because the way the pseudogene program's been going, enough people will be *us*, that we'll be the ones with the clout.

I hope we'll be nice about it. Maybe I'm kidding myself, but I think we will.

"Busby writes fine adventure stories, the kind that made us love science fiction in the first place. He tells one hell of a story."
—**Jerry Pournelle**

### F.M. Busby's
# THE REBEL DYNASTY
#### volumes 1 and 2

☐ **The Rebel Dynasty Volume One** (26954-2 * $4.95/$5.95 in Canada) is the first book in Busby's chronicle of the Hulzein dynasty. Including **Star Rebel** and **Rebel's Quest,** volume one follows Bran Tregare's brutal education at the notorious space academy, the Slaughterhouse, and his meeting with Rissa Kerguelen who joins him in his fight for humanity's future against Earth's imperial rulers.

☐ **The Rebel Dynasty Volume Two** (26988-7 * $4.95/$5.95 in Canada) continues the Hulzein saga with **The Alien Debt** and **Rebel's Seed.** Following in the footsteps of her parents, Lisele Selene joins in the rebellion against United Energy and Transport. But when she is sent to lead an ill-fated diplomatic mission, she must call on her Hulzein training to save her ship, her crew and her own life—as well as the future of the Hulzein Dynasty.

# CHERNOBYL
## —A novel by Frederik Pohl

"Forty years ago **Chernobyl** would have been far-out science fiction; now it is sober (and sobering) fact. Fred Pohl, one of the great masters of science fiction, would have done a good job of it as SF; he does an even better job of it now. Grim and gripping, with people as people, not caricatures." **—Isaac Asimov**

"Pohl movingly bestows a recognizable human face upon a catastrophe that could have happened anywhere." **—Publishers Weekly**

"A bright marriage of technofiction to disaster . . . As if Tom Clancy's **The Hunt For Red October** has been mated with Arthur Hailey's **Airport.** But Pohl officiates at the wedding with much more skill and style than either Hailey or Clancy . . . It has been months since I last read a popular novel so expertly done." **—Chicago Sun-Times**

"Along with a splendid cast in a gripping and vivid narrative, Pohl presents as balanced and insightful a picture of the USSR as may be found. A pro's pro in top form, tackling an inherently fascinating subject: the combination is irresistible."

**—Kirkus Reviews**

Buy **Chernobyl** now, on sale wherever Bantam Spectra books are sold, or use the handy coupon below for ordering:

# Special Offer
# Buy a Bantam Book
## *for only 50¢.*

---

Now you can have Bantam's catalog filled with hundreds of titles plus take advantage of our unique and exciting bonus book offer. A special offer which gives you the opportunity to purchase a Bantam book for only 50¢. Here's how!

By ordering any five books at the regular price per order, you can also choose any other single book listed (up to a $5.95 value) for just 50¢. Some restrictions do apply, but for further details why not send for Bantam's catalog of titles today!

Just send us your name and address and we will send you a catalog!

---

Read these other powerful novels by

# **David Brin**

☐ HEART OF THE COMET by Gregory Benford and David Brin (25839 • $4.50)—The first collaboration between two Nebula Award-winning novelists. The towering story of Halley's Comet's next return in the middle of the twenty-first century and of a daring mission to explore and colonize it.

☐ THE PRACTICE EFFECT (26981 • $3.95)—Physicist Dennis Nuel discovers a world that seems almost like our own—with one very perplexing difference.

☐ STARTIDE RISING (27418 • $4.50)—Winner of the Hugo and Nebula Awards for Best Novel. The epic story of the Terran exploration vessel *Streaker* which has crashed on the uncharted water world of Kithrup bearing one of the most important discoveries in galactic history.

☐ SUNDIVER (26982 • $3.95)—Circling the sun, in the caverns of Mercury, Expedition Sundiver prepares for the most momentous journey in human history. A journey into the broiling inferno of the sun . . . to find our final destiny in the cosmic order of life.

Buy these titles wherever Bantam Spectra Books are sold or use the handy coupon below for ordering: